PRAISE FOR DEADLY SLIPPER

"Wan hits her stride as a leading Canadian mystery writer. . . . [She] shows a mastery of mystery and an unmatched flair for the genre."
—*Edmonton Journal*

"Laden with local color. . . . A moody and elegant suspense story."
—*The Washington Post Book World*

"Full of vicarious thrills, offering sensory indulgences of the floral and culinary kind, with a dash of romance as spice. Lovingly written, with a sensuous style that lingers over the enticing or mouthwatering detail."
—*San Francisco Chronicle*

"Terrific . . . Wan's characters are well made and the story really clicks."
—Margaret Cannon, *The Globe and Mail*

"Transporting. . . . A cross between Peter Mayle and *The Orchid Thief*."
—*Los Angeles Times Book Review*

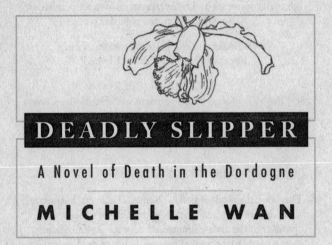

DEADLY SLIPPER

A Novel of Death in the Dordogne

MICHELLE WAN

SEAL BOOKS

Seal Books and colophon are trademarks of
Random House of Canada Limited.

DEADLY SLIPPER
Seal Books/published by arrangement with Doubleday Canada
Doubleday Canada edition published 2005
Anchor Canada edition published 2006
Seal Books edition published March 2008

ISBN 978-1-4000-2558-9

This book is a work of fiction. Names, characters, businesses,
organizations, places, events, and incidents either are the
product of the author's imagination or are used fictitiously.
Any resemblance to actual persons, living or dead, events, or
locales is entirely coincidental.

Text design: Deborah Kerner

Seal Books are published by
Random House of Canada Limited.

"Seal Books" and the portrayal of a seal are the property of
Random House of Canada Limited.

Visit Random House of Canada Limited's website:
www.randomhouse.ca

PRINTED AND BOUND IN THE USA

OPM   10   9   8   7   6   5   4   3   2   1

THIS BOOK IS LOVINGLY DEDICATED
TO TIM AND GRACE

ACKNOWLEDGMENTS

I am grateful to the many people who helped me along the way by providing local insights and factual information. I wish in particular to thank Alex Skelton for her friendship and valuable comments on the manuscript draft; Frances and Bill Hanna, Stacy Creamer, and Maya Mavjee for believing in this book; and my sister, Grace Anderson, whose generosity, encouragement, and wonderful house, La Charmeraie, were the beginning of everything. Above all, I wish to thank my partner, Tim Johnson, for his love, support, and botanical expertise. We have walked many paths together, and I look forward to walking many more with him. Among the many references used, Pierre Delforge's *Orchids of Britain & Europe* (Harper Collins, 1995) was my bible.

AUTHOR'S NOTE

The Dordogne (pronounced dor-DOHN-yuh) is an administrative *département* of southwestern France. Its landscape is diverse and dramatic; its history and culture rich; its people warm; and its cuisine justly famous.

This is a work of fiction, based in the Dordogne. All characters are imaginary. Invented places have been intermixed with or based on real locations. For example, the place-name Ecoute-la-Pluie was fashioned from the wonderful *lieudit* Ecoute-s'il-Pleut (Listen-If-It-Rains) because this one was simply too good to pass up. The geological, culinary, and botanical details of the Dordogne are accurate. Above all, the orchids (with one exception) exist and grow in the kinds of environments described. Their beauty is there to be admired, photographed, and, above all, respected. Wild orchids everywhere are endangered. Please don't pick, trample, or dig up the flowers.

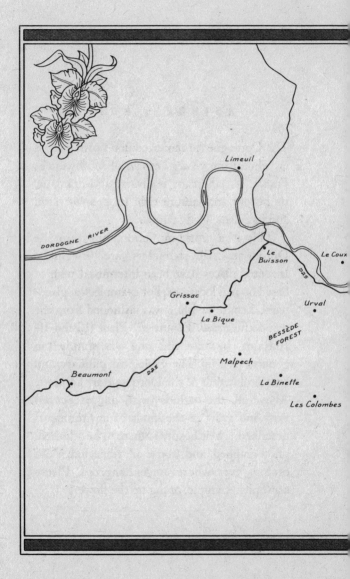

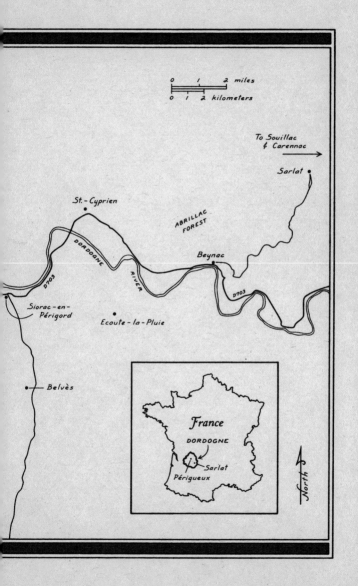

DEADLY SLIPPER

The Dordogne River springs out of the central highlands of France and flows westward through the region that bears its name, nearly five hundred kilometers to the Atlantic. The river, in its middle reaches, runs lazily through a narrow flood plain patterned with small farms. Here and there it swings between deeply undercut limestone cliffs. Small villages and fortified towns dot the landscape. Medieval castles rise from rocky prominences. Everywhere the earth is densely clothed in trees, for this is the heart of Périgord Noir—Black Périgord—named for the darkness of its great forests. Within their shadow, ancient footpaths wind over root and stone.

A young woman was walking on just such a forest path one day in the spring. Her stride was long, the stride of a seasoned hiker. On her back she carried a green canvas pack. She wore jeans and a blue windbreaker, the hood of which was pushed back, revealing dark, straight, shoulder-length hair parted in the middle and fastened at the temples with metal barrettes. Her ankle-high leather boots were caked with chalky mud. A camera hung unsheathed from one shoulder. Apart from the clatter of a nearby stream, the only other sounds to accompany the woman's passage were her own soft footfalls, the slight, rhythmical swish of her nylon jacket.

Her way now led uphill to an elevated meadow sprinkled with yellow cowslips, violets, and pale bladder campion. The woman paused, eyes searching until she spotted a scattering of odd-looking, greenish-red plants with hooded flowers, each formed around a deep throat. She approached to study them more closely, then took up her camera, slipping off her backpack at the same time for greater ease of movement. Carefully, she composed her shot, squatting low over one of the flowers, adjusting the lens meticulously for light and distance: first a close-up of the full plant, including basal leaves and inflorescence; then, shifting back with a crablike motion and refocusing to take in the immediate growing environment.

She capped her lens, gathered up her backpack, and walked on. Her path wound steeply upward over stony ground. Below her spread a rumpled panorama of wooded hills and valleys. Farther on, at the edge of a small clearing, she saw something that made her catch her breath: a plant bearing a single, fantastic blossom on a slender stalk. Her eyes widened and her lips curved in a smile as she crouched to marvel and admire. She prepared to photograph the flower at close range, adjusting her lens again, carefully pressing down the surrounding grasses for a better view. As she rose to back up for the longer shot, something—a streak of motion—cut across her line of sight. Startled, she looked up.

Talons outstretched, the buzzard struck so swiftly that the rabbit at the far side of the clearing had no sense of danger until it was pinioned with violent force. A shriek, a brief struggle, and the small animal was borne limply up beneath a beating canopy of wings. Raptor and prey disappeared beyond the trees. A moment later, a single feather, turning brightly in the air, drifted slowly to the ground. The woman watched transfixed.

Other eyes watched her.

"Maradonne," repeated the telephone voice. "I've been referred to you by someone who knows you, or knows of you—Monsieur La Pouge."

The accent was what he called straight-up American. Not a laid-back southern drawl. Not in-your-face New Yorkese, where "talk" rhymed with "squawk." But neutral, the tone slightly urgent.

"Ah," said Julian Wood, pushing his glasses up onto his forehead. He did not know any Maradonne. Or any La Pouge person, either.

"Because of your knowledge of wildflowers."

Julian thought hard. A fellow member of the Société Jeannette—Daffodil Society—the local wild-flower amateurs' club? Or an enthusiast who had come across his book, *Wildflowers of the Dordogne/ Fleurs sauvages de la Dordogne*, what he liked to think of as the bilingual bible on local flora?

He was standing in his slippers on the stone floor of his kitchen, which, since it was the best-lit and largest room of his ancient cottage, also served as his workshop. He fiddled with a sprig of dry-pressed pepperwort that he had been in the process of framing. He wanted to get back to it.

"I have a problem," continued the voice, "and I need your advice. That is, your expertise. I wonder if

5

I could ask for an hour of your time? On a consulting basis, of course."

Consulting? Well, he could consult with the best of them, but what on earth was this woman on about?

"I'm afraid—what—um—exactly is it that you want?"

There was a pause. "I just need a little botanical information. Look," she insisted, "can I come out to see you now? You live in Grissac?"

"Just outside, actually," he admitted weakly. He belonged to that species of middle-aged Englishman made nervous by pushy females.

"I can be there by—shall we say four?"

Turning his head, he looked out the window at rain, a cold March rain slanting out of an ugly sky that had hung for weeks over this region of south-western France. A sudden gust rattled his window-panes (in need of recaulking). He wondered, not for the first time, where Edith had got to.

"All right," he heard himself say, and told this Maradonne person how to find him.

•

Julian took one look at her and had a premonition of trouble. She was small, coming below his shoulder, with straight, black brows, a pointed chin, and an air of determination. Her face brought on a rush of uneasy associations with other determined women, dimly remembered, whom he had known. She was also soaking wet. That was because she had run through the downpour from the road, where she had been obliged to leave her car. She stood, hair plastered to her head, water coursing off her onto the flagstones of his gloomy vestibule.

"Mara," she seized his hand damply but firmly. "Mara Dunn."

"Julian Wood."

Reluctantly, he helped her out of her raincoat and hung it on his wobbly tripod rack. She scrubbed vigorously at her short, dark hair, flicking water everywhere. The action left it upstanding and spiky, making her look oddly like a hedgehog and younger than she probably was. Forty? Forty-five? He wasn't good with women's ages.

"Well," he said with a stab at heartiness, "may as well come through. Awful day. Tea? Coffee?"

"Oh, tea, thanks, if it's not too much trouble." Her brisk voice grated already on his nerves.

She ignored his invitation to be seated in his front room. Just as well. Since he lived with no one but Edith, whose habits were bohemian at best, housekeeping was not a strong point with Julian. He had tried to make a fire, which was smoking unpleasantly on the hearth.

Instead, she followed him right into his kitchen where her attention was immediately seized by a contraption standing at one end of the room:

"What is that?" she laughed, waving at a series of bulky, rectangular frames fastened together with immense wooden screws. "Some kind of medieval instrument of torture?"

7

"Floral press, actually," he replied stiffly and slapped an aluminum kettle on the burner. "Nineteenth-century. I still use it. For preparing herbarium samples."

"Herb—what?" Her eyebrows arched.

"Dry-pressed flora. Once the only means of providing type specimens for horticultural classification and botanical study." The hedgehog had asked for his expertise—by god, she was going to get it.

She looked perplexed. He relented a little. "For drying plant material. In fact a microwave does just as well for most things, but I find the old-fashioned method gives a more antique finish. It's a simple process, really. Clamp the plants in the press. It's lined with blotting paper to take up the moisture. Tighten the screws from time to time. Whole thing takes about six weeks. Thick bits like stalks and flower heads have to be pressed separately from petals and leaves and reassembled later. Then I mount and frame everything for sale."

He waved at an arrangement of flattened flowers and leaves laid out on a sheet of corkboard on his kitchen table. "It's my off-season trade. In summer"—he rinsed out a couple of mugs—"I'm a landscape gardener."

He eyed her warily as she approached his worktable to pick up a stiff cluster of pale-yellow blossoms.

"Cowslips," he told her. "What the locals call coucous. An early-spring bloomer found along hedgerows and shady footpaths."

"Oh!" Dark eyes swiveled to fix him intently. "Can you identify it like that? Where certain kinds of flowers grow, I mean?"

He cocked an eyebrow. "Well, yes and no. Most plants are habitat-specific. However, there are lots of hedgerows and footpaths around here. What do you have in mind?"

She took a deep breath, a diver about to plunge.

"Mr. Wood—"

"Julian."

"Julian. I'll get right to the point. If I showed you some photos of flowers, could you tell me—would you have any idea where they were taken?"

For a moment he entertained a suspicion that this was some crazy kind of test.

Quickly, she dug into her handbag and pulled out a thick brown envelope. "Please." She held it out to him.

With a sigh he slid his glasses down onto his nose and took it from her. It contained colored prints.

"But this is Beynac Castle," he objected, as the first shot revealed a fortified hulk perched on a cliff. It was a well-known local tourist site. "A few years ago, from the look of the cars."

"Yes. I left that in because it comes at the beginning of the roll. I thought it might give a general indication. There's also a *pigeonnier*." She fingered through to a print of a tall stone dovecote standing like a gaunt tower in the middle of a field. "But the rest of the photos are all flowers."

He frowned and flipped through them.

"Well," he said finally, "they're field orchids."

She waited, watching him tensely.

He shrugged. "Temperate species. Cousins to the more dramatic tropical varieties most people think of when you mention orchids. These are more modest plants, but every bit as beautiful, in a smaller way. And damned easy to miss unless you know how to spot them. But look here, these photos are in terrible condition. Some are almost impossible to make out. You want me to tell you where these things grow?"

"If you can." She had moved close enough for him to feel the dampness rising out of her hair and clothing, to catch a faint scent of sandalwood. He found the proximity slightly disturbing. He cleared his throat.

"Well, I can't. That is, not specifically. I mean, most of these, from what I can make out, are pretty widespread throughout the region. Beyond the fact that some like shade, others sun, and most grow in calcareous soils, it would be hard for anyone to tell you exactly *where*."

"But," she insisted, "you just said a certain kind of soil. Couldn't that be a clue?" She was not going to be put off.

"Calcareous?" He gave a harsh laugh. "Chalk. Pretty well describes the entire Dordogne Valley, certainly all of the middle reach, which is entirely underlain by chalky limestone."

The look of determination drained from her face,

to be replaced by something like desperation. "You're absolutely sure there's no way?"

"Look," he said dryly, "I'm not a psychic." He returned the photographs. Her insistence was becoming irritating.

"No. Of course not." She slumped heavily into a chair.

Julian saw that, whatever her reasons, his visitor had placed a lot of hope in him. Now she was disappointed. More than disappointed. Crushed.

The kettle rattled on the burner. He turned away to make the tea, feeling mystified and thrown off by their exchange.

"Milk? Sugar?"

She did not answer. He put the teapot down and eyed her again. "Or something stronger?"

She stirred, looked up dully. "No. Thanks. Look, if you don't mind, I think I'll pass on tea. Anyway, I'm interrupting your work." She rose jerkily, dropped her bag, picked it up, and fumbled in it. "Can I—can I pay you something for your time?"

"Good god, no." He felt insulted.

"Well, if you're sure . . . ?" She regarded him uncertainly. "Then I'll be on my way."

She did not wait for him to help her with her coat. He stood by as she struggled into it, feeling somehow that he had failed this odd, impulsive woman with her unreasonable expectations. She shook his hand stiffly.

"Thank you. You've been very kind."

Through the bull's-eye window in the vestibule Julian could see rain sheeting off the overhanging roof.

"Er—do you want an umbrella?"

She forced a brittle smile. "I'll sprint."

He opened the door for her. She pulled up her collar and stepped out. In the next instant something struck her full in the chest. With a scream, she skidded backward, threw up her arms. Her handbag flew, hitting the ground for the second time. Before Julian could catch her, she landed hard on the wet flagstones. A large, writhing form straddled her while a vigorous lash repeatedly struck the rickety coatrack, knocking it from side to side until it, too, went over with a splintering crash.

Julian waded in, lunging and grabbing.

"Dammit, Edith," roared Julian Wood, finally getting a hand on the collar of a large, very wet, exuberant dog. "Get off, you bloody beast! Get off!"

•

She had twisted her right ankle and had to be helped, carried by him really, back into his front room. It was an awkward, bumpy trip, and Mara was intimately aware of Julian's long, angular body, his thick pullover smelling slightly of damp wool, his rough, badly trimmed facial hair. She recalled his look of dismay—or was it shock?—when she had first entered his house, dripping water, mascara undoubtedly running down her face, and acknowledged with embarrassment that her attempted exit was even less graceful.

He deposited her on the sofa. Edith, a black-and-white short-haired pointer, was dragged away and shut up. Mara could hear her barks, whines, and frantic scrabbling from the back of the cottage.

"Better get that up." Julian swept away several days' accumulation of newspapers from the sofa so that she could raise her leg. Then he was gone again, retrieving her bag, placing it beside her, darting away into the kitchen, calling as he went, "Sorry about the dog. She just wanted to get inside. She hates the rain. I was wondering when she'd turn up."

He reappeared moments later with ice cubes wrapped lumpily in a tea towel. "Here. Get the swelling down. Nothing broken? Do you want a doctor?"

"No, no, I'm fine," Mara lied. Her ankle throbbed. Edith's howls were making the pain worse. "You ought to do something about her, you know."

"What? Let her out?"

"I meant, get her under control," Mara told him severely. "She's a liability."

He grinned, a sudden, attractive, boyish grin that illuminated his saturnine features. "Not guilty. Not my dog. Belongs to a farmer down the road, old Hilaire. Lets her run loose. She lives with me when she feels like it, and when she doesn't she buggers off somewhere else."

He shot away again. Mara closed her eyes. His comings and goings were making her dizzy.

However, the improvised cold pack was dulling the sharpness of the pain. She adjusted it around her ankle and looked about her: a low, small room full of mismatched furniture, threadbare carpets, and lots of litter. Pots of flowering plants crammed the window ledges. The walls were entirely taken up with books. Their worn spines suggested that all were well read.

He was back with a mug of tea and a couple of aspirins. "Here. Take these. When you feel better, if you can't drive, I'll run you back wherever you want to go."

Mara managed a smile. "Thanks. I'll be okay."

"No problem, really. Where are you staying?"

"Ecoute-la-Pluie." She opened her bag and gave him her card: *Mara Dunn—Interior Designer/ Décoratrice ensemblière*.

Julian looked surprised. "You're not a tourist?"

She shook her head. "I'm sorry. I should have made that clear. I'm Canadian, but I live here."

"Ah," he said, as if that explained something. "Of course." He lowered himself into a leather easy chair—obviously his favorite since the arms and seat were badly worn. "And the photographs? Look," he said, against his better judgment, "don't you think you'd better tell me what this is all about?"

Wearily Mara let her head fall against the sofa back so that she gazed past him at an indeterminate spot on the ceiling. "Yes," she said at last. "The photos." Briefly she closed her eyes. "You see, nineteen years ago, my sister Bedie—Beatrice Dunn—I think my sister may have taken those pictures."

He stared at her blankly, waiting for her to go on.

"In 1984, my sister, Bedie, disappeared in the Dordogne." Mara had told this story many times. With each telling, the recital became bleaker, more mechanical, reducing the people in it to mere essential facts. "She'd come over with her boyfriend, Scott Barrow, for a hiking holiday. They were camping not too far from here at a place called Les Gabarres. It was early May, and they'd had a lot of rain. Scott wanted to push on. Bedie wanted to stay. They had a fight about it, and Scott packed up and took off." Mara was silent for a moment. "When he came back to the campsite a couple of days later, Bedie was gone. Scott waited around for a few more days. He was sure she'd be back because, although she'd taken her backpack and camera, a Michelin guide, and a book on flowers, the rest of her things were still in the tent. We—none of us—ever saw her again."

Her eyes wandered to the windows. Darkness, the early darkness of remnant winter days, was closing in, but the rain was letting up. "The police launched a massive search. It was in all the papers. They questioned everyone in the area and followed up with campers who'd left during the critical period, anyone who might have seen her or given her a ride. A German family said they saw her go out of the campsite the morning after Scott left. Alone and on foot. No one else knew anything."

Throughout this narrative, Julian had been regarding his visitor with an increasingly troubled gaze. Now he stirred, rising to poke mechanically at the dying fire. He spoke with his back to her. "What about the boyfriend? Surely he must have had some idea where she might have gone?"

"No. In fact, for a time Scott was a prime suspect. The police were sure it was a crime passionel. They put him through hell, poor guy. Why did he leave? Why had he waited so long before reporting her missing? Scott told them that he had simply hitched a ride to Bordeaux and back, and that he hadn't been particularly worried about Bedie, at least not right away, because, as anyone who knew her could tell you, Bedie was perfectly able to look after herself. The police didn't believe him. On the other hand, they had no proof of foul play. There was no body, you see.

"My parents and I came over as soon as we were notified. We stayed on for three months, looking for her. Scott stayed, too. We showed her picture to everyone—hikers, campers, waiters, shopkeepers, farmers. My father offered a reward for any information about her. We had dozens of leads that went nowhere. Finally, the police told us we were complicating things by trying to run our own investigation. They told us to go home."

"And then?" Julian turned back to sit down again.

"And then, a couple of months later, in the fall, the French police contacted us again. Someone had found a woman's body in a wood near Carennac, over in Quercy. Her skull had been bashed in. They wanted dental records. But it turned out not to be—

to be someone else. The woman was later identified as a Dutch tourist. Bedie just went on . . . missing."

Julian scratched his beard. "It could have been an accident. The entire region is full of underground fissures and pits. She could have fallen down one of them. Or—or drowned in the river."

"We went through all that. We thought of mental breakdown. Amnesia. I pictured my sister wandering mad and nameless through the streets of Marseille. For years we all hung on to the hope that somehow she would just turn up. Eventually, my parents just found it easier to accept that she was dead."

"And you?" His tone was tentatively probing.

She shook her head. "It hasn't been that simple for me. You see, we were very close. Closer than ordinary siblings. We're twins."

She fumbled in her bag for a photograph, cracked and ragged at the edges, encased in a plastic sleeve. It was Mara's face, the same oval shape, straight brows, and pointed, determined chin. But taken long ago, frozen in time. The hair was different, longer and worn pinned severely back at the temples by metal clips. The eyes gazed out at the world with a challenging, quizzical stare. Find me, they seemed to say.

"I see," Julian spoke quietly. Unlike most people to whom she had shown this photograph, he did not display intense interest, merely glanced at it, then back at her, before placing it with a hint of distaste on the low table between them. He cleared his throat. "And so you came back to look for her?"

Mara shook her head. "Not right away. I got on with my life. I married, I divorced, I moved around. Finally, I realized I couldn't go on like that. I had to find out what happened to her. That's when I decided to make the move. My parents loaned me the money to set myself up in business here. I pushed to have the case reopened. The police haven't been very helpful. I tried myself to follow up old leads, but most were cold by then. The campground at Les Gabarres doesn't even exist anymore. People we had talked to at the time were dead, or moved away. It was hopeless, after so many years. But at least I was doing something. It made me feel somehow closer to Bedie, that I wasn't letting her down." She paused. "And then, a few weeks ago, I found the camera."

He raised his head sharply. "The camera?"

She nodded. "Last month I stopped off in Villeréal to check out a brocanteur I sometimes use—I'm always on the lookout for antiques for my clients, to go with their renovated barns and farmhouses. They like the genuine thing, or at least the appearance of it. Anyway, there was a big basket of junk. Dishes, figurines, books, and a camera, an old Canon. It was in pretty bad shape, the leather case all mildewed, like it had been stored for a long time in a damp place. It caught my eye because it was exactly like the cameras our parents had given my sister and me for our high school graduation. I looked at it more closely, and I realized, incredibly, that it was in fact the twin to mine!"

Julian regarded her doubtfully, eyebrows jacked up to the top of his head. "How could you be so sure? There must have been thousands of tourists with cameras like that coming through the Dordogne in the past—what did you say?—nineteen years."

Mara hesitated, then gave him her proof: "There were initials written on the inside of the case. *B.D.* Beatrice Dunn."

"Ah."

She set the ice pack aside, swung her feet to the ground, and sat facing him squarely. "But that wasn't all. Needless to say, I bought the camera. After I got it home, I found there was still film in it! I didn't try to have the film developed myself. I didn't want to risk a commercial lab. After all, it might be evidence, and the film was bound to be in a fragile state. I took everything to the police in Périgueux. They weren't very interested in reopening a missing person case nearly two decades old. However, I finally persuaded them to examine the film and have it processed in their lab."

"And these," he surmised grimly, "were the photos you showed me?"

She nodded. "It was a roll of thirty-six, intact, although in pretty bad condition, as you saw."

"Well, did the police at least try to trace the camera? What about fingerprints?"

"There were residual prints on the film, but they were too deteriorated to be analyzed. The police did try to trace the camera but got no further than I had. The *brocanteur* in Villeréal could only say that it had

19

come from a clear-out of someone else's stock, an old junk dealer named la Camelote who died last year. The police kept the negatives but gave me back the camera and a copy of the prints. They aren't willing to take it further."

Julian grunted. "I suppose to them it's an old incident. Cold file."

"That's right. Most of them weren't even around when it happened. However, there's one man I've had contact with on and off. Lieutenant La Pouge. He's retired now, but he actually worked on Bedie's case. I looked him up again. He wasn't very encouraging, though. He dismissed the initials as coincidence and said the photos could have been taken by anyone who'd done the usual tourist circuit and who liked wildflowers."

"He may have had a point."

"But that's just it," Mara cried, her frustration breaking through. "That was the most important part. Once I found out what the flowers were, I realized that was the link. *Bedie, you see, loved orchids!* She was what you'd call an orchid freak."

"I see," said Julian. He thought a moment and then nodded his comprehension. "Sure. Orchid fever. Gets in your blood. With some people it's an obsession, especially the tropicals. Fanciers spend big money on them. The field varieties you get around here are free but, for my taste, just as addictive. I know a Dutchman who hikes around France every spring with a donkey, just orchid hunting. His wife remains in Amsterdam. I'm not even sure they're still on speaking terms."

"Well, I'd say Bedie was obsessed. I tried to explain the importance of this to the police. I got nowhere. And that was when he thought of you."

"Who?"

"Lieutenant La Pouge. He'd heard you were something of a local authority."

"Oh well!" Julian lounged back in his chair.

"So, you see, I thought if you could help me . . ." She locked her gaze on his. "Julian, I'm not only convinced these photos were taken by my sister, I believe that somehow they're a clue to where she was before . . . before whatever happened to her."

He looked startled, almost aghast. "But they're just photographs of flowers. There's nothing in them that could indicate—"

"Maybe not directly. But I was hoping they could serve as a—a kind of signpost . . ."

She trailed off, not saying to where, but she could see him thinking it: a shallow grave?

"Please," she said after a long silence, "these photos are the only lead I have. Won't you have another look at them?"

TWO

There were thirty-four of them, each numbered on the back in order of exposure. Julian sat down next to Mara on the sofa and laid them out in a line on the coffee table. He put his glasses on and scanned the array. As he had noted before, all showed some degree of damage, streaks and staining, as if by light or moisture. Not surprising if they really had been taken by Mara's sister, with the camera lying about god knows where for nineteen years. It was a bloody miracle that the film had survived at all.

He was able to identify most of the flowers easily: dainty Helleborines; pink, conical Pyramidals; frilly Lady Orchids; white Butterflies. The final frames were the hardest to make out. They had suffered the greatest deterioration because they had formed the overlying tail of the film.

"What do you think?" Mara asked.

He sighed. "Well, I'll say this much. Whoever took these—your sister—knew something about orchids and had some experience documenting floral material. Look, each one's been photographed at least twice, once up close as a full-plant shot, showing the flower and the leaf base. That's important for identification. And then again from a few meters back to show the growing environment. For example"—he picked out a portrait of a compact spire of creamy florets lightly tinged with maroon—"this is *Aceras anthropophorum*, Man Orchid, so called because the labellum is shaped like a little man."

He saw that he had lost her, so he explained: "Orchids have three petals, surrounded by three sepals. The sepals are like—like a kind of cup holding the petals in place, you might say. One of the distinctive features of orchids is that the middle petal, the labellum or lip, is specialized, sometimes in fantastic ways."

He jumped up to fetch his botanist's loupe and held it out to her. "Here, see for yourself. The photo's got some bad patches on it, but you can just see that the labellum of the Man Orchid has four prongs, like arms and legs, with the sepals closing over the top to form a little head."

Obediently she peered through the lens.

He went on. "Now, the close-up is fine, but it's not that informative. All you get is the flower. So it's the habitat shot that's going to be the most useful for what you want." He pointed to the next photograph in line. "This is a middle-distance shot of the same plant. Here you can see that it's part of a scattered stand of Man Orchids, growing on a patch of rocky, sloping ground. So this tells us we're looking at, say, an eroded hillside, which would account for the lay of the land and the stones at the surface."

He skipped to a view of a grassy field awash in purple blooms. "Or this one. These are some kind of Marsh Orchids, which only grow in wetlands. So this has got to be a water meadow. The dark line there is probably a stream, and you can make out a wood in the background. This is an identifiable place. Of course, exactly where is the problem."

He continued scanning slowly, pausing with a grunt of approval over a portrait of a single brownish-yellow sprig. "*Neottia nidus-avis*. Bird's-nest Orchid." The grunt changed to a low whistle when he saw the companion photo. What he had initially dismissed as a badly stained exposure now proved to be a view of an extensive carpet of the plants. How big he couldn't exactly tell, because the plants filled the entire frame.

"Nice," he muttered admiringly. "A bloody great stand of them. Certainly bigger than anything I've seen."

Mara peered through the lens at a swarm of pale, fleshy specimens. "Those are orchids? They look like some kind of fungus."

"In fact," he nodded, "they live on fungi, and they're that browny-yellow color because they have no chlorophyll, no green in them at all. It's their matted roots that give them their name. Bird's-nests aren't that uncommon around here, but a big colony like this is extremely rare. Again, the problem is finding the location. If it even still exists," he added doubtfully.

He pored lengthily over the remaining photos. Suddenly, through the staining and speckling, he saw something that made him stiffen.

"My god!" he uttered.

"What?"

He grabbed the loupe from her to squint intently at a flower. It was taken in close-up, a startling plant bearing what looked like a deep-pink, swollen median lip flanked by two long, thin, spiraling, dark-purple petals. A blackish-purple dorsal sepal, arching forward like a hood, gave the flower an almost sinister appearance. Unfortunately, the picture was so badly damaged that he couldn't tell if he was truly seeing a slipper-shaped labellum.

"If I didn't know better"—he sprang up and carried the photo to where he could study it under better light—"I'd say it was some kind of *Cypripedium*."

Mara frowned. "What's that?"

He was at his shelves, pulling down reference books.

"*Cypripedium*? The French have various names for it—*Sabot de Vénus*, Venus's Shoe. *Sabot de la Vierge*, Virgin's Shoe." He thumbed rapidly through *Delforge's Orchids of Britain & Europe*. "In English we call it Lady's Slipper. The only known Western European species is *Cypripedium calceolus*." He flipped through a few pages and came over to show her a picture of a handsome flower bearing a bright-yellow slipper flanked by two twisted maroon side petals and backed by sepals of the same hue. "Here. The color and shape of the one in your photo are different, but it's definitely in the same genus. I'll be damned if I've ever seen the like of it, and certainly not around here.

"The problem is," he went on, more to himself than to Mara, "it's impossible. *Cypripedium* doesn't grow in the Dordogne. In fact, it's been wiped out in most places in Europe because of picking and habitat destruction.

"It's got to be the photo that's misleading me." He scowled irritably at the blackened print, slammed Delforge shut and plunged into Landwehr's double volumes on wild orchids of France and Europe. A serious orchidologist, he was sorely tempted to put the matter of Mara's missing sister entirely aside, itching as he was to pin down an identification. But there was only the single portrait of this tantalizing flower, and it was the last shot. Filming had stopped before the end of the roll. From what he could tell, the final couple of frames had not been exposed. He stood for a long moment, lost in thought.

Mara's voice brought him back. "If it's not a Lady's Slipper, what is it?"

He shook his head. "Damned if I know."

It was a question he would have gladly given everything he owned to answer.

•

They were sharing an omelet, the only food Julian had to offer. The bread was day-old, but the eggs were fresh, bought that morning from Madame Léon next door, the shells in fact still crotted with dung and feathers. He also had a decent bottle of Pécharmant on tap and a bit of chèvre, from another neighbor (Edith's putative owner), who made, in

26

Julian's opinion, the finest goat cheese in the region, smooth and mild, not rank and gritty like some.

Julian had finally coaxed the fire to life. They ate companionably before it. Edith, released from captivity, lay dreaming on the hearthrug. Mara, with her ankle propped up again, was in less pain now and looking better. Julian was aware of the way she sipped her wine, the rim of the glass pressed against her lower lip, the flickering flames glowing in her dark eyes, lending color to her cheeks.

"Julian, I need to know," Mara said. "Am I asking the impossible?"

He hesitated and then answered, "Yes. Apart from this"—he tapped the photo of the mystery *Cypripedium*—"most of these orchids are pretty widespread throughout the Dordogne. Even the Bird's-nest could potentially grow in any forested glade. This makes pinning down an exact location pretty hard. Also, although you have the sequence of exposures, there's no way of telling if your sister took all of these pictures within the space of a few hours— say, on a walk—or over several days. If she took them all in one go, that would simplify things because it would limit their range to a given area, whatever she could do on foot, assuming she was on foot. You could then try to find places where all of these flowers grow together and use the photos to create a sort of continuity—"

Mara cut in eagerly, "That was exactly my idea. I thought, if somehow I could find a starting point, I could use the photos as a kind of—of map to retrace her steps."

"But what"—he had to point out the other possibility—"if they were taken at different times? That means they were also probably taken in different places. Look, the lighting in this photo of Beynac Castle is dull, the road and stonework look wet. But the flowers were shot in dry, sunny conditions. That suggests that these were taken at different times, on different days and possibly in different locations."

"Or that it rained in the morning and cleared up in the afternoon. The weather in these parts can be very changeable, everyone knows that." She was not prepared to accept his complications. She fixed him with an obstinate regard accentuated by the set of her pointed chin.

He shook his head. "You also have the problem of this." He returned to the Lady's Slipper. "If this really is a *Cypripedium*, it's very doubtful it was taken anywhere around here at all."

"But Beynac Castle shows that the photos were taken locally."

"However, not necessarily the orchids, or at least not all the orchids. Your sister could have begun the roll in the Dordogne and finished off in—in the Gorges of the Tarn, for all I know."

"But I found the camera in Villeréal," she objected. "That's no more than thirty kilometers away."

Julian shrugged. "Junk travels."

Then he gave her the coup de grâce. "The real difficulty is that you're hoping to follow your sister's footsteps using floral landmarks of nineteen years ago. A lot could have happened in that time, Mara. Orchids are extremely vulnerable to changes in their environments. Their propagation patterns could have shifted. Their habitat could have been destroyed. You could be looking for something that no longer exists."

She was silent for a long moment, taking this in.

"All right," she said doggedly. "What about this?" She held up the photo they had so far ignored. The pigeon house. It was a distance shot, taken from an elevated point: a round stone tower, some fourteen meters high, with a rough, gray conical roof. It stood by itself, surrounded by poplars, at the bottom of a soggy-looking field. The specific features of the structure were hard to make out because of a large patch of speckling covering much of the print, but it appeared to have at least one window, a low door, and numerous holes for the entry and egress of birds.

"True," he had to admit. "In any case, a *pigeonnier* is a more permanent marker and a lot easier to spot than orchids. But, again, the Dordogne is full of these things. Every farm has some kind of a dovecote. Where do you start?"

She stared at him unhappily. "You think I'm crazy, don't you? Or maybe obsessed." She gave him a small, tight smile. "You don't have to be polite. I've heard it before. I have a friend—she used to live out here. She's gone back to New York now, but we still stay in touch by e-mail. She says it has to do with our twin psyches. She says I have a misplaced sense of guilt. Why Bedie and not me, that kind of thing."

"Sounds like the stuff of psychoanalysis," Julian grunted.

Mara gave a dry laugh. "Pretty good. Patsy is a psychoanalyst. And she may be right. But I think it's more than guilt. It's—it's something almost tangible, as if Bedie and I each had hold of a piece of string. Her end has gone slack, but I can't drop mine because I'm afraid if I do I'll lose her forever. So I have to keep hanging on. Sometimes I feel that if I could only follow the string out to its end I'd find my way to her . . ." She trailed off. "What I'm trying to say is, if I could only find out what happened, then we could all get on with our lives—Mum, Dad. And Scott. Because it's been worse for him in many ways, living all this time in the shadow of guilt."

"And you?" Julian prompted.

"I?" She paused and then said simply, "I could put an end to my nightmare."

"Ah," he said, as if he understood, but he wasn't sure if she were speaking literally or figuratively. This woman had an uncomfortable knack of knocking him slightly off balance.

Mara sighed. "You see, Julian, I have a recurring dream. A nightmare. In it I see my sister walking along a forest path. I'm behind her. I can make out the details of her jacket and the green canvas backpack she carried, the barrettes she always wore. She's walking very fast, and I'm hurrying after her because I have to warn her she's in danger. I shout her name, but she doesn't hear me. I start to run. Then, just as I'm about to catch up with her, she vanishes around a bend. I reach the bend, but she's gone. Now I'm alone in the forest, and I'm very frightened because I suddenly realize that the person behind my sister all along wasn't *me* but *someone else*. It's like I've been seeing her through *his* eyes, and now *he's* behind *me*. He walks very quietly, but I know he's there, and I can sense him closing in. I grab a stick, or sometimes it's a rock, to defend myself, and Bedie, too, because if I can stop him I can save both of us. I scream and swing around to face him. And then I wake up. I've had this dream dozens of times since Bedie disappeared. It's always the same dream, and it always ends like that."

He studied her silently for some moments. "Nineteen years of it is a long time."

Mara nodded somberly. The fire crackled. Edith whimpered in her sleep.

•

The rain had stopped. A strong wind had driven the clouds before it, leaving a half-moon and a sprinkling of stars in command of a clear night sky that promised fine weather on the following day.

Although her ankle was very stiff, Mara insisted on driving herself home. It was not far, half an hour at most. Julian walked her down the long path leading

31

from his house to the road, shining his torch ahead of them on the wet cobblestones. When they reached her car, parked beneath the dripping branches of a chestnut tree, she touched his arm in a gesture of parting.

"Thanks again, Julian. For everything. You've been really kind."

He shrugged. "Least I could do. But"—it seemed only natural for him to place his hand on her shoulder—"if you want my opinion, I'd say forget the photos. Leave your sister where she belongs. In the past. Move on." Even through the impersonal fabric of her raincoat he felt the shape of her, alive and warm. The sensation was both exciting and deeply disturbing. Easy, boy, he warned himself. Take your time with this one.

With unaccustomed gallantry, he reached out to open the driver's-side door. A terrifying, feral snarl erupted from the darkness within. Julian gave a panicked yell and dropped the flashlight, which went out with a sound of breaking glass, as something big lunged out to clamp his forearm with bone-crushing force.

Mara shouted, "Omigod! Jazz! No! No!"

There was a confused struggle, ending with a deep grunt, before Julian was freed from an excruciating grip of teeth that stopped just short of breaking flesh.

"Oh, Julian," Mara cried. "I'm so sorry. I totally forgot he was in the car. Are you all right?"

"Just a severed limb." Julian was still recovering

from his fright. "What in the name of hell was that?"

"My dog," she said sheepishly as a large, muscular body bounded from the car, fortunately with no further display of hostility. With a brief flash of tail it raised a leg against the rear tire of the car and let loose an urgent, copious stream of urine. "He wouldn't have bitten you."

"Thank you, the effect was just as good. You ought to do something about him," Julian told her severely.

"It's just that he's very territorial. A lot of dogs are protective about their space when they're confined, and he gets very cranky if he's left too long. . . ."

"Get him under control," Julian declared angrily. "A dog like that's a bloody liability."

"*Touché!*" she acknowledged, laughing softly.

THREE

April came on fitfully, with windy skies, bright patches, and sudden showers. Julian stood in the open doorway of his kitchen. The sun for the moment shone warmly. Wisteria bloomed on the crumbling stone wall between his land and the walnut plantation of Madame Léon, from whom he got his eggs. The cherry tree at the bottom of his garden was in full and glorious flower. A cuckoo rang out in the valley.

He should have been feeling satisfied with life. The sale of two dozen herbarium frames to a hotel in Le Bugue had replenished his bank account. The prospect of a new landscaping client (referred by Mara Dunn, and rich from the sound of it) made his immediate financial situation look even better. But he was restless.

First there was the *Cypripedium*. Its weird, beguiling beauty haunted him. Orchid fever, he had called it. Where tropical species were concerned, it drove a multibillion-dollar industry. Nice, ordinary people were compelled by a dark-side lust to possess these plants, to engage in the costly, competitive, and secret business of searching for and breeding them. For two centuries, European and American orchid hunters had trekked, at no little risk to their necks, into the jungles of the Amazon, Borneo, Sumatra in search of new, undiscovered species. Temperate-clime orchids commanded a less extravagant piece of this botanical market. All the same, the fanaticism of fanciers and collectors was no less acute. The possibility that a totally unknown species of Lady's Slipper grew in some hidden corner right there in the Dordogne made Julian almost frantic with desire. If it still existed, he knew he had to find it. But where to begin?

And then there was Mara Dunn. He recalled the flicker of firelight on her face, her dark eyes, the set of her chin. Not the kind of person, he sensed, to leave things as they were. He had been surprised and then relieved when several days had passed without a phone call from her. Nevertheless, he felt her looming ominously on his horizon. The thought brought on an unpleasant pressure behind his eyes, which always foreshadowed a headache.

He had been toying with a plan, more out of self-defense than a desire to help her. Now seemed the time to put it into action. Except that he wasn't sure if he should venture seeing Paul so soon. He hesitated, then made up his mind. Not bothering to lock his door—he rarely did—he set off down the road.

It was a brisk, fifteen-minute walk from Julian's cottage to the village of Grissac. Along the way, Edith loped up to join him. Pleased to have company, he gave a token scratch to her silky ears—much her best feature in his opinion. The vagabond bitch was exactly the kind of female that suited him: handsome, wayward (she came and went as she pleased), but constant (she always turned up at mealtimes); full of her own plans, yet often willing to give him the pleasure of her company for long rambles or drowsy winter evenings by the fire. Best of all, she was not his. Not his responsibility, not his blame.

Grissac consisted of a few dozen houses built in the style typical of Périgord Noir: tall, two-storied structures of warm, honey-colored limestone, narrow windows flanked by heavy wooden shutters, and roofs steeply pitched to bear the immense weight of overlapping layers of *lauzes*, rough-hewn limestone slabs, the traditional roofing material. Its main features were an incomplete thirteenth-century central arcade surrounding a grassy square, which doubled as municipal parking lot and marketplace (Thursday mornings), an elementary school, and the Chez Nous bistro. It was Friday, past noon, and, apart from the voices of children behind the high playground wall, there was little sign of life.

Chez Nous, a large, square building on a deep plot of land, was situated just off the *place*. Julian found his friend Paul Brieux at the front, washing winter's grit from the windows.

"Missed a bit there," Julian observed, playing the jolly kibitzer. His French was good, although it bore remnant traces of his English background. At the moment he was unsure of his welcome. In last Saturday's friendly rugby match (there had been nothing friendly about it), he had failed to stop a try in the final minute of play, which had put the dreaded team from Les Eyzies on top. It wasn't good rugby—mostly middle-aged men, short of wind and gone to fat, who met in occasional inter-village matches organized by Paul—but the play was serious. *Le rugby* being one thing sure to rouse passion in the breast of the otherwise phlegmatic Périgourdin, Julian was not an especially popular man with his teammates at the moment.

"I'm not talking to you," snarled Paul, wringing a rag into a bucket of soapy water. A bull of a man, son of a farmer near Issigeac, he played right-hand prop to Julian's fullback.

"Come on, Paul," Julian pleaded. "Christ, it wasn't my fault. Those guys from Les Eyzies are out of the Stone Age. How would you like having le Trog pushing *your* face in?" The one they called le Troglodyte was Les Eyzies's horrendous center, a brute with a forehead like a cliff and small, piggy eyes. "He nearly bit my ear off last year."

"You chickened out," Paul accused in a seriously aggrieved voice.

"I wanted to live!" Julian recalled his feeling of extreme vulnerability as le Trog advanced on him, head lowered, arm outstretched like a battering ram, fully intent on flattening Grissac's last remaining line of defense: Julian. Why did they call it a "line" when it always boiled down to one lone man?

"Anyway, why do I always get stuck with full-back?" He knew the answer: the position was his because no one else wanted it. Since their forward defense was not particularly good, he frequently found himself alone, deep in home territory, scrambling for the ball while a rush of attackers—loggers, farmers, abattoir workers—converged darkly on his field of vision. Admit it. He was getting too old for the game.

"All right," conceded Paul. "What do you want?"

"Well, I just stopped by to say hello," said Julian, feeling as wounded by Paul's unfriendliness as by the pounding he had suffered. He still showed the bruises.

"Go bother Mado."

"I intend to," said Julian, relieved to see that he had been forgiven.

"And leave that bloody thief outside," Paul roared, meaning Julian's canine companion, but Julian and Edith were already through the door.

Chez Nous could just as well have been called Chez Paul, or Chez Madeleine, but when the couple had first set up the establishment, they could not agree on whose name should go on the sign. "Chez Nous" was the compromise. In fact, Chez Nous had evolved, through economic necessity, into more than a bistro. It served Grissac also as *tabac*, newsstand, post office, general store, and community hall. The Brieux lived above all of this and worked below in the various capacities implied. If Chez Nous had failed so far to rise to the height of culinary fame originally intended by the pair, in fact the cooking was very, very good. Julian ate there at least once a week, as much for the company, which he genuinely enjoyed, as for Mado's confit of duck or Paul's *feuilleté au citron*. Despite his bulk, Paul had the lightest hand with pastry in the region.

There was no one in the front area, which served as the store. The bistro was through a bead curtain off to the side and consisted of a bar with stools, a dozen or so tables, and a mixed collection of chairs. Julian had a look in. The only person there was a morose type named Lucien Peyrat, who delivered bread to communities too small to have their own baker. The man was eating an early lunch. Julian gave him a perfunctory nod and wandered back to the kitchen. The appetizing odor of frying garlic filled the air.

"What's cooking?" he asked in both senses of the word, sticking his head through the door. Edith stuck her head in, too.

"*Ah*," cried Mado, a statuesque redhead with tawny, leonine eyes, "*c'est toi*." She was at the stove, pan-frying river sprats to a golden crispness, moving the fingerling fish about with swift, sure motions. She wore a loose knit jersey, which draped a magnificent bosom and left bare a pair of voluptuous arms.

"So—we haven't seen you for days," she accused. "Gone off my cooking?"

"I lust after your cooking and I was here last week," Julian defended himself. He had purposely let six days elapse before venturing back to give Paul time to cool down.

"For a miserable *apéro*," snorted Mado. She cared little for *le rugby* but could be as cranky as Paul when the mood took her. Julian fancied her in an off-limits kind of way, largely because she gave him a taste of what it would be like to live dangerously with a woman driven by temperament and steaming sexuality.

She jerked her chin in the direction of the bar. "Serve yourself. I'm busy. *Tiens, bibiche,*" she baby-talked the gourmand pointer, tossing out a tidbit which Edith snapped up midair. Mado adored all animals: dogs, cats, ferrets, donkeys, rabbits, although she had no qualms about gutting, skinning, and stewing the latter. She and Paul had no children.

"Thanks, love," Julian said, and wandered off to make himself a pastis at the bar.

By one o'clock, the bistro was busy. Julian had the prix fixe of the day: a terrine of aubergine for starters, followed by the sprats, hot, crisp, and dressed in garlic and coarse salt. They were accompanied by potatoes and spring asparagus poached in butter. He ordered a *pichet* of local white.

Paul, who had donned an apron, was now serving tables. A group of cyclists, dressed in colorful spandex, sun goggles, and aerodynamic helmets, pushed through the bead curtain. All walked with the mincing step of men treading on cleats who have been straddling bicycle seats too long.

"*Messieurs, dames,*" they gave the standard greeting to the room at large.

"Damned spacemen," Paul muttered to Julian in

passing. "Think they're training for the Tour de France. Drink nothing but Badoit."

Julian finished up with a dessert of crème brûlée. He drank a well-sweetened coffee and read the paper. Eventually, when the bistro cleared, Paul joined him at his table, followed by Mado.

"Listen, you two." Julian drained his cup. "I need to ask you something."

"What's up?" rumbled Paul. Mado lit a cigarette, dragging at it deeply.

"Do you remember a case involving a missing hiker, a Canadian woman, nineteen years ago? She was last seen at Les Gabarres. It's possible she disappeared in this area."

"Vaguely." Paul pulled a face. "Long time ago. Why?"

Julian told them about Mara Dunn and her sister.

"She should lean on the police, lazy *salopards*," Mado said. "She could be on to something with these photos. Why won't they take it seriously?"

"There's no real way of proving her sister really took them, except for some initials on the inside of the camera case, but those could be anyone's."

"The flowers tell you nothing?" Mado took another deep drag, tilting her head back to blow smoke upward to the ceiling, eyes half closed. Mado's smoking, Julian thought with pleasure, was an object lesson in sensuality.

"Probably not. However, there's a shot of a *pigeon-nier* in the middle of a field. Something like that is a lot easier to place than a bunch of flowers. It's long odds, I know, Paul, but you're from around here. I thought if you could look at the photo . . ."

Paul stared aghast. "*Bigre*! Do you know how many *pigeonniers* there are around here? In all the Southwest? For five hundred years, farmers have been building pigeon houses. Pigeon shit used to be worth its weight in gold, you know, as fertilizer. France was built on pigeon shit."

"Well, even if you don't know the *pigeonnier*, you might be able to recognize the general locality," Julian persisted doggedly.

"Oh, what can it hurt?" cried Mado, stubbing out her smoke with a quick, imperative gesture.

"Just look at the photograph," pleaded Julian.

"You know what you are, my friend?" uttered Paul. "You're a raving lunatic."

But he promised to have a go.

•

The drive to Toulouse took Mara much longer than if she had gone by the A20. But today she preferred the minor roads. She needed the soothing progression of villages and farms and rough, newly planted fields, of towns with names that rolled off the tongue: Villefranche-du-Périgord, Fumel, Tournon-d'Agenais, Montaigu-de-Quercy. Her dog, Jazz, also a lover of country drives, occupied the passenger seat, his broad head hanging joyfully out the opened window. The wind was heavy with the smell of wet manure.

A few days before, Mara had sat on a hard, upright chair in police headquarters in Périgueux, pleading again with Commissaire Boutot for the reactivation of Bedie's case. The Commissaire, a sad-eyed man with a drooping mustache, told her mournfully that the camera was very little to go on, the police had already made what inquiries they could with no result, therefore, *désolé*, there was nothing more they could do. "After all, madame, nineteen years!" His entire demeanor gave a weary conveyance of the Gallic shrug.

Depressed, Mara had e-mailed Patsy Reicher, her psychoanalyst friend in New York:

> *So once more things are at a stop. I told you I drew a blank with Julian Wood. Knows his flowers, but a bit of an oddball and in the end no help. Oh, Patsy, why did I have to find that damned camera? Just when I was beginning to let go, I'm plunged right back into it. I haven't told Mum and Dad yet, or Scott. Afraid to raise their hopes. Sometimes I feel as if Bedie were still alive, playing a game of hide-and-seek, daring me to find her.* <

For five years, tall, wacky, gum-chewing Patsy had been Mara's only real confidante in the Dordogne. The problem was that Mara's other friends were also her clients, and experience had taught her that business and intimacy—particularly something as heavy as Bedie—didn't mix well. With Patsy, however, it had been different. Mara pictured her—gangling, fifty-something, with frizzy, badly hennaed hair showing gray at the roots, a broad, freckle-splashed face, ironic green eyes—and missed her badly. But Patsy's time in the region had been a temporary midlife fling at sculpture. Her work, humorous, free-form, and too large to command a market, now stood moss-covered and forlorn in Mara's back garden, where it had resided since Patsy's return to New York and psychoanalysis. *Know when to cut your losses*, was Patsy's motto, a guiding principle she also applied to men—her marital career, like her art, being somewhat free-form.

From her uptown Manhattan office, Patsy had fired back:

> *Easy, kid. The only player here is you, and the game is solitaire. Yes, you can let it go. Finding out what happened won't bring Bedie back. Besides, you might not like what you dig up.* <

It was true. So focused was she on the hunt that perhaps she had not sufficiently considered its possible consequences. Suddenly the countryside she drove through took on a more forbidding aspect: wild woods and fields, a scatter map of isolated farms and small communities. The rough, clustered dwellings of the villages seemed to draw in on themselves, stubbornly closing down on secrets that the outsider would be hard put to dislodge. Terrible things could happen within their precincts and no one would be the wiser. Which one, she wondered, and where?

•

Mara's business in Toulouse included an importer of ceramic ware, a fat, voluble Spaniard named Pablo who had his shop in the old Fish Market. She had not dealt with him before. He gazed at her with warm, coffee-colored eyes while Mara gave him a purposely exaggerated notion of the size of her clientele, all with bathrooms and kitchens that they, as today's purchasers of picturesque Perigordian cottages, were disinclined to leave in the sixteenth century.

"Bueno." He drew back thick lips, disclosing square, yellow teeth, and offered her a negligible discount and a bag of sample tiles.

Lunch was a quick *croque-monsieur*, half of which she shared with Jazz, followed by a pass through the antique dealers on the Left Bank. The only thing she found of interest was a dusty bolt of vintage yardage that in the end wouldn't do for draperies because on unrolling it she discovered that it was water-damaged. All in all, a disappointing day.

She drove home in the gold-blue twilight, tired, still depressed, mechanically making the turnoff to the hamlet of Ecoute-la-Pluie. Translated literally, Ecoute-la-Pluie meant Listen to the Rain. Nomenclatures in those parts tended to be rendered in a kind of rural shorthand, reduced simply to the names of residents, or, in this case, to their prominent characteristics. Ecoute-la-Pluie referred to a small water mill that had once operated there—or, more whimsically, to the miller himself (as Mara imagined him), ear ever cocked for the sound of rain that would swell the little stream that powered his grindstone.

The hamlet consisted of a handful of dwellings, strung out along a bumpy gravel lane. At the head of the lane, someone had left a battered white Peugeot van, badly parked on the grassy verge. She veered around it. Her house was the third down, a rambling eighteenth-century structure. She loved her house, its honey-gold stone, its roughly tiled roof, its many windows. It was her one solid point of reference in a life that to date had been busy with making her business go, haunted by the imperative of Bedie, and too little given to comprehending where she herself fit in all of this.

She parked along the side and got out, breathing in the sweetness of lilacs that filled the evening air. Jazz dropped heavily to the ground behind her, did a dog's version of a full-body stretch, and sauntered off to water a bush. As she rounded the corner of the house, a tall figure broke from the shadows. She froze. Jazz was suddenly beside her, tail stiff, ears erect. He gave a low growl.

"Ah," said the figure, stopping mid-stride. "Julian Wood. You came to see me about some photographs. Is your—I've forgotten his name—is he okay?"

"Jazz," said Mara, slightly annoyed with herself for being frightened. In fact, now that she had recovered, she was glad of a visitor. She hadn't been looking forward to an evening of her own company. "Don't worry." She waved a reassuring hand. "He's very friendly, actually."

"I'm sure," said Julian with palpable skepticism.

•

"I just happened to be passing," Julian said, stepping bemusedly into her front room. Right away he didn't like it: a showcase of period furniture and objets d'art, all positioned for effect. A large floral carpet (genuine Aubusson? if so, worth a small fortune) lay on the highly polished walnut floor. The whole place had an uncomfortable, upmarket air, redolent of the sweetish smell of beeswax polish. He looked at her, and his discomfort deepened. This was not the hedgehog woman who had come to him for help the month before. Instead, a person to match the room, bone dry to start with, coolly professional, tailored silk dress belted at the waist, wedge sandals, hair artfully clipped. Stood to reason, he thought sourly. As her business card had announced, she was a designer, an arranger of the natural scatter of things.

And then there was her dog, a large, tawny beast, probably of pit bull extraction. In any case immensely strong, with a broad chest flashed with white and a very big head. It took up a protective position beside her on the Aubusson. Its eyes, Julian noted, were remarkably intelligent, golden-brown, and outlined in black.

Julian hadn't really been passing by. He had driven out on purpose. It was necessary to his plan that he see her in person. Not knowing which house was hers, he had parked at the top of the lane and ambled down, peering in the dusky light at names on mailboxes until he saw her sign. Now, taking in her furnishings, her dog, he decided to cut his visit short.

"Um, thanks, but I can't stay," he said in response to her offer of a drink and a chair (a hard-looking Louis Something fauteuil). "I really came by because I was wondering if I could have another look at those photos."

She tensed immediately. "Have you found out something?"

"No," he admitted. "I just thought—"

She didn't wait for him to tell her what he thought. "Come out to my studio," she said, and led him quickly across the room and out the back of the house through a set of double doors.

He had anticipated manicured turf and topiary to match her interior decor. He was surprised to find instead an unkempt ground studded with oversized statuary that made his patch look like the formal gardens of Versailles. Her studio was even worse. Housed in a converted stable, it resembled a bomb crater. The floor was littered with what looked like salvaged material from wrecking sites. A chipped marble mantelpiece and bolts of cloth leaned against the walls. There was a broken-down armchair loaded with manila files, a large workbench buried in paint

48

samples, plans, and sketches. The only relatively clear space was an L-shaped desk with a phone/fax, computer, and printer.

"Sorry," she apologized. "This is how it really is. What you saw out there is my storefront, where I impress my clients."

"I was impressed," he admitted grudgingly.

She laughed, a clear, friendly laugh. "You were meant to be. Everything in it is for sale. My cleaning woman treats it like a holy shrine. Honestly, she polishes the floor on her hands and knees with a brand of encaustic that smells like churches."

She went straight to the desk, pulled open the bottom drawer, and removed the now familiar brown envelope. Beneath it lay a dark rectangular object covered in plastic.

"Is that the camera?" he was moved by curiosity to ask.

She nodded, lifting it out, unwrapping it, handling it like a holy relic. He took it from her. The black leather case was brittle, crumbling slightly at his touch. Gently he unsnapped the top. A dusty smell of mold rose to his nostrils. The metal mounting and other hardware were corroded, but the box and lens looked intact. On the interior of the cover flap, he saw the letters, clearly printed: *B.D.* At that point, she took the camera back from him, as if his scrutiny had somehow become too personal.

Julian removed the photos from the envelope and fanned through them, purposely ignoring the Lady's

Slipper, singling out the shot of the pigeon house.

"Look," he said, "would you be willing to make copies of this print?" And he told her about Paul and Mado Brieux.

"Paul's from around here, you see. I thought, even if he doesn't recognize it, he has a lot of contacts, agricultural salesmen, farmers, market vendors, people who travel around the region every day. I've talked to him. He's willing to pass copies of this print around."

"Julian, that's brilliant!" Mara cried. Her pale face glowed with sudden hope.

"Oh well," he said, speculating on where the admiring light in her eyes might lead. "Nothing may come of it, of course. Still, no harm in making, say, a couple dozen copies, letting Paul hand them out, and seeing what happens." He was standing close enough to her to catch a remembered scent of sandalwood, to see the faint flutter of a pulse in her throat. It made him slightly uneasy.

"I can't begin to thank you—"

"Yes, you can," he said, taking a deep breath and stepping back. "Because I want something in return."

"Oh?" She was suddenly wary. "What?"

"A full set of these prints."

She looked surprised. "But the photos are awful. You said so yourself. Oh . . . I suppose you're interested in the Lady's Slipper?"

"Be crazy not to be," he admitted. "Something like this is a botanist's dream."

She frowned. "But why do you want . . . Wait a minute, I thought you said it was impossible to use these photos to trace my sister."

"Well, yes, there's really no way—" he began, but she cut him off.

"But you're going to try to find this *Cypri*—this flower. Using Bedie's photos. That means—"

"Now, hold on, Mara," he broke in. "No one said anything about trying to *find* the *Cypripedium*. After all, what are the odds? It's probably a mutant that bloomed once a long time ago and died. I just want a photo of it for, well, call it scientific curiosity."

"Fine," she said coolly. "If that's all you want, then you can have it. I'll make you a copy. But only this one. You don't need the rest. Not if, as you say, you're really not trying to track this orchid down."

He felt a sudden spike of anger. "For heaven's sake, this is ridiculous. It's not a lot to ask, and I would have thought—"

"You help me," she said, her awful chin snapping up, "and I'll help you. After all, in a way, we're looking for the same thing, aren't we?"

The admiring light in her eyes had hardened to a bargaining glare. The pulse in her throat pumped aggressively.

She had him.

"All right," he gave over. Bloody woman. At that moment, he felt like strangling her.

•

Julian got out of bed the next morning feeling terrible. He had slept badly, and the shadow headache of the day before, taking on substance, seemed to be trying to hammer its way out of his skull. A real thumper. Strictly speaking, his headaches were not typical migraines. He did not have, thank god, the nausea, the incapacitating pain, but they were bad enough. He stumbled blindly into the bathroom, groped for his pills, and swallowed them down with tap water. Seeking Mara out had been a big mistake, like dropping a rock into the placid puddle of his existence. Grudgingly, he had to hand it to her. She had seen through him pretty damned quickly. With a sigh he shambled unsteadily into the kitchen to make himself a mug of tea. Stirring in four sugars, he squinted dizzily at his list of appointments—there was only one, but he wondered if he really would feel well enough to make it. It also occurred to him that Edith hadn't been around for her morning snack. In fact, he hadn't seen her for a while. She was in heat. Probably off coupling with every dog in the valley, the slut.

By eleven o'clock, the pills had kicked in and Julian was feeling better. He slicked down his hair, put on a clean shirt, and drove out to meet the new client whom Mara had referred. She proved to be a glamorous, retired Chinese American advertising executive named Prudence Chang. Looking over her property, Julian cheered up considerably. He fervently hoped the woman had money to burn. If he was given his way, her renovated farmhouse, fronted by a wonderful walled-in cobblestone courtyard, was about to become *la plus belle site de la région*.

The client, standing with him in the sunny courtyard, listened while he enthused over the microenvironment of walls, the characteristics of *Rosa gallica* versus heady floribunda. He was developing a theme of wisteria over the archway of the double gate when she tipped down designer sunglasses and looked at him with tired, slim-line eyes.

"Look. Julian. I've got two questions. How much is this gonna cost, and do I get to see any of it before I die?"

Sadly, he realized that what she really wanted was instant garden—hostas, bedding plants, and *pret-à-porter* hanging baskets. It was like that with most Americans. She read the disappointment on his face and offered a compromise.

"Okay, listen. I'm giving a bash here next month. You get things looking nice—I don't care what—just whip it into shape—in time for my party, and you can plant roses up the ying-yang for all I care."

"Fair enough," he said. But he wondered what "whipping into shape" meant to a woman like Prudence Chang.

•

There was a message on his *répondeur* when he returned to his cottage: *Julian, Mara. I've made two dozen color photocopies of the* pigeonnier. *Can I bring them over?*

She turned up at the end of the day, accompanied inevitably by Jazz. They went straight round to Chez Nous, where they found Paul working in his *potager*, turning the soil carefully around herbs that had wintered over, and setting out tomato and lettuce seedlings with a delicacy that belied his size. He gave Mara a muddy fist to shake, scratched Jazz's ear, and jerked his head toward the house.

"*Apéro*," he stated rather than asked, and led the way inside.

Mado was within, talking at the bar with Gaston, the fat, big-nosed postman, who was finishing up his rounds with his usual *coup de blanc*. Lucien Peyrat, as thin as the baguettes he sold, was also there, eating a solitary ice cream at the back of the room.

"Her husband's in the hospital," Gaston was saying. "Liver. It's serious."

"Ah, Paul, did you hear? Yvette's old man is dying." Mado pecked Julian and sized up Mara before saying briefly, "*Bonjour, madame*."

They sat down near the window. Julian had a pastis, Mara accepted coffee, Paul drew himself off a pression, Mado smoked a cigarette, and Gaston, who himself looked like a candidate for a serious liver complaint, joined them for another *coup*.

Mara gave them a shortened version of her sister's disappearance and her discovery of the photos, more for Gaston's benefit, since Paul and Mado had already had it from Julian. It was the first time Julian had heard her speak French. She was fully fluent, although he found that she had an oddly flattened accent and a way of swallowing her vowels that he could not immediately place.

"Wait a minute." Gaston scooted forward in his chair, his beetroot nose quivering with emotion. "I remember! Years ago. *La canadienne disparue—c'est ça?*"

"Yes, that's right," cried Mara eagerly. "The Vanished Canadian. That's how the papers described her."

"And she was your sister? A terrible business, madame. To come all the way from Canada to disappear like that. Montreal, wasn't it?"

"Yes," replied Mara. "We're from Montreal."

"Ah," said Mado knowingly. "Montreal."

Gaston went on, "I remember because all of us *facteurs* were told to be on the lookout for her. Or anything suspicious. For me, that was the bad part. I have daughters, you see. It could have been someone from around here. It made me think, I tell you."

"The countryside is full of cretins and perverts," snapped Mado, drawing hard on her cigarette.

They all looked at the photocopies of the pigeon house that Mara handed round.

"It's a very bad photograph," said Gaston. "Eh, Lucien," he called to the thin man as he slid past on his way out. "You seen this?"

Lucien, who had pale eyes set very wide apart, giving him the look of a startled horse, stared at Mara rather than at the photocopy that Gaston held out. He shook his head, left money on the bar, and slipped like a shadow through the bead curtain.

"Scared of his own farts, that one," Gaston grinned, as Lucien's battered vehicle shot off in a spurt of gravel.

Paul, who had been studying the photocopy intently, blew out his cheeks. "Needle in a haystack," he concluded. Absentmindedly he fondled Jazz's massive head. The dog gazed up at him adoringly, great jaw agape in an idiotic grin. A moment later, however, something on the wind caused the animal to tense and shoot out the door.

Mara said, "Isn't there anything—those poplar trees, for example—that could give you a clue?"

Paul said, "There have been half a dozen big windstorms in the past ten years alone. Poplars grow fast. Then they rot. They could have all blown down. Or been cut for firewood."

"Nothing at all distinctive about the *pigeonnier*?"

Gaston pushed his lower lip out. "Plenty like it. This one might not even be still standing."

"Or recognizable," added Paul. "Big ones like this are being converted into holiday homes nowadays."

Mado had been studying one of the copies with slit eyes through a cloud of smoke. She tapped it with a red-enameled nail. "That's a sheep."

They all craned forward. The object she indicated was faintly outlined and could have been anything because it was largely obscured by a stain.

Julian had to admit that he hadn't spotted it

before. "Looks more like a goat to me."

"Sheep, goat. So what?" said Paul.

"Not everyone raises sheep," said Mado.

Paul said, "It's *one* sheep."

Mara asked, "Is there any record of—of sheep farmers in the region?"

"Are you kidding?" This was from Gaston, who had slumped back in his chair.

"You have to find someplace with a *pigeonnier*, poplar trees, and sheep—nineteen years ago. It won't be easy," Mado concluded, not unsympathetically, nodding in Mara's direction.

"I'm prepared to offer a reward." Mara sounded desperate. "One thousand euros."

"Seriously?" asked Gaston, sitting forward again.

"Seriously."

Gaston's bulbous snout twitched. "Not bad, that."

Paul shrugged. "Still a needle in a haystack."

Gaston drained his glass and stood up. "Well, I'm off." He held up a copy of the print. "Can I take one of these? I'll ask around. You never know."

He saluted the company and went out, also leaving money on the bar. They watched as, a moment later, his canary-yellow minivan, with *La Poste* scripted on the side, trundled down the road.

"Poor Gaston," said Mado. "He has seven kids. All girls. On a postman's salary."

Julian and Mara rose to leave. Paul walked out the front with them and around to the side of the house, where Mara had parked her Renault.

"Look, I'll show my father this picture. He may come up with something, or one of his cronies may remember this *maudit pigeonnier*—" He broke off abruptly. For a moment he stared unbelieving at what was happening in his beloved *potager*, then stuffed the photocopy into his back pocket and gave an outraged bellow.

Jazz was humping Edith lustily among the newly planted lettuce and tomatoes. For her part, the bitch, tail flagged coquettishly to one side, appeared to be trying to walk away, requiring Jazz to hop athletically behind her and causing a widespread trampling of young seedlings. Human attempts to move or separate the coupling dogs—the scene by then had attracted a small but interested crowd—only resulted in worse damage. There was little to be done except stand back and let nature take its course. It lasted nearly half an hour, during which time the dogs wound up end to end before Jazz finally came free. He was panting hard but looking smug.

"Oh, Paul, I'm so sorry," Mara moaned, surveying the wrecked garden in dismay.

Paul seemed to come out of a trance. Slowly he shook his head. "*Quel dogue!*" he breathed in admiration.

"Swine," muttered Julian.

•

"I'm going to have to persuade Prudence to hire Mado and Paul to cater her party," Mara said as she drove Julian back to his cottage. "It's the only way I can make it up to them for their garden."

Jazz, tongue lolling, lay splayed out across the backseat. Edith, who had never in her life accepted a ride home, had trotted off on business of her own.

"Oh, don't worry about Paul," said Julian tartly. "He'll get over it. Besides, he liked you. Did you notice the way he wouldn't look at you? Whenever he refuses to look at a woman, it means he fancies her."

"I've never heard anything so ridiculous in all my life!" Mara laughed. "However," she said after a moment, "Mado has her eye on you."

"Eh? What makes you say that?"

"The way she checked me out. She regards you as her property. You two haven't got something going, have you?" Her tone was bantering.

"I hunger for her cooking, not her body." Julian replied with mock dignity. Nevertheless, his conscience twanged as he spoke the words. There had been one or two occasions, usually when he had drunk too much on a Saturday night after rugby, when he had found himself swirling like a drowning vole in the vortex of Mado's powerful attractions. "Besides, Paul's one of my best friends, practically family."

"That's why they call it a *ménage à trois*," Mara said.

•

"She's French Canadian," Mado said to Paul when they were alone. "Did you hear her accent?"

"What accent?" Paul sat on one side of the bar, studying rugby scores in the local daily, while Mado dried glasses on the other. In a region where people spoke a lazy patois and where all words were drawled out to end in "ng," an accent was hardly a thing to be remarked on.

"*Joual.*"

"What're you talking about?"

"*Joual.* She speaks *joual.*"

"What *joual?*"

"It's the Montreal argot. That's how they say 'horse.' They eat their words, so *cheval* winds up sounding like *joual.* I think she's got her eye on Julian."

"About time somebody did." Paul buried himself more deeply in his paper.

Mado watched him. "Are you going to show that photo around?" she asked a moment later.

"Sure. Why not?"

"Well, like Gaston said, it could have been anyone around here. You'll want to go carefully. Don't forget, the man was never caught."

"How do you know for sure it was a man?"

"Use sense. It had to be."

"Well, who?"

"Anyone. Lucien Peyrat, for example. It's usually the repressed type."

Paul looked up. "For Christ's sake, he's a bread man, not a murderer."

"Or old Benoît. Being a butcher, killing would have been easy for him. Even you."

"Are you joking?" Paul gaped, incredulous.

"All I'm saying is, you could stir up something. Especially if she's really offering a reward. A thousand euros is a lot of money."

"*Hou!*" Paul went back to his sports page. "I'll wave the photo under people's noses. No one's going to identify this *bougre* of a *pigeonnier*. Besides, the boyfriend probably did it, even though they couldn't hang anything on him. Or else the sister drowned in the river or fell down a hole."

Mado shrugged. After a pause, she resumed, "She's not his type, you know."

"Who?"

"This Mara. She's all wrong for Julian."

Paul threw his paper down at last to squint ferociously at his wife.

"What's right? The problem with Julian is, he's got no staying power. He takes up with a woman for a while, and just when things start to look serious, *fsst*. It fizzles out. Sometimes I think he doesn't really like women. He wants them, but he doesn't like them."

"He likes me," pouted Mado.

"You're different," her husband pointed out. "You're safe."

"Safe?" The redhead bristled.

"Unavailable. Married. He can fantasize without running any risks. In any case, he has no idea what makes a woman tick."

"You do?" Mado challenged, rubbing the glassware hard.

"At least I'm not scared of them." Paul retreated from possibly thin ice. "Anyway, if this Mara's putting moves on him, she's as good as any. Julian needs a woman, any woman. He's going to seed. You should have seen him watching that dog of hers hump Edith. Pure envy."

Mado gave a throaty laugh, put away her towel, leaned across the bar, and nuzzled her husband's ear.

"Poor Julian," she whispered throatily. "Poor, poor Julian."

FOUR

He had been christened Armand some fifty years ago, but round about they simply called him Vrac. The name meant "in bulk" or "loose goods." He grew up large and brutish, with an oversized head, slack mouth, and pale hair that stood up in tufts. He lived with his mother in a grim farmhouse, eking out an existence from a few hectares of soggy land in a valley below the village of Malpech.

The mother, Marie-Claire Rocher, otherwise known as la Binette, was herself no beauty: a hulk of a woman, with a massive jaw rising out of a creased dewlap, and a livid birthmark covering one eye. Her nickname suited her, for the word binette meant "hoe," an implement she had once nearly decapitated a man with for trespassing on her land. Its more archaic meanings, "visage" and "wig," could equally be taken to refer to her unsettling face or to the coarse yellow clump of horsehair that sat on her head like a turkey's roost.

Of Vrac's father, nothing was known. Everyone suspected it had been old Rocher himself. "*Mon dieu, his own daughter and barely thirteen!*" they had exclaimed those many years ago as the smock front of the young Marie-Claire grew daily shorter for all to see. Over time, Vrac the child and Vrac the man came simply to be accepted by the scattered farming community as an unpleasant feature of existence, like bad weather or mud. If he was shunned—children ran when they saw him, and women crossed themselves at his approach—he was at the same time tolerated and even protected by the fierce local loyalties that defined a region where in times past a person's entire universe was measured by how far he or she could walk out and back in a day.

In fact, it might even be said that Vrac enjoyed a kind of ill-favored celebrity. Local farmers sometimes employed him to fell trees and heave tractors out of ditches, for he was enormously strong. He also had a certain understanding of the darker side of machinery and was often able to bludgeon exhausted and antiquated farm equipment, which normally would have been left on a hillside to rust, into some level of fitful functioning. These odd jobs gave Vrac cash in his pocket, a tenuous claim on society, and a kind of preposterous self-conceit.

All the same, Vrac understood murkily that he was not wanted. Even his own mother called him names. These rejections filled him with an inarticulate rage that erupted from time to time in crude acts of violence perpetrated randomly against inanimate objects and living things that chanced to cross his path.

Like a bear, Vrac covered a vast territory, killing and taking at will, poaching on reserves and fishing on private land where the streams and rivers of the region formed pools attractive to pike and perch. There was only one place that he avoided—a deep pond in the forest where tall reeds whispered and frogs and small fry abounded. For reasons known best to him, he would not eat things taken from its muddy depths.

La Binette was a more complex being. She assessed the world about her with a cynicism that usually worked to her benefit. Her son she treated like an animal, with a bitterness that arose from her belief that he was a punishment for past sins. He was of her making, and he never should have been made. Nevertheless, need arising, she probably would have defended him to the death. And if she attended but minimally to his bodily needs, it must be said that she did no more for herself.

For the rest, la Binette tended her sheep and made a surprisingly good cheese from ewe's milk. In fact, her *brebis* was something of a local specialty, which she sold at nearby periodic markets, arriving with much backfiring in an ancient wood-paneled truck. Occasionally, she augmented the household income by picking up unwary hitchhikers or motorists in distress, driving them not to where they wanted to go but to some isolated spot where she demanded a *forfait*, usually what cash their wallets contained, for "transportation services rendered." Most paid and were then dumped, shaken but relieved, to make their way back to civilization as best they could.

Curiously, mother and son slept together. Whether

they joined in an incestuous relationship was beside the point. The point was that, apart from routinely cooperating out of necessity to till the soil or harvest or slaughter, these two creatures went their own way from dawn to dusk. At night, however, like beasts made uneasy by the dark, they drew together, sharing a sagging double bed. Vrac had slept with his mother since his first day of life, when she had given him the breast, the only bounty he had ever received from her, and continued to do so unthinkingly into adulthood and middle age.

In a region where places took the names of the inhabitants, the Rocher farm was simply referred to as La Binette. Its narrow fields lay between the forest and the road. The house, built over a byre, a style more typical of Quercy than Périgord, stood in a wooded combe.

The byre, once used for stabling animals, served la Binette (the woman) as a cheese cellar and Vrac as a storehouse. There Vrac kept his fishing tackle, gutting knife, shotgun, and other items—a book (he could no more read than fly, but he liked the pictures of the flowers); a dog collar; a canvas backpack; old boots; a green bicycle bearing the stamp *Phoenix Made in China*, which he occasionally rode.

For the most part, the mother was incurious about the son's treasure hoard, her only interest being the possible value of a given object. However, one day many years ago, la Binette happened to notice that a camera had been added to the collection. She picked it up and examined it because it looked to be expensive. Then she heard a noise behind her. Turning, she saw her son's form, framed in the low doorway of the byre, blotting out the light.

"No," Vrac croaked hoarsely, hands dangling heavily at his sides. "Put."

Dropping the camera back onto the pile, la Binette pushed roughly past her son to the outside. Sometime after that, she saw that the camera had gone.

•

High on a prominence above La Binette (the farm) and at the top of a tortuous road, stood the grand but decrepit château of Les Colombes. It, too, was heavily screened by trees—from most angles, nothing more than its numerous chimneystacks could be seen. To the northwest, it looked across a broad valley to the village of Malpech. In all other directions, it was surrounded by forests and fields.

At one time all of the land for leagues around, La Binette included, had been part of the Seigneurie of Les Colombes, owned by the powerful de Sauvignac family. However, over the course of ten generations, the Seigneurie had been so parceled, hacked, sold, and ceded that only the château, with its adjoining woodland, remained. Nevertheless, the fact that the estate was still in the hands of an unbroken line of de Sauvignacs was a matter of local pride.

How la Binette's father, a drunken day laborer with never two sous to rub together, had come to acquire a corner of Les Colombes was a mystery. "Silence is golden," the more cynical locals said knowingly, tapping the sides of their noses, suggesting that the scoundrel Rocher had rooted out something about the family worth the price of a parcel of land. When Rocher died—"Fetched by the devil," they said, for he had been found in a ditch one winter morning, frozen stiff, mouth wide open as if midshout—the farm had passed to his stony, antipathetic daughter and her son. And so things had continued over the years, with la Binette and Vrac tending their sheep and wresting their harvest of root crops from the wet, exhausted soil.

•

La Binette was on the big-nosed postman Gaston's route. For years, his canary-yellow minivan had bucketed past the place, making only infrequent stops. There was rarely any mail for the residents, mostly circulars and bills that the *facteur* deposited in a rusty iron box set on a cairn of stones at the roadside. Never had he needed to negotiate the narrow track leading from the road to the farmhouse itself. Just as well, for Gaston, like others, preferred to stay well clear of mother and son.

However, on this afternoon there was a delivery requiring a signature. From the Electricité de France, so it had to have something to do with the electricity. As he turned off onto the muddy, rutted lane, Gaston reflected that, in all the time he had come down the valley, he could not recall actually having spoken to either of the La Binette pair. Today, he wondered nervously if Vrac would be around. Of the two, he thought he would rather deal with the woman. Once or twice he had seen Vrac standing on a hillside roaring unintelligibly at the sky, or glimpsed him in the rain, moving like an animal among the trees. Besides, he didn't think Vrac could read or write, let alone sign his name.

Gaston pulled up in front of the farmhouse. The day was turning overcast and windy, with the suggestion of an impending storm. Reluctantly he heaved his bulk out of the minivan. A crow rose flapping from the roof.

"*Allo?*" he shouted from the bottom of the six deep steps leading up to the front door. In addition to its unusual style, he noted that the house was built of darker stone than normal, giving it a damp and secretive air.

Laboriously, he climbed up to the elevated stoop. He knocked. Silence. The front of the house had one window. Peering through grimy glass, he could make out nothing of the darkened interior.

Not here, he concluded, considerably relieved. He wondered if he could get away with putting the EDF envelope and the signature form in the mailbox at the roadside with a note instructing la Binette to sign the form and leave it for him to pick up the following day. He wasn't really supposed to do that, and he had no reason to believe she would comply. Ah well, he supposed he'd just have to try again.

As he turned to descend the steps, he saw, with a sense of shock, that la Binette was waiting for him at the bottom. She wore overalls tucked into knee-high rubber boots, and a black jersey with the sleeves pushed up. With her massive forearms and her birthmark obliterating one eye, she reminded Gaston uncomfortably of a beached pirate.

"Ah, madame," Gaston stammered. Perhaps she had been in the byre at her cheesemaking, for her hands were wet, and her wig, the color of dirty straw, was tipped askew over her forehead. Fleetingly he wondered what had become of her own hair, not that he would have dared to ask.

"What?" she said. Her voice was hollow and harsh, like wind blowing down a chimney.

"Er," he said, "it's this. For you." Tentatively he held out the electricity board envelope.

She ignored it, glaring balefully into his face.

"What do I want with that?"

"*Eh bien*, how am I to know?" he gabbled apprehensively, realizing that it was probably a final notice of arrears. "However, as you can see, it requires your signature."

She spat, aiming for a spot just off his right toe.

"Madame!" Gaston pulled his foot back. "I am only doing my duty."

At that point Vrac appeared, rounding the corner of the house and stopping up short behind his mother. Together the pair of them blocked the *facteur's* way like standing stones. Gaston thought how

much bigger Vrac seemed up close. He wore dungarees over a greasy sweater and a pair of steel-rimmed
sunglasses with one lens missing, giving him a patch-
eyed look and the bizarre appearance of parodying
his mother's birthmark. The expression on his large,
misshapen face was not friendly, and he smelled
strongly of sheep.

Gaston tried affability. "Come. I'll leave it here,
shall I?" He placed the envelope on the third step.
"And if you'll just sign this. A mere formality." He
extended the required paperwork.

Vrac gave a sudden, braying laugh. He moved
close enough to poke Gaston hard in the chest and
plucked the form from the postman's hand.
Scowling, he goggled at it upside down and right side
up, turned it over, and gave another burst of mirthless
laughter. Momentarily, Gaston was taken in by this
dumb show. Then he caught a gleam of malicious
cognition in Vrac's eye.

"Monsieur," he cried, somewhat shrilly but with
all the dignity he could muster, "I really must—"

But Vrac merely stuffed the paper inside the bib of
his dungarees and stalked away.

"Madame," Gaston appealed to the mother, who
still barred his path, "I regret to trouble you, but I
must have that back. With your signature."

"*Toi*." Her eyes had never left his face. "*Va t'faire
foutre*," she directed, telling him crudely what he
could do with his form and his signature together.

It was not a hot day, but Gaston found as he edged

71

past—she left him barely enough room to get by without actually having to brush up against her—that he was perspiring heavily. Defeated, he scrambled into his minivan and drove rapidly away.

•

Les Colombes was also on Gaston's route. He had no mail for the de Sauvignacs, but after his experience at La Binette, Gaston felt that he owed himself a stop at the château. He needed something to calm his nerves. He was so shaken that he ground his gears twice as he downshifted to take the steep ascent.

The château was, of course, altogether a different matter, for the de Sauvignacs had once been, and for many remained, the first name in the land. Henri de Sauvignac père, now long dead, was still remembered with affection as a dotty old gentleman with a passion for botany. The son, the present Henri de Sauvignac, was a more worldly character, known in his heyday for his elegance, high living, and appetite for women. He had taken his wife, Jeanne Villiers that was, a willowy, compliant creature, from a well-to-do bourgeois family. In the sixties, the couple had made a handsome grouping with their two little boys, driving about grandly in a shiny new Citroën with hydropneumatic suspension, the first of its kind in the area.

Of the two de Sauvignac sons, Alain, the elder, had grown up, studied civil engineering, and gone abroad to work in places like Gabon and Cameroon. Patrice, the younger, had not grown up because he had drowned in a pond in the woods below Les Colombes when he was seven. It was a terrible tragedy, and some said that Jeanne de Sauvignac had never fully recovered from the loss.

Now in their seventies, the de Sauvignacs lived almost like recluses but still commanded respect. Aristocratic folk, Gaston called them, with an old-fashioned sense of *ce qu'il faut*. Even on days when he had no mail for them, he frequently made the steep drive up just to look in on the old people. In winter Monsieur was often good for a small tot of rum, in summer a refreshing *coup de blanc*, either of which Gaston took standing on the stone floor of the cavernous kitchen.

In return, the *facteur* gave them the latest local gossip and ran the odd commission, rub for Madame's rheumatism from the pharmacy in Belvès, cigarettes and newspapers for Monsieur from the Chez Nous emporium in Grissac.

The de Sauvignacs still had their Citroën. Like them, it had grown old but retained a certain dusty cachet. From time to time, Monsieur might still be seen puttering sedately along the roads, raising a hand in greeting to the locals, and stopping occasionally to offer, with seigniorial courtesy, directions to lost motorists and rides to bewildered hitchhikers passing through his *territoire*.

•

As he neared the top and turned onto the path running up to the rear of the great house, Gaston remembered that he had been meaning in any case to ask the de Sauvignacs about the *pigeonnier*. If nothing else, it would give them something to chat about and be good for his *coup de blanc*.

He had shown the photocopy earlier in the week to his fellow *facteurs* (keeping quiet about Mara's cash incentive), with no luck. Now, standing in the vast, damp stone kitchen of the château, he watched anxiously as Henri de Sauvignac studied the, by now, much-wrinkled photocopy. Before looking at it, the old gentleman had first taken his glasses from his jacket pocket and polished the lenses with care before setting them on his beaklike nose. A once imposing man, he was now stooping and cadaverous, but still meticulous in his habits.

"Hundreds like it in the region, m'boy." He shook his head and passed the photocopy to his wife. Jeanne de Sauvignac, trailing several layers of shawls, looked about for her glasses, could not find them, and ended by squinting ineffectually at the paper at arm's length.

"Dear me," she murmured with an absent, lopsided smile that always made Gaston think of village idiots, even though he was ashamed to harbor such a disrespectful thought in association with someone belonging, if only by marriage, to the first family of the region.

"You'll have a time finding one among so many," Monsieur observed. "Things have a way of blending in. One gets so used to seeing them, buildings, people, one no longer in fact sees them, not for what they really are." He seemed to imply that Gaston would be destined to pass by that particular *pigeon-nier* every day of his life and never recognize it.

Gaston thought disconsolately that this might be true. He tried to envision all the pigeon houses that he routinely encountered. Many were attached to houses. Others, like the one Mara was looking for, were solitary, freestanding towers. It could have been one of them or none of them. Pity the detail was so hard to make out. *Merde* of a print. Why couldn't the *pigeonnier* have been one of the really distinctive ones, like that self-important cross-timbered block set on six stone pillars he'd once seen in Quercy?

"She's offering a reward." Gaston felt it appropriate to impart the information to the de Sauvignacs. A thousand euros wasn't to be sneezed at and would establish that his inquiry was serious.

"Hmmm," said Henri judiciously. "As much as that. But you have only her word that she'll pay up."

"She seemed sincere," Gaston ventured cautiously. "Of course, I know with foreigners it's say one thing, do another. Still, it's worth keeping one's eyes open."

"Of course. You do that, m'boy," agreed Henri and offered Gaston the longed-for *coup*.

"But what does this person want with a *pigeon-nier*?" Madame's watery blue eyes goggled at the postman. Her dry, yellowy-gray hair was as faded as her face. "Will she buy it?"

"Ah. There's a story," exclaimed Gaston, enjoying

the cool trickle of wine down his parched throat. And he then spun the de Sauvignacs his version of Beatrice Dunn, enjoying their scandalized attention.

"Funny how life brings things back around," he wound up his narrative with a deep, philosophical sigh. "First *la canadienne disparue*. Now, all these years later, the sister."

"Indeed," Henri said dryly.

Jeanne, bony beneath her shawls, stirred restlessly.

"Well," said Gaston, feeling it was time to change the subject, "what do you hear from—where is he now?"

"Douala," Jeanne said at once.

"Ah, yes," Gaston nodded knowingly. Their son, Alain, was off in Africa, constructing roads. It seemed to the postman that he could have built a superhighway all the way around the continent, he'd been at it so long. For twenty years at least, Gaston had carried up letters bearing colorful stamps from places like Abidjan and Libreville. "Still building things?"

"Bridges." The mother gathered her draperies primly about her. "He's their, what do you call it, washout expert. Very important work."

"Head operations engineer, actually," corrected her husband.

"It rains a lot out there, you know," Jeanne confided. "Bridges are always washing out. He works terribly hard. Of course, it has its compensations. He's much in favor with influential people in the Cameroon. He's been to the *presidential palace*, you know." Her rusty voice pealed with pride. "And he speaks the local patois quite well."

Gaston had heard much of but never clapped eyes on this prodigy, who seemed to like living in places where things collapsed in the wake of tropical storms. For his part, the *facteur* couldn't understand this preference for the jungle, with mosquitoes and snakes, over the healthy Dordogne countryside.

"His contract has just ended, so he's coming back to be with us." Madame's puckered cheeks went pink with pleasure. "For a visit, before he lines up something else. He'll be home any day now."

That was another side of the Dordogne, Gaston reflected. Young people fleeing for lack of work, only the old remaining. A countryside abandoned to foreign holiday cottagers, or people from Paris who spent two weeks a year in run-down family houses that stood empty and shuttered the rest of the time. How many were like the de Sauvignacs, left stranded, waiting eagerly and pathetically for the next visit from children who had moved on to other lives, other worlds?

Although, in the de Sauvignacs' case, Gaston had heard that it was some problem between father and son that had caused Alain to leave home and stay abroad. Something to do, perhaps, with Alain's objection to his father's profligate ways, his chronic fondness for a bit of skirt. No doubt about it, the old fellow had been a spender and chaser in his day. Women from Limoges to Bordeaux, until his wife's money had given out. It was rumored that this was the bone of contention: Henri de Sauvignac had run the estate into the ground, and the son sweated in Africa to keep Les Colombes in de Sauvignac hands.

Outside, it had grown very dark, even though it was the middle of the afternoon. A wind was building up. Tendrils of ivy tapped fretfully on the small panes of the kitchen window, and Gaston could see trees swaying in the distance. He drained his glass, saluted—for some reason with the de Sauvignacs he always raised a respectful forefinger to the side of his cap by way of greeting and leavetaking—and hurried out to his van.

The first drops of rain were already smacking down, forming big craters in the dust on his windshield. He looked back. Husband and wife seemed to be clinging together in the obscure opening of the kitchen doorway, Madame's draperies whipped by a moist wind. He had the impression of a pair of ragged crows balancing precariously on their perch.

Rapidly he backed out of the overgrown courtyard, where in better times tradesmen had called with crates of champagne, oysters in season, truffles, and foie gras; and where nowadays few but Gaston, with his belly and beetroot nose, ever came.

In the cover of the shrubberies at the corner of the house, a large shape stood motionless as the postal vehicle bumped off down the narrow lane. Vrac stepped out onto the weed-choked, rain-spattered flagstones.

Jeanne saw him first and uttered a startled cry. She stamped her foot. "Go away. Shoo!"

Henri looked up and frowned. Then he said, "Ah, it's you. Come here."

FIVE

"You've got a *fouine*," said Mara.

She was balanced precariously on the courtyard wall, peering at the rough tile ends of Prudence Chang's roof. Down below, Jazz was whining and trying to scramble up after her.

Prudence, dressed in a smock like the figures in the Quimper ware she collected, frowned. Sunlight gleamed on her faultless casque of black hair. "I'm from L.A.," she complained. "The only wildlife you get there is Homo sapiens. So what's a foo-een in *anglais*?"

"A marten. Like a weasel." Mara shooed Jazz off and jumped down. "They like old stone houses. Look, you can see where it's been getting in. That hole right there. It's made its den in your roof."

"Oh, swell," said Prudence.

Like many of the expatriates coming back to the region for the summer, Prudence had called Mara first. If the toilets didn't work, if mice had chewed the wiring over the winter, if renovations were needed, Mara knew exactly what to do and whom to contact—fixers like Edouard, who would block up Prudence's roof; Kranz, the plumbing whiz; masons and painters who attended to damage done over the winter by wind and water. She also subcontracted work to a quaint trio of unmarried sisters in Limeuil who specialized in custom sewing.

"You'll have to leave it," Mara advised, brushing her hands off on her jeans. She had stopped by to check on a delivery of tiles from Pablo for the renovation of Prudence's kitchen. The stainless-steel double sink had been installed, but the new tiles for the counters had not arrived, despite the dealer's fervent promise to expedite them.

"Leave it?" Prudence objected. "Mara, it crashes around up there at night like a drunk husband. I'm losing my beauty sleep. And it smells."

"It'll smell worse if you close the hole up now. It's rearing a litter up there, and the lot of them will die. Wait until the babies are grown and leave the den. I'll get someone to seal it up for you then."

"Oh goody," said Prudence unenthusiastically. "I can hardly wait."

"By the way," said Prudence, walking Mara to her car. "That landscaper you set me up with."

"Julian Wood?"

"He's been asking questions about you."

"Oh?" Mara felt her cheeks go warm. "Like what?"

"Like what do I know about you. If you're attached. I think he's interested. Sweetie, you're turning pink."

Mara gave a snort of laughter. "He's fixated on orchids. I doubt if he thinks about anything but flowers. Besides, he's not my type. And I haven't turned pink."

Prudence cocked an Oriental eye at her. "What's your type, then?"

Mara was sure that the pink was now a dark red. "Oh," she said evasively, "someone a little more urbane. Less—less botanical. For heaven's sake, Prudence, I don't know."

"That's your problem," Prudence said, stepping back to regard her severely. "You really don't. I've known you now for—what?—two years? And in all that time I don't think I've ever seen you with a man. I mean, not seriously. What's wrong, gone off them?"

"Not at all." Mara was now on the defensive. "But I've been there before, don't forget. Marriage, divorce, the whole bit." And she had. Hal, her ex, had been a brilliant architect specializing in old stone structures. Everything she knew about restoring houses she had learned from him. Hal also had an ego bigger than the buildings he worked on and a love affair with the bottle that she simply couldn't compete with. Other relationships had followed for her, none of them satisfying. For some reason, she seemed to gravitate toward men who, though outwardly unlike Hal, inevitably revealed the same underlying trait: 150-proof self-worship. Although Julian didn't seem eaten up by conceit. Or was he? She knew nothing about him, really.

"Time to move on, don't you think?" suggested Prudence.

"When I'm ready," said Mara, ending the conversation.

Spring was Julian's favorite time of year. The lilacs were just finishing, but the locust trees, coming into bloom, gave a heady sweetness to the air. The hillsides were burnished with golden *genêt*, the local variety of broom, and poppies brightened the fields of newly planted wheat. Edith, Julian noted, was beginning to take on a sleek, self-satisfied look.

Spring was also Julian's peak time for gardening. He had a dozen or so properties that he maintained regularly. Throwing in Prudence Chang's courtyard, which was requiring a lot of work, he found himself hard at it from dawn to dusk. Not that he didn't welcome the business. He knew that things would die down for him later, when it got too hot to do more than nurse seedlings along. Business would pick up slightly in September and October, with fall plantings and beddings down, before dropping off entirely for the winter.

When he had time to think about anything else, his mind was taken up almost entirely with the *Cypripedium*. Almost, because it was hard not to think about Mara, too, given that she was so tightly bound up with this botanical puzzle. He felt a little sorry for her. But also resentful because her position amounted to nothing short of blackmail. Much good it would do her. He knew his chances of tracking down the Lady's Slipper were close to nil, which was exactly the odds he gave Mara's hopeless search for her missing twin. The thought filled him with a certain spiteful satisfaction.

·

More than a week had passed since Mara had distributed the photocopies. She knew that Julian would have phoned if the *pigeonnier* had been located, so she assumed he had no news. On the other hand, if he had been asking questions about her, as Prudence had said, she wondered that he hadn't found another reason for calling. She thought things over and decided to take matters in hand.

·

He was just pouring himself a late-morning mug of tea when the phone rang.

"Julian? It's Mara. Are you busy?"

It was Sunday morning, Julian's day of rest.

"Er—no," he said and wondered what he was letting himself in for.

"Well, I was hoping to invite you to lunch."

He was pleasantly surprised. "In that case, entirely at your disposal."

"Great. I'll pick you up at noon. And by the way, I hope you don't mind, there's someone I'd like you to meet."

"Oh?" He was wary once more. Whom did she mean? A boyfriend?

"Look, I've got to run now. Tell you about it when I see you. *A bientôt*." She rang off.

Julian put the receiver down. What the hell was she up to? It was something he really disliked about her, always tipping him off balance, speaking fluent French, albeit with peculiar vowel sounds, having a dog that lunged out of the dark to take off your arm, turning nasty over the photos. And now inviting him to lunch so she could introduce him to somebody else. Still, she was paying. He showered and put on a clean pair of slacks—well, they had a couple of not-too-visible splotches on the knee (Mado's crab mousse?)—and a freshly laundered shirt.

He waited for her at the roadside to save her the walk to his front door. She pulled up, and he got in. She looked glamorous in dark glasses and an orange short-sleeved dress. Her arms were slim, her neck graceful. Had she done something to her hair? It was shorter than he recalled, sleeker.

Jazz was in the back seat of her Renault, but no one else. So where was this person she wanted him to meet? He risked the French cheek-to-cheek greeting, keeping an eye out for any sign of jealousy from Jazz, but the dog only favored him with a careful exploration of the back of his neck with a cold, wet nose.

"So—where are we going? Or am I allowed to know?"

"Bergerac. There's a restaurant there I'm dying to try. And then Duras. Didn't I say?"

"No, you didn't." Bergerac first and then Duras? That would take the rest of the day. Really, Julian thought, feeling a little put out by her easy assumptions regarding himself. To make matters worse, her dog was now resting his heavy head on Julian's left shoulder.

"Sorry." She executed a three-point turn. "It's just

that the person I want you to meet lives in Duras. Louis—although he prefers to be called Loulou—"

The boyfriend, Julian confirmed with irritation and shoved the head away. It returned with a gust of malodorous breath. Why on earth invite him to lunch and drag him to Duras just to introduce him to a clown named Loulou?

"—La Pouge," she finished. "The retired policeman I told you about. The one who put me on to you."

"Ah." The one who had referred to him as—what was it?—a local authority. That was all right. Mollified, he reached back absentmindedly to scratch Jazz's neck.

"I phoned him yesterday. He wants to meet you." She braked before turning onto the main road. "I figured we could swing by Duras on our way back from Bergerac. It's not much out of the way. He's the one who was involved in investigating Bedie's disappearance. I told him about your idea of handing out copies of the *pigeonnier* photo, by the way. He said it was a very clever strategy."

"I'm afraid I haven't heard anything from Paul or Gaston," Julian had to admit.

"It's early days yet, Julian." She turned to him with a smile. The dark glasses flashed. Her voice had a huskiness that got him in the base of his spine. "Anything could happen."

Anything could, he thought, and warmed to the possibility. Suddenly he felt quite happy to be rocketing—she drove too fast—across the countryside with her. Glad about lunch in Bergerac, glad about Duras and Loulou.

•

Cyrano de Bergerac had nothing to do with Bergerac. Still, this did not prevent the Bergeracois from embracing Rostand's romantic hero as their own, even raising a statue to him, nose and all.

When Julian and Mara arrived in the old part of the town, they saw that the area around Cyrano's statue had been torn up. Consequently, parking was impossible, even on a Sunday. They had to leave the car below the Ancien Port and walk back up along the quai where in times past *gabarres*, the workhorses of the Dordogne, had discharged lumber from upcountry for making barrels and taken on casks of Bergerac wine. Nowadays it seemed the boats were mostly used to shunt tourists about.

Their destination was in the old town, a small restaurant called, with a grammarian play on words, Le Plus-que-Parfait, the Pluperfect. An elderly waiter waved them in and seated them at a shady table on the terrace at the rear. With a dignified tread, he brought Jazz a bowl of water on a tray before even considering Julian and Mara's needs. The French were like that. Nutty about dogs.

The lunch, living up to the restaurant's name, was more than perfect. Julian started with grilled foie gras of duck topped with thin parings of summer truffles and went on to a fish dish of *merluchon* baked in cream. Mara had oysters, followed by quail in a delicate pastry basket. She chose the wine, a crackling dry white Bordeaux. Cheese was roundels of *cabécou*, lightly grilled, dessert fresh Garriguette strawberries dipped in dark chocolate and topped with crème anglaise. Julian took the opportunity to point out that the strawberry, unlike most fruit, wore its seeds on the outside.

"The red pulpy bit that we think of as the strawberry is actually what's called the pseudocarp."

"No kidding," Mara commented with her mouth full.

Jazz sampled everything except the oysters, which Mara said made him sick. Mara liked the way Julian let her handle the wine, deferring to her choice. So many men she knew seemed to need to take charge of the wine, as if it were some kind of male preserve.

Their conversation throughout the meal was relaxed, verging at times on intimate as they disclosed to each other selected details of their lives.

"My people? Oh, your garden-variety Brits." Julian leaned back with a pleasant feeling of repletion. "I grew up in Essex, oldest of five. Did a degree in horticulture at Wye. In those lighter, swifter days of my youth," he sighed with exaggerated but perhaps not mock regret, "I played wing forward for my college rugby team."

Had he ever been married? Well, yes, he had. At the age of twenty-three, he had fallen hard for a stunning French au pair and moved with her to the Dordogne. It was the seventies, life was easy, and theirs the romance of the century. Unfortunately, like so many relationships, it hadn't worked out. Véronique had developed other interests. By then, however, he had taken root in French soil. He had been gardening in the Dordogne ever since. If Julian neatly glossed over how deeply the au pair's defection had hurt him, the chaos it had made of his life, and the anger he had experienced, still felt sometimes, he did so because that had been twenty-five years ago, and, where Véronique was concerned, the less said the better.

Mara described her background. Grew up in Montreal. Crazy hybrid family, Scottish father, French-Canadian mother who came from a tiny place in Quebec with the unlikely name of Saint-Louis-du-Ha! Ha! She explained that the "Ha! Ha!" (complete with exclamation marks) had nothing to do with laughter but was an old French word for "dead end." Many archaic terms no longer used in France still survived in Quebec.

"Mum's *pure laine*, one-hundred-percent *québécoise*," she informed Julian, "and a staunch separatist. Wants Quebec out of Canada. Dad says, Dream on, it'll never happen. They argue endlessly about it. It's their way—" She paused and drew breath "—of not talking about Bedie." She turned her wineglass about slowly, concentrating on the shifting level of the liquid.

"You know," she said, "when we were kids, Bedie and I hated being twins. We fought a lot, and we were horribly competitive. If I beat her at tennis, she had to beat me in skiing. We were always trying to put distance between us."

"Isn't that typical?" offered Julian. "I mean, with twins?"

She shrugged. "I suppose. Anyway, I left home in the seventies, did a couple of years at the Ontario College of Art, got a job with a design firm in Toronto. Bedie stayed on and did a degree in wildlife biology at McGill. After a few years apart, I think we realized, like it or not, we were joined. It was only then that we began to be friends."

After Bedie's disappearance, Mara had drifted, freelancing in Ottawa, Vancouver, and Montreal. She touched briefly on her failed marriage to Hal. Like Julian, she felt the less said the better. Bedie continued to haunt her dreams. Cutting ties in Canada to come to the Dordogne had not been easy, especially since it meant she had to start up anew in a place where she was unknown and where she knew no one. However, timing had been in her favor. With the boom in holiday cottages and the influx of expats, her line of work was now very much in demand.

"I have something for you," Mara said over coffee. Ceremoniously, she presented Julian with a duplicate set of the photographs.

"Ah," he said. "Thanks."

Tucking them in his shirt pocket, he had to

acknowledge that she had come through with her end of the bargain. Now he would have to make some sort of effort, even if halfhearted, to do his part. A deal was a deal.

SIX

They reached Duras around four in the afternoon. The buildings of the town ambled pleasantly along a breezy escarpment above the broad, green valley of the Dropt. Vineyards stretched away below them. Mara parked in front of a narrow stone-faced house just off the main road. They left Jazz in the car, head thrust disapprovingly through the open window. Julian sincerely hoped no one would pass within lunging distance of the vehicle.

"So, madame, we meet again!" Loulou La Pouge swept Mara an exaggerated bow. He pumped Julian's hand, greeting him in rapid, voluble French. He was a tubby, energetic man, pushing seventy, with remnant strands of hair plastered across a speckled scalp and a round face creased from smiling. Julian thought that he looked less like a retired cop than a superannuated cherub.

"*Entrez. Entrez.*" He led them into a narrow parlor crowded with furniture. An upright piano stood at one end of the room. Family photographs took up every available horizontal surface. There were more photographs on the walls. "Sit down. Sit down."

Julian and Mara perched stiffly on small overstuffed chairs while their host brought out a chilled Monbazillac.

"You know this wine?" Loulou held the bottle aloft. "Pure nectar. A specialty of the region. Gets its sweetness from a fungus, what we call *la pourriture noble*, the noble rot. It makes the grapes split open and shrivel up, a horrible sight, but it creates a very high sugar content. Did you know the harvest is done grape by grape, with special clippers?" He trotted away and came back with little glass dishes of shelled pistachios.

"*Santé!*" Loulou plumped his sizable haunches onto a plush-covered sofa and raised his glass. "Now we have our little chat, eh?" He poked a forefinger at Julian. "You must, of course, wonder how I got on to you in the first place. Well, I saw your slide show, eight, maybe nine years ago. In Bergerac. The wife talked me into going. She was keen on flowers. When she was alive. You gave a talk at the public library. Something about orchids. Unforgettable."

"Ah." Julian was gratified but unremembering.

"You tripped on the cord—ha-ha! The carousel went on the floor. Slides flew everywhere." The cherub gestured expansively.

"Ah," repeated Julian, placing the event.

"Everything was out of order. You kept saying, Sorry, sorry. All the same, when Mara looked me up, I remembered you. Thought maybe you'd be able to spot something in those photos. Couldn't recall your name, of course, but a fellow at the library was helpful. Still, I expect you'll have a time trying to trace those flowers."

Mara cut in, "Julian's very knowledgeable about orchids."

Loulou chuckled, as if she had just told a mildly funny joke. "Of course. However, as I already told you, your first problem is establishing that the camera really was your sister's in the first place."

Mara's chin shot up. "I'm positive it's the twin to mine. I'd know it anywhere. Besides, her initials were on the case."

"*Alors*, the famous initials." The cherub twinkled mirthfully. Another joke. "But we must look at the facts, eh? You found this camera where? A junk shop in Villeréal. How did it get there? Part of a lot purchase from another dealer. Where did this other dealer get the camera? Only *le bon dieu* knows because the person in question is now dead, and when she was alive, la Camelote showed up at every estate sale from Bordeaux to Toulouse. First the undertaker, then la Camelote. Where did she get it? She left no records of acquisition, that one! It could have been part of another lot purchase from another *brocanteur*, for all we know. I sympathize, but you must understand that the lads in Périgueux need more to go on than hearsay."

"Hearsay!" Mara was indignant. "Loulou, I'm convinced Bedie took those photos. This is the first positive lead I've had, and if the police aren't willing to do anything about it, I"—she glanced quickly at Julian—"*we're* going to follow it up."

Julian caught her shift of pronouns and fidgeted

uncomfortably in his chair.

"*Très bien*." Loulou threw up his hands. "Let's say, for the sake of argument, that's how it was. Then let's review the course of events. Before her disappearance, your sister and the boyfriend, Monsieur Scott Barrow, were camping at Les Gabarres. According to him, they had already visited—let me see—the Caves of Lascaux, Sarlat, Domme, La Roque–Gageac, Castelnaud. To get around, they walked or hitchhiked. Then they have the falling out. He wants to move on, she wants to stay. He goes off on the eighth of May, she remains at Les Gabarres. He comes back two days later, on the tenth. Their tent and equipment are still there, but your sister is not. On the thirteenth, Monsieur Scott becomes worried and calls the police.

"Now, if Mademoiselle Beatrice took those photos"—Loulou held up a finger—"mind, I don't say she did. But if she did, then she could only have done so *after* she and Monsieur Scott separated because in his *déclaration* he made no mention of having been to Beynac, which is on the first couple of frames of the film."

Mara shrugged. "Why not? It's a major tourist attraction. It was fairly near the campground. And, don't you see, the fact that she and Scott *hadn't* already visited Beynac is a kind of negative proof that Bedie took those pictures. Because if Bedie had already been there she would have had no reason to return."

Julian found her reasoning unncessarily complicated.

Loulou merely looked unconvinced. "But how much better if the photographs actually tied in with places your sister was definitely known to have visited? Or, better still, if there were a shot of her in front of the castle keep?"

Julian spoke up, realizing as he did so that he was nailing down Mara's earlier use of "we," but something, he knew, was expected of him. "Look, in my opinion, what you've really got to deal with is the *discontinuity*."

"*Comment?*" asked the ex-*flic*.

"I mean, after Beynac the quality of the light changes from overcast and wet to sunny and dry. Okay, admittedly, the weather can shift pretty rapidly in May. But also, and what's more important, the film goes from a castle in a built-up area to flowers that mainly grow in forests and undisturbed areas. Now, I know orchids pop up in the damnedest places—roadsides, airfields. Nevertheless, it really seems to me the critical piece is how Bedie got from Beynac to wherever she photographed this lot."

"Bravo," cried Loulou, clapping Julian on the shoulder. "You, *mon ami*, will make a detective yet." He tipped a handful of pistachios into the red hole of his mouth and scooted forward in his seat. "So," he said, munching loudly, "this suggests an interesting scenario. Mademoiselle Beatrice meets someone. They get to talking. She tells this person she's interested in orchids. He says, I know a place where the ground is covered with them. She goes with him. They drive to some isolated spot. Then—*tac!*—both Julian and Mara jumped—"he does away with her."

"But not right away," objected Julian. "Don't forget, she had the chance to take thirty more photographs. If this person intended to harm her, why wait?"

Loulou shoveled more nuts in his mouth and considered. "Maybe he didn't mean to. Maybe something happened along the way. Our man makes a pass. Mademoiselle Beatrice resists. Or perhaps he simply needed to lure her to a sufficiently isolated spot . . ."

Mara shuddered. "All the same," she persisted, "if this person knew where to find the orchids, then it means he must have been local, from the area. And if we can find where those orchids grew, it's possible they could lead us to him."

Loulou pulled a face. "What's local? Do you remember the Dutch tourist we dug up in Quercy? Hanneke Tenhagen, student from Eindhoven, twenty-one years old." He addressed himself to Julian. "Let me tell you something about Mademoiselle Tenhagen. Multiple fractures to the skull, as if the killer had been in a frenzy. Possibly raped. Her corpse was pretty badly decomposed when we got to it. A truffle hunter and his dog found her. Shallowly buried and then covered over with branches. Maybe the killer was disturbed in the middle of concealing the body. How did she get there? We interviewed an elderly couple who remembered picking up someone fitting Hanneke Tenhagen's description at the beginning of August outside of Millau. Drove her as far as Rodez. Three months later, her body turns up in the woods near Carennac, one hundred and twenty kilometers away, *mon dieu!* And between Carennac and Beynac, it's another eighty kilometers. So you see"—Loulou pivoted back to Mara—"your idea of local doesn't work. If he had a car, our killer could have come from anywhere, gone anywhere."

"He has a point," Julian conceded. Mara glared at him.

Loulou continued: "Even if you find out where those photos were taken, where do you start? Do you question everyone in the vicinity? Do you dig up the forests? You must comprehend, Mara, your sister's case was difficult because there was no evidence of a crime. I was working in Missing Persons at the time. We had very little to go on. I'm afraid she simply remained for us *la canadienne disparue.*"

Mara felt suddenly tired. The visit was taking a discouraging turn that she had not expected. Had Loulou invited them merely to justify the lack of interest on the part of the police? She glanced at Julian, who seemed disappointingly willing to capitulate. She was thinking of terminating their stay as politely as she could, when Loulou raised a hand.

"Of course, you haven't yet asked me the most important question."

Mara blinked. "What's that?"

"So far we have Mademoiselle Beatrice and the Dutch woman. But *were they the only ones?*"

Mara and Julian stared at him.

Mara found her voice. "There were others?"

Loulou savored his moment, rising to pour another round of wine and taking care to give the bottle a half-turn each time, to avoid drips. "Have more nuts," he said maddeningly.

"You see, my friends"—he addressed his guests but spoke as if a much bigger audience filled the room—"after I talked with you yesterday, Mara, I got to thinking. I used to keep a journal, rough case notes, to help me on the job, so to speak. I thought, who knows, maybe one day I'll write my memoirs. Well, anyway, I looked through them last night, just to refresh my mind." He paused, bottle in hand.

"And?" they asked in unison.

"*Eh bien*, there were *subsequent events* that might interest you."

They both sat forward. "Subsequent events?"

He nodded, pleased with his effect. "Just that. At intervals, spaced out over the next fourteen years."

"Bodies?" Julian asked.

"No," Loulou admitted regretfully, "but vanished, like Mademoiselle Beatrice. One was a woman from Souillac, Julie Ménard, thirty-five, married. Summer of '89 it was. Another was a middle-aged spinster, Mariette Charlebois, from Le Buisson, July 1993. Then there was a teenager, Valérie Rules, from the hamlet of La Bique, set out after school one day, never arrived home. That was in June 1998."

"They've never been heard from since?"

"Missing to this day. Every one of them." Loulou had the self-satisfied air of a magician making rabbits disappear. What he actually did, however, was to put the bottle down and go over to the piano bench. As he lifted the top, Julian and Mara could see that it was filled not with sheet music but with square copybooks with shiny red covers, such as schoolchildren used. "It's all," he said, proudly displaying his archive, "in here." Despite the cheap melodrama of it, they were impressed.

"Naturally," Loulou went on, "we did the usual routine questioning—family, friends, employers, teachers, parish priests. Even talked seriously with a couple of *types*."

"Well?" Mara pressed.

"*Phut!*" He dropped the piano bench lid with a resounding thud.

"Wait a minute." Mara turned suddenly to Julian. "La Bique. Isn't that just down the road from you?"

Julian, about to help himself to pistachios, paused. "Well, yes. Yes, it is. Oh, I see. Valérie Rules. Now that you mention it, I do remember hearing about her. I believe she went to school in Grissac. Everyone said she ran away from home."

"Who knows?" Their host pulled up a chair opposite them and sat down on it. "Let me tell you something. I'm speaking as a cop now, with many years' experience. With missing persons, psychology is very important. Julie Ménard, the woman from Souillac, husband claimed she went off with another man. Personally, I always thought the husband did her in. But her clothes were gone, and she did have a certain reputation. Or la Charlebois. Nursed her invalid *maman*, vicious old trout, rich to the gills, but never let her daughter have a life of her own. So one day poor Mariette just walks out and doesn't come back. Who can blame her? As for *la petite Valérie*, alcoholic father, neurotic mother, she could have run away. Kids do that. Is she dead? Or working the streets in Marseille?"

Loulou leaned forward. "Even Mademoiselle Beatrice. She and her boyfriend had a quarrel serious enough to cause Monsieur Scott to leave. Maybe your sister, out of spite or disgust, simply went off, too."

"But we would have heard from her," Mara cried out. "She would never have left us without word all these years—" She bit her lip, deeply troubled.

"But of course." Loulou waved a hand. "Undoubt-edly, something unpleasant occurred." Mara found it a perverse kind of comfort. "The question is, what? You see, Hanneke Tenhagen aside, where the other women are concerned we have to consider the possibility that *no crimes were committed at all*. Valérie, Mariette, and Julie could have simply left for reasons of their own. Beatrice could have met with an accident—"

"No," Mara objected. "The camera changes all that. Who-ever found the camera would have also found her body and reported it."

"Not necessarily, if she dropped the camera first. Picture it. She slips, drops the camera, tumbles off a cliff into the river, her body is never recovered. My point is simply that some or all of these missing women may still be alive."

"You don't believe that!" Mara cried.

Loulou tugged meditatively at the fatty wattle beneath his chin. "No," he said finally. "I don't. And this leads me to the second possibility and my little theory. Because, you see, if we say that these women, including your sister, are all dead, then we must also consider the possibility that their deaths were not unrelated."

Mara tensed. "Are you saying that we're dealing with a serial killer?"

Loulou cocked his head to one side. "It's something to think about, *n'est-ce pas*? And it leads us to an interesting speculation. Taken all together, the disappearances tell us a little about the person, if it is one person, whom we seek. *Primo*,"—he stuck up a big, flat thumb—"it was certainly a man, and one who chose his victims at random. Why? Because only Beatrice and Hanneke Tenhagen had anything in common. Both were tourists, similar age and build, both hitchhiking. Little Valérie Rules, on the other hand, was a schoolkid, fifteen, no breasts, skinny like a stick. La Charlebois, forty-two, fat, face like a cow pat. Julie Ménard, thirty-five, glamorous in a cheap way, liked the bright lights. So he took them as he found them.

"*Secundo*,"—a forefinger shot out to join the thumb—"he probably was, how should we say, *comme il faut*, presentable. Maybe even"—he grinned at Julian—"an orchid amateur like yourself. Oho! You are discomfited. But it's logical. Who better to attract someone like Mademoiselle Beatrice, who loved orchids and who would be easily approachable by anyone who shared her interest? Tell me, were you in the Dordogne nineteen years ago, monsieur?"

Julian looked aghast. "Was I—? Well, yes, I was."

"And you undoubtedly heard about *la canadienne disparue*?"

"Of course I did," cried Julian irritably. "It was everywhere on the news. But there was absolutely no mention of orchids at the time."

"True," admitted Loulou. "That's something that has only come to light just now. Always assuming, of course, that the photographs were taken by Mara's sister."

"They were," said Mara doggedly.

"Regardless," Julian persisted, "you can't honestly believe—"

"*Assez*. Enough," Loulou chuckled. "Just my little joke. All I say is, whoever it was, his victims must have trusted him. Hanneke Tenhagen was hitching rides, very possibly Mademoiselle Beatrice and Valérie Rules as well. Would any of them have gone willingly with Quasimodo?"

Julian parried, "He could have forced them or taken them by surprise."

"You mean followed them to a lonely spot and then—*couic!*" Loulou drew his forefinger sharply across his throat.

Mara winced.

The ex-cop shook his head. "It doesn't fit. Take Mariette Charlebois, fat, asthmatic. Or the Ménard woman. Unlikely that either of them would have been wandering alone in the forest. More probably our predator met them in a more conventional way. Say la Charlebois is sitting disconsolately in a *salon de thé*, dipping a macaroon and thinking about her horrible mama. A stranger befriends her. He is *sympathique*, offers her a ride somewhere. Or Julie Ménard. Picks her up in a bar.

"*Tertio*, it's probable that our man lived or worked somewhere in the region, or traveled, for whatever reason, within Périgord-Quercy. And, finally, he must have had some form of transportation because the disappearances were widely distributed."

Julian developed this train of thought. "So you have a body in Carennac and four others missing, last seen in Souillac, La Bique, Le Buisson—and Beynac, if we accept that Bedie was there. All of these places lie in an east-west line *exactly following the Dordogne*. Have you considered that the person you're looking for might work on the river? A barge hand, for example. Or someone who works on those tourist *gabarres*."

"Hmm," said Loulou. "Yes, we thought of that. Except my theory is, it's not the river but the road.

Every one of those places is also on the D703, the major east-west artery, or the D25 where it joins the D703. Who knows, maybe he was a trucker with a delivery route along that stretch."

Mara came in. "The dates of these incidents. Except for Bedie and the Dutch woman, which occurred in the same year, the others were—what?— roughly four or five years apart? You said the last one was Valérie Rules, in 1998. So nothing's happened since then?"

"Not within the region. Not so far." A hard glint came into Loulou's eyes. "Makes you wonder, doesn't it?"

"Yes, it does."

"But surely women have gone missing in other places," Julian objected.

"*Certainement*. Over the years there have been disappearances elsewhere—Limoges, Bordeaux, Biarritz."

"Then maybe your man's not from around here after all. And maybe the four-to-five-year gap doesn't hold, either. In fact, as you pointed out, every one of these women could have gone off for their own reasons. You could be looking for a killer and a pattern that don't exist."

"Hanneke Tenhagen was most definitely and brutally murdered," Loulou reminded him sharply.

"Of course," Julian conceded, looking vaguely troubled. "I wasn't referring to her."

"And my sister," said Mara. "She didn't disappear

of her own volition. I'm sure of that. I think Loulou's right. I don't know about the women in other places, but for my money, Bedie, Hanneke Tenhagen, Julie Ménard, Mariette Charlebois, and Valérie Rules are connected somehow. I think there's a killer loose in the Dordogne, Julian, and he's probably looking for his next victim right now."

They were all silent for a long moment.

Julian was the first to speak. "All of this is very interesting. But what are we supposed to do with it?"

"Do?" Loulou looked startled. "In my opinion, nothing. But of course, that's up to you." He peered closely at Mara and shook his head. "I fear, however, that Madame is very much the one for action."

"I'm convinced the orchids are trying to tell us something, at least where my sister is concerned," she said.

"*Eh bien*, what about you, Monsieur the Orchid Expert? Do these flowers also speak to you?"

Julian blinked. "Well," he said after a moment, "it so happens the section of the Dordogne Valley between Souillac and Le Buisson is a part of the region I know well because of the mapping and field research I did for my book." Not in his wildest dreams had he ever expected *Wildflowers of the Dordogne/Fleurs sauvages de la Dordogne* to be put to such a bizarre application. "Offhand, I'd say that most of the orchids in the photographs could be found there. Trouble is, they can also be found in other places, scattered pretty much throughout the region." He shook his head. "When all's said and done, it's precious little to go on."

By the time Loulou saw them out, the day was coming to a spectacular end. A fierce sunset bathed the western face of the town, lingered redly in the windows of the houses. The vineyards in the valley below stood in shadow.

"*Bonne chance!*" Loulou shook hands energetically with them. "I think you have much work ahead of you. Keep me informed. I'll be very interested to know how you progress." He added gravely, "But be careful. You realize, do you not, Mara, that you place yourself in great jeopardy?"

"Me?" Mara was startled.

"But of course. If our killer is still operating in the area, you could come as a nasty shock." And since she still looked puzzled, he explained: "Your face, Mara. Your face. You will remind him unpleasantly of a woman he murdered nineteen years ago. Our man will not be happy finding you on his trail. Having killed before, how easy it will be for him to kill again." Loulou regarded her searchingly. In a moment of genuine solicitousness, he took her hand once more.

"If you really want my advice, I say give it up. Take it from me. Some things are better left alone."

•

"I'm not sure how useful that was," Julian grumbled as they left Loulou's house. "All we know now is that four other women, apart from Bedie, have gone missing, and the police haven't been able to find them. And I'm not including Hanneke Tenhagen."

"But there's the possibility that one person might be behind the disappearances," said Mara. "It puts everything in a different light."

"Humph," said Julian.

As Mara drove out of the town, she reflected that Julian had played it rather cagey about Bedie and Valérie Rules. He clearly remembered the cases well enough but for some reason had been reluctant to admit his knowledge. Was he just one of those people who didn't like talking about unpleasant things? Or was there something more behind his reticence?

"Are you going to take his advice about giving it up?" Julian asked, noting that she had gone quiet.

"Of course not," said Mara, downshifting into a turn.

Far away, against a fiery sky, a buzzard circled lazily, on the hunt.

SEVEN

Mara e-mailed Patsy:

> > Look, Patsy, I know you don't do criminal psychiatry, but do you have any thoughts on what the profile of a serial killer might look like? <

In her Manhattan office, housed on the third floor of a dignified if dingy brownstone, Patsy frowned as she read Mara's message. She rubbed her nose, made a noise that sounded like "Sheew!," and tapped out a response.

> > Not until you tell me what's behind this, kiddo. <

> > Loulou La Pouge, the ex-flic I told you about, thinks we may be dealing with a serial killer. He's collected information on other women who have gone missing from the area. Bedie and Hanneke Tenhagen, whom you know about, both date from 1984, but after that there was someone named Julie Ménard from Souillac who disappeared in 1989, then a Mariette Charlebois from Le Buisson in 1993, and a schoolgirl from La Bique in 1998. The problem is, except for Hanneke Tenhagen, there was no evidence of a crime in any of the cases,

they're all simply missing persons. Nevertheless, Loulou thinks they were all the victims of foul play by a single perpetrator. <

> *Okay, I get you. Look, like you said, I'm no forensic shrink. There's a range of psychiatric disorders that can turn nasty, given the right push. But what you're talking about is a whole different twist. However, at a guess, I'd say your subject would probably present as someone with a lot of unresolved anger, obsessive, a loner, socially inept. Although not necessarily a geek. In fact, this person might have to be capable of projecting a lot of charm in order to get near his victims. Don't forget, some of the most horrific mass murderers have behaved like thoroughly nice people. At least at first.* <

> *Right. My next question is, what would drive this person to seek a victim at regular intervals? The dates of all these incidents are roughly four to five years apart.* <

> *Hoo boy. You don't want much, do you? At a guess, and this is no more than a guess, I'd say any situation that causes the demons to rise, say an adverse life change or some sort of personal crisis. On the other hand, it might be as simple as noncompliance with medications. Say we're dealing with a severely paranoid individual on antipsychotic drugs who quits taking his Thorazine every*

so often and starts hearing voices. It could also be something that moves this person periodically out of circulation. Say a series of prison sentences or a history of repeat psychiatric hospital stays. Then again, maybe he simply goes by an inner clock. However, the real question for me, Mara, is not the timing, but what makes a serial killer in the first place. Is it simply hard-wiring? Some kind of significant precipitating conditions? A combination of both? Answer that question, kid, and you could make psychiatric history. <

It was something to go on, Mara reflected as she read Patsy's reply. Except how did she set about commandeering the incarceration and release records of every person who'd served time in a French jail since 1984, or the admission-discharge information of psychiatric patients? She doubted Loulou would be willing or even able to twist arms to help her. And what about Patsy's question. Was the killer she sought triggered by cyclical events? Or was he driven by an inner impulse, like a spring wound tighter and tighter until it caused the mechanism it governed to burst apart?

•

Paul gave out the photocopies of the *pigeonnier*. Like Gaston, he did not mention Mara's money incentive. He did not see his father until the following week, when he and Mado went to the family farm outside Issigeac for Sunday lunch. His uncle Emile and Sylvie, Emile's wife, were also there.

Paul's mother had prepared a haunch of Quercy lamb, lightly rubbed with garlic and so tender it made one sigh. They had, in addition, fennel in cream sauce with pan-roasted potatoes, a compote of prunes, a plate of local cheeses, and a Savoy cake, light and moist as only Tante Sylvie, a Savoyarde from Bonneville, could make it. The wine was a robust red from the family's own vineyard. Fresh figs finished off the meal. Paul's mother believed, for reasons of her own, that figs would help Mado to conceive.

"By the way," Paul said as the women cleared the table for coffee and Armagnac. He pulled out a crumpled copy of the dovecote photo and handed it across to his father and uncle. "Does this look familiar?"

His father adjusted his glasses, smoothed out the paper, and peered at it. "It's a pigeon house," he said finally, handing it on to Emile.

"Right," said his brother, who suffered from a left-veering amblyopia.

"I mean," said Paul, "do you know it?"

Uncle Emile, bad eye wandering up the chimney, reached for a toothpick. "Sure."

"You do?" Paul sat forward. "This very one?"

"Well, maybe not this very one. *Zut!* You can stand on a hilltop and see half a dozen like it any day."

"Not so much around here, though," said Paul's father.

"What's wrong with around here?" asked Paul.

"Well, they didn't go in for pigeons as much. Pigeons eat too much grain."

"And the roof of this one is different," offered Uncle Emile.

"How so?"

"It's made with *lauzes*. Around here it's mostly tile."

"What's so special about this one, anyway?" Paul's father tapped the photocopy.

"Nothing," said his son, "but if you can locate it, there's money in it."

Father and uncle looked interested for the first time. "How much?" they asked together.

"One thousand euros. Split two ways, five hundred for me, five hundred for whoever can tell me where to find it."

"One thousand euros." Uncle Emile screwed up his face in the effort of converting currencies. He still thought in francs, would never get used to euros. "*Bigre!* That's almost seven thousand francs."

Both older men looked more carefully at the photocopy.

"Where do you come in?" asked the father after a while.

"Brokerage fee," grinned the son, leaning back in his chair, content for the moment to digest his excellent meal.

•

Slowly breasting the hill, the ancient wood-paneled truck came to a groaning, fumy halt at the summit. The young German hitchhiker ran forward gladly, swinging his rucksack onto his back.

113

"Sarlat?" he inquired with a broad smile, naming his destination to the driver.

The driver, a farmer in a shapeless, broad-brimmed hat, barely glanced at the hitchhiker, gave a grunt and a nod, and signaled with a thumb for the young man to climb onto the bed of the truck.

"*Danke! Merci!*" the youth shouted. He trotted back and hoisted himself lightly up over the tailgate.

The vehicle revved up with a shuddering jerk, moved forward, and gathered speed on the downhill run. The German, whose name was Hans, slipped off his pack and lowered himself beside it, squeezing down onto the floor of the truck bed between a stack of empty crates and an assortment of muddy tires and dented milk cans. On the other side of the crates was a heap of dirty sacking. A thin, good-looking youth traveling *auto-stop* through France for the first time, Hans had been lucky. From Carcassonne, two rides in swift succession had brought him this far. He calculated that this lift would bring him to Sarlat within the hour. He leaned back against the wooden slats of the side frame, stretching his long legs out before him, and congratulated himself on his good fortune. With the heel of his boot he shoved one of the crates aside to make more space. The sacking next to it moved. Hans was startled to see that he was not alone. A hand flapped in the air, as if driving away flies. Then the sacking sat up. Hans saw a flat, misshapen face perched neckless on a massive pair of shoulders. One eye was obscured by a dark lens. The other glared at him balefully.

"*Bitte*," said Hans faintly, forgetting momentarily what little French he knew. The uncovered eye continued to fix him unpleasantly.

"I go to Sarlat." Hans struggled. "You go also to Sarlat?"

The face gave no indication of intelligent reception.

Hans smiled weakly. Nervously, he dug into his rucksack for his guidebook and made a great display of poring through it. Sarlat-la-Canéda, the German text informed him, boasted some of the finest examples of medieval secular architecture in the Dordogne. The town had grown up around a ninth-century Benedictine abbey. The thirteenth and early fourteenth centuries were the golden age for Sarlat, which waxed in importance as a market town. But the Hundred Years' War left it weakened and depopulated.

Hans stole a nervous glance at his companion, who had not left off staring at him in a way that made the young German increasingly uncomfortable. It was at this point that Hans realized that they had left the main highway and were bouncing crazily over a dirt road, headed in a westerly direction, trailing a plume of dust behind them.

"Hey, wait a minute," he shouted in German. "Stop! Where are you going?"

If anything, the truck picked up speed. With difficulty, he stood up, steadying himself against the side rail, and worked his way forward. In order to reach the cab, he had to step over the legs of his fellow passenger.

"*Bitte*," he said again and banged with his fist on the metal roof. "*Halt!*" The wind cut at his blond hair as he stood swaying with the side-to-side motion of the vehicle. "*Stopp! Stopp!*" The landscape of Black Périgord, which he had so recently been prepared to admire, flew past him, wild and unfriendly. Then the truck took a sudden turn that sent him sprawling over the other man, upsetting the crates, which, being loosely stacked, went spinning against the tailgate. The patch-eyed man, with intentional malevolence, seized the hapless German by the collar and shoved him backward with a force sufficient to land him winded against the opposite side of the bed.

"Hey!" shouted Hans, terrified but prepared to defend himself. "What did you do that for?"

For answer, Vrac gave only a hoarse, unpleasant laugh.

Hans took in the size of the man's hands and the fact that they were now jolting through alien forest over a deeply rutted road. Tall trees rose up gloomily all around. Mutely, he sank to the floor of the truck bed.

After what seemed like an interminable time to the young German, the truck came to a rocking halt. The cab door slammed, and the driver got out and came to the back.

"Listen." Hans rose to his feet and stopped. He

now perceived that the driver was not a man but a woman, but that did not improve his situation. Seen full-on, hat pushed back, her aspect, with its gargoyle features and a purple mark over one eye, was enough to make his mouth go dry.

"Wh-what do you want?"

"Cash." La Binette held out a blackened hand as hard and horny as a hoof. She never took traveler's checks or credit cards.

"Haven't got any," Hans squeaked, which was near enough to the truth.

"Your wallet," la Binette demanded.

"I give you money, and then what?" he demanded spiritedly in his rudimentary French.

Again, Vrac gave a loud, braying laugh. "Give!" he roared, rising to his feet.

Frightened though he was, Hans was a quick thinker. Also a fast sprinter.

"All right," he said and picked up his pack as if to comply. In one fluid motion, he leaped over the opposite side rail and was off through the trees, running like a hare.

Vrac gave a tardy bellow and lumbered forward.

"Leave it," snarled the mother. The German was already lost to view. With a stoical grunt, la Binette climbed back into the cab, turned the truck around, and set off in the direction they had come. Vrac lay down again and resumed his nap. His mother drove until they rejoined the D703. She turned onto it and proceeded slowly west. At this time of year there wasn't much traffic, and fewer hitchhikers. From June on, she knew things would improve.

EIGHT

She stood still, her heart pounding. Once again she heard the sounds, a soft rustling in the undergrowth, the snap of a twig.

"Who's there?" she called. And turned, staring wildly about her.

From the dark shadow of the forest there came only breathless silence.

Panicked, she groped for a stick, a rock, anything with which to defend herself. Then she glimpsed it moving behind the screen of trees. Slowly it broke into view, coming on her with an implacable tread. In horror, Mara saw for the first time the large, shapeless thing that had been behind her, the creature through whose hungry eyes she had watched her sister on the forest path. Desperate to buy escape for Bedie, Mara did the only thing she could do. Shouting an inarticulate challenge, she ran straight at it.

•

She awoke with a thundering in her head. *A dream*, she told herself. *It was only a dream.* Abruptly, she sat up in the darkness, breathing hard.

And then she froze in terror. *It had been no dream.* There was something in the room with her, a black, featureless form standing motionless at the foot of her bed. She opened her mouth to scream. Nothing

119

but a strangled whimper came out. As she cowered there helplessly, the thing raised its arms, and she saw in that awful moment that it had no head. In a rush it was on her, enveloping her in a sudden, suffocating wave of red.

•

Mara lay facedown, drenched in sweat, heart hammering in her chest. The blankets were twisted around her legs. Gradually, familiar sounds reached her. Jazz's light snoring beside her on the bed. The early-morning sound of birds. She raised her head. Gray, misty dawn filled her window.

With a sob, she stumbled out into the cold, damp air, ran barefoot across the wet grass, fumbled with the latch of her studio door. Once inside, she switched on her computer with trembling fingers, dialed up and pounded out her electronic cry for help.

> . . . *My god, Patsy, what does it mean? Why headless, why red, and why now, after all these years?* <

•

Patsy Reicher opened Mara's e-mail hours later, at the start of her day by New York time. She ran her fingers through her crazy gray-red mop of hair. Thoughtfully, she moved a wad of gum from one side of her mouth to the other. The air in her office was stale. She got up from her desk, shoved open a window. The smell of the day, the grind of traffic, a sudden blare of car horns reached her from the street below. She returned to her desk and tapped out a response:

> *Calm down, Mara. Headless because so far he's faceless. Red? Well, he ain't Santa. Try red for danger, red for predator. Hunters always wear red, don't they? And why now? Because you've got new information, you're processing it, and you're beginning to believe that things are finally breaking open on Bedie. Maybe they are. Go carefully, kiddo. You may not like what you find.* <

·

She was at his door again, sweeping past in a rush of air, taking possession of his front room. "Julian, we need to make a start."

"Eh? What are you talking about?"

It was nine o'clock on a Friday evening. Mara's knock had jerked him out of an armchair doze, dog-tired as he was from a day of heavy labor. He had been assisted in this enterprise by his neighbor's grandson, Bernard, whom he employed casually, partly because Madame Léon was a lovely old girl, partly because he valued fresh eggs, and partly because Bernard was the closest thing Julian had to a bulldozer. He really didn't want to deal with Mara.

"Our search for the orchids. And the *pigeonnier*." She was depositing an assortment of maps on his dining table.

Christ! There it was again, this coming at him blind-side. Julian shook himself awake. He needed to take control of the situation.

"Look here, Mara, you simply have no idea what you're asking. Do you know how much area we'd have to cover? On foot and bending from the waist?"

She paused, clearly lacking the faintest notion of the enormity of her demand. "Why bending from the waist?"

"Because, dammit, terrestrial orchids aren't that bloody easy to see! They grow in tall grass and among other plants. They're widely scattered. Anyway, I already told you, you're looking for a specific place that might never have existed, where a certain sequence of flora grew. Nearly twenty years ago. It could have been plowed up, grazed over, or wiped out by herbicides. Or simply buried under a meter of cement!"

She was taken aback by his vehemence. "But you agreed to help me. I can't do it alone. You know the terrain. You've got the field notes."

"Okay. Sure. But I'm telling you, it's not that bleeding easy."

"Right." She raised her hands, palms forward. "That's where I thought the *pigeonnier* would come in. I've worked out a system. We'll look for it first, as our main point of reference, you see? Once we find it, we can use the orchids to work from there."

"If we find it, don't you mean? Don't forget, Paul, Gaston and god knows who else have been looking. So have you, so have I—"

"Well, I've just figured out a way of making the job easier," she announced, waving at the maps. "The Série bleue. I got one for every section of the

Dordogne and including the western part of Quercy. They show everything. I don't know why I didn't think of it sooner."

Julian was fully familiar with the Série bleue maps. They were a necessity to someone like him, whose customers resided on isolated hilltops, in the hidden folds of valleys, and down unmarked lanes. The maps, on a scale of one centimeter to 250 meters, and based on National Geographical Institute surveys, depicted not only contour lines, geological features, land use, and types of vegetative cover, but every road, every footpath, every man-made structure on the landscape. He could, for example, pick out his own cottage—fifth dot on the right on the road going west out of Grissac. But it was difficult to say, unless you knew beforehand, what was what.

"Look," he pointed out, "they show everything, sure, but these maps aren't foolproof. Or what if the *pigeonnier* we're looking for no longer exists? Besides, on paper, buildings show up only as black dots. Things aren't labeled 'house' or 'barn,' you know. How will you be able to tell a dovecote from a—a pigsty or a *cabane*?"

"Simple. The *pigeonnier* we're looking for is in the middle of a field, away from other buildings. All we have to do is look for isolated dots in the middle of open spaces."

"All we have to do—? Mara, there must be thousands of isolated dots in the middle of open spaces all over the Dordogne. Are we going to check out every one of them?"

"Listen," she said, a flinty edge coming into her voice, "we had a deal. You got your photographs. Now help me find my sister. Or at least the path she walked before she disappeared."

He gave in. In a perverse sort of way, he was even relieved that she had kick-started the process. He had been sitting on the fence for days, wondering how to deal with her, what to do about the Lady's Slipper, wanting it but knowing it to be impossible. Now she had given him a possible means to resolve both issues. But he'd have to work fast. Orchids had a limited flowering season. It was already coming on to early May. It had been a hot, wet spring, with early flowering, meaning that many of the specimens captured in the film would not be much longer in evidence. Using the maps to identify possible *pigeonniers* made sense. At least it shortened the odds.

"All right," he said. "Give me a couple of days. I'll see what I can do."

•

Thus, Julian found himself spending his Saturday afternoon after rugby (Grissac won for a change, twenty-three to fifteen, in their "friendly" game against La Grotte) at home, instead of celebrating at Chez Nous in the company of teammates. Forgoing Mado's mouth-watering veal pie, he settled down at his kitchen table with the photographs and a solitary, sorry lunch of tinned cassoulet, washed down by quite a bit of wine.

The only way through an impossible task, he decided, was to be systematic. He got a pad of paper and lined off the top sheet into three columns. In the first column, he listed the orchids in the photographs by common rather than taxonomical name and in order of their appearance. There were fourteen different species in all. The first seven—Helleborines, *Limodorum*, Common Spotteds, Military Orchids, Bird's-nest, Butterfly, and Pyramidal Orchids—were followed by the *pigeonnier*. Then another seven: Marsh, Bee, Lizard, Man, Lady, Tongue, and Fly Orchids. Finally, the Lady's Slipper. Next to each, in the second column, he jotted down what he knew of the growing environment. Orchids were habitat-specific. Each required well-defined growing conditions: sun, dappled light, deep shade, varying degrees of dampness and soil conditions. Some proliferated on hilltops and open meadows; others grew shyly in woodlands and forests. Some occurred in conjunction with certain trees; some were transitional plants, occupying the edges of clearings; still others could only be found in wetlands.

When he had completed this task, he saw that the information, organized in this way, told more of a story than he had realized. In fact, he had created a specific progression of landscapes, like beads threaded on a string. However, the problem was locating where this particular combination of habitats was to be found. For the region in its entirety provided endless possibilities: pine and deciduous forests, grasslands, fields, swamps, seepage zones, scree, scrubland, all characterized by the calcareous, alkaline soils on which most of the species he had listed thrived. Again, he was ominously aware of the immensity of the undertaking ahead of him.

His only recourse was to fall back on actual sightings. These were documented in field notes that he had made over the years, as well as hundreds of prints and slides, everything stored topsy-turvy in an old metal cabinet.

He began by pulling out anything related to the orchids captured on the film and entering known locations in the third column. For most, he had numerous sightings, and in some cases this proved more problematic than helpful. For example, the purple Pyramidal Orchid, an aggressive colonizer, grew everywhere. Next to it he simply wrote: *widespread, abundant*.

Then it occurred to him that he really needed to focus on sightings dating from around the time of Bedie's disappearance in 1984. Here he met a more serious roadblock. In those days he had not been particularly systematic in charting floral distributions, except for the notations he had done for his book, and even these were casual scribbles on the backs of envelopes and so forth.

"Merde!" he uttered, shoving his glasses up to the top of his head.

Inevitably, his thoughts drifted to the *Cypripedium*. He rose to stare in fascination at a blowup of the print that he had pinned to his kitchen wall. There was now no doubt in his mind about the slipper-shaped labellum, although a more objective observer might have pointed out that the stain running across the print made identification iffy. A remarkable flower under any circumstances, magnified five times it seemed almost nightmarish. The deep-pink labellum looked swollen, veined, and slightly obscene, although some of these effects could have been owing to the graininess of the enlargement. Two wildly twisted lateral petals, springing stiffly away from the slipper, resembled fantastical, blackish-purple mustachios.

"*Merde!*" he said again, turning away from the blowup in frustration. Why did this have to be the worst of the lot, and the only one to lack a habitat shot? Not that this in itself would have pinpointed a location, but at least the surrounding growth and leaf litter might have furnished him with something to go on. It occurred to him (he was in a maudlin mood) that it was all too emblematic of his life—doomed to clutch hopelessly at the things he wanted most, desired objects dangling just out of reach. More wine reconciled him to his fate.

He was slumped in an attitude of defeat when Edith appeared in the open doorway. She looked at him speculatively. Julian considered the fag end of his dinner, congealing palely on his plate.

"All right, you opportunistic bitch," he muttered and scraped the remains into her dish. Watching the pointer gulp it down, Julian gave in and decided to call for help.

•

"*Allo?*" Géraud Laval's voice thundered at him through the telephone.

"Géraud? Julian. Julian Wood. What? No. Géraud—yes, yes, I know. Géraud, look, I've—er—got a problem. No, not personal, floral. I said floral. Are you and Iris busy? Well, I don't want— Oh, all right, if you're sure. Great. Be there in half an hour."

Julian did not like Géraud. Put plainly, the man was insufferable. He was also Julian's main rival in the Société Jeannette's Bring and Brag, as Julian called it. The club, which attracted wildflower enthusiasts from Mussidan to Rocamadour, met monthly in different locations. The end of each meeting was always set aside for members to show off important botanical finds. Julian vied bitterly with Géraud for primacy in this area.

On the other hand, Géraud Laval was the only person who could help him. A vastly knowledgeable orchidologist, he bred tropicals in a hot room attached to his house and grew plantations of temperate species on his property near the village of Malpech. Géraud lived with Iris Potter, a cheerful woman from Lancashire whom Julian did like, in a long-standing but on-and-off relationship. That is, every now and then Iris declared Géraud to be impossible to live with and moved out. Her goings were always noisy, with everyone taking sides; her returns surprisingly uneventful, word simply going round that Iris was back. She had been back, as near as Julian could reckon, for nearly half a dozen years.

Resignedly, Julian grabbed his notes and Mara's photographs (imagining Géraud's sneers at the poor quality) and headed for the door. Then a better idea struck him. A malicious grin spread over his face. He turned back and reached for the phone. There was no reason, he thought, why Mara shouldn't help to bear the brunt of Géraud's obnoxious personality.

•

Mara had spent a frustrating day. Wealthy American friends of Prudence had purchased a charming nineteenth-century manor house and were now complaining about the rudimentary state of just about everything, especially the water closet. Their problem was now Mara's headache, since she had agreed to put things right. It came with the territory, she had to admit. Without people who bought things they ultimately couldn't live with, she would be out of business. Her difficulty at the moment lay with Kranz, the plumbing whiz, who had stubbornly voiced several objections, mainly structural, to her redesign. Stare as she might at the sketch before her, she could see no other way of repositioning the narrow little recess that currently housed the toilet. She was glad, when Julian called, for a reason to quit her studio.

Now she was crammed into the front seat of his van, feet on a coiled hose, knees jammed against a plastic sack of fertilizer, as they sped off in the direction of Malpech.

"Géraud Laval's a retired pharmacist," Julian informed her. He swerved around a pothole. "And, to hear him talk, the world's leading mushroom authority."

The edge in his voice made Mara look at him sideways. She had been in the region long enough to know that pharmacies routinely dispensed, along with pills and enemas, advice on the edibility of wild mushrooms. From late summer onward, the woods swarmed with people in search of apricot-hued chanterelles, black-capped *têtes de nègre*, and other edible cèpes. Every year, people got sick or even died from failing to distinguish an innocuous fungus from a deadly cousin. The easiest way of knowing was to consult your local pharmacist. So maybe this Géraud's claim wasn't as far-fetched as Julian made it sound.

"He's also as vain as a prima donna," Julian went on. "And twice as temperamental."

"Then why are we going to see him?"

"Because," Julian admitted grudgingly, "he's as good as they get where orchids are concerned. Breeds fancy tropicals and has a fine collection of European orchids right in his own backyard. Which he got from rootstock, not seed, I might add."

"Meaning?" His tone was ominous, but the significance escaped her.

"Meaning the bugger digs up wild plant material rather than gathering the seed and growing his orchids in vitro, as any"—Julian downshifted angrily—"decent conservationist would do. And by the way, Mara, while we're there, it might be better if you let me do the talking."

"Let you—? Oh, be my guest!" Mara rolled her eyes. Really, if he wanted her to keep her mouth shut, why bother having her along?

•

Iris met them at the door, a short, dumpy person with a round, weathered face, very blue eyes, and wispy gray hair. She wore a paint-smeared smock over baggy trousers, and her broad, flat feet were strapped into leather sandals.

"So glad you came," she welcomed them in English after Julian made the introductions. She gave Mara a friendly but frankly curious once-over before adding, "Visitors. Always relieves the tension." Not bothering to lower her voice, she informed them as she led them in, "He's been absolutely awful these last few weeks, you know. Honestly, I really think it's time I left him. What do you think, Julian?"

"By all means." Julian seemed to take the question in his stride.

Mara did not know what to think. She focused instead on the walls of the front room, which were covered with bad impressionistic floral paintings that seemed to match the condition of Iris's smock.

"You're the artist?" she inquired.

The other woman giggled. "Awful, aren't they? But they sell surprisingly well. Come on. Don't want to keep his nibs waiting."

"Ha! Julian Wood!" roared a short, powerfully built man, emerging from the depths of a glassed-in area attached to the back of the house. *"Entrez, entrez!"* The space was crowded with moss-filled hanging baskets and clamorous with blooms.

Iris left them, and Julian made more introductions, this time *en français*. Everything from that point on switched to French. Conversations in the Dordogne, which was rapidly filling up with English-speaking expatriates, were apt to be like that, a mix of languages according to the speakers.

"Enchanté, madame," Géraud boomed. He stared avidly at Mara, then bowed and kissed her hand. His prominent head, bald on top, was made fantastic by wild sprouts of white hair springing like horns from the sides. Tufts of darker hair grew out of his ears. Mara wondered if they impeded his hearing, causing him to shout the way he did. "Are you as well an orchid amateur?"

"Débutante," Mara admitted. "What lovely flowers. But why is everything hanging from the ceiling?"

"Because," said Géraud smugly, "these are tropical epiphytes. *C'est-à-dire*, in their natural jungle habitat, they grow on trees to get light, and their root systems are designed to capture airborne nutrients. I mimic here the same conditions. Whereas orchids that grow in the ground, such as our local species, put out tubers or rhizomes. Do you know," he leered, "why I consider the orchid to be the most sexual of flowers?"

"I have no idea," said Mara, not liking the leer but enjoying the look of disgust on Julian's face.

"Why, because the tubers are—ahem—testicular in shape, hence the name 'orchid.' From the Greek, *orchis*, you see, which means testicle—"

"Yes, yes." Julian moved in to stem Géraud's verbal foreplay. "While you're at it, why not tell her that 'orchidotomy' means castration, and 'orchialgia' means pain in the balls?"

Géraud glared at him. "Come." Skillfully he steered Mara away. "Let me show you my new *Paphiopedilum*."

Proudly, he walked her over to a large, glossy flower rising imperiously from a slender stalk. A tropical species of Slipper Orchid, it had a greenish, tubular labellum, ripple-edged side petals, and a yellow dorsal sepal that flared up showily, like a sultan's fan.

"*Que c'est beau!*" Mara exclaimed, sincerely impressed. Julian's expression as he trailed along behind was decidedly sour. Serve him right, she thought, for that crack about doing all the talking. She laid it on thicker. "*Absolument magnifique*. Did you—er—breed this yourself?"

"But of course," the other preened. "Bulldog hybrid. Just in bloom."

Their host took advantage of her show of interest to point out other of his botanical achievements. At one point, Julian simply left them. When, at last, Géraud led Mara out to a terrace at the rear of the house, Julian was already there, seated at a wooden table with Iris, a half-empty, sweating bottle of sparkling Vouvray between them. An unopened second was on standby in a bucket of ice.

"So—what's this all about, eh?" boomed Géraud, seating Mara with an excess of gallantry.

"We need," said Julian, "to draw on your knowledge of local flora to place a certain sequence of orchids." He made a show of informing Mara, "Géraud's terrifically knowledgeable about terrestrial as well as tropical orchids. If anyone can tell you what you want to know, it's Géraud." It was a shameless priming of the pump, and they all, including Géraud, knew it. Julian laid out the photographs in order on the wooden garden table.

Their host squinted at the array. "What's this? Terrible quality. Who took this rubbish?" He glanced at Mara, then turned on Julian. "And you expect me to tell you where this muck grows? What's this all about?"

"Treat it like a botanical puzzle," Julian evaded. Mara caught the warning glance he shot her. Bringing Bedie into the conversation, the look said, would simply sidetrack the purpose of their visit. She raised a hand: *Your show*.

"Oh, goody," cried Iris. "A mystery. I love mysteries."

Géraud gave his visitors a suspicious glare.

"Come on, Géraud," Julian wheedled. "I just need some information from you. My notes don't go back far enough."

Grudgingly, Géraud picked up the first photo, a

composition of dainty white Helleborine florets springing from a single stem. The habitat shot included a cluster of similar plants against a shaded backdrop of beech saplings.

"*Cephalantheria longifolia*," their host declared, holding fussily to taxonomical names. "Bah. Impossible to place. Grows along every footpath in the region. You ought to know that."

Julian said with forced patience, "I was hoping to identify a possible location through all of the orchids, taken together."

"Hmmph. So you said. What's next?" The older man frowned at a portrait of a dark, leafless stalk bearing deep-violet flowers tightly braided up the length of the plant. This was followed by a middle-distance view showing a trio of the same, blossoms beginning to unfurl. They stood in a light-dappled litter of conifer needles. "*Limodorum abortivum*," he identified.

"It's growing here among what looks like Scots pine—"

"I can see that for myself, thank you."

"—but my notes show it mainly in conjunction with oaks and chestnuts, especially along tree-root systems—"

"*Quelle merde*," scoffed Géraud. "You're about to tell me *Limodorum* is parasitical."

"Who said anything about parasites? They're saprophytes."

Iris leaned forward to peer at the photo. "Well, for

that matter, *I've* only ever seen it growing near rotting stumps."

"You wouldn't recognize *Limodorum* if it bit you," Géraud snapped. "Look, take it from me, *Limodorum*'s mostly found, when it's found, in mixed deciduous-coniferous woodland. That describes most of the Dordogne. So where does that get you?"

Not very far, Mara acknowledged silently. Julian looked grumpy.

Géraud grunted dismissively at the shots of *Dactylorhiza fuchsii* and *Orchis militaris*, but his attitude changed abruptly when he saw the Bird's-nest Orchids. Startled, he reared a pair of tufted eyebrows. "*Mon dieu!*" he shouted. "*Epatant!*"

"Thought you'd be interested." It was Julian's turn to look smug.

The eyebrows waggled. "And why not? *Neottia nidus-avis* is not that common. A stand like this is entirely remarkable. Whoever took this photograph was damned lucky—not you, was it? No, couldn't be. You wouldn't be here picking my brains. Well, as you undoubtedly know, *Neottia* likes damp shade, so this would have had to be found under forest cover, most probably deciduous."

"I don't suppose you've ever seen anything approaching this size?"

Géraud stuck a lip out. "Well, not quite this big." A quick look at Mara, as if assessing how much she knew. Then at Julian. "You?"

"Oh, couple of sightings." Julian's tone was casual.

"Wait." Géraud appeared to think hard. "Maybe."

Julian grinned. "I'll tell if you will."

The other glowered. *Julian one, old fart nil*, Mara marked the score with amused interest.

"Go on," rumbled Géraud.

Julian referred to his notes. "One fair-sized scattering, Forêt de la Bessède, south of Urval, just below the junction of the main logging roads. And a small growth along the footpath north of Doissat. Your turn."

"Hmm." Géraud rubbed his chin. "Abrillac Forest."

"You couldn't be a little more precise, could you? Abrillac covers a big area, as you well know."

"Nearer Le Double, actually." Géraud gave grudging directions.

Mara felt a quickening of the pulse. She had once done a small job for someone near the hamlet of Le Double. "That's just north of Beynac," she broke in.

"Date?" Julian persisted as if she had not spoken. "I'm interested in anything around 1984."

Géraud frowned. "Why?"

"Oh, just curious."

"Very well. Nineteen eighty-two."

"How can you be so sure?" Julian objected. "Just a moment ago you said you didn't have anything—"

"Of course he has," crowed Iris. "He has stacks of notes, all in Latin and Greek and teensy-tiny coded numbers so no one else can read them. He's terrified someone will steal his precious information. Go on."

She gave her lover a hearty shove. "Show the lad."

Scowling murderously, Géraud strode off into the house. He returned with a long wooden file drawer. It was labeled *E–N*, suggesting a wealth of other material spanning the rest of the alphabet. The older man riffled through tightly packed, minutely inscribed index cards while Julian looked on with obvious envy.

"As I said"—Géraud surfaced after a moment—"nineteen eighty-two." And since Julian was eyeing him meaningfully, he reluctantly imparted minimal directions.

This interchange put their host in a bad mood. He sneered at the shots of *Anacamptis pyramidalis*—"Common as straw!"—and quarreled angrily with each of Julian's subsequent identifications.

"*Platanthera bifolia*, Lesser Butterfly Orchid," Julian said.

"*Bifolia* my elbow!" This aimed at a graceful stalk of spiky white blooms. "It's *Platanthera chlorantha*, or Greater Butterfly, if you must. Use your eyes, *mon vieux*. Regard the positioning of the pollinia!"

"You can't *see* the pollinia. At least, not very well. I make it out to be *bifolia*."

"Rubbish. When was this taken?"

"Early May."

"That proves it. *Clorantha* blooms before *bifolia*." Géraud flashed a look of triumph in Mara's direction. Julian looked huffy.

One–one, Mara tallied over the rim of her glass.

Iris created a temporary diversion by snatching up the next photo in line and interjecting, "Ooh, look, a *pigeonnier*! I once lived in a converted pigeon house."

"You would have," intoned her temperamental consort through gritted teeth.

"I also painted a lovely series of them. For greetings cards. Sold very well."

"Did you?" Mara was immediately interested. "You don't recognize this one, by any chance, do you?"

"Oh dear." Iris studied it lengthily. "I don't think so. I mean, it was years ago, and there are so many, and one is very like another, don't you think?"

But the two men were off again, sparring over the distinguishing features of subspecies of *Dactylorhiza* and arguing heatedly about a plant that Julian said was one variant of Marsh Orchid and Géraud another. Géraud's temper grew shorter as the condition of the photographs deteriorated. "What did you do with this film? Flush it down the toilet?"

Iris, on the other hand, was unperturbed by the awful quality. She crooned over a discolored clutch of fat, velvety blossoms. "Bee Orchids. The darlings, so sweet, with their little furry bodies. And Snakes!" She pounced on a blackened portrait of a tall spike just coming into bloom, the lower blossoms of the spike releasing what looked like pale, wildly flying ribbons. "My absolute favorites."

Géraud closed his eyes and pushed air noisily out his nostrils. "Do me a kindness. *Himantoglossum hircinum*. What you English refer to as Lizard Orchid, although the locals call it *orchidée bouc* because it smells damnably like a billy goat in rut."

"Don't be pedantic, dear. Snakes, Lizards, whatever. But so dramatic, don't you think, with their twisty things?"

Géraud glared. "Those 'twisty things,' as you call them, happen to be much-elongated median lobes." He said for Mara's benefit, "Thinly but widely distributed. They typically populate open fields and sometimes roadside verges, but where, my dear, is anyone's guess."

He waved in disgust at the rest of the shots. "What the devil do you expect me to do with these?"

Julian said acidly, "Well, I was hoping you had some sightings."

"Sightings?" Géraud threw up a pair of short, hairy arms, demonstrating that he had reached the end of his limited patience. "*Parbleu*, what do you think? I have been hunting orchids in the Dordogne for forty years. Of course I have sightings!" Fulminating, he picked up and slapped down each of the remaining photographs in turn. "*Aceras anthropophorum*? At least three dozen stands between here and Bergerac. *Orchis purpurea*? Ditto. Aha, *Serapias lingua*, what my beloved here would call *Tongue* Orchid"—he roared out the word "Tongue"—"well, I can give you a damned fine spread of them on a hillside above Le Grand Mas dating back to 1972, but the land was bought last year by some Belgians, so you can't get in there anymore!"

Iris shook her head at Mara. "You see? Absolutely impossible. I really shall have to go. I was saying, dear"—she raised her voice over her lover's bellows—"that I shall have to leave you. Oh, no point looking like thunder, Joujou. It's for your own good." She turned back to Mara: "Always pulls him up short, and gives me a break. He's as good as gold after."

Julian struggled to get the conversation back on track. "I was talking about sightings that could tie in with the others."

"*Bof!*" Géraud slammed his hand down on the table so hard that the glasses jumped. Then he said what Mara was most afraid of hearing: "What you're asking is impossible. You can't seriously expect me to take this garbage and give you a location."

At that point Iris leaned forward confidentially. "If I tell you something, you two, will you promise to keep it a secret? There's a lovely little cluster of Fly Orchids right behind the Chapel of Our Lady of Capelou that I can show you if you're interested. I visit them every year around this time, when I go to get spring water."

"*Ah, ça, enfin!*" exploded Géraud.

There was one photo left: the Lady's Slipper. Géraud seized it irascibly. Mara held her breath.

"What in the name of *le bon dieu* is this?"

"It's probably," said Julian carefully, "a very bad photo. I was just curious to know what you make of it."

"Julian thinks it's a Lady's Slipper," Mara cut in, tired of the verbal fencing.

"What?" Géraud roared.

Julian said stiffly, shooting her a furious glance. "Well, yes, I did rather think it might be—er—some form of *Cypripedium*."

"Impossible!"

"I know. But you have to admit the structure is awfully similar."

"You're mad. First, *Cypripedium* is exceedingly rare. Second, it doesn't grow here. It likes cooler, subalpine conditions."

"Only the labellum isn't yellow but deep pink," Julian persisted. "And these appear to be unusually long lateral petals. I thought maybe a mutant, and if so, did it propagate, and where?"

"*Balivernes!*" shouted Géraud. "Absolute rot! I tell you it doesn't grow here. If it doesn't grow here, how can you have a mutant?" He paused, frowning intensely. Despite himself, he was intrigued. "*C'est ça?* No other photo?"

"Unfortunately, no."

"And you think you've made a rare find. What do you plan to call it? *Cypripedium woodianum?*"

The tone to Mara's ears was viciously mocking, revealing a seriously nasty side to Géraud's intense competitiveness about floral matters. As he held the photo up to catch the light, the reddening sky behind him outlined his head with its hairy horns, giving him an infernal, demonic look.

"Oh, Julian." Iris clasped her hands in suppressed excitement. "A find. How wonderful for you!"

"Cease the raptures, woman," Géraud muttered wearily. "And this, I suppose, is what the charade has been about? If you wanted me to help you locate this dubious specimen, why didn't you say so straight off, man?"

"Come on, Géraud. Admit you're fascinated."

The other glared at the photograph again. "Let me put you out of your misery. If this is some kind of *Cypripedium*, I can tell you it wasn't taken here. *C'est final.* Don't get visions of grandeur yet, *mon vieux*. Come." He reached into the ice bucket for the second bottle of Vouvray and turned to Mara with a ghastly grin. "We've had enough of orchids and execrable photography, wouldn't you say, my dear? More wine."

•

"You didn't make things any easier," Julian said coldly as they drove away, "telling him I thought it was a Lady's Slipper."

"Oh dear," snapped Mara, "and here was me thinking that was what it was all about."

•

By the time they had picked up a selection of deli items from a charcuterie and returned to Mara's house to assemble their findings, an unspoken truce had been established between them. They ate their food hurriedly, sitting cross-legged on the Aubusson, which in Julian's opinion was a damned sight more

143

comfortable than her chairs. The Série bleue maps were spread out edge to edge before them, showing the entire region in cartographic detail. They were able to follow the lazy looping of the Dordogne, flowing west through a patchwork flood plain of fields and farms. Its ancient bed wound between limestone cliffs crowned with stark medieval fortresses (black dots) and pleasure châteaux (more black dots) built by the gentry over the centuries. *Gentilhommières*, they were called. Julian traced the path of the D703 with his finger. It followed the contours of the river from Souillac as far as the town of Siorac-en-Périgord, where it swung north. Westward traffic was carried along the D25 on the next map of the series, until it turned south at Le Buisson. Jazz, banished to the hardwood floor, looked on, deeply offended.

Julian got right down to business. "We have to make a critical assumption: that Bedie took the photos in one go. After visiting the castle in Beynac"— he circled the town on one of the maps with a red marker—"your sister somehow found herself on a shady footpath. *Where* is the question, and how she got there, of course, the missing piece. But once there, she was likely walking through light woodland, say, something like a second-growth copse, which is where she found the Helleborines, *Limodorum*, Common Spotteds, and Military Orchids. From there she went into dense tree cover for the Bird's-nests." He gestured widely, indicating numerous green areas on the maps affording a plentiful choice of forests.

He went on. "But then she came out into open country again. That's indicated by field dwellers like the Pyramidal and Butterfly Orchids."

"And after that," Mara put in, "she found the *pigeonnier*."

"Right. Then the water meadow, where she saw the Marsh Orchids. The maps show contour lines and elevations, so they'll be some help in locating low-lying bogs. The rest of the flowers suggest a transition onto higher, drier ground, and again we can use the contour lines: Bee, Lizard, Man, Lady, and Tongue Orchids are all pretty adaptable, but they prefer sunny, well-drained areas—hillsides, high meadows, embankments, that kind of thing."

"And the Lady's Slipper?" Mara asked.

Julian frowned. "The Lady's Slipper would have probably grown on even higher ground, say a cool, shady, north-facing ridge. And that," he finished abruptly, "is where the trail ends."

Mara stared at him. "But—but that could be any-where!"

"It's what I've been trying to tell you." Julian found her dismay intensely satisfying. "Worse than that. If Bedie took the photos at different times and in different places, then, like I said before, we have no continuity at all, and even less to go on. Which brings us back to the Lady's Slipper. You heard Géraud. He thinks I'm mad to even think it was locally occurring mutant of *Cypripedium calceolus*. So we have to consider the possibility of another discontinuity—your sister found it in an entirely different location. Or we're looking at something quite different."

"Are you saying it's *not* a Lady's Slipper?"

He shook his head. "More like an unknown variant of Lady's Slipper. You see, the genus *Cypripedium* consists of around a hundred and ten species. Only one, *Cypripedium calceolus*, is native to Western Europe. But who's to say your sister didn't stumble on an unknown, highly localized type that grows in one spot in the Dordogne and nowhere else?" For a moment Julian let his mind drift as he considered the possibility. "Blimey, wouldn't that shake up the botanical world!"

Mara regarded him somberly for a moment and then called him back to more practical considerations. "So how should we go about this?"

He sighed. "Right. Well, we have three distinctive photos to go on. First the *pigeonnier*. Then the *Neottia* or Bird's-nest Orchids. And, finally, the Lady's Slipper. Let's try your idea of identifying possible pigeon houses using the maps. But, rather than looking for any isolated dot, we can narrow things down a lot, at least at first, by focusing on dots in the vicinity of known sightings of Bird's-nests. We've got three sightings, two of my own and one from Géraud. Let's start with Géraud's. It's just about here, above Le Double"—Julian drew a red "X" on the map—"which, interestingly enough, is only a few kilometers north of Beynac."

"I tried to tell you that."

"What? Oh. Well, I hope you realize it's the only useful piece of information that bloody man gave us, and you saw how I practically had to pull worms out of his nose to get an exact location. Now, if we concentrate on a walkable area within a radius of, say, ten or twelve kilometers around this point—"

"That's walkable?" Mara asked faintly.

"Nothing for an experienced hiker," he replied breezily and penciled in a rough circle around the "X." "What does that give us in the way of single black dots?"

Together they scanned the map.

"Here's a couple outside Le Glandier." Mara pointed at two specks that Julian duly marked. "And one there, north of La Fage, and another south of Lavergné."

In all, they found a dozen candidates. Several Julian rejected straightaway. "Too big for a pigeon house. Things may not be labeled, but they're more or less to scale. And these are probably cottages. You can tell by their orientation to the road. Luckily, we'll be able to check most of these out by car, or with the aid of binoculars. Except this one." He tapped a spot on the map. "It's in the middle of woodland. Have to walk in for that." He eyed her severely. "You'd better come prepared to trek, you know. Even if we're lucky enough to find your pigeon house among this lot, we'll still have to hike in for the *Neottia*."

"I don't see why, if we have the *pigeonnier*," she objected. "Why not just go from there? Look for the orchids that come after it?"

"Because finding both will help us establish that Bedie took these photos in a single walk, which, don't forget, is the critical assumption. The other orchids, except the Lady's Slipper, are simply not rare enough to go on. Also, the pigeon house and the *Neottia* together will give us the direction of Bedie's approach, since we know the Bird's-nest is before the *pigeonnier*. Any evidence of orchids that come after the *pigeonnier*, say, like the Marsh Orchids in the water meadow, will help us fix her forward path."

Mara was silent for a moment. Finally, she said, "It all boils down to the Lady's Slipper, doesn't it?"

Julian frowned. "Unfortunately, yes. Without that, we can't really know where she ended up. We're always faced with the possibility that your sister began the roll of film in this area, and finished up somewhere else, like in the Lozére."

She said somberly, "I don't think you understand what I mean, Julian. You told me Bedie was systematic about photographing her orchids. She took them close up and at a distance, right?"

"Sure. It's standard practice."

"Except the Lady's Slipper. She only took one shot of it. I've been asking myself why. There were at least a couple of frames left on the film. It occurs to me that the only explanation is that something must have interrupted her. Julian, I think the reason Bedie didn't take any more photos was that she couldn't." Mara paused. "By then she may have been dead."

N I N E

They agreed to meet at eight the following morning behind the Parc Archéologique in Beynac. Mara arrived first. She parked her car and let Jazz out to mark trees while she leaned against the front fender of the Renault. A thin mist, rising from the river, hung delicately in the air. Below her, the town, stacked against the face of a jutting cliff, still slept. The tour buses would not appear for another two hours. A fat woman in slippers came out of one of the houses, threw open the ground-floor shutters, and waddled inside again.

Above Mara soared the massive ramparts of Beynac Castle. French stronghold during the Hundred Years' War, the fortress glared upriver in the direction of equally hulking English Castelnaud. Both fortifications had played key roles in the bitter fighting. At Castelnaud, Mara had once seen a full-scale working model of a *trébuchet*, a giant medieval catapult, with which the English had once hurled boulders at the French. She had found the brutish engine of war daunting, even at a remove of five centuries.

Mara wondered how the day would go. She felt energized, finally having something concrete to focus on: Géraud's *Neottia* and a scattering of black dots.

At the same time, she was wary of entering Julian's turf, his world of leaves and flowering plants. Julian had a deadly seriousness and quick irascibility where botanical things were concerned. Would he tell her to keep her mouth shut while he stared at the ground? Make her walk until she dropped? Would he even notice? She was sure that the only thing that mattered to him was his damned Lady's Slipper. Fixated, that's what he was. And, curiously, alone. Like her, she had to acknowledge. Her world was bound by work, the reconstruction of dank water closets and primitive kitchens. And Bedie, nineteen years gone. It occurred to her that, viewed from this perspective, she and Julian had a lot in common after all.

He came roaring up twenty minutes late with a bump and a screech of brakes. He jumped out, looking harried.

"Sorry I'm late." He traded quick pecks with Mara and sidestepped Jazz's snout, directed at his crotch. "Had to get Bernard started on some digging for Prudence. The lad works hard, but he's got a very short attention span."

He wore jeans, sturdy boots, and a wide-brimmed hat. He bristled with equipment: binoculars, camera, compass, canteen, rucksack. She wore cotton slacks and light canvas running shoes. Her only provisions were a tube of sunscreen and a couple of ham sandwiches that she stowed in Julian's pack.

They left her car and went in Julian's van, Mara navigating them along the edge of the Abrillac

Forest, down bumpy lanes, past wood lots and pale-green fields of newly planted maize. It took them over an hour to locate six dots, all of which they could see from the car. Two were in fact *pigeonniers*, but square structures unlike the one they sought. The others were a barn, a couple of sheds, and a conical shepherd's hut built of darkly weathered stone.

"It's down to this one," Mara said, studying the map.

Julian leaned over to peer at the final dot, situated in forest.

"Hmm. I make it about five or six kilometers north of Géraud's *Neottia*. I suggest we go back to Le Double and hike in for the orchids first and continue from there on foot."

He let out the clutch, and they started off down the road. As they approached the hamlet, Mara read out Julian's scribbled notes of Géraud's directions. " 'Bark'—no, 'park bend in road.' Slow down. I think this may be the spot we're looking for."

Julian pulled off onto the narrow shoulder and set the hand brake with a jerk.

" 'Path N,' " Mara continued, squinting at his cryptic scrawl, " '2 k. Function'—? Oh, 'junction—W 2 k.' Then something 'oak.' 'BN 100 m S.' "

"We have to look for a footpath on the north side of the road," Julian interpreted. "We follow it for two kilometers until we hit a junction of trails. Then we branch off west for another two kilometers until we find a very large oak tree. The Bird's-nests are off-trail, about a hundred meters in a straight line south."

A beige Deux Chevaux was parked farther down from them. At the roadside, a big man in a blue jacket was stringing a length of orange plastic tape around a framework of wooden stakes. The man looked up, recognized Julian, and waved.

"*Salut!*"

"Bother," muttered Julian. "I'll have to say hello."

As they approached, Mara could see that the framework surrounded a clutch of what she was pleased to be able to identify as Lizard Orchids. They were tall plants, most still tightly in bud, but two had already begun to unfurl gaily twisted labella, like pale-pink party streamers, to the breeze. It was the first time Mara had seen them in the leaf, as it were, and she was impressed by their dramatic oddity.

Julian introduced the man as Maurice Bourdon, secretary of Les Vigilants, dedicated to the protection of endangered flora.

"The mowers will be coming through next week," Maurice explained for Mara's benefit. "The barrier alerts them to leave the orchids. Trouble is, they don't always cooperate. You see," he went on, his broad red face earnest, "one has to act. Orchids are vanishing from our woods and meadows. Most people don't care, so it's up to the few of us who do to do something. With force, if need be." And he cited instances of violence, of greed and corruption driving the development of lands where protected species grew. "I tell you, these canailles will stop at nothing. You don't believe me?" He rolled up a trouser leg. Mara beheld a massive, hairy shin cut across by a jagged weal.

"See this? Last year, three of us were guarding a pair of Summer Lady's-Tresses. They're dying out everywhere, you know. We were taking it in turns, just until they had time to bloom, because roadwork was going on, and we were planning to move them to a safer spot. Construction crew came through, trucks and earthmovers. I told them to bugger off. Cracked me on the leg, the bastards did, with a shovel."

Julian cut off the flow of further tales by asking Maurice about the Bird's-nest and the *pigeonnier*.

The other shrugged at the photocopy of the dovecote. One was much like another. As to the *Neottia nidus-avis*, he thought they might find a few plants round about, but nothing like what they were looking for.

"Your trail head is over there." He directed them about twenty meters farther down. "It's marked by another one of those damned *bornes*." The entire region was criss-crossed by ancient cart tracks and paths. Some, like the one Julian and Mara sought, had been designated with markers as hiking trails by the Dordogne Tourism Service, a phenomenon that Maurice vigorously cursed. "It's just inviting more destruction of orchid habitat by hikers and those *fichu* all-terrain bikes." He waved his arms to take in the surrounding countryside in a gesture of despair.

They left him to his taping.

Their trail ran between pastures and newly planted fields that shaped themselves to the contours of the surrounding hills. The air was rich with the smell of overturned earth and dung. Cattle stared placidly at them from the other side of electrified ribbon fencing. Jazz rushed them, and they lumbered off, hooves squelching on the muddy ground. Along the way, Julian was surprisingly chatty, pointing out common wildflowers for Mara's benefit. The tall flower there, looking like a tiny purple candelabra, was tassel hyacinth. That was wild sage; if she crushed the leaves between her fingers, she could smell its pungent aroma. Buttercups she knew, but she didn't know that the locals called them *boutons d'or*, or gold buttons. Mara warmed to his brisk authority, his long, swinging stride, and hurried to keep pace with him.

They entered a meadow awash with Pyramidal Orchids, hundreds of purple cones made up of small, tightly packed blossoms balancing atop single stems. Mara knew the flowers—they grew plentifully in fields near her house—and wondered that she had never before stopped to admire their beauty. She bent to pick one. Julian's hand closed over hers swiftly.

"Lesson number one, Mara." His face was very near hers. A vein in his temple flickered. "Never pick an orchid. Look, photograph, but don't touch. *Ever.*"

"Sorry." She backed away. "But there are so many of them. And you pick flowers. What about your herbarium samples?"

"I only take common plants," he said coolly. "Never vulnerable species."

Farther ahead, as they clambered over a fallen tree, he waved despairingly at a cluster of withered Lady Orchids.

"This is what we're up against," he complained. "Things are going fast. In a few more weeks we may not see much in bloom."

"Think positively," she grinned, to lighten things up. "I need you at your very best."

He glanced at her slyly. "Botanically speaking?"

"Of course."

They walked on. Then something caught his interest. "Look." He grabbed her arm and pointed to the top of an embankment.

She saw a scattering of slender plants topped with plump, dark blossoms. "What is it?"

"*Ophrys apifera*." He climbed up, placing his feet with care, beckoning her to follow. "Bee Orchids. You have some on your film. Here, if you look closely you can see why they're called that." He selected a flower, cradling the labellum gently, almost intimately. Standing close beside him, Mara made out a furry, blackish-brown lobe with yellow markings.

"But," she marveled, "it looks exactly like a bumble-bee."

"Exactly." He uncapped his camera. "And there's a reason for that. It's— Wait!" he broke off tensely. "Don't move!"

For a panicky moment Mara thought she was

about to tread on a snake—she had heard there was some kind of poisonous viper in the Dordogne. But it was only a bee, the real thing. Hastily, she waved it away.

"For Christ's sake, Mara," Julian hissed furiously. "Don't do that! Look, just stand back, will you?" He scowled and crouched, camera at the ready, waiting for the circling insect to return. After some moments, it alighted on an orchid. Waggling its body, it mounted the fleshy labellum, probing its head down the flower's throat, tiny feet treading busily. She heard the snick of the shutter. "Got it!" Julian exclaimed.

"Got what?" she asked resentfully. It was an aspect she didn't like about him, this overbearing, downright tetchy underside to his congenial surface.

"Pseudocopulation. False mating. Well, you said you wanted me at my best botanically."

"Oh, absolutely," she replied. "Do go on."

He gave her a searching look. "All right. You see, the sexual reproduction of orchids is very complex. Some orchids try to appear like other kinds of nectar-bearing flowers in order to attract pollinators. In fact, you often find them growing among the flowers they model. Now, with the Bee and Fly Orchids, which belong to the *Ophrys* genus, it's different. They've evolved flower parts that not only mimic the bodies of female insects but also put out pseudopheromones to lure males into false copulation. The live insect lands on the fake one, gets covered in pollen, which it carries to other orchids, which of course is the whole point of the exercise. Am I boring you?"

"Not at all," she told him coldly. "It's fascinating, all this pseudocopulation and fake pheromones. Makes one quite dizzy. Tell me, are the orchids that do the attracting male or female?"

"What? Oh, both. That is, orchids are hermaphroditic. In fact, they're quite capable of pollinating themselves."

"Now, that," said Mara softly but with meaning, "is boring."

•

They set off again. This time Julian did not bother to help her over logs but strode ahead, leaving her scrambling to keep up. Jazz ran, nose to ground, back and forth between them. The sun, riding high overhead, was hot. She found herself lagging behind. She wished she'd thought to wear a hat.

"Julian. I need a rest."

He allowed her a brief pause and a swallow from his canteen.

Then he was off again. "Come on," he called over his shoulder. "Chop-chop. We've got a lot of ground to cover."

"Look, I'm going as fast as I can."

"Well, don't complain. This was what you wanted."

She was grateful when they plunged into shady woodland. Helleborines, each plant bearing clusters of delicately nodding white bells, embroidered the shoulders of their path. Eventually, beech and pine gave way to a dense forest of oaks and chestnuts whose branches met overhead, creating a greenish net of light that shivered down through the leafy canopy. Here great vines hung like curtains, and ferns carpeted the forest floor. The air was fresh and cool, redolent of leaf mulch and growing things. Mara leaned against a tree, breathing hard. Julian drew up beside her.

"Forests," he murmured softly near her left ear. "Mystery, creation, and evolution." It was poetically, almost seductively said, and she turned to him in surprise. His eyes, brown flecked with gold, held hers for a moment. He placed his hands on her shoulders. Her heart gave a leap.

"Look," he whispered, turning her about, and pointed out purple spears of *Limodorum abortivum*, rising from the litter of the forest floor. "You see how they follow the root system of this old beech tree? One up on old Géraud."

•

Their chief difficulty lay in finding Géraud's landmark oak. There were so many, all clotted with balls of parasitic mistletoe, but not a *Neottia* in sight. An hour of off-trail searches into likely growing areas produced nothing more interesting than a giant bracket fungus adorning a tree like a huge, fleshy lip.

"We're not going to find it, are we?" Mara said, seating herself wearily on a rock. Jazz flopped down panting beside her.

"Wouldn't put it past the old fox to have purposely misled me," Julian fumed.

They abandoned the search and ate their sandwiches. It was a bizarre kind of investigation they were conducting, Mara thought, taking in her leafy surroundings. One in which the sole witnesses to Bedie's disappearance were silent and ephemeral, their only evidence the existence of a *pigeonnier* and a certain pattern of plants. How, she wondered in bemusement, do you question a flower?

"Do you suppose," Mara mused aloud after a long silence, "that what Maurice said is really true?"

"What?" Julian, deep in his own reflections, surfaced.

"That people commit violence over orchids?"

He replied cautiously, "It's been known to happen. I've heard worse stories than Maurice's—double-dealing, even murder—but mainly to do with tropicals, the showy ones that collectors go mad over. Avid fanciers can get pretty unbalanced. Why?"

"Well, supposing it wasn't a serial predator that Bedie met but an orchid fanatic. Supposing this person never really meant her any harm. Only she did something, accidentally, to an orchid that he was trying to protect . . ."

"What, stepped on it?" Julian was incredulous.

"Or say Bedie found a rare species, like the *Cypripedium*, that this person wanted to keep secret. Bedie might not have been exactly cooperative if she thought the world should know about it. This person could have seen red, struck out blindly—"

"You mean Géraud?" Julian looked interested. "Admittedly, he's bloody obsessive about his favorite stands . . ." He trailed off, frowning, then shook his head. "I don't see it," he concluded regretfully. "Géraud's a right prick, but not even he would go to that extent. Anyway, what you're saying puts every amateur orchidologist in the region under suspicion. In fact, every bloody member of Société Jeannette—I can give you the subscription list—to say nothing of Maurice's Vigilants lot."

"Well, there is something else. Iris says she leaves him periodically."

"What's that got to do with it?"

"The four-to-five-year cycle. Adverse life changes. Her departures could set him off."

"What are you saying, every time she walks out he goes on a rampage?" Julian gave a sharp bark of laughter. "Oh, he's impossible to live with, I'll give you that. In fact, I don't know how Iris puts up with him. But that doesn't make him a serial killer. And anyway, you keep saying 'he.' It could just as easily have been a woman. Females can be pretty violent, too."

Mara sighed and took off her shoe to examine a developing blister.

"It was just a thought," she said.

Julian opened the map and took a bearing with his compass, orienting them toward their final dot.

"Rather than go all the way back to the main trail, what say we save time by angling through the woods and picking it up farther ahead? It'll mean some crashing through the bush, if you think you're up to it."

"Sure," Mara agreed, although she was quite certain she wouldn't enjoy the crashing part.

Farther on, as they plunged deeper and deeper into forest, Julian remarked, "You know, peasants used to give this area wide berth. It's full of swamps and once had a bad reputation as the hideout of brigands and wolves. Even werewolves."

"Brrr."

"Of course, that was a hundred years ago. Still"—he paused to glance back at her—"even today you wouldn't want to get lost here."

"No. I would not."

But she did get lost. It was after Julian had led them over a ridge and down into an extensive bog. Dragonflies hovered thickly in the air. The earth was spongy and full of standing water. As usual, he strode ahead of her. Soon he had vanished behind a gray-green wall of willow bushes. Jazz, off on business of his own, was nowhere to be seen. Mara found herself struggling through high swamp brush that obscured her view, cursing the ankle-deep, sucking mud, and falling farther and farther behind.

It was an eerie, claustrophobic place full of rustling vegetation. A frog erupted suddenly in front of her, landing on her foot. She choked back a yell of alarm as she shook it off. Not, of course, that Julian would have heard her. Where was he? She fought her way forward. Quite unexpectedly and with a feeling of immense relief, she broke through into an open water meadow.

"Julian?" she called, shading her eyes to look around her. "Jazz!"

The meadow grasses rippled in the wind. She was utterly alone.

"Julian," she shouted, louder this time. She stood still to listen. Silence. A slight feeling of unease gripped her. On the far side of the meadow, a dense wood rose up. A gap in the trees revealed a path. *Dammit*, she thought, *he could have waited*. Furious, she made for the trailhead.

"Julian?" she called doubtfully, peering into a tunnel of greenery that led uninvitingly into a twilight world.

"Bastard," she muttered and started unwillingly down it. Suddenly a brownish blur exploded in front of her. She screamed and ducked. The thing passed so close to her head that she felt a great rush of air lift her hair. She had an impression of rapidly beating wings, an open beak, cruel, bright eyes. Seconds later, she realized that she had startled a buzzard from its perch. She saw it now, through a gap in the trees, lofting powerfully, angling sharply against the sky. Shaken, she stumbled back out into the sunshine.

"Shit!" It was as much an exclamation of fear as of real anger with herself for being afraid. Anyway, it was ridiculous to think she was lost. Somewhere along the way, Julian would find her. In fact, he was probably looking for her at that moment. And if he didn't, well, screw him, all she had to do was to return the way she had come until she found the path they'd taken when they branched off in their search for the Bird's-nest Orchids. Working back through the swamp, as much as she disliked the hissing world of towering reeds, would be easy. She could simply follow the swath broken by her original passage. But finding her way through the uncharted forest to rejoin the signposted main trail might not be so simple. She had not paid particular attention to the way they had come, merely followed Julian as he pushed through the understory of the trees.

"Shit," she cried again and recrossed the water meadow.

She almost stumbled on him, crouching behind a thicket of willows.

"Julian," she cried out, half in relief, half in exasperation. "Where were you?"

He peered up at her. "What do you mean, where was I? I was here."

"Well, *I* was lost. Didn't you hear me shouting for you? You—you left me behind!"

"I did no such thing." He sounded indignant, but she thought he looked a little guilty. "And no, I didn't hear you. Or, if I did, how was I to know you were lost? I mean, how could you get lost? All you had to do was follow me. Anyway, look what I've found." He pointed triumphantly to a pair of tiny, green spires rising bravely out of a saturated patch of moss.

164

"*Hammarbya paludosa*," he said with satisfaction as he uncapped his camera lens. "Bog Orchids. Very early on. Won't flower for another month or so. This species is special because the edges of the leaves put out tiny bulblets that eventually grow into new plants. It's an unusual form of vegetative propagation. Bog Orchids are rare. I've only ever seen them once before, around Le Bugue."

At that point, Jazz trotted up, muddy and looking pleased with himself.

"I don't get it," Mara mused wearily as Julian knelt to photograph his find.

"Get what? Look, Mara, d'you mind moving? You're throwing a shadow."

She stepped aside. "People like you. Bedie. This—this *thing* with plant life." Her tone, she knew, was brittle.

He edged around crabwise for a close-up from another angle. She took in his avid, soiled presence and turned away.

"What thing? Anyway," he said blandly, moving back for a final shot, "without 'people like me' you wouldn't have a hope of tracking your sister. Do you have any idea how many hours of collective field observation—mine and Géraud's, not that he's been much bloody use—you're drawing on?"

He stood up and took a reading on his compass. Then he dug into his rucksack for a notebook, in which he recorded his find, its precise location, and the date. "I'll come back in a few weeks to check on how they're doing," he said. "I'll be able to get them in flower then." He seemed to expect her to be as cheered as himself at the prospect.

"Speaking of your sister," Julian said as he packed his notebook away. "I've been meaning to ask you. How did she get going? On wild orchids, I mean?"

"Oh," said Mara, ruefully aware that Julian had yet to show as much curiosity about her. So much for Prudence's speculations. "It started one summer when she got a job with the Ontario Ministry of the Environment. They sent her up to map orchids on the Bruce Peninsula."

"Ah." He looked interested. "Did you know that you have something like five species of Lady's Slipper in Ontario?"

"Whatever. Anyway, Bedie spent three months wandering around in the woods, sleeping in a tent, and living on peanut butter. She got eaten alive by blackflies and lost some of her gear to a bear—our woods aren't as tame as here—but she came out with fifty rolls of film and happier than a tick in an armpit."

He studied her critically for a moment. "Different from you."

True, Mara acknowledged. For the first time in her life, she had an inkling of her sister's mind, the passion that ruled true amateurs, motivating them to spend countless hours bending at the waist, as Julian had said, all for the sake of discovering and documenting the existence of a single flower or the breeding ground of a particular species. There was an avaricious, competitive side to it, too, she decided, remembering Géraud's possessiveness as well as Julian's recent expression of gloating, which caused them to hoard, like gold, the sighting of a rare plant.

"We only look alike," she replied dryly, and it occurred to her how much more Julian would have had in common with Bedie than with her. Together they could have tramped the length and breadth of the Dordogne, delighting over the discovery of a *Platanthera* this or an Ophrys that. As Patsy had put it in one of their e-mail exchanges, *Whaddya have to do to make it with this guy? Speak Latin?* Unreasonably, Mara was suddenly made uneasy by a stab of jealousy directed at her missing but darkly present twin.

"I see," Julian said, and applied himself to capping his camera. They walked on in silence.

•

The remaining dot proved to be a disappointing pile of rubble. Mara looked at it briefly, taking in the dimensions of the foundations, and shook her head. Julian concurred.

It was past four by the time they returned to the road where they had left the van. Julian was pleased with his find of Bog Orchids. Mara was footsore, filthy, and stumbling with exhaustion.

•

> . . . *the thing is, Patsy, he was behind some bushes all along, and he must have heard me*

shouting. Honestly, for a moment I thought he'd been trying to lose me. Of course, right away I saw how ridiculous it was. He was merely gloating over some orchids, and when he's like that, I think a bomb could go off without him even noticing. <

Patsy e-mailed back:

> *Orchids shmorchids. If he heard you yelling, why the heck didn't he come looking? Just how much do you know about this Julian character anyway?* <

The following day, Mara had business in Bergerac, so Julian offered to go alone to Doissat to check out the first of his own Bird's-nest sightings, dating from 1988. Secretly, Mara was relieved. It was her hunt, she knew, but she had blisters on both heels, and her experience in the swamp had deflated her enthusiasm considerably.

He called her that evening to report.

"Well, it's no longer there."

Admittedly, the stand as he remembered it had been patchy. Now he expressed his dismay that not only the *Neottia* but also much of the shady woodland that had once bordered a little watercourse no longer existed.

"The trees have all been cut down," he told her, sounding seriously aggrieved. "There's nothing left but rotting stumps and soggy fields full of cows and flies. And the dots you circled as *pigeonniers* were a cottage and a ruined shed."

•

There remained only Julian's final sighting in the Bessède Forest.

Julian was not free again until Thursday. He suggested they meet at four at the Intermarché in Siorac-en-Périgord. The supermarket parking lot, when

Mara pulled in, was full of shoppers trundling grocery carts. Many had the pale look of English summer residents just arrived to open up holiday cottages. Behind the parking lot, the grounds of the Camping Municipal showed a sprinkling of tents and *caravanes*—the early phase of the tourist invasion. The day had turned cool and overcast, threatening rain.

Julian bumped up in his old Peugeot a few minutes later. He climbed out of his van, looking tired and dusty. In addition to trying to complete Prudence's courtyard before her party deadline, he complained, he was putting in a rockery at the back of her house.

"Does that have to be finished in time for the party, too?" Mara asked.

"No," he said grumpily, "but it involves shifting about a hundred tons of Mediterranean stone."

They went in Mara's car this time. Jazz, relegated to the backseat, once again made his presence felt by driving his chin painfully into Julian's shoulder. Julian was too knackered to push him away. He directed them west out of the town on the D25 and then south. En route, they viewed three out of five dots circled on the map by Mara, none of which were *pigeonniers*.

"We'd better leave the rest and go after the Bird's-nest," Julian said, squinting pessimistically up at the sky, "while the light lasts." He was beginning to feel the pressure behind his eyes that preceded a headache.

A few kilometers past the village of Urval, he pointed her onto a logging road that cut straight into the heart of the Bessède Forest.

"Look, Mara," Julian warned as they lurched along, "I don't want you to get your hopes up. This stand of Bird's-nests dates from quite a few years back. There's been a lot of logging in this area. Chances are it's been totally wiped out."

"It's the only sighting we have left," she said, unnecessarily and a little desperately.

He made no reply.

"Stop here," he ordered eventually. He got out and peered up and down the road. Tall trees rose up around them, admitting a fitful, livid light. He got back in the car and slammed the door. "This isn't it. Keep going."

A few minutes later, he said again, "Stop here."

He got out once more and this time walked a little way forward. He returned and spoke to her through the car window.

"Pull up a bit. There's more space to park farther ahead. I think this might be it."

The way was so narrow that Mara had to nose the Renault into a ditch. She wondered if they would ever get out again.

From there, they went on foot. Twenty meters or so down the road, they found a trail opening to their right.

"Is this what you were looking for?" Mara asked.

"Yes," said Julian dully.

He's fed up with this, Mara concluded to herself. *With me. I'm making him look for something we both know we'll never find. It's hopeless.*

She followed him dispiritedly along a scree-covered path that wound uphill through tall pines. At one point Jazz routed a badger. The animal held its ground, snarling ferociously and showing jagged yellow teeth. Julian prevented a bloody scene only by a timely grab at Jazz's collar.

"Look, can't you leash him?" he roared, hauling at her lunging dog while the badger disappeared into the bushes. "And for pity's sake, Mara, mind where you walk." He freed a hand to gesture irritably at a couple of pale sprigs poking up through the grass.

"Well, excuse me!" Angrily she secured Jazz. "What rare species did I nearly tread on?"

"*Listera ovata.* Common Twayblade," he informed her sulkily. "Better get a move on. This weather's not going to hold."

And then there's my dog, she went on to herself. *But really, the man's impossible. He lives, thinks, and breathes orchids.* Seconds later, she realized that it was why she had come to him in the first place.

•

"It ought to be right around here somewhere," said Julian, scanning the forest floor. He pivoted slowly around. "Damn!"

"How can you be sure this is the place?" Mara gazed about her at the dense, undifferentiated wall of

172

trees and bushes. "It must all look the same, and after so many years."

"I would have sworn this was the spot. The problem is, my notes weren't terribly exact in those days. I was less systematic, didn't take compass bearings."

"Oh. Then what?"

"We'll have to keep searching, won't we? If the stand survived, it's got to be around here somewhere. As I recall, it was a thin, extensive scattering that I thought might have been the remnants of a bigger stand. We'd had a series of dry years, and I figured a lot of the plants had probably died off."

He gazed glumly into the middle distance. "Look, we have to be systematic. We'll take this beech as our reference point." He indicated a tall, smooth-barked tree. "Imagine a guide line running north and south of it. What we'll do is walk out together along the line ten paces to the south. Come on." He led them the required distance. "Okay. Now we split up. You go ten steps to your right, then right again twenty, so you're heading back in the direction you came, and right again another ten. That'll bring you back to the guide line, ten paces to the north of the beech. I'll do the same on the left, so that we each pace out half a twenty-by-twenty square. Scan for the Bird's-nests on either side of you as you go—you know what they look like from the photos. If they're still here, you won't miss them. We'll meet up at the top of the square."

They did it.

"Okay. We'll have to expand the square. Out another ten, and this time you go to your left twenty paces, thirty back down the way you came, and twenty in again. Are you with me?"

She was.

"That's the problem with orchids," he complained after they had completed a second, more lengthy interval of scrambling through the bush. "They're among the most highly evolved and specialized of all flowering plants but bloody temperamental. They can bloom in strength one year and put out only a few straggling plants the next. *Neottia* are the worst. They're sporadic. Sometimes they even flower underground, in which case we won't see anything." He looked deeply offended.

Something on the run shot suddenly across their path. Jazz, off leash again, gave a single, sharp "gruff" and set off in immediate pursuit. There ensued a diminuendo of barks and crashing sounds followed by ominous silence.

"Jazz!" Mara yelled. "Here!"

The dog did not return. "It's all right," Mara said, avoiding Julian's accusing eye. "He always comes back."

Julian looked about to say something, but didn't. Instead, he pinched the bridge of his nose between finger and thumb. The throbbing in his skull was starting. He cursed himself for not bringing his pills with him. But, then, his headaches usually gave him a couple of days' warning. This one, dammit, was moving in fast and promised to be a thumper.

"Try again?" she asked, with a false brightness that irritated him beyond bearing.

"Of course we'll try again!" His voice came out hoarse in his effort not to shout at her. *Stupid cow. Stating the obvious.*

He saw her startled reaction and muttered, "Another ten, and this time thirty, forty, and thirty."

"Are you all right?" Mara asked, but he was already striding away.

Mara pushed off through the brush, pacing out her segment of the square, scanning from side to side as she had been instructed. Julian, she thought, looked appalling. His face was drawn, and he had ugly dark shadows under his eyes. Or maybe it was the light in this damned forest. Everything had a dead, greenish cast. Once or twice she thought she heard Jazz. She called and whistled. The dog did not come.

At the point where she expected to meet up with Julian, she found herself in a small, gloomy dell, hip-deep in bracken. She waited. The air was muggy. Clouds of gnats began to swarm about her head. In the distance she heard a faint rumble of thunder. Julian was taking his time getting there.

A noise in the bushes alerted her.

"Jazz!"

No dog appeared. Only the gentle rustle of a quickening breeze, bringing with it the smell of rain, broke the stillness. She gazed about her. She was surrounded by a wall of trees, towering, ancient, and faintly ominous. Was this the kind of place Bedie had gotten to? she wondered. And then what?

A twig snapped. She swung around sharply.

"Jazz? Come, boy!"

Silence.

"Julian? Is that you?"

If it was, he made no reply. A slight prickling of alarm tickled her scalp. There was another soft movement in the undergrowth, off to the right this time. Slowly Mara turned her head in the direction of the sound. She saw nothing but leaves and branches. Pushing down her growing fear, she began to walk very quickly out of the dell. The sounds of something stepping quietly through the undergrowth followed her.

"Who's there?" she demanded, turning to stand her ground. Then, as her gaze swept the dark understory of the forest, she saw a pale blur, there one moment, gone the next. It took only a split second for her to realize what it was—a face, featureless except for a pair of glittering eyes. The shock of it left her momentarily paralyzed. Then her lips parted in a thin cry. She wheeled about and ran.

Whatever it was ran with her, unseen but keeping pace easily, tracking her as she zigzagged through the trees. With no sense of direction, she clawed her way through the tangled brush, dodging trees, tripping over roots. A large fallen pine blocked her path. She veered, running around the great upheaval of roots at its base. In that moment, a dark shape stepped out suddenly before her. She screamed. Hands grabbed at her as she stumbled and pitched forward. She went on screaming.

"*Calmez-vous, madame,*" a deep voice addressed her. "I have you."

She found herself being lifted and steadied just as Julian broke into sight a little way behind her.

"Mara, are you all right?" he demanded, out of breath. "What's going on?"

The man who held her was tall and strongly built. He had sandy-brown hair, and his eyes were a blue so dark they seemed almost black. As he stared intently at Mara, reading her fear, an odd expression came over his face. Slowly he raised his gaze, to address Julian in fluent if slightly accented English. "I could ask the same thing of you, monsieur." And to Mara, "Are you all right, madame?"

"Yes." She was shaking but standing unsupported now, and she moved a little away from both men. "I'm all right."

"I heard you shouting," Julian said. He looked pale and agitated. "What—what happened?"

She stared at him, breathing hard. "There was someone back there," she spoke finally. "Watching me through the trees."

Julian peered about him. "I don't see anyone."

The sandy-haired man asked more helpfully, "What do you mean, madame, when you say some-one was watching you?"

"A—a face. I saw a face."

"For pity's sake, Mara," Julian cried impatiently, "this place is riddled with public footpaths. Look." He pointed to a break in the trees that she had not noticed. "There's one right over there. You saw someone on the path. People come and go in the woods all the time." He came forward and drew her toward him. She resisted at first, but finally let him put his arm around her. Her body, however, was stiff, unyielding. Julian spoke over her head to the man, who watched them curiously.

"Look—er—everything's fine. Thought she was lost. Got panicked. It's happened before."

The man looked unconvinced. "But perhaps madame requires some assistance?" He regarded Julian with slightly narrowed eyes.

"Oh—no." Mara gulped. "I—I'm fine. Thank you."

"Not at all. As long as you're sure you really are all right." The man spoke with careful insistence. He waited for a moment before raising a hand to them in a gesture of parting and moved off through the trees and down the trail. However, he glanced back once, his expression doubtful.

Mara pushed roughly away from Julian. "I did *not* think I was lost," she said through gritted teeth. "And there was someone—or some*thing*"—she waved her hand angrily—"following me."

He shrugged. "Probably a deer. Their tracks are everywhere. Get hold of yourself, Mara. You're letting your imagination run away with you."

"I suppose so," she relented. "I'm sorry. I feel quite stupid."

•

Julian was leading Mara back in the direction they had come when she clutched his arm.

"Listen."

"What?"

"Barking. Over there." She pulled him toward the sound.

"That dog's a bloody nuisance," Julian grumbled. Hurrying in her wake was making his head worse. He was about to add something sarcastic about the protection of wildlife when Mara stopped so suddenly that he bumped into her, knocking his mouth sharply on the back of her head.

"Shh," she warned. "He's got something cornered."

They found Jazz whining frantically at the base of a tall oak while an enraged marten hissed furiously from the safety of a branch. At that point, Julian forgot his headache and forgave the dog everything, even his rapidly swelling lower lip, for carpeting the forest floor around the tree was a splendid stand of Bird's-nest Orchids, proof that, if left alone, nature went about its procreative business as it should.

"Amazing," he marveled. The swarm of fleshy flowers was almost ghostly in the gloom. Each plant rose from an erect stem, the upper half of which bore an elongated cluster of brownish-yellow blooms. "This is it. This is really it. I thought this colony was a goner. It's come back triple the size!

And a lot denser. This is bloody magnificent!"

"Do you think it's the same one Bedie photographed?" Mara, ever practical, asked.

"What? Oh, right." Julian scratched his beard. "Well, it's hard to say. She didn't give us much of the surroundings. Otherwise I'd have been able to place it straightaway. And, of course, the stand as I originally saw it was a mere shadow of what she found and certainly bears no resemblance to what it is now. But is it the same?" He puffed out his cheeks. "Based on the law of probability, I'd say yes. Almost certainly yes. A stand this big is rare, Mara. *Neottia* propagate slowly. Something this extensive would have taken years to establish, and the chances of there being two like it are low."

Carefully he paced out the immense length and breadth of the colony, shaking his head in disbelief. "Another one up on old Géraud."

He took several close-ups, cursing the fading light, and more mid- to long-range shots to capture the extensiveness of the growth. In the last photograph, he positioned Mara in the foreground.

"Just to get a sense of the scale," he said, managing to grin for the first time.

"Great," she said dryly. "I'm a marker. Thank you very much."

"Smile."

She smiled for him, her left cheek dimpling. Framing her in his viewfinder, Julian had a momentary desire to fix her there indefinitely.

"Come on," he cried, energized. "We've got our *Neottia*. Now all we need is a *pigeonnier*."

There remained two isolated dots. Both were situated at the forest's edge, adjacent to farmland. One proved to be a byre. As they drove toward the final dot, Mara was acutely aware that a match on the dovecote, combined with the Bird's-nests, would give her proof that Bedie had come this way, that she was now treading the path that her sister had walked nineteen years ago. Julian's thoughts were entirely on his *Cypripedium*.

They came upon it in the twilight, just as a light rain began to fall: a tall tower rising out of the shadows at the far side of a meadow. Wider at the base and tapering upward to a broken cupola, it leaned drunkenly to one side, as if the land on which it stood had shrugged. They both studied it carefully through Julian's binoculars. But even with the naked eye, they could tell that it was all wrong.

ELEVEN

Edith was missing. Julian heard about it the following morning through Madame Léon when he went for his eggs.

Shortly after, old Hilaire himself, gnarled and weathered, turned up on Julian's doorstep, belligerently demanding his dog back. His bald, wrinkled head always reminded Julian of a pickled walnut. He was missing most of his front teeth, and he smelled strongly of goat.

"But I don't have your dog," objected Julian. "I haven't seen her for days."

"Then you should have told me, monsieur," said old Hilaire reproachfully and unreasonably, but somehow Julian knew what he meant. The farmer always addressed Julian as "monsieur," just as Julian always referred to him as "old Hilaire." Edith and cheese were the sole things they had in common, their only interaction being the exchange of money for excellent-quality *fromage pur chèvre*.

The long and the short of it was that Edith had not been seen for several days, not by any of the neighbors, including Julian, or by old Hilaire himself. The goat farmer was extremely worried.

"She's a valuable animal, monsieur," Hilaire whistled through the gap in his dentition. "There are thieves about who'd steal a good dog like that, use her in experiments. Besides," he lowered his voice, "she's *in that way*."

That, to the old man, was the worst of it. She needed care, regular meals. In that way or not, Julian was not inclined to be overly anxious about the way-ward bitch. She did occasionally go walk-about, and he knew she would eventually turn up. To placate his neighbor, however, he agreed to keep an eye out for Edith and to inform him if he saw her.

•

Julian told Paul and Mado about Edith, and they in turn told Gaston. The postman also promised to keep an eye open for the pointer on his rounds. That made two things he had to look for—the *pigeonnier* and Edith.

In fact, he was on his way now to Les Colombes to have a word with the de Sauvignacs about the dog. He had no mail for them and didn't really expect them to have seen her. The château lay at the eastern end of his route. Little chance Edith would have wandered that far. But it was a hot day, the kind of weather that Gaston believed to be particularly try-ing for men of his physique. He saw himself as heav-ily built as opposed to fat, and it was people like him who suffered most from heat. He looked forward to the *coup de blanc* that Monsieur de Sauvignac would certainly offer him. It was a point of honor with such people. Real gentry, not like some.

His minivan had been giving him trouble again.

The motor was dying for no reason. Gaston suspected it had something to do with the battery or maybe the alternator. He sighed. He would have to fill out yet another maintenance request at the end of the day. He bumped down the muddy lane past La Binette. As usual, there was nothing for them, either, especially (he was relieved) nothing requiring a signature. He began the rough, steep climb out of the valley bottom toward Les Colombes. He was about three-quarters of the way there when the engine coughed. He downshifted quickly. The engine died completely.

Merde! Why did these things always happen to him? He set the hand brake and considered his options. He was almost through his route, but this meant he'd have to call in to the depot for help. This would make the fourth time in a month, and his boss was giving him sour looks for running up maintenance costs and late deliveries. As if it were his fault. These tin-pot PTT vans, couldn't hold up to the roads.

Well, he could walk up the rest of the way to the château and phone from there. He got out, glumly studying the steep incline before him. Really, it would be simplest to wheel the van around, get it pointed downhill the way he'd come, jump in, and kick-start it on the run. So much for his *coup de blanc*, but, provided he didn't stall, he'd probably make it back to the main road, maybe even all the way to the depot.

He opened the driver's-side door and was setting his shoulder to the frame when it occurred to him that before releasing the brake he'd better do something about preventing the car from rolling backward. He went to the opposite verge to gather some rocks. As he did, his eye caught something below him through the screen of trees. He walked farther up the road to get a better view. He was now looking down at a corner of La Binette, a perspective he normally did not have of the farm. It was a peaceful scene, a low, hummocky field dotted with grazing sheep, old poplars in a line, and a stream heavily overgrown with willow brush at the bottom. Gaston stood very still, a huge grin spreading over his features.

"*C'est vachement fort, ça!*" he exclaimed softly. Really, it was too rich. Luck landed in your very hand when you least expected it.

He hurried back to the van, maneuvered it around—it was infernally hard work because he had to push it uphill a bit first in order to turn it downhill—jumped in, and let it roll. The engine caught on the first kick, and he was away, joyfully bucketing at speed back down the steep, rocky lane, past trees and hedges, approaching the grassy track winding off to La Binette. It was a fairly straight run down, except for the curve at the bottom, one he'd done thousands of times. As he entered the bend, he never really saw, much less had a chance of avoiding, the log lying in the middle of the road, only felt the tremendous shock as his front tires hit it. The van sailed through the air and came down on its side in a long, gouging slide of gravel, shattered glass, and grating metal. Gaston lay stupidly in its wreckage, bleeding profusely from the nose and mouth. His last view of the world, before the darkness gathered in, was of the day's mail littering the grass like confetti and a swollen, one-eyed face hanging upside down above him like a bilious moon.

•

It was *la canadienne* that he called for, her name that he muttered insistently. When Mara arrived, the tall female doctor said disapprovingly that she could stay for a couple of minutes, no more. Gaston's fat wife and seven daughters, huddled together like chickens at one end of the waiting room, glared at her with tear-filled, hating eyes. They now knew her to be the mistress whom slow, fat Gaston had cunningly concealed from them all these years. That's what came of letting foreigners live among you. They included Mara's companions, grouped at the other end of the room, in their outrage. Mado paced like a caged animal, smoking furiously despite a *défense de fumer* notice. Paul huddled massively in a plastic chair that threatened to give way beneath his weight. Julian sat next to Paul, long legs outstretched, gazing at the opposite wall.

Mara followed the doctor's straight white back through the swinging doors and down the long pale-green corridor leading to the intensive-care ward. She returned shortly. Everyone's eyes were on her.

"He's in very bad shape," she said unnecessarily. "He could barely talk. He's full of tubes. I think—I think he was trying to tell me something about the *pigeonnier*." And she burst out crying.

•

The village of Malpech perched atop a rise and consisted of two dozen dwellings. Mara and Julian approached it along a narrow, winding road. As they entered the village, the first thing they saw was an empty, dusty square flanked at one end by a small, mossy church and at the other by a newish community hall. It was noon, and there was no one about, not even, to Jazz's disappointment, a dog. The houses had a hot, closed look. The only movement centered on a public notice board where badly tacked posters flapped lazily in the breeze.

Beyond Malpech, the road took them down into a leafy valley, over a humpbacked bridge spanning a stream and continued past a thin scattering of farms, with not a pigeon house in sight. Several kilometers farther on, they drew up at the bend in the road where they were told the accident had occurred. Julian braked the van. They got out. Apart from a few shards of glass and plastic, the rutted, gravel road showed no sign of violence.

From where they stood, they were in a kind of bowl with wooded hills rising up around them. The sound of cicadas, sawing drowsily, filled the air. A light, sere wind rustled the foliage, but otherwise the landscape was very still, as if everything were caught in a kind of hot, midday enchantment. Only Jazz was animated, following his nose avidly along the grassy verge. Back and forth he ran, tongue lolling, now loping ahead, now stopping to investigate a smell long and lovingly. Wordlessly, his human companions trudged after him, past a rough field grazed by a few sheep, the only sign of agricultural activity in the immediate vicinity, and past stacks of logs cut from fallen trees and left at the roadside by the work crew after the last windstorm. From there the road led straight up. Slowly they took the steep ascent.

"You don't suppose Gaston was delirious, do you?" Julian hazarded. As far as they could see, an unbroken canopy of treetops spread away beneath them. The only visible man-made structure was much higher up, where the roofline and chimneystacks of an imposing house could barely be made out through a screen of greenery.

"I don't know. He seemed to think he'd found something. He was very insistent, especially about the money."

"Well, if he did, it wasn't here. In fact, odds are it was somewhere else. His route takes him all over the place."

Mara made no reply.

"It would be simple enough to check it out," Julian offered a moment later. "His route, I mean."

"I suppose we could," she said without conviction. Since the facteur's accident, she had little stomach for pursuing her quest. Gaston had suffered a concussion, a broken arm, four fractured ribs, a broken nose, internal injuries, and facial lacerations. His condition was serious, and he remained heavily drugged, lapsing in and out of consciousness. She had not been able to question him further. For the sake of the family, the doctor had ordered Mara to keep away. She, too, believed that Mara was Gaston's secret companion of joy.

"I'm thinking of giving it up, Julian," she told him finally.

He stopped short. "You're not serious?"

"Very." Her small face was pale, the dark, straight brows knit together.

"But why?"

"I feel responsible. It's pretty obvious Gaston's accident was somehow tied up with that damned *pigeonnier*."

"Oh, come on, Mara, you're not to blame for what happened."

"All the same, he's been badly injured, probably because of a thousand euros and my need to know. Bedie's been missing for nineteen years, is probably dead. I think the time has come for me to let it go."

She called for Jazz. "Well, we've been, we've looked, and now I'd like to go home."

"Of course, it's up to you," Julian conceded as they turned back down the hill. Why did he feel so disappointed when really he should feel relieved? The search for Bedie Dunn was something he had entered into with the greatest reluctance. He was now free to continue looking for the Lady's Slipper alone, without impediment, without the nagging worry of what Mara's presence might mean in his life, of what ultimately he might have to do with her. Her and that dog of hers. But deep down he knew that her withdrawal took the heart out of the chase, and the chase, after all, was what had been driving them—him—from the beginning.

For her part, Mara was convinced of the rightness of her decision. The time really had come to say goodbye to Bedie. A sudden sense of lightness flooded her, as if, having put down the weight of her sister, she could now stand straighter, move without encumbrance. Savoring the relief of the moment, she raised her eyes and saw her surroundings clearly as if for the first time. A dusty country road, shimmering with heat. Below them a peaceful wooded valley. Through the trees, a meadow running down to a stream, thickly bordered by willows and poplars. Her eye rested there, picking out the occasional flash of the watercourse. Then she saw something that made her heart lurch.

"Julian," she cried sharply.

"What?"

Dragging him back uphill to a point where they both could get a better view, she pointed frantically. There in the distance below them, rising from the meadow and still largely obscured by foliage, was a *pigeonnier*. Craning their necks and leaning this way and that, they put together enough glimpses of it to make it out: a tall, round tower built of local limestone with numerous entry holes for the birds. The steeply pitched roof, what they could see of it, was conical and covered in *lauzes*. From where they stood, part of a shuttered window and a door were visible. They stared at it wordlessly, as if by speaking they feared to dispel an illusion.

At last Mara stirred. "This was not," she said with conviction, "on the Série bleue."

Julian was actively scanning the panorama of forested hills and valleys around them. Eventually, he pointed to his left. "My stand of Bird's-nests can't be more than three to five kilometers northwest of here." He paused for Mara to take in his meaning. "Easily within walking distance. So we know which direction she came from."

"And all we have to do," Mara finished, "is work out where she went."

They walked quickly down the hill. At the bottom, they passed an iron box placed on a small cairn of stones at the side of the road. Speculatively they paused before it. The name BINETTE was crudely lettered on the front. In several places the paint, once red, now weathered almost black, had run, so that the words had a ghastly, dripping look. At right angles to the road, an overgrown, rutted track led across a rough sheep pasture and down toward a heavily wooded combe. The tip of a chimney showing through the treetops indicated a house.

"At a guess," said Julian, "I'd say the *pigeonnier* belongs to this farm."

Something was moving on the track—a large man on a small bicycle, coming toward them not in haste but steadily. As the bicyclist approached, they could hear the faint rattling of the frame on the uneven ground and the soft, regular squeaking of the crank set with each revolution of the pedals. *Grinch. Grinch. Grinch.* The scene had such a dreamlike quality to it that Mara and Julian stood transfixed, watching it unfold. Now the bicyclist was nearing the point where the track met the road. The rider made the turn in their direction. As he drew even with them, he slowed but did not stop. Nor did he greet them, only fixed them with one bulging eye—the other was covered by a dark lens—craning his neck slowly around as he rode past to keep them, particularly Mara, in view as long as possible. Jazz gave a low growl. Mara retained a vision of pale, ragged hair standing on end and a large, misshapen face resembling an oversized, semi-cooked hunk of engorged goose liver.

"Dear Lord," whispered Mara once she could find her voice, "what was that?"

•

"*Eh bien,*" said Loulou La Pouge, "you have found a pigeon house."

"*The* pigeon house," Mara said firmly. Once again they were in the ex-policeman's parlor, perched on overstuffed chairs, being served Monbazillac and nuts. "So that's proof, isn't it?"

Loulou shrugged and threw up both hands. "Proof

of what? That it exists? *Soyez raisonable*, Mara, you still have not definitely connected the photographs to your sister, and until you can do that, what is your case?"

"But the photos were taken with her camera," Mara cried impatiently. "Her initials are on the case. How much more do you want?"

"Ah." The old fellow cocked his head at her with a knowing look. "Always we return to the initials. I'm afraid, mon amie, you did not help your own cause there."

She paled. "What do you mean?"

"*B.D.* Presumably for 'Beatrice Dunn'?"

"Well of course!"

"But written *over* the accumulated deposit of dirt and mold. A more recent addition, don't you think?"

Julian started. "A more recent addition? Are you saying someone added those initials at a later time?" He turned to stare unbelievingly at Mara, who flushed a deep red.

"You knew all along!" she burst out furiously at Loulou. "All right. You caught me out. I wrote them myself." Unrepentantly, she glared at Julian, whose eyebrows were hovering near his hairline. "Don't you see? It was the only way I could make the police take me seriously."

"*Au contraire*," Loulou said gravely. "I can tell you that those of us, myself included, who still remember the case would have liked nothing better than to take you seriously. After all, we still have the unsolved murder of the Tenhagen woman and several disappearances on the books. But we needed more than supposition and—*pardonnez-moi*—flimsy chicanery! It doesn't do"—he wagged a fat forefinger in her face—"no, it doesn't do at all to try to trick the police!"

"So you're saying this camera could have belonged to someone else?" Julian asked.

"No, it did not," Mara almost shouted. "Forget the initials. That camera was Bedie's. I'd know it anywhere. Oh, why won't anyone believe me?"

The two men regarded her in silence. She looked near to tears.

Julian drew a deep breath. "Okay." He turned to Loulou. "It seems to me you do have proof of a sort. First, Mara recognized the camera as her sister's, even if she did falsify the initials. That ought to count for something. Second, whoever took those photos knew orchids, how to identify and film them. According to Mara, Bedie was an experienced documenter of orchids. Taken together, I'd say these things argue strongly in favor of the camera's provenance."

Heartened, Mara persisted. "And there's something else. We told you the pigeon house is on a farm called La Binette. What we didn't tell you is that it's also just up the road from the spot where the *facteur*, Gaston, had his accident. He was asking around about the *pigeonnier*, you know, showing the photocopy to everyone on his route. Don't you find it odd that he crashed just there? Besides, we got a look at the farmer. He's . . ." She hesitated. How could she say that he was the embodiment of the nameless terror of her nightmares? "There's something horrible about him—brutal, ugly. Maybe you won't be convinced by gut feeling, but I tell you, I *know* he had something to do with my sister's disappearance. Can't you persuade the police at least to question him?"

Loulou shook his head, clicking his tongue softly against his teeth. "Mara, you must understand that your credibility with the lads in Périgueux is not— how shall we say—particularly famous. They see you as someone who has already tried to doctor evidence and who is quite capable of doing so again. Moreover, you bring me nothing more than highly circumstantial information, an argument based, as you put it, on a reaction of the viscera. A *pigeonnier* and an ugly farmer do not make a case. Supposing this man is questioned and denies all knowledge of your sister, as he most certainly will. What then?"

"Ask questions. Make people talk. The police can do that. Someone is bound to know something, to remember something."

Loulou smiled indulgently. "For you it seems so simple. But you don't understand how the rural mind works. Make people talk. *Ma foi!* The locals will simply close ranks. This man is one of them, and the tendency is always to cover for one's own, regardless. Besides, what you need is something much more concrete than local gossip, Mara. A solid link tying this man to your sister. That's what you must establish, don't you see?"

Mara rose, chin set firm. "Loulou, all I can see is that the only thing that will convince you is finding Bedie's body on that farm. Well, if that's what it takes, that's what we'll do!"

Julian, who found himself hurrying out the door after her, wished, not for the first time, that she would be more sparing in her use of the first person plural.

TWELVE

Gaston felt like his hero, Marshal Ney. Or, rather, what he imagined Marshal Ney must have felt like as he planned and directed the victorious battles of Friedland, Smolensk, and Borodino. The son of a barrel-maker from Saarlouis, Ney had risen to fame and glory in the days of the Empire. Gaston was also from a line of barrel-makers, from Bordeaux.

First, there was the triumphant moment when Mara had presented him with a check for one thousand euros. This had been in the recovery ward in the presence of his wife and daughters. Now that they understood the situation, they had forgiven him and embraced Mara enthusiastically. Even the once-disapproving doctor shook Mara's hand. The other ward patients thought Gaston had won the lottery. Although his eyes were bruised and bloodshot, tubes still ran out of nearly every orifice, and most parts of his body, including his nose, were heavily bandaged, it had been the best day of his life.

Then followed a deeply gratifying conference with Mara and Julian, both of them hanging on his lips, as it were.

"So you see," Mara appealed to him, "what we need is a way of getting information on those La Binette people without arousing suspicion."

"It's more than that," said Julian. "We need to be able to get onto their land."

"Hrrr," Gaston spoke with difficulty around his tubes. "You ha' to be ca'ful. I heard sub preddy fuddy stories aboud dem."

Mara and Julian nodded. Their sighting of Vrac— the man on the bicycle could have been none other— made them alive to this advice.

In the end, Gaston advised them to talk with the people in the château on the hill, Monsieur and Madame de Sauvignac. He knew them personally, having delivered their mail for nearly thirty years. If there was anything to be gotten on those La Binette folk, the de Sauvignacs would have it. He then gave Mara and Julian a barely intelligible version of the history of the de Sauvignacs as he knew it: the early death of one son, the estrangement of the other, the mother gone right off her head. He finished by describing the present melancholy state of affairs in which the old couple lived out their days alone, rattling about in a great cave of a mansion.

The nurse came in to warn Julian and Mara not to tire her patient.

"Good lug," Gaston gurgled happily after them as they departed. "Leb be doe wha' habbens." And he touched the side of his bandaged nose knowingly with his good hand.

•

When Mara telephoned Henri de Sauvignac, she mentioned only her interest in the *pigeonnier*. The old gentleman was courteous but wary and surprisingly evasive. From this she judged that Gaston must have, at some previous time, given the de Sauvignacs his undoubtedly gruesome version of *la canadienne disparue*. To them, she was only a stranger with unpleasant questions to ask. Henri de Sauvignac made the excuse that his wife was not well, apologized, and said they could not possibly receive her at the moment. However, if she would be good enough to leave her number . . . She did so.

She was extremely surprised when, the following morning, Henri de Sauvignac telephoned and suggested that she come out to the château at four o'clock that afternoon.

•

Les Colombes stood high on its prominence, surveying a great sweep of rumpled hills and valleys. As Mara drove up the steep, winding approach, she could barely make out the dimensions of the château, so overgrown was it with shrubberies. Then she rounded a bend and found herself in an empty, dusty forecourt giving onto a broad, ivy-covered facade. Once grand, no doubt, Les Colombes now had a shabby, forlorn air. The roof looked in bad condition. Many of the tall upper-story windows were shuttered. The broad front of the château was dominated by a central portal above a balustraded terrace. A crumbling pair of Baroque staircases curved down from either end of the terrace.

Mara parked in the shade. Jazz looked hopeful

and then disappointed at being left. As usual, he hung his head out the window and moaned disapprovingly at Mara's retreating back.

Henri de Sauvignac must have been watching for her, for as she climbed the weed-choked steps the great front door swung back. He stood in the opening, tall and gaunt.

"Madame Dunn?" His voice was suave, like old velvet, his deeply lined face still handsome. He wore a tired but well-made suit of an old-fashioned cut, a shirt of dubious whiteness, and a paisley cravat.

"Monsieur de Sauvignac?"

Gallantly, he stooped to brush the back of her hand with lips as dry as autumn leaves.

"How good of you to come at such short notice." His practiced regard, wandering covertly over her body, revealed a libertine beneath the gentleman. "And how clever of you to find us. Rather out of the way, I'm afraid."

"Your directions were excellent."

Her host stepped back to admit her into an echoing vestibule. An impressive stone staircase rose at the back of it to the upper reaches of the house. Passing near him, Mara caught a whiff of eau de cologne, suggestive of a still-potent sexuality but underlain by a faint smell of decay that he seemed to share with the house itself. It was an odor that Mara recognized from her own work in restoring dank places long uninhabited.

"I think the library will be most comfortable." He

ushered her through a pair of handsomely paneled doors opening off to the right. "Please. Sit down. May I offer you something? An apéritif?"

Mara preferred tea but accepted vermouth because she thought it would be easier for him. She somehow doubted that the de Sauvignacs kept domestic help. With a small bow, he withdrew.

She had been invited to sit, but Mara remained standing, glancing curiously about her. The library, he had called it. Certainly it contained books, but it looked more like a furniture warehouse—Louis XVI armchairs pushed against the walls, an antique armoire, a dainty Restoration console, an eighteenth-century ebony escritoire. There were little touches of domesticity, too, suggesting that the de Sauvignacs spent much of their time there: a pair of worn velvet settees drawn up to an oil heater; a small television on a scarred mahogany stand; a sewing basket full of scraps of material. The back of the room was entirely taken up by a baronial dining table, set about with sixteen chairs (Mara counted them). It was stacked with papers and bric-a-brac, but a telltale litter of crumbs at one end told her that this was where the couple took their meals.

The paneled doors creaked. Mara turned. It was not Henri de Sauvignac; instead, a tall elderly woman clad in a dress that hung unevenly at the hem, a voluminous green, fringed shawl, and dressy high-heeled shoes.

"Ah," said the woman, fixing Mara with vague

kindliness before wobbling toward her in a clattering, jerky gait, like a marionette in the hands of an inexpert puppeteer.

"You must be Madame Dunn? I am Jeanne de Sauvignac. How very kind of you to call." Her rusty voice was pleasant, and she spoke with almost childish pride, as if she had initiated the meeting. She extended her hand to touch Mara's with formal courtesy. "Do sit down." Up close, she emitted the same musty odor as her husband.

Mara seated herself on one of the velvet settees, Jeanne on the other, drawing her shawl about her with care, smoothing its shiny nap with the palm of her hand. Mara studied her with interest. The old woman's clothing was like the room, a gathering of oddments from better times, the dress of fine but much-worn gray silk jersey, the scuffed satin pumps dating from another era and too big now for the bony feet. The grayish-yellow hair was swept up at the sides and held haphazardly in place by two tortoise-shell combs, giving the woman's head a flyaway look. The shawl struck a curious note. Mara realized with a mild sense of shock that it was in fact one of those souvenir tablecloths that one bought at seaside resorts; the word "Biarritz" was emblazoned down one side.

Jeanne was also staring at her, not just curiously but with a hungry interest that made Mara uncomfortable.

A slight, wondering crease crumpled the old

woman's brow. "You are so much—" she began eagerly and then broke off.

So much what? Mara wondered, but at that point the husband returned with a small tray bearing glasses and a bottle of Martini & Rossi. He seemed momentarily surprised to see his wife in the room, but merely said as he handed Mara her drink, "Ah, my dear, here is Madame Dunn, who has come to see us." He served his wife and then himself before sitting down beside Mara.

He raised his glass. "*A votre santé, madame.*"

"*A la vôtre aussi*," Mara toasted them both in return.

"How nice to have a visitor." Jeanne de Sauvignac favored her with a crooked smile of naive and vacant sweetness. "We often used to have visitors in the afternoon. For tea, you know. I always liked to take afternoon tea, in the English manner, is that not so, Henri?"

"Of course, my dear," murmured her husband. He delved in his pocket and drew out a thin black marocain case, snapping it open with a thumbnail. "Do you smoke, madame?" When Mara declined, he said, "I hope you will permit?" and applied himself to removing a cigarette, striking a match, lighting up, and placing the burnt matchstick in a plastic Cinzano ashtray, each movement carried out with fastidious care. His smoking fascinated her: both greedy and precise, as if he hungered for the taste and smell of the tobacco but apportioned each drag sparingly. With every inhalation, he tapped the ash carefully into the ashtray.

They were clearly waiting for her to begin. For the moment, Mara really had no idea how to go about it. Gaston had not prepared her for such penurious eccentricity. In the end, de Sauvignac saved her the trouble.

Clearing his throat, he said, "You expressed an interest in the *pigeonnier*, I believe?"

"Yes, of course." It was her ostensible reason for coming.

"Unfortunately, I don't know how much I can tell you." He tapped the cigarette. "It was built sometime after this house, probably in the late 1600s, and at one time stood on land that belonged to my family." Momentarily, his voice took on a ring of pride. "In times past, the Seigneurie of Les Colombes extended some ten leagues east to west, farther than a man could walk in a day. In fact, until the last century, Les Colombes was one of the most important holdings in the region. Of course, things are now—how should I put it—much reduced."

"I see." She did not know what else to say.

"However, to return to the *pigeonnier*. But perhaps you are not aware of the historical importance of pigeons in France?" Once more he sucked deeply on the cigarette. Twin trails of smoke streamed thinly from his nostrils. "For centuries they were valued for meat, eggs, and fertilizer, especially here in our southwest, where we have little livestock. In my grandfather's, even in my father's day, pigeon dung was so precious that it was given as dowries and passed down from generation to generation.

"It's not surprising, therefore"—a wave of the hand—"that there are thousands of such structures scattered throughout the Dordogne. However, ours is one of the largest." Again the note of pride. He craned around to frown at the bookshelves. "I believe somewhere there is an architectural drawing showing it in cross section so that you can see the niches set into the interior wall for the birds to nest. At one time we may have had over one thousand nesting pairs. I remember there was a tall, pivoting ladder in the middle for the keeper to climb up. In my father's time, however, the bottom nests were blocked off to reduce the number of birds. Pigeons"—he gave a sardonic smile—"eat a lot of grain."

He paused reflectively. "It no longer belongs to us, of course. The land was sold a long time ago, the *pigeonnier* with it." His gaze traveled to the windows and beyond. "You know, I haven't set eyes on that dovecote in years. I didn't even recognize it when Gaston showed us the picture." His eyes returned to Mara. "Is this sufficient information? I'm really not sure how much more I can tell you."

"Yes. At least where the *pigeonnier* is concerned." Mara hesitated, then plunged. "Monsieur de Sauvignac, I haven't been exactly open with you. It's not so much the *pigeonnier* that I want to talk to you about, although that does come into it. I expect

205

Gaston has already told you something about me . . ." She drew breath. De Sauvignac waited for her to go on.

"My real reason for being here, as you've probably already guessed, is—I've come for my sister." She was putting it awkwardly, yet she *was* there for Bedie, because of her and on her behalf.

If Henri regarded her impassively, the effect on his wife was electrical. The smile slipped completely from her face. Jeanne gaped at Mara in acute alarm, bordering on panic, as if Mara were a madwoman accusing them of body snatching. "But she's not here!" she cried, appalled.

"I mean," Mara corrected, feeling her cheeks go hot, "it's about my sister that I've come."

Quickly, to cover her gaffe, she gave them her version of Bedie's disappearance and the link, through the photograph, with the dovecote. Throughout the telling, the deepening crease in Madame's brow hung like a question mark in the air. When Mara finished, wife and husband were silent for a long moment.

De Sauvignac ground out his cigarette. "Terrible for you, of course, but I don't quite see how we can help you."

Mara explained. "I'd like to approach the people who own the farm below you, where the *pigeonnier* stands. The woman known as la Binette and her son, Vrac. I'd be extremely grateful if you could assist me in this regard."

He frowned. "La Binette and Vrac?"

"I understood from Gaston that you have some influence with them."

"Influence?" De Sauvignac gave a dry laugh, like a cough. "Only in the sense that we are, how should I put it, long acquaintances. I'm afraid those two keep very much to themselves. They don't like strangers, and one has to respect their privacy."

"Could you at least tell me something about them?"

He considered this, then shrugged. "What is it you want to know?"

"Well, how long have they been here? What kind of people are they?"

"They're from these parts, of course. La Binette's father, old Rocher, was a day laborer. Took on odd jobs round about—woodcutting, harvesting. La Binette and her mother did the rough washing for the house. When I was a lad Madame Rocher and little Binette used to wheel their wooden cart up here once a week to collect the dirty things, which they'd take to the stream down below because the communal *lavoir* in Malpech was too far away. La Binette's boy, Armand—the one they call Vrac— grew up simple."

Mara found it curious that he referred to the creature she had seen on the bicycle as a boy.

"I don't like nicknames, do you?" Jeanne de Sauvignac interjected suddenly, pulling the tablecloth tightly around her. "They can be so cruel. Poor Binette had a perfectly proper name once. I can't remember it. Can you, Henri? Oh yes, that's right, Marie-Claire. Such a pretty name. And to call her a thing like that. All because she had that dreadful *tache* on her face. She was born with it, madame, a purple birthmark over one eye. When she was a girl, she always used to try to hide it with her hand, as if she were shading her eyes from the sun."

The old woman leaned forward, addressing Mara with gentle indignation. "Do you know what *binette* means, madame? Of course, most people nowadays think it merely means a hoe, the thing you use in the garden. But in the old days, it meant "ugly mug," and also one of those big old-fashioned wigs, because of course poor Marie-Claire lost all her hair after she had her baby and had to wear that ugly old horsehair thing. I remember well when Vrac was born. Two days she was in labor. When her baby came out his head was badly deformed, and he never was right as a result, poor thing. It affected his brain. Everything shook loose. That's why they called him Vrac."

"I've seen him," Mara ventured. "Frankly, he looks quite terrifying."

"Oh," the wife said softly, "you mustn't be put off by appearances. He's perfectly harmless, one of God's creatures. If you tell him to go away, shoo, like that"—she waved her hand as if she were scattering chickens—"he just fades into the trees. He never bothers anyone."

"Nevertheless," Mara persisted, "Gaston mentioned . . . certain rumors."

"Rumors?" The couple glanced quickly at each other.

"Odd behavior. I'm sorry to ask this, but I have to know. Would he have—has there ever been any history of incidents with Vrac?"

Henri, reaching for another cigarette, paused. "Incidents? I'm not sure I understand what you intend, madame."

"Violence, attacks on people, that kind of thing."

"Ah." Her host was silent for some time, studying her speculatively. Finally, he asked simply, "Are you suggesting that Vrac had something to do with your sister's disappearance?"

Mara chose her words with care. "The photo shows that Bedie was on their land. It may not be that he was involved, but he might have seen her, or else he or his mother might know something that can help me."

"Madame . . ." De Sauvignac's voice was controlled. He replaced the cigarette unlit, snapping the marocain case shut. Mara noted that his hands trembled slightly. "This affair of your sister happened many years ago. You must comprehend that Vrac can't remember things from one month to the next. I doubt he would be able to tell you anything. In any case, as my wife said, he's quite harmless, but simple, you see. It would be . . . entirely inappropriate for you to question him."

"Monsieur de Sauvignac," Mara appealed to him, "having come this far, I'm afraid I can't just leave it.

The *pigeonnier* is the first concrete lead I've had in nineteen years."

"Indeed. All the same, I must ask you to avoid upsetting him." His tone grew emphatic. "When all is said and done, Vrac is one of us. I would feel required to intervene if I thought he or his mother was being harassed."

"I don't want to harass anyone," Mara insisted, "but you must understand I have to find out the truth. You see, I have reason to believe my sister came to harm on la Binette's farm."

"You have proof of this?" Henri inquired sharply.

"No," she admitted. "Only the photo of the *pigeonnier*."

He regarded her stonily.

"I don't want to involve the police." It was Mara's only trump, a weak one. "But if I have no other choice . . ."

A dark stain spread slowly over de Sauvignac's face. He spoke with cold dignity. "You must do as you see fit, madame. However, I assure you that neither you nor the police will find anything of interest in these parts." He rose stiffly. "Now, I fear my wife is growing tired. You must excuse us if we bid you good-day."

She had no choice but to rise, too, and follow him out. As she passed from the room, Jeanne's voice wavered after her uncertainly: "Au revoir, madame. Do come again. For tea next time."

The massive front door closed behind her with

heavy finality. Bleakly, Mara descended the stone steps. Well, the de Sauvignacs had received her. She'd asked her questions, and they had told her nothing. She knew the house would not be open to her again. She crossed the forecourt dejectedly, making for her car. Just before she reached it, a tall figure came striding around the corner of the house. She had to swerve to avoid a collision.

"You!" Mara exclaimed.

The man stopped short with a look of startled recognition. "Ah, of course. Bonjour, madame. We meet again. I hope in calmer circumstances?" He peered doubtfully down at her and extended a large sunburned hand. "Alain de Sauvignac."

"Oh," she said, taking in the significance of his name. "Mara Dunn."

They shook hands, he holding hers fractionally longer than Mara thought necessary. He had his father's handsome face, only more square-cut and deeply weathered. His sandy-colored hair was shot through with gray. A curious light came into his dark-blue eyes. "If I may ask, how is it that you're here? When last we met you were the frightened rabbit in the woods." It might have been teasingly said, but his look was serious.

"I came . . ." She paused, uncertainly.

"Of course!" he declared, remembering. "To see my parents. Papa said something about a visitor."

She asked a question of her own. "Then you live here?"

"Not at all. I work abroad. I'm only back for the moment, visiting the old ones."

Mara made up her mind swiftly. "Monsieur de Sauvignac, I know it's awfully forward of me, but I wonder if I could impose on you. . . ?"

"At your service," he smiled gallantly. "What can I do?"

"It's rather complicated. You see, I—I would very much appreciate the chance to talk to you. It would mean a lot to me. But I'm afraid it would have to be in confidence."

"In confidence?" He frowned. "What about?"

She shook her head, dug in her bag and gave him her card. "Not here. This is my number. Can you call me? This evening, if possible? And please, will you say nothing of this to anyone?"

He looked perplexed. "Is it so important? But why the mystery?"

She had no time for more. The massive front door was swinging open.

"Until tonight, then," she said and hurried to her car.

As she backed out, she saw that Henri de Sauvignac had emerged from the house. He made no move to join his son, only stood on the terrace, like a frozen sentinel, overseeing her departure. She caught a final glimpse of him in her rearview mirror as she pulled away. His expression gave her quite a shock. His face was white, his eyes staring, his lips pulled back in a rictus of fear.

THIRTEEN

The bead curtain flew apart noisily. Mara strode into the bistro. Jazz's entry was more sedate, snout first, a quick survey of the room, then a rambling approach to Julian, who was sipping a pastis while watching Paul do accounts at the bar. Julian looked up.

"Well? What happened?"

"They're hiding something," she cried, and hopped onto a stool beside him.

"Eh? Like what?" Paul slapped down his pencil.

She threw her hands up in frustration. "That's just it. I don't know. But it has to do with Vrac, and they won't tell me because *Vrac is one of them.* The husband is especially secretive. He doesn't want me anywhere near La Binette. Virtually warned me off."

"What about the wife?" asked Mado, coming out from the back of the bistro, where she had been setting tables in preparation for the evening crowd.

"She seems sympathetic," Mara ventured doubtfully, "but I don't think she's altogether there."

"D'you mean gaga?" Paul produced glasses and a bottle.

Mara considered the possibility. "No. Just somehow slightly out of focus—or absent. I mean, as if she weren't quite in the room with you, but listening at the door." And she told them in detail about her

213

conversation with Henri and Jeanne de Sauvignac, as well as her encounter with the son.

"The man we met in the woods was Alain de Sauvignac?" Julian queried. Finding Jazz's head within reach, he scratched it.

They all fell silent as Paul filled three glasses with white Bordeaux and topped up Julian's pastis. Mado lit a cigarette. Finally, through a screen of smoke, she said:

"It'll have to be you, Julian."

"Eh?"

"You'll have to go there and snoop around."

He gaped at her, incredulous. "What? Search the château?"

"Not the château. La Binette. The farm holds the clue to everything."

"Why me?"

"Well, *you're* the orchid expert."

"Oh, thank you very much."

"Mado's right," Mara pressed him earnestly. "Don't you see, Julian, if we can identify even some of the orchid sequence on La Binette land, it'll prove Bedie was actually there."

"I thought the *pigeonnier* already did that."

"Not good enough. From the angle of the photo, she could have taken it from the road."

"You can't *see* it from the road," Julian objected.

"Nineteen years ago, there may have been less tree cover. We need to prove that she was actually on that farm."

"I wish you wouldn't keep saying *we*, when what you really mean is *me*."

Mara stared into her wine and made no offer to accompany him.

"So you want *me* to search the whole bloody farm?" Julian glared at each of them in turn. They avoided his eye. He drained his pastis and banged the glass down in disgust. "*Par pitié*, make me a sensible suggestion for a change."

"Take a shotgun with you," Paul advised with a spark of malice.

In the end, Julian gave in. It was true that reconstructing Bedie's path would give Mara something concrete to take to the police. Let the gendarmes do the digging, he thought grimly, and then focused on the more cheerful, if faint, possibility that, if his quest were *really* successful, he would have his Lady's Slipper.

•

Alain de Sauvignac's phone call came at ten o'clock that evening. Mara snatched eagerly at the receiver.

"Yes, hello?"

"Madame Dunn?" His deep voice had a seductive quality to it. "Perhaps now you will be kind enough to tell me what this is all about?"

Mara took a lungful of air, exhaled slowly and told him as much as she thought he needed to know.

•

His terms were simple: information conditional on lunch. He came directly to the point. "I'd like to see

215

you again. Under more conducive circumstances."

So now they were sitting on the terrace of La Vieille Guinguette, a little waterside restaurant upriver from the town of Maussac. Jazz dozed at Mara's feet. The day was sunny and the fare simple, mainly traditional dishes like braised sheep's tongues and tripe cooked with leeks. They ordered *tourain*, bread-thickened soup heavy with garlic and duck fat, a meal in itself. By the time they were adding red wine to the dregs *à la Périgourdine*, they were on a first-name basis and speaking French.

"I admit I was intrigued by you," Alain said, pushing his empty bowl aside. "Who wouldn't be?" He gave her a glance that was half admiring, half speculative, then retreated onto safer ground. "You speak French well. But your accent is unusual. I can't place it."

"Montreal," she grinned, "and absolutely unique. We slur and drawl, flatten our vowels, and compress our sibilants. The point is, can you get us—Julian— onto La Binette land?"

"Your orchidologist friend?" Alain drew down the corners of his mouth. "I wouldn't like to do so *à la dérobée*, as they say. I don't hold much with sneaking. And what you're asking is trespassing, after all. You also have to realize that, if you've already approached Papa and he refused to help you, you're putting me in a damned difficult position."

She shifted uncomfortably. "I suppose you think me deceitful."

He flipped a hand in the air. "*Oui—et non*. If you truly believe Vrac had something to do with your sister's disappearance, I can understand that your desire to know might override all—well, all scruples. However, you must also comprehend my father's reticence. It might sound terribly old-fashioned to you, but Papa has a strong sense of noblesse oblige toward the people of the *territoire*, particularly la Binette and her son. The family worked on the estate, you know. La Binette and Vrac still do the occasional odd job. Local loyalties run deep."

"Even to the extent of protecting a possible murderer? Other women have gone missing, too, you know."

Alain shook his head. "No one's protecting a murderer. Oh, I agree that Vrac and la Binette sometimes get up to things they oughtn't, but Vrac's not a killer. You demonize him because he's ugly and mentally—shall we say incomplete? When really he only represents the dark side of all of us. Look, I've known him all my life. When my brother, Patrice, and I were little and Vrac a few years older, he used to jump out of the bushes at us, screaming and making horrible faces. He'd chase us through the woods, threatening to bash our heads in. I admit, we were terrified. However, I suppose, like most boys, there was also a side of us that relished the gruesomeness of it. I suppose you might say we turned it into a kind of game. We ran, he hunted us down. A variation of *cache-cache*."

"Hide-and-seek? A rather nasty form of it."

Alain grinned ruefully. "We took care not to let Vrac find us, let me tell you. The consequences could be pretty dire. In fact, it became a rule of the game. The hunter could do anything he wanted to you if he caught you."

"Such as what?" Mara asked faintly.

"Oh, mainly shoves and punches. Vrac didn't have the imagination to be very refined in his punishments. But far worse than that were his seizures. It was really frightening, watching him flail around and foam at the mouth. La Binette would have to hold him down until he grew calm again. Otherwise, he'd break things or hurt himself. But I can assure you, he never did us or anyone else any real harm. Everyone around here knows that."

Mara leaned earnestly across the table. "Alain, that was Vrac as a child. Nineteen years ago, Vrac would have been a man of—what?—thirty? thirty-five? If he found my sister on his land, what do you think he would have done?"

Alain went silent, his gaze drifting unhappily out over the water. Restlessly, he shoved his shirtsleeves up, exposing tanned, muscular arms lightly furred with golden hairs. "In my opinion, Mara, apart from a few threats and obscenities, nothing."

She fixed him somberly.

"And if he came across me alone in the forest? It wasn't my imagination, you know. Someone was stalking me that day. Purposely trying to frighten me. Or worse. I find it hard to believe that a chance passerby simply happened to decide to chase me through the trees."

Alain tossed a heel of bread to the ground for Jazz. "So do I. But only because there were no passersby." And when she looked puzzled, he went on to explain. "You see, you'd strayed onto Saint-Hubert terrain, the grounds of our local hunting association. My father is the association president. That day, it so happened that he asked me to do a routine check of the area, the posting of hunting-reserve and parking signs and so forth. I was on that footpath and in that stretch of forest for over two hours, Mara. During all that time I saw no one, apart from you and your botanical friend."

Alain's eyes met hers. In the sunlight, the dark-blue centers were surrounded by aquamarine. She held his gaze. At last, he sighed, slumping back in a gesture of defeat.

"All right. I suppose it could have been Vrac. He wanders around a lot, and the woods where you were aren't that far from his land. But if it was he, I can assure you he would have only wanted to frighten you. I doubt he intended you any harm."

Mara smiled tightly. "Another game of *cache-cache*? You don't," she challenged him, "really expect me to believe that?"

•

Julian's first consideration was how to implement the search. He made it clear that this would not be so easy, since no public footpath or hiking trail gave legitimate access to La Binette terrain. Going under cover of darkness was impossible for obvious reasons—he needed light to see and photograph the orchids that Mara required as evidence. The search would have to be conducted in broad daylight and at risk of Julian's neck.

It was Gaston who came up with the only feasible strategy. However, he played up shamefully, refusing to talk on the telephone and insisting that all of them come to "consult" with him at his house in Le Coux. He was out of the hospital by then and being assiduously nursed by his wife and seven daughters, who treated him as if he really were a battle hero. Which was only right. He had, after all, been in something very like the wars. And still was because his boss was giving him trouble, sloughing responsibility for the accident onto Gaston in order to cover up his own track record of shoddy vehicle maintenance. But if Gaston's engine hadn't given out, he wouldn't have been freewheeling down the road in the first place.

The four of them drove out on Monday evening, when the bistro was closed. They found Gaston in the garden, eating a roll of *petit-suisse* mashed up with sugar, like a schoolboy. White flecks of the creamy cheese stuck to his teeth. The bruising around his eyes had faded to an unattractive yellowish-green. His nose, no longer bandaged, was the color of an underripe aubergine. Paul and Mado gave him chocolates. Julian, who carried the flowers that Mara had brought as a get-well present, dumped them unceremoniously in the *facteur*'s lap.

Gaston dragged it out as long as he could. First he commanded his daughters to bring chairs. The guests were then served apéritifs and a tasty homemade pâté spread on little slices of grilled bread. After that he and his family had to hear in detail about Mara and Julian's encounter with Vrac and her visit to the château. Gaston was particularly fascinated by Mara's description of the interior of the house, for he had never been farther than the kitchen. He was dismayed that the de Sauvignacs had refused to help her.

"Hmm," he said judiciously. "More to this than meets the eye. But why would they cover up for Vrac? It doesn't make sense."

"They tried to make him out as simple but harmless," Mara said. "Alain, too. But I don't believe it for a moment. I'm sure he had something to do with Bedie's disappearance. We've got to find some way of searching the farm without their knowledge."

"She means me," Julian pointed out unnecessarily.

Gaston rubbed his chin.

Finally, what he told them was this: Vrac fished, and la Binette went sometimes to market to sell cheese. That was their opportunity, when the two of them were away from the farm.

"And when exactly would this be?" Julian inquired sarcastically.

"Well . . ." Gaston pushed his fat lips out and considered. "The old woman sometimes goes to the market in Le Bugue, which is on Tuesdays. Or some-times she sells her *brebis* over in Montignac, which has its market day on Wednesdays. However, she doesn't go every week. Only when she has cheese to sell. But since it's May, you're probably in luck because the ewes are milking. Now, if it were winter, that would be a different story."

"What about Vrac?" asked Julian. "He's the one I'm worried about."

"I'm getting there. Don't rush me. Vrac, on the other hand, comes and goes like a wild animal. Why, I've seen him standing still as a heron, up to his hips in the lower reaches of the Nauze one day, and prowling around the north shore of the Dordogne the next. The trick, as I said, is to hit on the very day when both of them are away together."

"How?" they all wanted to know.

"It'll take some planning," Gaston admitted. "However, if you just give me a little moment, I think I can come up with *une stratégie* that'll work."

He then went deep into thought. Mara stared at him in frustration. Paul slumped in his chair. Gaston's wife and daughters sat forward in theirs, goggling. Mado paced at the edge of the group, blowing smoke in the direction of the rosebushes. Damaged though Gaston was, Julian had to resist an urge to shake him until his neck snapped.

"What I suggest you do," Gaston said slowly, coming up and squinting into the middle distance, "is go out early on a Tuesday or Wednesday morning.

222

There's a copse above the farm, just below where the road winds up to Les Colombes. Hide your car in the trees, walk down, and find a spot where you have a good view of the farm. But you'll have to keep a sharp eye out for the people in the château, too. That's important because Madame walks in the woods every day and Monsieur still likes to shoot the occasional rabbit. You don't want them to see you. It would give everything away. Monsieur de Sauvignac would be perfectly in his right to order you off since all of the uphill land around there still belongs to him."

"What about the son?" Julian wanted to know. "He might be wandering around."

"Hmm. You'll have to take your chances there. Anyway, wait until you see la Binette and Vrac go off. The old woman drives the truck. Sometimes she takes Vrac with her and drops him somewhere along the way. Other times he goes off on that bicycle of his. That's the chance you want to watch for. But be careful. The mother's usually back before noon. Her *brebis* sells out fast. With him, it's hard to say. Sometimes he can be away for days. People say he sleeps in the woods."

Julian thought it a hit and miss plan and said so, but no one had anything better to suggest. He sulked in the car all the way back to Grissac. The following day was Tuesday, and he had been prevailed upon by the others to go out to La Binette at the crack of dawn. He pictured himself in the misty chill, crouching in wet grass, peering through leaves, while others slept. He liked to start his day out slowly, with several cups of well-sweetened tea, which he sometimes shared with Edith on the occasions that she chose to drop in. Except that Edith was still missing. Old Hilaire was beside himself, and the entire population of Grissac was worried and on the lookout for her.

"*Courage, mon vieux*," sniggered Paul. "If you're not back by the end of the day, I'll send in the gendarmes."

"It'll come off fine, *chouchou*," Mado assured him. "Afterward we'll all have a big lunch at Chez Nous. I'll make you something absolutely to bring water to the mouth."

His own susceptibilities got the better of him, but just. *Chouchou* was what she called dogs and cats. Rabbits, too, before she slaughtered them.

•

So it was agreed that Julian would set out at first light the following day, armed not with a shotgun but with his camera and binoculars. He was to take photographs of anything that could be used as evidence linking Bedie to the farm. He was expected to report back at Chez Nous by noon.

Mara turned up at the bistro at a little before twelve to find it doing unusual business, owing to the car-crash death of France's legendary soccer goalie, Jimmy Bartholème, otherwise known as le Mur, the Wall. Patrons sat at the tables, talking in hushed tones. The newsvendor portion of Chez Nous had sold out of papers early; indeed, Paul said that every copy of *Sud Ouest* in the region had been snapped up by eleven that morning.

By one o'clock, there was still no sign of Julian. Paul, in his multiple role as garçon, barman, and caissier, repeatedly went to the door to scan the road leading into the village. Mara brought periodic reports to Mado in the kitchen.

"No sign of him yet."

"But it's nearly two!"

"I hope he hasn't run into Vrac."

"*Dieu l'en garde!*"

The afternoon slid by. Mara, as an alternative to nervous collapse, lent a hand clearing off the tables. Jazz slept unconcernedly in the doorway, where everyone had to step over him.

It was not until half past three that Julian's battered van finally pulled up. He had scarcely pushed his way through the beaded curtain before they jerked him out of the hearing of a last, lingering pair of customers and cornered him at the far end of the restaurant. No one seemed to notice that he was tired, muddy, and scratched.

"Well? Did you—"

"What happened? I was worried—"

"What the hell took you so long?"

Julian avenged his lost morning by refusing to tell them anything until he had been allowed to wash up and was seated with a beer. Even so, he doled it out slowly with each course. By then they had the restaurant to themselves. Over a white bean soup, he

informed them that he had left his car in the spot
Gaston had described and walked down through the
woods in the direction of the farm. He had found a
place where he could watch the farmhouse from a safe
distance and had seen la Binette drive off at around
six-thirty, backfiring through a cloud of smoke.

"I got a good look at her through my binoculars,"
he told them. "She's about six feet tall, wears rubber
boots, and has a face that would stop a clock."

Over a next course of *foie gras en croûte*, he
informed them that Vrac had not appeared until
much later.

"Mado, this smells terrific." He broke off to fork
open a steaming dome of light, flaky crust and
allowed himself the luxury of a slowly savored
mouthful of baked goose liver before continuing.
"Then he spent the morning sticking sheep."

Paul ceased chewing, nudged Jazz away with his
knee, and glared at Julian in disbelief.

"By the way, he has two good eyes. I saw him
without those sunglasses of his. Anyhow, he had this
long pole with a sharpened end, and he went down to
the pasture and poked sheep. He wasn't rounding
them up or anything, just chasing and sticking them
for the hell of it. He seems to be the type who enjoys
random acts of violence."

Mara moaned and put down her fork.

Julian went on in a pastry-thickened voice: "I was
about to give up, thinking he'd be at it for the rest of
the day, when suddenly he went back to the house

and came out again with a shotgun. Then he stalked off through the trees. I sat tight, I tell you. The last thing I wanted was to run into him and have to explain my presence on his land. If he even gave me the chance to explain."

He paused while Mado brought out the principal dish, a *ballottine* of pork braised in wine and served in a cream sauce. It came accompanied by asparagus and his favorite, *pommes de terre sarladaises*, potatoes richly browned in goose fat and dressed with parsley and garlic.

Breathing deeply, he resumed. "I waited for what seemed like forever. Eventually, when he didn't come back, I figured he'd gone hunting for the day. It seemed too risky to approach the house, but I was able to check the *pigeonnier* out. It's the same one all right. I photographed it from roughly the same angle as in Bedie's photo and had a quick look inside. It was full of junk, old farm implements, empty bottles. No pigeons, though, because the nest holes are all blocked up. And nothing suggestive."

"Such as what?" asked Mado.

"Er—signs of digging. Of course," he added lamely, "there wouldn't be by now, would there? Anyway, by then it was nearly ten. I figured I had a couple of hours tops before the old woman got back. But I was less worried about her than him, roaming around with that shotgun. However, since he'd gone off in one direction, I did the only thing that made sense. Went off in the other, which took me east along the stream at the bottom of their land. It was very soggy going and fairly open in parts, so I was at a disadvantage from the viewpoint of my personal safety. That is, I expected at any moment to get a backside of shot or manual strangulation, if Vrac spotted me groping around on his property. Not that any of you would care, of course." His sarcasm was lost in a mouthful of hot, succulent pork.

"Did you find any orchids?" Mara demanded, watching him enjoy his food with barely concealed impatience.

He swallowed. "I'm coming to it. I floundered on like that for a bit until I came to a footpath that veered off through the trees. And suddenly I found myself in a water meadow, up to my knees in *Dactylorhiza incarnata*. Early Marsh Orchids to you. The lay of the land looked damned similar to Bedie's photo. Naturally I took pictures for comparison. Now, I assume you all see the importance of the Marsh Orchids . . ."

He paused for another mouthful and also to let them take this in. Since no one offered any comment, he explained: "The point is, they were the next photo in sequence after the *pigeonnier*. So, if it was the same spot, this clearly established that Bedie had come in from the west, which is where the Bird's-nests are, through the forest, along the bottom of la Binette's farm, past the pigeon house, and onto the footpath leading into the water meadow. It's also possible that Bedie did this in a single walk, which answers our question about continuity. It's no more than four or five kilometers between the Bird's-nests and the Marsh Orchids—nothing for a seasoned hiker like Mara's sister."

"*Parbleu!*" uttered Paul.

Julian fell to plying his fork and knife, giving them more time to admire his deductive skills.

"What remained, of course," he mumbled, coming up after a bit for air, "was to figure out where she went from there. If you remember, Mara, the final sequence of orchids all needed higher, open ground. But I had three problems."

"What?" The others watched as he mopped up a pool of sauce with bread and chewed lengthily.

"First, the water meadow was low-lying and enclosed by forest, so I couldn't get a clear view of the surrounding area. Second, the trail branched off in three different directions. And, third, I was beginning to feel a little nervous because by that time I really had no idea where Vrac was." Pushing away from the table, he leaned back with a sigh.

"So?" Paul inquired, rising to clear away the plates.

"So there was nothing for it but to follow my nose. I assumed Bedie would have stayed on a path, so I picked the first branch and followed it for a couple of kilometers. It went through the woods and then into some fields, and for a while things looked promising, scatterings of Butterfly and Bee and Man Orchids, but then it led down into big pine forest with lots of ferns. I knew the soil there would be too acid for most of the orchids I was looking for, so I turned back and tried the second path."

He paused to help himself to cheese, which Paul had set out. "This one took me up to a hanging meadow. I saw lots of Pyramidals mixed in with sage and daisies, tons of Twayblade, and a nice pair of Monkey Orchids along the way, but nothing indicative. So I went back and tried the third path, which I must admit seemed the least likely of the three because it led straight down into wetland. But then it wound up along the face of a hill. Things started looking promising when I found some Lizard Orchids. Then a scattering of Bees and Flies intermixed with lots of Man Orchids with a few dried out Ladies here and there. Then I came to a beautiful big stand of *Serapias lingua*, Tongue Orchid. Of course, you realize what this means, Mara."

And while she was working it out, he cried, "Well, dammit, don't you see, those were all the orchids in the photographs, in order of appearance. I'd pretty much reconstructed the forward part of Bedie's path!"

"*Mais, c'est incroyable!*" breathed Mado.

Paul whistled appreciatively.

"And the Lady's Slipper?" Mara asked eagerly.

"Ah. Yes." Julian scratched his beard. "The *Cypripedium*. Well, obviously, I knew if I could find that, it would be the clincher. I also knew the most likely place for it to grow would be on elevated, cooler ground. Now, I'd spotted a long, high, wooded ridge off to my left, just the kind of habitat I was looking for. So I made for it. At one point, I was surprised to realize the path I was on had actually taken me in a wide arc running below Les Colombes. By the way, what's for dessert?"

"Apple-and-prune upside-down cake with crème fraîche," said Mado, placing the handsome confection before him.

"My favorite! Mado," Julian declared, "you're a twenty-first-century Brillat-Savarin. Curnonsky would have devoted chapters to you alone." He leaned over and gave her a greasy and, since Paul was looking, chaste kiss on the cheek.

"Get on with it," growled the husband.

"Okay. Okay. It was quite a rocky climb, pretty much straight up. En route I found a great patch of gentians. Quite a few Butterfly Orchids as well. It's a splendid view from up there, by the way. I could make out Géraud's house on the road beyond Malpech quite clearly."

"The Lady's Slipper?" Mara reminded him exasperatedly. "Did you find it?"

He paused to pick his teeth. "Er . . . no."

Their collective letdown was palpable. Julian was especially sensitive to the disappointment on Mara's face.

"Look," he burst out defensively, all of his accumulated grievances surfacing. "You didn't really think—I mean, I was possibly looking for a single flower, for pity's sake. I want to find it as much as you, Mara, but it was hopeless doing it like that. The only way is to go back and do a proper search, square off the area, and this time all of you can get off your backsides and help." He threw down his napkin in disgust.

Mara was immediately contrite. "I'm so sorry, Julian. I didn't mean to sound ungrateful."

"Well, that's how it came across."

"I think you did very well," soothed Mado.

An awkward silence persisted through to coffee. Julian dumped more sugar in his cup than he really needed and stirred angrily. Mado lit a cigarette and sat leg over knee, dangling a backless sandal. Mara stared bleakly at the floor.

Paul, after some inner struggle, heaved himself away from the table, disappeared momentarily, and returned with a dusty bottle of very fine old cognac, possibly by way of amends. Reverently, he served out four small glasses. They had by then been over two hours at table. The afternoon was drawing to a golden finish. A soft breeze stirred the curtains at the open windows of Chez Nous. They sipped in meditative silence.

Eventually, mollified by the cognac, Julian said, "While I was out there, I did a lot of thinking."

"*Parbleu!*" intoned Paul.

"I mean, I'd established to my own satisfaction that part of Bedie's trail cut across La Binette land. But what I started wondering was how she'd got there in the first place. I don't mean to La Binette. I mean to the *beginning of her path*, which was off a logging road in the middle of the Bessède Forest. If her last stop was Beynac, she couldn't have walked there. It's nearly thirty kilometers away."

"Someone gave her a ride." Mado shrugged.

"But why there?"

Paul suggested, "If she was hitchhiking, she could have been on her way someplace else and simply got put down there."

"But in the middle of the forest, Paul," objected Julian. "It just doesn't make sense."

Mara shook her head impatiently. "How or why she got there isn't as important as what happened to her afterward. We've always thought the Lady's Slipper was the key to everything, Julian. Unfortunately, it's the one flower you couldn't find."

"Oh, look, don't rub it in, will you?" he snapped.

FOURTEEN

Julian put all of his other contracts on hold so that he could concentrate on Prudence's courtyard. With luck, everything would be ready for her party that weekend. It wasn't the kind of work he particularly liked, but he had to admit that the effect he'd created was nothing short of a marvel of container landscaping. She had wanted a tropical look. The walls dripped with hanging baskets of fuchsia and bougainvillea. The pièce de résistance, on which he was still working, was a kind of botanical tour de force built up in the middle of the courtyard, a temporary jungle of potted palms, lacy umbrella plants, flame coleus, and even orchids (rented from Géraud at exorbitant cost) in beds of sphagnum moss. He had not yet presented Prudence with his bill, but she was looking so pleased with everything that he hoped she wouldn't care.

"You should make a business of it," she advised, ever with an eye to the market. "Theme landscaping. Its time has come. Even here. You'll be at my do, of course," she added by way of invitation. "It'll be chock-full of Americans with dollars to burn who'll all want your services, once they see what you can do. Besides, I need people who can *parler français* with the French. And by the way," she added, "Mara's coming. The two of you should get together. I think she's interested in you."

He called Mara, got her answering machine, and left a message: "Look, Mara, there's this thing on at Prudence's on Saturday. I know you've been asked, too. Why don't I pick you up? Or, if that won't work, we could meet up there and go on someplace after."

Mara didn't reply. Too busy, he suspected. He knew she'd been working on Prudence's kitchen, whipping it into shape, with the same deadline as he.

On Saturday evening, the narrow country lane running past Prudence's house was clogged with cars. Among them Julian spotted the Chez Nous van. Guests from Bergerac to Brive filled the courtyard. Mado and Paul, who were catering the affair, moved among them, pouring champagne and replenishing trays of hot and cold hors d'oeuvres.

On entering, Julian was immediately press-ganged by Paul into helping to shift more champagne from the van. Staggering under the weight of a crate of bottles, he spotted Mara through the crowd. She wore a long black dress that made her look as lean as a knife and provocatively dangerous. Her only splash of color was a large, red silk flower pinned to the shoulder.

"Fancy meeting you," he called out as he deposited his load. A moment later, he sidled up and presented her with a refill of champagne. "Let me guess. You are a mysterious double agent posing as an interior designer."

"Clever of you." Mara smiled, tossed her head, and exchanged her empty glass for the full one he offered. She waved at the courtyard. "Very impressive. I didn't know you were so good."

"Oh, I'm very good. What are you doing for afters?" he whispered into her ear in a way he hoped was suggestive.

"Looking after my date," she told him archly and ruined his evening by introducing him to someone whom Julian had difficulty for a moment placing, and then recognized as the sandy-haired man from the forest.

They shook hands. So this was Alain de Sauvignac. He was bigger than Julian remembered, no taller than Julian but more solidly built in that muscular, athletic way that Julian loathed. Attractive, too, he supposed, if you liked the tanned, tourist-brochure look. Instinctively, Julian distrusted him.

Prudence arrived to sweep Mara away, leaving the two men together.

"So you're the orchid expert," Alain said, studying him with an assessing eye. He opted to speak English, which was another thing Julian held against him. As if his own French weren't good enough.

"Amateur," Julian corrected with the false ha-ha voice he used when he was not enjoying himself.

"Nevertheless, Mara tells me you've managed to locate the entire orchid sequence between the Bessède Forest and Les Colombes. Quite a botanical feat."

"The full sequence but one," Julian corrected

again. "She might have mentioned that we're missing a *Cypripedium*." He wondered how much Mara had told Alain about her sister and their search for Bedie's trail.

"Ah. Yes, come to think of it, she did say that."

"You work abroad, I hear."

"Right. Gabon, Ivory Coast, Senegal. Most recently Cameroon. I'm a civil engineer. Government-to-government projects. Back on home leave. In between contracts for the moment, actually."

It was Julian's turn to say, "Ah."

The conversation languished. Unhappily, Julian wandered off to do his French bit with the locals and chat up his hostess's wealthy compatriots. That was what he was there for. Over a bumper of champagne, he covertly observed Mara returning to Alain's side, saw him slip his arm around her waist, and felt another headache coming on.

He had drunk too much, eaten too little, and needed air. On his way out to the courtyard, he snagged a couple of *escargots en brioche*, one of Paul's specialties, waved off a compliment or two on his handiwork, and found himself alone in the lane. The evening was filled with distant laughter. An early moon rose through the trees. Sourly, Julian pictured the after-party scene. Alain and Mara would go back to her place. He couldn't see them sitting on her impossible chairs. That left her bed or the Aubusson rug. He scowled and viciously ground a patch of nettles to shreds under his heel.

A low moan caught his attention. It came from Mara's Renault. Jazz was in the car, head thrust through the open window. A slow, malicious smile crept over Julian's face. If there was a God, he thought, Jazz ought to be counted on to take Alain de Sauvignac's head off at the very least.

•

As it turned out, Jazz did not have a chance to do his work because Alain and Mara had come separately to Prudence's party, Alain arriving in his father's old Citroën.

"It's good to get the old *guimbarde* out on the road," he had explained to Mara. "Papa drives it so little nowadays. But also it's easier this way. I think you realize Papa would be very upset if you turned up for me at the door after he sent you packing."

More than upset, Mara thought, remembering the expression on the elder de Sauvignac's face. The father had been frightened—no, terrified—of something. What? There was something Alain was not telling her. One way or another, she intended to find out.

•

The existence of Alain in Mara's life was a new dynamic that had been thrown, clanging like a spanner, into Julian's consciousness. He knew she had the right to see whomever she damned well pleased. Nevertheless, after all the effort he had put into helping her with her damnable orchids, he felt that she might have shown him a bit more consideration. It was always like that, it seemed. Just as you got interested in someone, they turned on you, kicked you in the balls.

He confessed all this to Paul and Mado a few evenings later, over a solitary dinner at Chez Nous.

"He *was* very good-looking," Mado affirmed.

It was not what Julian wanted to hear.

"What I mean," he said plaintively, shoving new peas about his plate with his fork, "is that to her I'm just a means of tracing her sister. I doubt she even sees me as a person. Frankly, I feel used."

"Hah!" Mado contrived to look sympathetic and intensely gratified at the same time. Paul merely gave an exasperated snort and demanded what the hell Julian expected.

"Well, not a lot," said Julian defensively.

"What you need," Paul began and stopped. *Bigre!* He didn't quite know how to tell Julian that what he needed was to cash in his chips and settle down. Put crudely, he needed a combination of mothering and regular sex, which he clearly wasn't getting; otherwise, he wouldn't be going around looking like he was holding in a belch and a sour taste in his mouth.

Julian and Mado were regarding him expectantly. Paul shook his head and retreated to the bar.

"What you need," he repeated, fetching back a bottle, "is something for the digestion."

•

That night, Paul was restless as he lay in bed beside Mado. He had been having a spell of *nuits blanches* recently: white nights, in which, although his body

239

was numbed by the desire to sleep, his inner eye stared dry and lidless at a moving jumble of worries, the detritus of the day-to-day thrown onto the conveyor belt of his mind. The transmission of the van needed attention. Last month's restaurant receipts were down. Julian's face, disembodied, slid by, came past again. Paul exhaled noisily.

"What's wrong?" Mado murmured thickly, turning to curl against him.

"Nothing," he grunted. Her breathing was slow and soft. "Except . . ."

"Mmmm?"

"I was just thinking. About Julian."

She said sleepily, "What about him?"

"Oh, I don't know. There's something funny about him. I mean, have you noticed how none of his relationships seem to last?"

"He's shy. Besides, he always hooks up with the wrong sort of person." Mado was fully awake now. "Domineering types who like to push him around."

Paul wondered if his wife meant Mara. He didn't think she was domineering. Strong-minded, maybe, but nothing a real man couldn't handle. He folded his arms behind his head, staring up into darkness. Anyway, it wasn't that Julian was shy so much as inept. Of the few relationships he'd known his friend to have, it had always been the woman going off Julian rather than the other way around. And go off she did, because she never showed her face around these parts again. Like that skinny *anglaise*, Coco

Somebody, a few years back. Julian had been very offhand about her departure. "Oh, she went back to England," he had said in passing one day and had not referred to her again.

"Well, he's not getting any younger," Paul went on. "Time he settled down. Got married."

"He was married once," Mado reminded him, raising herself up on one elbow. She trailed her fingertips over her husband's chest. "I don't think he liked the experience. Anyway, why are you worrying about Julian at this time of night?"

"He's a pal," said Paul. The stroking was creating a pleasant, tickling sensation.

"He's a big boy." Tenderly Mado seized his right nipple between her teeth.

"Oh, what the hell," said Paul, dismissing his friend and giving himself over to a certain way of getting a good night's sleep.

•

> *I tell you, Patsy, it's as if I don't really exist for him except as a botanical exercise. Honestly, if it weren't for that damned Lady's Slipper, I think he'd be very happy to forget he ever met me. But you should have seen his face at Prudence's party when I introduced him to Alain—very attractive, by the way. You'd like him. I could tell it had never crossed Julian's mind that I might have a life!*

Mara sighed, reached down to scratch Jazz's ear, and went on typing.

> *The problem with Julian is that he's terribly private. He never really talks about himself. It's like there's some part of him that he's afraid of revealing, that he wants to conceal.* <

Patsy wrote back:

> *What do you mean? Like he's some kind of a Bluebeard hiding a closet full of dead brides? Ease up, kid. He sounds to me more like a disaster victim, someone who's survived rather than murdered past relationships.* <

> *What I'm trying to say is, he invites no intimacy, and I'm not even talking sexually. The truth is, the only really personal thing we've ever discussed is Bedie. In fact, he seems far more interested in her than me. Otherwise, he talks about flowers. And he's so damned pedantic. I mean, why does a snapdragon have to be an* Antirrhinum *and everything belong to the buttercup family? And you should hear him on the sex life of the orchid.* <

> *Hey, I'd like to! But, you know, it can cut two ways. Have you ever considered that maybe Julian knows as little about you as you do of him? Or that what he sees is too much of Bedie and too little of Mara? I mean, shackled to your leg like she is, figuratively speaking, she does tend to dominate*

It was true, Mara reflected, and Patsy had said things like this before. However, try as she might, she could not give up her dead. Less now than ever, with the discovery of the *pigeonnier*. Or was it Bedie who would not give her up? For she was always there, standing in shadow at her side, mute but heavy with appeal, asking for—what? Life? Whose life? Mara shuddered.

•

This time lunch was on her. Except that Mara made it dinner at her favorite bistro in Trémolat. On the day, she left her work site early, something she rarely did, and drove home not by the country roads but by the shortest route. Instead of a quick shower, she allowed herself a long soak in a hot tub. She rose from it and stood streaming and naked before her bathroom mirror, careless of puddling the floor, staring at her body. Her flesh gleamed back at her. She was conscious of a sag here or there, but, standing straight and sucking in her stomach, she saw that she was still firm, still attractive. Her dark, wet hair clung to the oval of her face, her chin, as ever, giving a strong finish to her own particular kind of beauty.

That evening Alain did not meet her at the restaurant but instead let her pick him up, although not at the house. He walked down from the château and met her at the roadside.

"Better this way," he said as he got in her car.

Mara wore an off-the-shoulder dress of sapphire blue. She had made up her eyes to accentuate their boldness, outlined her lips in vivid red. She was aware that his cheek-to-cheek greeting lingered like a caress, that he seemed to take her in appreciatively, that his eyes stayed on her the entire time she drove.

At the bistro they took a table inside because the evening was cool. Alain continued to gaze at her steadily over their drinks.

"*Très belle*," he said finally, but with meaning. He was not, it seemed, a man to use words unnecessarily. In him, his father's suave courtliness and covert sexuality had been distilled to a more direct, casual virility. He had inherited a more rugged version of his father's aristocratic good looks. Unlike his parent, Mara was glad to note, Alain did not evoke the moldy reminder of damp places. He gave off instead a musky scent of aftershave. He wore light-gray slacks, a charcoal silk shirt under a loose-fitting cream-colored linen jacket, a gold Rolex. Building things in Africa must pay well, Mara thought.

"Have you made any further progress?" he asked as they tucked into a platter of steaks served very rare with frites.

Mara shook her head. "Things are rather at a standstill."

"But you have your orchids. Or all but one of them, according to your friend."

"The police, I'm afraid, weren't sufficiently impressed. Circumstantial evidence, they called it."

"I see. So they're not pursuing the matter?"

"No."

"Then what will you do?"

She looked at him lengthily. "That, I think, depends a lot on you."

"Me?" he put down his fork with surprise. "How so?"

She had come prepared to challenge him. "There's something you're not telling me, Alain. Something that you know or suspect but don't want me to know. I assume it has to do with your father . . . or Vrac."

He toyed with his food for a moment before meeting her gaze. In the dimness of the restaurant, his pupils were very dark, reflecting no light. "I take the matter of your sister seriously, Mara," he said at length. "I also lost my brother, Patrice, although at a much earlier age. So you see, in a way, we're alike. Please believe me when I say that, if I could help you in this regard, I would."

She urged, "Then tell me what your father is afraid of. What does he think I'm going to stir up?"

He shrugged. "It's very simple, really. Papa believes you're victimizing Vrac by accusing him unfairly. Despite appearances, Vrac is vulnerable, like a dumb beast. Papa feels obliged to stand between him and the forces you could, with your questions, unleash against him."

He stopped. She waited, unconvinced, forcing him with her silence to continue. Reluctantly, he gave ground.

"Also, perhaps, in disturbing the waters, you could cause my father a certain amount of public discomfort, and he is a man who has much to feel uncomfortable about. Oh, nothing really serious, I assure you. It's just that Papa has always been a man of, shall we say, appetite." He shrugged. "Some men are made that way. From my earliest boyhood, I remember the locals making sly remarks, off-color jokes. Thing-in-his-pocket, they called him, the stallion *en rut*. Of course, it was only when I was older that I came to understand what those things meant. In short, my father's excesses have caused my family much embarrassment . . . and expense. It's also been a source of anger and bitterness between Papa and me, largely because of the pain it has caused my mother. So now you see, Mara, there is no great mystery to unravel. Merely a rather sorry story of seigniorial misconduct."

Alain's mouth went momentarily tight with distaste. "To be quite frank," he resumed, "although Papa's main concern is the de Sauvignac name, as far as I'm concerned, that's his lookout. Old sins cast long shadows, as they say, and he's sinned enough for five men. Let him take what's coming to him. However, your questions, if they probe too deeply, could cause considerable unhappiness to Maman, who, quite frankly, doesn't deserve to have old scandals raked up."

They both fell silent.

At length, he spoke again. "If you don't mind, I'd like to change the subject. I want to know about you."

He reached across and took her hand, turning it palm up and studying the crisscrossed lines on its surface "You have," he observed, "very delicate fingers. And"—he frowned slightly—"a very short life line."

"I think that's my heart line you're looking at," Mara corrected, but she allowed her hand, with its fingers, which she had never thought of as delicate, to continue resting where it was. "And it's not short, just broken. Look, Alain, I'm grateful for your honesty. I'm sorry. I had no idea . . ."

"Then be candid with me in your turn," he proposed with a smile.

"What?" She drew her hand back.

"Your friend Julian. Is he an important part of your life?"

"No," Mara answered simply.

"Then let me ask you something else. How much do you trust him?"

"Julian?" She thought about it. "I don't know. Why do you ask?"

"Because"—Alain was watching her closely, judging her reaction—"I'm starting to wonder if *he* wasn't the person who was stalking you that day in the forest."

Mara laughed. "But that's crazy! It was Vrac. You said so yourself."

Alain shook his head vigorously. "I said it could have been. I now realize that was impossible."

"What do you mean?"

"Mara, on the afternoon you were in the woods,

Vrac was in Saint-Cyprien, picking up a new motor for a water pump. Our pump, in fact. I can show you the printed invoice for it, with date and time, together with Vrac's scrawl. And he spent the rest of the day at the château installing it."

"I don't believe it," Mara declared. But the words were scarcely out of her mouth when she was reliving her panicked flight, her encounter with Alain, and Julian *coming up behind*, crashing through the bushes only seconds later.

"But why?" she whispered, horrified. "Why would he do that?"

"To frighten you? To put you off the hunt? Mara, are you sure this Lady's Slipper is Julian's only reason for helping you?"

"Oh yes. He's desperate to find it, of that I'm sure."

Alain thought for a moment. "Look, let's approach this logically. You believe that someone was responsible for your sister's disappearance. You don't know who this person is. Your only clue is a set of orchid photographs. But maybe the answer has been in front of your nose all along: Julian. He's an orchidologist. Your sister was an orchid amateur. Supposing she met him by chance, went with him?" He paused, raking his fingers through his hair, leaving it pushed back and tousled.

Mara stared at him. Loulou had said something like that: Bedie would have been easily approachable by anyone who shared her interest. She would have gone trustingly with Julian into the forest.

248

"And you," Alain went on, "you could have come as a nasty shock to him when you turned up, the spitting image of your sister, asking him to help you find a woman he might have killed nineteen years ago!"

Again, had not Loulou warned her of exactly the same thing? *Your face, Mara. Your face.* She recalled Julian's look of shock when he had first opened his door to her.

And yet something did not fit.

"No. It doesn't make sense," she cried. "I swear Julian was genuinely amazed at the photo of the Lady's Slipper. If he'd been with my sister at the time she took it, wouldn't he have seen it, too? Why would he need her pictures to trace it? He'd already know its exact location."

Alain frowned. "What if," he said slowly, "she took the photos before she met him?"

"But even so, why would Julian try to help me? He's known all along that the whole point of reconstructing my sister's trail was to find out what had happened to her. Why would he want to lead me to himself?"

"Maybe," Alain suggested grimly, "that's part of the kick."

Mara's eyes widened. Her experiences in the forest and in the bog came rushing back to her. "Are you saying this is all part of some kind of sick game?"

"Maybe. Or perhaps," Alain added after a moment's reflection, "it's simpler than that. You see, it really hangs on the camera. You're convinced it belonged to Bedie. But don't you think her assailant—Julian—would have destroyed such a vital piece of evidence? Especially the film it contained? But he didn't. So it really argues the case that the camera you found can't have been your sister's. *And the only person to know that would be Julian.* In which case, there would be absolutely no risk to him in searching for an interesting sequence of plants that some other, totally unrelated person had photographed. Particularly if it led to a rare orchid that he very much wanted to find."

In fact, Mara realized, she'd virtually blackmailed Julian into it. No help, no photos. Those were her terms.

Then reason asserted itself. Julian had behaved oddly, even inexplicably, at times. She knew very little about him; he gave nothing away. He was every bit as irascible and botanically obsessive as Géraud. But none of this made him a psychopath or a killer.

"I don't buy it," she told Alain.

He said gently, "I'm sure what I've said comes as a bit of a shock, Mara. But I'd like you at least to consider it. You can't afford to ignore the possibility that Julian may be the very person you're looking for."

She turned away, glancing through the restaurant window at the gathering darkness outside. "I don't know what to think," she murmured dully.

"Then don't. For now, at least." He took her hand again. This time he did not examine her palm, but cradled it in his own. "Let me tell you instead," he said quietly, "about dawn in the Cameroon highlands."

•

Mara drove Alain back to Les Colombes. He let her take him all the way up the narrow lane leading to the rear courtyard. It was late, the old ones would be asleep, and there would be no risk of awkward questions from his father.

The dark mass of the château rose above them as she cut her headlights before pulling up. She keyed off the engine and turned to him.

"You know," she said, "there's no way of proving if your suspicions about Julian are true."

"I agree. You need hard evidence."

"Such as what?"

"Something tying him to your sister? Or any of the other women. If he's responsible for their disappearances, maybe he kept something of theirs. I don't imagine it will be easy to find. Julian seems to have covered his tracks well." Alain sat facing her in the car. Moonlight glinted on his brow, the strong profile of his nose. The rest of his face was cast in shadow.

"Whatever you do, Mara, I don't want you to take any stupid risks. Remember, I'm here if you need me."

He leaned across, cupping her face in both his hands. "This is for luck," he whispered. And he kissed her, long and hard.

Mara watched him slip away from her. His form was quickly swallowed in darkness. There had been something of hunger in his kiss, almost of ferocity. The feeling of his mouth on hers stayed with her, his smell, a faint musky odor, filled her nostrils. In that kiss something indefinable had sprung up, a brief frisson, like electricity arcing momentarily between them. Mara was shaken to acknowledge the depth of attraction she felt for Alain de Sauvignac. It expressed itself in a lurch of the heart, a yearning she had not felt for years. In fact, not since Hal. The realization disturbed her. She put her car in gear and circled about, tires crunching quietly on gravel until they met the rough surface of the lane. A warning sounded in her brain. Hal had been a bastard.

FIFTEEN

Mara chose a morning when Prudence could confirm that Julian was working in her garden.

"He's digging more of those trenches, he and that brawny helper of his," Prudence informed her when she phoned. "Don't ask for what. Why do you want me to call you on your cell phone if he leaves?"

"Too complicated to explain. Just do it the minute he goes, will you? And thanks, Prudence."

"Whatever helps, sweetie."

•

Julian's front door was locked. His back door, as usual, was not. Mara opened it and stuck her head inside.

"Hello?" she called, just in case.

No response.

She made rapid work of the kitchen, ignoring the clutter of pots and pans, the dirty dishes in the sink. His shelves were stocked with cans of cassoulet and beef ragout, packets of dry soups, rice, sugar, instant coffee, a canister of tea. A lower shelf was taken up with large tins labeled *Borax, Silica Gel, Glycerine*. For drying plants, she assumed. What exactly she was looking for she did not know. Something to tie him to Bedie, Alain had suggested, or to any of the other women. A part of her was equally interested in any intimate information on Julian. Family photographs, love letters, birthday cards, anything to give him a past, dimension. She was torn between wanting to condemn him and to prove Alain wrong, to find nothing more incriminating than the sundry silly, embarrassingly personal desiderata that clutter any normal person's life. She would have been dissatisfied and yet relieved to walk away empty-handed, allowing Julian to continue undisturbed with his earthy if eccentric pursuits.

The scarred dining table at one end of the front room displayed the remains of past meals and a bilingual clutter of old newspapers: *La Presse*, *The Observer*, and the monthly *News*, serving the local English-speaking community. There was an old desk, its surface covered in bills. A glance informed her that Julian was none too prompt about paying his accounts. The drawers stuck. She pulled them out with difficulty: more bills, bank statements, string, a dried-out bottle of glue, paper clips, a hunk of beeswax, leaky pens, a broken watch, loose batteries, nursery catalogues, letters. This man was a hoarder. The letters were all business correspondence: queries from interested customers, confirmations of landscaping projects. One was a complaint regarding plants that had lifted the coping around a swimming pool. Mara wondered that there should be so little clue to Julian himself. Or perhaps that was how he wanted it.

The shelves sagged with books. Texts on wildflowers, orchids, and plant physiology. She spotted a field manual: *Wildflowers of the Dordogne/Fleurs sauvages de la Dordogne*, by Julian Wood. She pulled it out. It had been published in 1983 and bore the dedication: "To lovers of wildflowers everywhere." The biographical information on the back cover described the author as an authority on local flora, living in Grissac, and showed a photograph of a younger Julian, smiling, with slightly fuller features and no facial hair. It made Mara realize that she rarely saw Julian smile.

Mara flipped through the book. It was filled with photographs of all kinds of wildflowers, taken, as Bedie had done, close up and at a distance and annotated with details on plant structure, habitat, and flowering season. Many were orchids that she recognized. Pyramidals, Bees, and Lizards. Lady and Man Orchids. She saw a portrait of a Bird's-nest Orchid with an accompanying view of a thin scattering of the plants. There was no doubt that it was the same location she and Julian had found in the Bessède Forest. The oak in which Jazz had treed the marten was just visible in the background. *Neottia nidus-avis* was described as thick-stemmed, fleshy, yellowish-brown, with sepals and petals curving into a hood, and labellum pendant. It flowered between May and late June, liked shade, and was partial to beech and coniferous woodlands. These plants, Julian had noted, were possibly representative of a much larger stand, which, owing to several years of dry conditions, was either in decline or semi-dormant. Both photographs were dated 1980.

Suddenly the kitchen door banged. Mara dived down behind the sofa.

"*Allo?*" cried a woman's voice. "*Julian? C'est moi, Francine Léon. Vous avez oublié vos oeufs.*" There was a silence as Madame Léon waited, with the eggs that Julian had forgotten, for a response.

"*Bon,*" Madame Léon called, even though it was apparent that Julian wasn't there. "*Je les mets dans le frigo.*"

Mara heard the refrigerator door open and close, and then the clack of the kitchen door as Madame Léon left. Raising her head, Mara saw Madame Léon cut across Julian's back garden on her way to her own, adjoining property.

Mara let her breath out and moved to the bathroom. The medicine cabinet was full of bottles and tubes, including a vial of prescription tablets and a jar of something that, as best she could make out, was a preparation for hives.

In another room she found a dented metal cabinet crammed with cardboard boxes stacked precariously one atop another. The boxes were filled with prints and slides of not only flowers but plants of every description. The backs of many of the prints were inscribed in Julian's untidy script, providing cryptic details on identification, date, and place.

She had only the bedroom to go. The bed was unmade. Clothes trailed over every piece of furniture. One leather slipper, trodden down at the heel, had been kicked under a scarred walnut armoire; the other lay by the door. She checked out Julian's bedside table, stirring around in the contents of the single, shallow drawer: reading glasses, nail clippers, throat lozenges, buttons. Her cell phone went off.

"Hello?" she answered tensely.

"Mara? That you? You sound funny. It's Prudence. Look, I know you wanted me to ring you if Julian left. Well, he took off just around twelve."

"But it's nearly twenty past," Mara exclaimed, with a glance at her watch. "Why didn't you call me straightaway?"

"Couldn't, sweetie," returned Prudence's voice. She seemed to be blowing on something. "He went right in the middle of me doing my nails. Takes an age for them to dry. Matter of fact, they're tacky even as we speak."

Mara cursed as she disconnected. If Julian were returning for lunch, he could be walking through the door at any moment. So far she had come up with nothing.

She rammed the drawer shut and hurried back into the front room. Julian's wildflower book still lay on the floor behind the sofa where she had left it. She scooped it up and shoved it back on the shelf, not where it had been, but at the end of a row of books, wedging it upright with a small plastic box. Her hand hesitated over the box. She took it down and flipped back the hinged lid. It was filled, as she had expected, with personal and business cards. She riffled through them quickly, spotting her own among them, and then another card that caused her to catch her breath. She pulled it out and studied it with narrowed eyes, puzzling over it, and then coming to a conclusion. She did not know if she was sorry or exultant as she slipped it into her pocket.

A volley of barks at the front of the house alerted her. Through a window she glimpsed Jazz, head thrust out of her car, happily greeting Julian's arrival. By the time Julian walked in the back door, Mara was seated at his kitchen table, reading a crumpled newspaper. The kettle was heating on the gas burner.

"Hi," she said, affecting casualness although her hands were shaking. She had to force herself to look at him. "Hope you don't mind me making myself at home. I just dropped by and was about to leave when Prudence called." She gestured at her cell phone. "She happened to say you might be on your way here, so I thought I'd wait. I—er—I'm making some tea."

"You're a stranger," he said coolly. He seemed on edge, suspicious of her presence in his house. Nevertheless, he must have thought tea was a good idea because he took down a couple of mugs and rinsed out the teapot. "What did you want to see me about?"

"Oh." She stopped. What *did* she want to see him about? She glanced nervously at the newspaper which she had found on the kitchen counter, hoping for inspiration. A front page photograph of le Mur's mangled Ferrari, in all its graphic detail, saved the moment. "I just wondered if you'd gotten the film developed. The one you shot at La Binette."

If it occurred to Julian that she could have as easily phoned for the information, he didn't show it. In fact, he looked evasive. "Er, no. Not yet." He stuck his head in the fridge and pulled it out again. "Haven't had time. Have you had lunch?"

"Who, me? Oh, don't worry about me. I can't stay." Figuratively she kicked herself. That was stupid. She had just said she'd been prepared to wait. "That is, just the tea. Then I have to run."

"Close call," she told Jazz as she drove off ten minutes later. She reached the intersection with the main road and turned onto it, trying to collect her thoughts. The card pointed her in an unexpected direction. However, she still lacked anything tying Julian directly to Bedie.

Or did she? Alain had suggested that Bedie had met Julian by chance, gone with him because of her interest in orchids. An idea began to form in her mind. *Wildflowers of the Dordogne/Fleurs sauvages de la Dordogne*, 1983, which included many species of wild orchids. Bedie could have seen Julian's book in any bookstore and bought a copy. In fact, hadn't Scott said that Bedie had taken some kind of book on flowers with her? Given her keen interest, she would not have hesitated to seek Julian out—he was described in the biographical blurb as "an authority on local flora living in Grissac." And it would have been easy—she could have simply looked him up in the phone book, just as Mara herself had done. The more Mara thought about it, the more plausible her idea seemed. It could be the very link she needed. But was it enough?

An oncoming truck bearing a load of chickens rumbled past, crowding her onto the verge of the narrow road. Then she remembered the Bird's-nest Orchids. She threw her head back in mirthless laughter.

"Damn it, Jazz," she cried. "It's been staring me in the face all along."

Julian had pronounced Bedie's photo to be an almost certain match with his colony in the Bessède Forest, based on the law of probability. *A stand this big is rare*, he had said. *The chances of there being two like it are low.* By the same argument, if the colony was as exceptional as Julian claimed, what were the odds that Bedie had simply stumbled on it by herself? Mara had seen the spot. It was in the middle of nowhere. Julian himself had raised the question of how Bedie had come to be there. The only reasonable answer was that someone who had known about the colony had led her to it.

"And that person," she addressed her dog with grim finality, "could only have been Julian."

He had been clever, initially feigning astonishment at Bedie's photograph, carrying out the charade of consulting Géraud, pointing out that the stand as he had originally seen it was scarcely recognizable as the one Bedie had captured on film. But he had guessed that the colony was representative of a much larger growth—his own words in print gave him away—and as the expert he should have made the connection. Finally, Julian's photo was dated 1980. This meant that, when Bedie had turned up in 1984, he had already discovered the plants and would have been able, and for his purposes more than willing, to guide her to them.

Yet Mara was still nagged by a troubling point. She did not accept Alain's idea that the camera had belonged to some unknown third person. Her sister had taken those photos, she was sure of it. The Bird's-nest Orchids clearly placed Julian with Bedie near the beginning of her trail, so Julian must have known that Bedie had a camera with her and that she was photographing orchids. Maybe he had even helped her set up some of her shots. So how was it that he did not know about the *Cypripedium?* And why, as Alain had asked, didn't he destroy the camera? The only conclusion she could draw was that Julian must have left Bedie before she found the Lady's Slipper. But why would he have done that?

A sickening picture began to form in Mara's head. Bedie alone in the forest. Something, perhaps a sound, alerts her. She looks back, listens. Uncertain, she moves on. Other sounds, soft, persistent, follow in her wake. Looking over her shoulder, she begins to have her first intimation of real danger. Her pace quickens to a rapid walk. Now, as she realizes the full nature of her peril, she begins to run, fleeing in terror, throwing off her backpack, her camera, all encumbering gear, to speed her flight.

A car honked frantically as it swept past, missing the Renault by centimeters. Mara careened wildly, downshifted, and pulled to a lurching stop onto the verge of the road. She pressed her face into her hands, trying to get her breathing under control.

It wasn't good enough for Julian to attack and kill. The predator needed to stalk his prey. Just as he had "lost" her in the bog and directed her to pace off squares in the forest in order to afford himself the pleasure of the chase, so must he have sent Bedie on her way and then, cruelly and at his leisure, hunted her down. Orchid freak though he was, his focus would have been entirely on his victim, not on what she was photographing. He never thought about the camera she had been carrying. He never knew about the flower that he now coveted so greatly. And the irony of it was that she, Mara, had put the evidence of Bedie's remarkable discovery right into his hands!

Then something else occurred to her that further underscored Julian's capacity for duplicity. The cheapness, the gratuitousness of it almost made her cry with rage. The newspaper she had been pretending to read in Julian's house had been a copy of last Tuesday's *Sud Ouest*. Every paper in the region covering le Mur's fatal accident had been sold before midday, according to Paul. So how had Julian, who was supposed to have been at La Binette from the crack of dawn until late afternoon on Tuesday, gotten a copy?

"The bastard," she fumed to Jazz, putting the car in gear and shooting forward in a spurt of gravel. "It was a lie. He never went there at all." The whole thing had been a fabrication from start to finish.

•

"Mara was around yesterday," Mado called out from the back of the bistro. "She was asking questions about you."

Julian paused, thumbtack in hand. He had stopped by to post a notice on the Chez Nous bulletin board for old Hilaire. In fact, he had helped the farmer to compose it: *Perdue. Chienne pointer blanche et truitée noir. Très gentille.* Lost. White-and-black-spotted pointer bitch. Very gentle. Julian had wanted to add *très gourmande*, but had held his tongue.

"Oh? Like what?"

"Oh," the redhead said evasively, coming up to peer at his hand-lettered sign, "your background."

"My background? What d'you mean, my landscaping qualifications?"

"Of course not," said Mado, giving him a shove. "Your romantic background, *abruti*."

"Cut a long story short," broke in Paul from the bar, "I think she's making moves on you. She was asking me about your love life, former girlfriends, names, dates, the lot."

"Names—?" Julian was extremely alarmed.

"Don't worry," Paul grinned. "I didn't tell her much. Anyway, she already knew about your ex. I just said that since then you've had a couple of girlfriends, nothing serious. Oh, and she wanted to know if any of them were still in the area."

Julian looked aghast. "What did you tell her, for Christ's sake?"

Paul shrugged. "Well, what could I say? I mean, I've never seen any of them since, have I?"

"She's got a bloody nerve!" Julian fumed. "It's a damned invasion of privacy." And it wasn't the only one he had experienced of late. Someone—he now knew exactly who—had been in his house, rummaging about in his mess. Nothing had been taken, but the telltale signs of disturbance were everywhere.

"Take it from me, *mon vieux*," Paul advised, enjoying his friend's discomfiture, "when a woman starts checking up on you like that, it's a serious sign. They only ever ask those kinds of questions if they're planning on moving in."

•

The card was slightly soiled, printed on heavy buff stock in Garamond type. Alain studied it carefully, holding it between thumb and forefinger.

"It was the very last place I looked," Mara exclaimed. "I could so easily have missed it."

"Things happen for a reason," Alain said softly.

"You see what it could mean, don't you?"

"Yes."

Then she told him what she wanted them to do.

He thought about it for a moment. "All right," he said. "I'm game."

Later that night, Mara dialed a number and spoke

with a woman named Ingrid. Swedish, Mara judged, from her up-and-down accent.

•

The property, situated outside of Souillac, was set into a hillside well off the road. A modern wing—mostly glass, from what Mara could see—had been added to the original stone structure, giving the house the appearance of being at odds with itself. The result, Mara thought, of a combination of money and bad taste.

Ingrid, or so Mara guessed, answered their knock. She was tall, white-blonde, friendly, and wore a bikini that left most of her buoyant breasts and buttocks bare.

"Bonjour. Yes? *Ah, c'est vous*. You must be the one who called last night," she said, mixing singsong English and French.

They introduced themselves. She smiled broadly and shook their hands. Mara was amused to note that Alain seemed to regard Ingrid, and at the moment he was regarding quite a lot of her, with a look of stern disapproval.

"*Entrez*. Jackie is on the phone, but I can show you around, if you want." She took them through a large room furnished in glass and chrome and out to a rear terrace.

The garden, Mara had to admit, was magnificent, built on several levels to accommodate the uneven lay of the land. Steps led down past beds of perennials to a free-form pool bordered by bamboo and fed by a fall of water running over deeply pitted boulders, giving it the air of a secret grotto. A winding path led the eye away to a line of cypress standing like sentinels against a clear blue sky. The sloping side of the garden was built out as an extensive rockery.

At that point, Jackie appeared, cell phone clamped to his ear. He was a short, square man in his fifties, dressed in swimming trunks and a pool robe, which was open at the front, exposing a hairy chest and a creased belly. His skin was tanned to a deep mahogany, his lips were full, and his eyes took in Mara appraisingly as he ended his conversation and switched off.

They introduced themselves and raised the matter they had ostensibly come about:

"We're thinking of landscaping our property," Alain lied with surprising fluency. "This fellow Julian Wood gave us your name. Said he'd done work for you. Must say I'm pretty impressed with what I see. I take it you'd recommend him?"

"Sure," said Jackie. "Mind you, he's not cheap. And he took his own sweet time finishing."

"How long ago was this?" asked Mara.

Jackie shrugged. "*Parbleu!* Fifteen—no, fourteen years ago. Eighty-nine, it was."

Yes, Mara thought, the timing fit.

"Do you"—Alain looked around him—"still use him?" Someone had to maintain the place.

"*Pas question!* Not at his prices. I have a gardener come in from the town."

Jackie showed them out, leading the way with Mara. Alain lingered behind with Ingrid. Together they paused to inspect a flowering bush.

"So," Jackie said, taking Mara's left elbow to steer her unnecessarily along the walkway, "you're interested in gardening?"

"Oh," she extemporized, "it's really more my husband."

Jackie let his large, square fingers slide lightly down her arm. He raised her hand. "No ring? Pretty woman like you needs a ring. People might get the wrong impression."

"These visible signs of ownership, rather passé, don't you think?" Mara parried, rather smoothly, she thought, and freed herself from his grasp. At the same time, she seized the opening he had provided. "Speaking of that, Monsieur Ménard, I think I used to know your wife."

He stopped to study her carefully. "Which one?" he asked bluntly.

"Which—? Oh. Julie. You were married to Julie Ménard, weren't you? Or have I made a mistake?"

Jackie Ménard's stare was now coldly assessing. "No mistake," he said after a moment. "But you couldn't have known her very well or you'd have heard. She took off. Left me. Years ago."

"Oh dear." Mara contrived to look genuinely flustered. "I'm terribly sorry."

"I'm not. Quite frankly, she was a bitch in heat." He turned on his heel and walked on.

Bingo. Mara turned to shoot a triumphant glance over her shoulder. She was in time to see Ingrid jump as Alain slid a hand casually over her protuberant and inviting bum. Men, Mara thought, only partly amused. So much for disapproval.

•

> . . . *So you see, Patsy, the evidence is stacking up against Julian. He worked for the Ménards at the critical time, and he said nothing about it when Loulou mentioned that Julie was one of the missing women. For that matter, he had to be pushed before he'd admit that he'd even heard about Bedie and Valérie Rules. But Valérie lived just down the road from him. She probably walked past his house to and from school every day. He could have given her a ride, and then, who knows what happened. As for Bedie, I suspect she bought his wildflower book and contacted him from the information on the cover. He's a local orchid expert. It's also unlikely that she found the Bird's-nest Orchids on her own. Much more probable that Julian took her there.*

> *There are other things, too. He really did look pretty rattled when I turned up, as Alain said, like a face out of the grave, asking him to help me find a woman he might have murdered. His past is pretty cloudy. Paul told me that all of the women in his life seem to have dropped out of sight. And although I'm sure Julian genuinely wants to find his mystery Lady's Slipper, I think he faked the orchid hunt to throw suspicion on Vrac and the de*

Sauvignacs. It's true that the pigeonnier is on La Binette land, but apart from that, we only have his word that he actually reconstructed Bedie's trail leading from there to Les Colombes. And, finally, I'm now convinced that he purposely "lost" me in the swamp and stalked me in the forest. His version of fun and games. Oh, and by the way, do you remember what you said about psychos going off their medications? When I was searching his house, I checked his bathroom cabinet. I found some pills, something something acétaminophène. *Does this mean anything to you?* <

Patsy wrote back:

> *For Pete's sake, Mara, what have you got by the tail? Look, you need to understand that you could be dealing with a seriously sick and dangerous person. Corner him and he becomes a land mine. Hidden but highly explosive. Be sensible and turn this over to the flics!*
> *P.S. To answer your question, the something* acétaminophène *is probably the French version of prescription-strength Tylenol. Maybe our boy suffers from bad headaches. Not surprising if what you're telling me is true.* <

> *Don't worry, Patsy. I intend to hand this over to the cops. And I don't plan on taking any stupid risks. According to Loulou, this predator has always*

269

chosen his victims so that he can't be linked to them. That's why he's never been caught. I figure too many people have seen me in Julian's company and know about Bedie for him to try anything. Nothing more serious than his sick games of cat-and-mouse, that is. <

> Mara, don't count on it. Moreover, being careful also means not jumping to conclusions. Above all not trusting anyone. And while we're on the subject, there's something I think you're overlooking. Julian isn't your only candidate for stalker. Alain de Sauvignac was also there in the woods. I know you think you fell into his arms. Or did he lunge out and grab you? <

SIXTEEN

Mara was sitting very upright on the same hard wooden chair she had occupied two months ago in Commissaire Boutot's office at Périgueux Police Headquarters. This time she was there at the Commissaire's invitation. He sat facing Mara across his desk. With his baggy eyes and wilting mustache, he looked more melancholy than ever. Nevertheless, he had been listening to her with evident interest for thirty minutes. While she spoke, he rolled a blue pencil between his palms. His hands were dry, and the friction of the rolling made a scratchy, rhythmical sound. Loulou, who had set up the interview, was strolling about the office, chuckling softly at framed photographs of former *commissaires*, as if sharing a private joke with each of them. He paused to squint at a book on a shelf. It proved to be a biography of master thief-catcher Eugène François Vidocq—Boutot was something of a classicist when it came to crime.

"*Alors, madame*, your information is interesting," the *commissaire* said when she had finished. "As long, of course, as it is sans spurious embellishments."

Mara blushed at his reference to the faked initials. "Did you check Scott's statement to find out if Bedie had a copy of Julian's wildflower book?"

271

Boutot was cautious. "In his *déclaration* Monsieur Barrow did state that your sister had taken with her a Michelin guide to Périgord-Quercy and a book on wildflowers in the Dordogne."

"I knew it!" Mara exclaimed.

Boutot shook his head. "We can conclude nothing from this. Even if she had a copy of the book, it doesn't follow that she met up with Monsieur Wood. Indeed, I must point out that much of your so-called evidence against him is circumstantial."

"Maybe." She was undaunted. "But when so many things come together, as they do here, I think the coincidences stop being mere chance."

Boutot considered this, temporarily ceasing his pencil rolling. He dipped his head from side to side. "In fact, we have begun inquiries. Loulou has forwarded a rather interesting theory."

"Landscaping," pronounced the chubby ex-*flic*, bustling over. "You see, at first I thought our perpetrator chose his victims at random along major roads. I now think the link is landscaping. Julian is a landscape gardener. What better than to use his jobs to size up potential victims? Moreover, the distribution of the disappearances suggests the perpetrator was someone who moved around a lot. Julian's work—*mon dieu*—it takes him all over the region. He also has a van. Handy for transporting bodies."

Loulou plopped himself down on a chair next to her. "Look at it this way. Landscaping lets him get near his victims, observe their habits in situ, as it were. Picture that he's trimming the hedges around the house." He pumped his arms together in an enthusiastic hedge-clipping motion. "The target gets used to seeing him about. He's just the nice English fellow who tends the garden. That meets the criterion of trust. Child's play for him to get to know her routine, follow her somewhere, or even make an assignation, and *paf!*" Loulou slammed his right fist into his left palm with a look of shining satisfaction. The *commissaire* winced.

"Of course," Loulou conceded, "we still need to find out if our man also worked for Valérie Rules's parents and the Charlebois woman." He looked at his former colleague. "Any feedback on that, Antoine?"

Boutot sighed. The pencil started up again. "Monsieur and Madame Rules are now divorced, but one of my men spoke with the wife, who says they never employed a gardener and she's never heard of Monsieur Wood."

"Ah," said Loulou with a vigorous wag of a forefinger, "but in that instance perhaps he didn't need to work for them. He only lived a couple of kilometers away. He would have had ample opportunity to approach the kid."

"To the mother's knowledge, Valérie didn't know him, either. But maybe, as you say, he noticed the girl and events proceeded from that. As to the other, old Madame Charlebois died a couple of years ago. So there's no way of knowing if she or her daughter,

Mariette, employed our suspect. However, I have someone questioning the neighbors."

"But in any case, Julian's link to the Ménards is solid," declared Mara. "He worked for them the same year Julie Ménard disappeared. We've established that."

"*Bien sûr*, we are also reexamining the Ménard affair," the commissaire assured her. "All the same"— he thrust his chin in Loulou's direction—"I have a little problem with your landscaping theory."

"What problem?" demanded Loulou.

"It doesn't explain Madame Dunn's sister or the Dutch tourist whose body we found in the Quercy woods. Neither of those two had any connection with landscaping. Your idea, moreover, implies a certain amount of planning. Yet the Tenhagen woman was probably hitchhiking, suggesting a random encounter. Mademoiselle Bedie was probably a chance meeting, too. Valérie Rules?" He shrugged. "And Mariette Charlebois, who knows?"

"In Bedie's case the link was orchids," Mara said. "Maybe Hanneke Tenhagen had an interest in orchids as well. Have you looked into that?"

The *commissaire*'s hands paused again. His mournful gaze fixed on her. "No. We didn't know about the orchids at the time. But it's an interesting angle to pursue. However, what about the other missing women? Were they also interested in orchids?"

"Pooh," said Loulou with an explosive breath. "I

think we're making it more complicated than it needs to be."

Boutot cast a weary look at the chubby ex-lieutenant. "And your idea is?"

"Why, simply that, in addition to using his landscaping contracts to size up his victims, our man also seized his openings as they came, whether his victims were clients or strangers, as in the cases of Mara's sister, who might have approached him; the Tenhagen woman, who was hitchhiking; or *la petite* Valérie on her way home from school. As for Mariette Charlebois, maybe he did work for them."

The *commissaire* shook his head. "I still don't like it. It's too messy. In my experience, *mon vieux*, serial killers almost always adopt a consistent approach. That's not the case here. It's almost as if"—this time Boutot put the pencil down; his baggy eyes were unhappy—"we're looking for two different people."

•

Patsy e-mailed Mara:

> *Well, I'm glad you've quit playing cops-and-robbers and turned this over to the professionals. But listen, kid, if landscaping really is a thread running through all this, and if we're looking at a four- or five-year cycle of events, then I'd say your killer is overdue for another victim. I think you'd better forget about Bedie for the moment and concentrate on Julian's client list and who could be his next target.* <

My *god*, Mara thought when she read Patsy's message. *Prudence*. Julian had been digging around her property for the last three weeks. And hadn't he said something about a rockery? Where else had she seen rockeries? Was Julie Ménard buried beneath a hundred tons of Mediterranean stone?

Mara keyed in Prudence's number. Come on, come on, she whispered as the phone at the other end rang. And went on ringing.

•

Mara pulled up in front of Prudence's house with a screech of brakes. She raced to the front door and hammered on it with both fists.

Prudence took her time opening. She was wearing another of her Quimper-style smocks, and her hair and nails, as usual, were perfect.

"Oh," said Mara, taken aback. "Are you okay?"

"Fine. Why shouldn't I be? *Entrez*. Or do you just want to stay out there and beat down my woodwork?"

"I called you." Mara followed her inside. "You didn't answer."

"I must have been out in the back. Inspecting the trenches."

Mara said, "Prudence, about those trenches. I—I need to speak to you. Do you have any idea why Julian is digging them?"

"Something to do with drainage for my rockery. But if you're really that turned on by technical details, why not ask the expert?" In a lower voice, she added, "Lover Boy is here."

"*Here?*"

"Hullo, Mara," said Julian quietly, stepping into view. "Why should that surprise you?"

"It doesn't," said Mara. She took a deep breath and faced him squarely. "That is, I came to have a word with Prudence. Privately, if you don't mind."

"Oh?" He glanced at Prudence, who only shrugged. Then he smiled. "No problem. I can always come back another time. I'll leave you to it, shall I?

•

At the town of Le Buisson, the D25 swings away from the river, to run south through fields and forests. In May, traffic along it is sparse.

Along this stretch, a green Peugeot was coming to a coughing halt. The driver nosed the car as far as possible onto the grassy verge. The engine gave a final sputter and quit. In dismay, the driver, a prim, pretty woman named Arlette, stared at her fuel gauge and realized that she was out of gas. Only then did she remember that she had meant to fill up after leaving Toulouse. How stupid to have forgotten. But with so much on her mind . . . Her neatly packed suitcase lay on the backseat, silent witness to her flight.

Anxiously she checked the car clock against her watch. The car clock said six-thirty, her watch six-thirty-five. She always set her watch five minutes fast. But here she was, already an hour late because she'd missed a turnoff, and only *le bon dieu* knew how long it would take to get gassed up again. *Merde!*

She couldn't have that much farther to go, but with an empty tank, it might as well have been the other end of the earth. *Calm down*, she thought, and fumbled in her purse for her glasses and her cell phone.

Merde again! Her phone card had expired. She yanked her glasses off, jerking loose a strand of blond hair from the tight little bun perched on the top of her head. Where was this godforsaken place she had gotten to? She could not remember the name of the last village she had passed. Everything here was trees. Trees and fields. She got out of the car, slammed the door in frustration, and gazed angrily up and down the road in either direction. She recalled passing a farm not too far back. Perhaps someone there could help her. She locked the car, hooked her purse over her shoulder, and set out on foot in the direction she had come. The rough verge made walking difficult, especially in wedge sandals. The shoes were new. She cursed as she stumbled more than once. Why in heaven's name could she not have worn more sensible footwear?

But then, what she was doing was not sensible. Of course, she acknowledged as she trudged along, sense was what had kept her locked up within herself all these years, mutely complying with the expectations of family, friends, associates. Like a bad actor, she had gone through the motions of a role she had long ago ceased to want to play. Well, that was over now. All but the shouting. Suddenly she felt glad, despite running out of gas and her treacherous shoes, glad she'd thrown convention aside, glad of her leap into the void.

A car with foreign plates swung around a bend, coming rapidly toward her. She waved frantically, but it whizzed by. Another, but this one, too, passed in a gust of wind. Once again the road lay empty. Futilely, she tried her cell phone once more. Dead.

A vehicle appeared ahead of her on the horizon. Momentarily, she lost it behind a bank of trees. Then it broke into sight again, moving at a leisurely pace. Standing as far into the road as she dared, Arlette semaphored her distress with outstretched arms. The vehicle rumbled past, and she thought that it, too, would continue on. However, to her great relief, and with a grinding of gears, it slowed, stopped, and began to back up. When it was even with her, the driver rolled down the window.

"Bonjour," said Julian, sticking his head out. "Problems? Can I help?"

SEVENTEEN

They were back at La Vieille Guinguette, eating an excellent confit of duck. Alain had listened gravely as she told him what she had learned from Commissaire Boutot. Now he leaned forward.

"*Ecoute*, Mara, I have to be away for a few days this week. While I'm gone, I want you to be very careful. Do nothing until I get back. Do you understand me? Landscaping and orchids tie Julian in with Bedie and Julie Ménard. He could be a very dangerous man. I want you to promise that you'll wait until I return before taking further action."

Reluctantly, she agreed. "But where are you going? How long will you be away?"

His mouth turned down. "Paris. To negotiate another contract. I'm taking the TGV up on Wednesday. I'll be back Sunday."

"Another contract?" she echoed.

Alain nodded. "It's a multiyear stint in Mauritius, starting in September." He broke off to look earnestly at her. "I want to be honest with you, Mara. If I'm offered the job, I'll have to take it. I've worked abroad for the past twenty years because—well, partly because it pays better than anything I can get in France, and Les Colombes requires a lot of upkeep. But I make you this commitment. I won't go until this matter of your sister is resolved."

September, she thought with an unexpected feeling of impending loss. Three and a half months. So little time.

He reached out to cover her hand with both of his, blue eyes serious. "And when it is, when this is all over . . ." He paused, took a deep breath, and said huskily, "I want you to consider coming out to join me. No, don't answer now. Think about it. It needn't be right away. Just when you're ready. You'll like the scent of frangipani on the sea wind. I promise you."

•

On Tuesday, Mara drove to Limeuil to pick up an order from the three elderly sisters who did all her custom-sewing commissions. The women had names, but were referred to by everyone as l'Aînée (elder sister), la Cadette (the younger), and la Benjamine (baby of the family).

As usual when she called, the trio seated her in their tiny parlor and treated her to a small but potent glass of la Cadette's plum wine. They huddled around her, wispy and gray and smelling of mothballs, reminding her of a triplicate version of Jeanne de Sauvignac.

"Leslie Caron," exclaimed l'Aînée, who was always comparing Mara to one or another film actress. Last month it was Audrey Tautou, whom they'd seen in *Amélie*. This time she drew inspiration from a rerun of an old American film they'd watched on television.

"My dear, you look so much like Leslie Caron. You know, in *Gigi*. *Très gamine*. Don't you agree, sisters?"

La Cadette and la Benjamine did.

•

On the return journey to Ecoute-la-Pluie, Mara's mind strayed laterally to Jeanne de Sauvignac. The memory of her lopsided smile and gentle, kindly air of derangement unsettled Mara almost as much as the husband's secretiveness and fear. Or was it something more concrete than that? Yes, Mara decided, sifting through her impressions of their meeting. In fact, it was something the old woman had said, words that at the time had been lost in her general oddity but that now plucked at Mara's consciousness with a vaguely troubling resonance. Because one of the sewing sisters had said it, too. Or something like it.

That night she e-mailed Patsy Reicher.

•

On Wednesday, as Alain was taking his train to Paris, Mara drove to Toulouse to negotiate an order of tiles from Pablo. Instead of her usual quick *croque-monsieur*, she ended up having lunch with her supplier at the Brasserie des Beaux-Arts, overlooking the muddy waters of the Garonne. They opened with an apéritif of light, fruity muscat on ice. Pablo had an intense way of leaning his fat body across their little table when speaking. She half expected him to turn amorous, but his ardor proved to be reserved for food alone.

"Shall we say a half-dozen each of the number three?" he murmured huskily, referring to the oysters.

•

An hour later and an ocean away, as Mara watched Pablo climax on a dessert of *mousse au chocolat*, Patsy opened her morning and her electronic mail.

> *Patsy, it's me again. You remember my telling you about my visit to Les Colombes a couple of weeks ago? Well, there was something I forgot to mention that struck me as odd at the time, and I still can't make it out. See what you can do with it. When she first met me, Madame didn't say "enchantée" or "comment allez-vous" or any of the usual chitchat. Instead, she goggled at me in that nutty way of hers, and then she said, or started to say, "You are so much . . ." The actual words she used were: "Vous êtes tellement . . ." She didn't finish because her husband came into the room at that point. All the same, I had the feeling that she was about to make some kind of personal remark, which I find extremely peculiar because French women of her class and generation simply don't make personal remarks. At least, not right away. So much what?* <

In her uptown office, Patsy popped a tablet of gum into her mouth and chewed thoughtfully. She pushed away from her desk, leaning back in her chair and glancing through the window at an ugly Manhattan sky. The light outside had taken on a peculiar greenish tinge. A sudden clap of thunder shook the building.

So much what? Patsy sat motionless. The phone purred on her desk. She ignored it. Rain began to slash against the windowpanes. Yes, Patsy thought, that's got to be it. She tapped out:

> > *Mara, try "so much like your sister." I think Madame has seen Bedie, at least once. The question is, alive or dead?* <

•

Parts of the puzzle were beginning to interlock, but the full picture was still incomplete, critical pieces missing here and there. Although Commissaire Boutot had talked of two separate perpetrators, Mara felt in her bones that one person—Julian—was responsible for the death of Hanneke Tenhagen and the disappearances of the other women. Yet the de Sauvignacs were also somehow involved. Madame had seen Bedie before; the expression of fear on Henri's face was enough to tell Mara that the man was covering up much more than past sexual excesses; Alain had to know more than he was telling. And where did Vrac and la Binette fit in?

Confusedly, Mara grappled with the necessity of making some connection between Julian and the de Sauvignacs. Landscaping? She doubted it. Then she remembered something Gaston had said: "Madame walks in the woods every day, and Monsieur still likes to shoot the occasional rabbit." Had Jeanne or

Henri witnessed the attack on Bedie? But why hadn't they reported it? Perhaps the woman was so far gone she hadn't realized what she had seen. Or, Mara pondered, reflecting on the lack of funds so evident at Les Colombes, perhaps Henri had been using the knowledge to blackmail Julian. It couldn't have been for much. Julian was not a wealthy man. Unless, she concluded, a steady bleeding year after year was the reason.

If this was so, Mara knew that Henri would never talk. It was down to Jeanne, the link in the chain of lies and duplicity most likely to give. Mara's plan, therefore, was simple: return to Les Colombes and ransack Madame's knowledge for the missing puzzle pieces. To do that, Mara had to get her alone.

•

Thursday morning found Mara crouched in a thicket with a view of the rear courtyard of the château. Gaston had no idea when, between dawn and dusk, Madame's walk in the woods took place. Mara came prepared for a long stakeout. The problem was which door to watch. Châteaux of the style of Les Colombes had many doors, most connecting directly with interior staircases linking the various levels of the house. She counted on Jeanne's using the scullery door. In any case, Mara could not be in more than one place at a time.

By noon, Mara concluded that the worst of the exercise, not that she had any experience to go by, was the boredom. Apart from the listless waving of a rag on a sagging clothesline and the PTT—Gaston's substitute was a young, dark-haired fellow who left the mail on the scullery-door stoop—Les Colombes seemed devoid of life. Only a series of dormer windows, serving to light and ventilate the high loft of the château, seemed wakeful, peering down at her like quizzical, deep-set eyes. One of them, she noticed, had been blocked off at the bottom.

By three o'clock, Mara was cramped and stiff from sitting on the hard ground. Her sandwiches had long ago been eaten, her thermos of tea drained. In the valley below, a cuckoo voiced its lonely, intermittent call. The utter stillness of the place made her wonder if the de Sauvignacs were even there. She decided to risk a reconnoiter. As she pushed through wilderness that had once been formal garden, a tall, shadowy form suddenly barred her way, arm outstretched accusingly. She choked back a sharp yell of fear as she realized that she had come upon a small park of statuary, lost in the shrubbery.

Late-afternoon shadows were filling the courtyard when Henri de Sauvignac emerged from the scullery door. He carried a shotgun, broken at the barrel—off to bag his rabbit, no doubt. Mara held her breath as the old man paused, gazed up at the sky, and finally stepped off the stoop. With a stiff gait, he crossed the courtyard, walked down the lane running past the back of the château, and disappeared into the forest.

Swiftly, she darted from her hideout. She had anticipated intercepting the wife away from the house.

With Alain in Paris, this would do as well. The scullery door opened into a vast kitchen where old and new mixed oddly: a massive hearth, big enough to roast an ox; a white enamel stove where a simmering pot of soup gave off an aroma of celery and onions; a deep stone sink; a portable dishwasher; and, near the old-fashioned larder, a small refrigerator, gurgling faintly, like a hunchbacked and displaced dwarf.

She made a quick search of the pantry and the ancient *lavoir*, the wash area. No one was there. Stone steps, concave with use, led her up to the main floor. She passed through a progression of vast, empty chambers, each giving onto another. In one salon, where the smell of mold was particularly strong, the walls were covered in stained, yellow brocade that hung in tatters, like the ruined finery of a dead queen. Eventually, she found herself at the library where she had interviewed the de Sauvignacs. It was unoccupied.

Mara took the steps of the great central staircase two at a time. The first-floor landing gave onto a wide, windowed gallery that ran the entire width of the building. At the near end of the gallery was a narrow archway. A quick look told Mara that it accessed a dimly lit spiral stairway that wound up to the loft and down to the lower story of the château. The servants' staircase, no doubt.

Rooms, most of them empty, opened off the north side of the gallery. Everywhere was the same complexity of smells—damp stone, old wood, the odor of decay, of things closed off. She paused before a partly opened door, listened, gave the door a push, and stepped inside.

Jeanne de Sauvignac was standing just to the right of the door, gripping a large pair of tailoring shears.

"Is it you, then, my dear?" Jeanne de Sauvignac was clothed this time in a soiled blue dress, a shapeless cardigan, and grubby carpet slippers. Her hair had the same flyaway look, and the lower half of her face gawped in the same silly smile. She crossed the distance dividing them, eyeing Mara avidly. Involuntarily Mara took a step back.

"Madame de Sauvignac," she broke out jerkily, "forgive me. I had to talk to you. There seemed no other way."

"Of course." The other seemed to regard Mara's presence as natural. She waved a hand. "Do sit down."

Apart from a chair drawn up to a little table by the window, there was nothing to sit on. In fact, the large room contained no other furniture than a high matrimonial bed, an armoire, and a chiffonier cluttered with photographs—a wedding picture, the groom distinguished by a bred-in-the-bone arrogance apparent even today; the slim, pretty bride, swathed in such quantities of white tulle as to render her somehow inconsequential. Portraits of two small boys, the older wide-eyed and serious, the younger grinning a lopsided grin that reminded Mara of the mother.

Madame crossed the room and seated herself in the chair before the table.

Mara followed. "I came," she began awkwardly, "I came to talk to you about my sister. Beatrice Dunn."

If Jeanne de Sauvignac heard her, she gave no sign. Taking up a man's shirt, she began to hack it into random pieces with the shears, an aimless act of minor destruction that only strengthened Mara's impression that the woman was barking mad. What was it Gaston had said? She had lost a child and had never been right since. The glinting blades made a sharp, bright, and, to Mara's ears, awful sound.

Mara positioned herself squarely before the table. "Please listen to me, madame. I believe that nineteen years ago a man named Julian Wood brought my sister to the forest below your château. Something happened there. I think you were a witness."

The shears paused over the ravaged shirt.

Mara gripped the table's edge. "Madame, I need to know what happened."

Unwillingly, Jeanne raised a troubled face, eyelids fluttering like withered petals in a faint stirring of air. Her gaze fixed on Mara. Then she said it: "*You look so much like her.*"

Mara's heart lurched. "Yes," she breathed. "You saw the likeness the moment you met me. And the only way you could have known is if you'd already seen my sister." Gently but firmly Mara removed the shears from the other's grip and set them aside. "You were there, weren't you? You saw it all. What did he do to her?"

"Oh, my dear." Jeanne recoiled, looking genuinely shocked, as if Mara were broaching a socially embarrassing subject. "One doesn't speak of such things. *Ce . . . ce n'est pas convenable.*"

Pas *convenable*. Not seemly. The arid gentility of the old woman's choice of words made Mara want to shake her. She gripped Jeanne's arm. "Madame de Sauvignac, I have to know. *Tell me what happened to my sister!*"

"As to that," a voice spoke harshly at her back, "it's a question you would have been much better not to ask."

Mara whirled around to face Henri de Sauvignac. He stood in the doorway, breathing heavily and white with fury. Under his arm he still carried his gun. It was pointed at the floor, but this time the barrel was not broken. "You should be more careful where you park your car, madame."

Mara confronted him accusingly. "You! You know, don't you!"

"Enough!" Henri cried in a choking voice. "Why couldn't you let it be? Go away from here. Go now, before it is too late!" He brought the gun up sharply so that the barrel pointed at her breast. His eyes burned darkly in their sockets. He was old, but not without force or malice.

In desperation, Mara swung back to the wife, grasping at the slender thread that held her to Bedie. "Madame, for the love of God, tell me! What happened to my sister?"

"Jeanne!" The husband strode across the room. "Jeanne, I forbid—"

But Madame, hands fluttering up like frightened birds, cried out before he could stop her mouth. "It was her head," she moaned, rocking as if with pain. "Her poor, poor head!"

·

That evening, Julian, carrying an envelope of slides, arrived at the monthly meeting of the Société Jeannette. It was held in the Sainte-Anne community hall, which had once been a primary school. The words *garçons* and *filles* were cut into the stone lintels above the doorways of the separate boys' and girls' entrances. It was a good turnout—some thirty members. Iris and Géraud were there, Géraud looking smug, Iris cheerful and heavy with wooden beads.

"Come sit with us, Julian." Iris patted the empty chair next to her.

"I give you fair warning," she confided in a mock whisper as Julian settled himself. "Géraud's full of himself. Wait till the members' bit."

"Just let *him* wait," Julian grinned. "I've got something that'll knock his socks off."

The meeting started off with general business. Julian took the opportunity to alert the gathering to Edith's disappearance. They then moved on to nominations for the Prix Vénus. This was a prize awarded annually to the member who had contributed most to furthering the society's botanical knowledge or to the protection and public appreciation of flora in the region. In practice, this meant whoever had provided the best Bring and Brags. Inevitably, Julian and Géraud were nominated. Julian, who had joined the society only half a dozen years ago, was regarded as the upstart contender against Géraud, who won the prize with boring regularity. Julian was damned if he was going to be beaten out again.

The last part of the meeting was always reserved for the Bring and Brag. Here, there was usually a slight tussle as to order. Because Julian and Géraud almost always had something to show, it was understood that any other members wishing to make presentations (invariably inferior in point of botanical interest) had right of way. The issue of contention between Julian and Géraud was not which of them went next, but who went last, claiming the honor of rounding off the evening with the main spectacle, so to speak. The two men generally engaged in a species of wrangling, disguised as polite deference, each urging the other to precede him.

This time a resident German, Wilhelm Schroeder, led off with a nice series of slides of mountain wildflowers he'd snapped while hiking in the Ariège. When he stood down, there was a ripple of appreciation followed by a pause. Heads turned expectantly to Julian and Géraud. Julian sat back, knowing that what he had to show was well worth waiting for. To his surprise, Géraud did not demur but edged past him to the slide projector without ceremony.

"Just *un petit amuse-gueule*," he snickered at the gathering, "to whet the palate for the undoubtedly splendid botanical pièce de résistance that I'm sure my colleague Julian Wood has prepared for us." And he projected a close-up which caused Julian to sit forward agog.

"Saprophytes, as some of you may know, live on decomposing matter and are relatively rare. This fine example of the saprophytic *Neottia nidus-avis*, popularly known as Bird's-nest Orchid, is not at all common in the region. In fact, in all my years of spotting, I've come across very few examples—"

"Voyou!" Julian choked, outraged, to the consternation of those who sat within hearing.

Géraud continued unperturbed. "—and certainly nothing to match this magnificent colony, which I just happened to come upon recently." Julian's stand, in all its dense, brownish-yellow glory, flashed on, covering the screen.

"The immense size of this colony," Géraud went on, "is an excellent example of successful vegetative propagation. As you know, orchids, in addition to dropping seeds, spread underground through rhizomes or tubers, which clone off more plants, and so on. This way, quite massive carpets of a species like the *Neottia* here can grow up over time . . ."

Amid the murmurs of admiration, Iris turned to Julian. "What did I tell you?"

There was loud applause as Géraud wound up his presentation and sat down.

"*Pirate!*" Julian spat out as the other sidled past. "*Voleur!*"

Géraud smirked. "No such thing, mon ami. Believe me, your directions were more of a setback than a help. But don't keep us waiting. *Allez*, the show is all yours."

Julian glared. "Bugger the show!"

EIGHTEEN

A scampering sound brought Mara to her senses. Rats. Or more probably a *fouine*, a stone marten, she figured once she realized where she was; for she could make out a paleness that resolved itself into a dormer window. She was somewhere in the loft of the château. Judging from the quality of the light, it was early evening. Her head throbbed terribly. She tried to move and found that her hands and feet were bound. She rolled over on her stomach and attempted to push herself into a kneeling position. The effort made her sick and dizzy. With a moan, Mara collapsed onto a hard, filthy mattress that bore traces of her own blood.

The pain was mostly concentrated on the left side of her head. That was where Henri de Sauvignac had struck her, hard, with the butt of his shotgun. She remembered now his look of desperation and fury as he crashed the weapon, held like a club, into her skull. Her last conscious thought had been that he intended to kill her.

She tried again to raise herself up to a half-reclining position against the wall. Another rush of nausea and dizziness. When her vision cleared, she saw that she was in a small garret containing only the bed she lay on. The space, which had been walled off from the rest of the loft, had an air of long abandonment. The floor was thick with dust.

She sensed movement. A small door at the far end of the garret opened. Jeanne de Sauvignac stepped into focus, carefully balancing a basin of liquid before her. Reaching Mara's side, she stooped worriedly over her.

"How are you, my dear?" She seated herself on the bed. Dipping a cloth into the basin, she began to dab very gently at the side of Mara's face. The pungent smell of vinegar hit Mara with such force that she recoiled.

"Lie still," the old woman murmured, pausing in her ministrations. "This will do you good. You've had a very nasty fall."

"Fall!" Mara gasped hoarsely. "Your husband tried to kill me. Surely you must realize that?"

"Ah." The other thought for a moment. "But *then* you fell."

With a sinking feeling, Mara recognized that Jeanne de Sauvignac was either crazier or more cynically sane than she had thought.

"Untie me. You can't keep me here. I'm hurt. I need a doctor."

"Hush," said Jeanne, studying her patient with interest. "I'll take very good care of you. I know a great deal about head injuries."

It occurred to Mara that Jeanne herself might be the product of a head injury. Then she remembered Bedie.

"What happened to my sister?" she croaked. "Did someone hit her on the head?"

Jeanne's regard shifted to the basin. She fingered the wet cloth. Mara waited, her own temples throbbing, willing the other to talk. At last, the older woman spoke. "He was born that way. He couldn't help the things he did." She said it simply, as if of some beast shaped by nature to violence, and with a compassion that sounded somehow out of place.

Was the woman talking about Julian? Fighting against an overwhelming drowsiness, Mara forced herself to concentrate. Her blackmail theory seemed insufficient reason for the violence of Henri's reaction. Surely the de Sauvignacs would not go to the extent of attacking and tying her up just to protect their hold over Julian and what had to be a meager source of money. Unless, of course, it was their own complicity they were desperate to hide. Then her thinking cleared, and she realized there was a simpler explanation. She turned to the woman at her side, who was now gazing distractedly into the basin as if seeking something in its cloudy depths. Jeanne had not been referring to Julian at all, probably had no inkling of who he was.

"Vrac," Mara said with a long release of breath. "It was Vrac all along, wasn't it? You knew, but you did nothing. Because he and his mother are 'your people' you kept silent. *Mon dieu*, you probably even helped them dispose of her body! But why?" She pulled away in revulsion from the other's touch. "Why did you cover up for him? Why did you risk so much to protect someone who's probably a psychopathic killer?"

Mara had her answer even before she finished her question, guessed it from Jeanne's quickly averted face, heard it in her silence. Henri's sense of noblesse oblige. The games of *cache-cache*. There was only one reason why children of the château would have been allowed to play with a common washerwoman's spawn.

"The blood tie," she concluded. "That's what binds you to him, isn't it? Vrac is your husband's bastard."

"Let me go," Mara cried. "People will be looking for me. "They know I'm here. Your son—" an uneasy thought crossed her mind—"does Alain know about my sister?"

Jeanne sighed, a soft, sad rush of air. "My boy was away. In Africa. Building roads and bridges. His father won't let him live here. That's why he works abroad."

"Well, your boy is going to be back on Sunday," Mara challenged. "How will you explain me?" Then doubt edged in. Would they tell him? Would he even know she was up there in the garret? Would he help her if he knew?

•

She had no idea what the de Sauvignacs intended to do with her, only that she was one against many. A half-mad woman. Henri, arrogant, desperate, and armed. Behind him, the lurking specter of Vrac. And la Binette. Mara balked a little at the thought of Henri taking his pleasure with someone whom she had heard Gaston describe as big as a tree, ugly as a troll. But perhaps, when young, the woman had offered a brief attraction. Where had it happened? Mara wondered. At the stream where she routinely took the washing? Had the young milord taken her from behind, like an animal? She did the rough, the old man had said with fine distinction. How many couplings had it required to produce her misbegotten son?

Finally, there was Alain. Was he really ignorant of what his parents had done? Could they have kept something so monstrous from him? She wanted desperately for him to have no taint of collusion. Because if Alain had known, then his silence made him as guilty as they.

•

Later that night, Jeanne returned with a blanket and a bowl of soup. Mara caught the disheartening whiff of celery and onions. The soup was greasy, oversalted, and thickened with bread. The woman seemed to take pleasure in helping Mara to eat, cradling her torso against her own bony, stale-smelling body, lips moving in sympathetic movement with each mouthful that Mara took. Despite her revulsion at the physical contact, Mara ate it all. She needed her strength to fight against them. The light from a single, naked bulb suspended from the ceiling threw their shadows against the wall in a slow, wavering duet of motion.

When Mara said she needed to relieve herself, Jeanne offered her the use of a dusty chamber pot that she pulled from under the bed. Mara refused and insisted on being taken to a proper toilet. Jeanne untied her legs and escorted her out of the garret, down the spiral stairs to the floor below. Any thought Mara had of making her escape faded when she realized how weak and dizzy she was. She could hardly walk, let alone run. The water closet, situated off the gallery, was none too clean. Since Mara's hands were still bound, Jeanne had to help her. Mara recoiled from the intimate physical contact, but at least the woman was quick about it, pulling down her jeans, wiping her as efficiently as a nurse. Also surprisingly strong. Then Jeanne brought her back and tied her legs again, but not as tightly as before. With a murmured "*bonsoir*," she clicked off the light. Mara heard the grating of the key in the lock.

She waited breathlessly in the dark. The great house was absolutely still. Awkwardly she dropped her legs over the side of the bed and slid to the floor. It was a painful process, rolling over the hard floorboards, and she had to stop many times to let her swimming head stabilize. When she reached the door, she pushed herself up to a standing position. She slid her cheek against the wall until she found the old-fashioned switch and flipped it on with her chin. Once again the single bulb came to life, filling the garret with a weak light.

Her exploration of the garret told her a few

things. The door was made of solid timber with no knob or handle, only a metal plate housing a dead-bolt lock, an unusual fitting for a garret. No hope of escape there. The dormer window was boarded off at the bottom. That was enough to tell her it was the one she had noticed from the rear court-yard during her stakeout. She stored up this pre-cious piece of information. At some point the PTT van would drive up the rear lane and park by the scullery door. If there was some way she could open the window, she could shout for help when the dark-haired *rouleur* arrived with the next mail delivery.

But how to do it? The window was set high in the wall, and the boarding made it impossible for her even to see out of it. There was no chair or table in the garret, nothing to climb on. She would have to shift the bed over to the window somehow. She tried moving it the only way she could, by rolling onto her back and shoving it with her feet, using the power of her legs. It was extremely heavy. She managed to slide one end of the bed a small distance from the wall before a sudden wave of nausea overcame her. She rolled onto her side and vomited a pale-yellow liquid in which gobbets of undigested bread floated. Exhausted, she closed her eyes. She slept.

•

The following morning broke cool and overcast. Julian was standing sleepily in his kitchen, pouring himself a first mug of tea. He took it well sweetened, with a dash of milk. The back door was open, admitting a moist breeze. The phone rang.

"Julian?" It was Iris.

"Yes?" he inquired coldly, the memory of Géraud's scoop making him uncivil.

"Look, I've been stewing about this since last night. I felt I simply had to call you."

"About what?"

"Géraud, of course!" Iris's indignation crackled in his ear. "He told me what he did to you. He was laughing about it all the way home from the Société meeting. For what it's worth, I think it was a perfectly filthy trick."

"Oh that. Finder's rights." Behind feigned indifference, Julian was still furious. The only thing that had saved the evening for him was the fact that he had arranged a double billing: the *Neottia*, which he did not show—what was the point?—and his slides of *Hammarbya paludosa*, the Bog Orchids he had discovered on his first day out with Mara. The effect, however, had been much discounted by the fact that they were not yet in flower.

"But you don't know the worst of it," Iris went on.

"There's worse?" He pulled up a chair and sat down heavily.

"Géraud purposely misled you to buy time for himself. He *made up* that Bird's-nest colony outside Le Double! Meantime, he checked out your locations, which, of course, were genuine."

Julian swore. The thought had crossed his mind,

but he had been unable to believe that Géraud would stoop so low.

"Listen, Julian, I think it's too bad, what he did. I want you to know I had no part in it."

"No, of course not."

"However, to be fair to Géraud, you're always trying to one-up him, too, and he feels the pressure. Everything's so competitive nowadays. In fact, it's perfectly disgusting, the tricks some Société members play to outdo each other. In old Henri de Sauvignac's time, such things would never have happened. All the same, I think Géraud needs to be taught a lesson. The only way to punish him is to hit him where it hurts."

"Where's that?" Julian asked with interest.

"The Prix Vénus. He's won it seven years running. Beat him out for it."

Julian snorted. "How, if he's prepared to cheat?" All the same, he was gratified by Iris's blatant betrayal of her lover.

"Well, *I* don't know. You're the botanist."

Something Iris had said earlier only now registered with him. "Wait a minute, Iris. *Who* did you say?"

"Géraud, of course."

"No, before that."

"Henri de Sauvignac? He founded the society, didn't you know? But, of course, that was well before your time. Lovely old gent. Absolutely gaga about wildflowers. You'd have liked him."

"Are you talking about the de Sauvignac of Les Colombes?"

"Well, not the present *châtelain*, of course. Henri de Sauvignac père. Avid orchidologist. Both of them."

"Both of who?"

"He and his daughter-in-law. The two of them used to prowl the countryside collecting specimens for their plantations. Had them dotted all over the estate. He named the society for her, you know. 'Jeannette' is a *jeu de mots*, the diminutive for 'Jeanne,' which is her name. It also stands for *jeannette jaune*, yellow daffodil. He died years ago, god rest his gentle soul, but Jeanne de Sauvignac is still around, flitting through the woods."

"And her husband, the present Henri de Sauvignac, does he share this interest in botany?"

Iris gave a peal of laughter. "More interested in *les jeunes filles en fleur*, budding young women, than daisies, if you get my meaning. A real lady-killer in his day, with a penchant for rough sex, or sex in the rough."

"What do you mean?"

"Well, he had a liking for village wenches and he took it where he could get it, in field and forest. They say his youngest son drowned in a pond because the maid who was supposed to be looking after him was otherwise occupied in the tall grass with her employer. It destroyed his wife, which was very sad, especially as it's poor Jeanne de Sauvignac who's had to pay out all these years to hush up her husband's sexual indiscretions. She's the one with the money, you see. Or was. They're poor as church mice now, but he refuses to sell that barn of a place they live in. Family pride. Still, give the devil his due, after the old man died, Henri fils did his bit as Société president for many years, made pretty speeches at the annual assembly, handed out the Prix Vénus, which his father also founded, that kind of thing. Neither the present Henri nor Jeanne has come to meetings for donkey's years, of course."

Julian's mind was racing. "The Prix Vénus . . . That wouldn't happen to have been named after the Sabot de Vénus, would it?"

"Why, now that you mention it, I believe it was. Yes, I'm sure of it, because I remember that Henri senior and Jeanne once tried to grow Sabot de Vénus on the grounds of their château."

Julian was on his feet and gaping. "Are you saying they tried to breed *Cypripedium calceolus* here?"

"What?"

"*Cypripedium calceolus*. Sabot de Vénus. Lady's Slipper."

"Ah. I forgot that's what you experts call it. Well, yes, come to think of it, I believe they did. From rootstock they took from, mmm, I can't remember where."

"Look, I'm not just talking about one or two show plants, Iris. I mean, do you know if they actually tried to establish a viable plantation of them?"

"Might have." He could almost see her shrug. "Although, if they did, I doubt it came to very much."

"However, you don't know for certain that they failed, do you?" Julian was breathing hard.

"Oh," Iris murmured vaguely, "I rather think that if old Henri had succeeded we'd all have heard about it."

"And does Géraud know about this attempt to grow *Cypripedium?*"

"Bound to. But you know Géraud, vain as a peacock, scoffs at anything anyone else tries. Doubt he ever believed in it."

Until, of course, Julian thought sourly, *I turned up with that photo.* Aloud, he said, "Thanks for telling me this, Iris. You're a real treasure."

She chuckled conspiratorially. "Just give the old devil what's coming to him, all right?"

"You're on," he assured her.

Julian hung up with two thoughts driving everything else from his mind. First and foremost, if *Cypripedium calceolus* had been established at Les Colombes, then the plant could have mutated and the resulting flower could have been the one Bedie had photographed nineteen years ago. Second, Géraud, nobody's fool, was, like himself, on the hunt for the Lady's Slipper, probably closing in on it at that very moment.

A panicky urge to rush back to Les Colombes seized him, but he restrained himself. Les Colombes and the surrounding forest encompassed a large area, and he might be looking for a single plant. *If* it had survived. The logical approach would be to find out from Jeanne de Sauvignac where she and her late father-in-law had tried to establish the *Cypripedium* rootstock. That at least would narrow the search. Assuming the woman could remember. She sounded barmy, from Mara's description.

He took it for granted that he could count on Mara's cooperation. She wanted to find the *Cypripedium* as much as he—for different reasons, of course. However, he was aware that a coolness had set in between them ever since that damned Alain had happened along. Julian was quite certain that she looked at him differently of late, almost as if— Well, it was past thinking. All the same, it gave him a stab of uneasiness.

He drove straight out to Ecoute-la-Pluie. There he found Mara's front door open and the cleaning woman, a bony person named Madame Audebert, on hands and knees in the main room, vigorously waxing the floor. The smell of encaustic hung sweetly in the air. She looked up at Julian with eyes like olive pits. He asked if Mara was in.

"But her bed has not been slept in, monsieur," Madame Audebert told him sardonically, as if to imply that, if he did not know why, then it was none of his business.

Alain, Julian, concluded wrathfully.

The *femme de ménage* added that she came at nine twice a week and let herself in with her own key. Sometimes Madame Dunn was there when she arrived and sometimes not. This time not. Regardless, she got on with her work. She gave him an acid look.

"Oh, right—" He was about to leave her to it when he was startled by a deep bark. "Wait a minute. Is Jazz here?"

By way of answer, Madame Audebert jabbed her hairy chin in the direction of the back of the house. Julian strode across the room. Through the glass panels of the double doors, he could see the dog straining at the end of a chain, looking anxious amid the Patsy Reicher statuary.

"He hates the vacuum," Madame Audebert muttered at his back, "so I put him in the garden. He barks a lot because he doesn't like being tied up." She seemed to imply that Julian should do something about it.

"Look," Julian said, "I want to leave Mara— Madame Dunn—a message." He peered about for something to write on. The woman was unhelpful. He settled for the back of a bill he found in his pocket. Hastily he scrawled: *Mara—where the hell are you? Call me. Urgent. Julian.*

"I'll put it here, shall I?" He placed it conspicuously on one of the Louis Something consoles.

"*Comme vous voulez, monsieur.*" From the floor, Madame Audebert pursed her lips, as the French picturesquely called it, *en cul de poule*. It was a fitting description, Julian thought nastily. Her puckered mouth really did resemble a chicken's arse.

No sooner had he returned to his van than he regretted leaving a message at all. What was the point of waiting for Mara to take her sweet time getting back just to tell her about his discovery? Now that she was so thick with Alain, he wouldn't put it past her to cut him out, use the son to get the information from Jeanne de Sauvignac, and try to find the *Cypripedium* herself. Just to spite him. And the damnable thing was, the bloody woman might succeed. After all, her sister had stumbled on it. His anger and his resentment mounted.

He was considering retrieving his note when another volley of barks, desperate this time, sounded from the garden. Julian hesitated, then walked around to the back of the house. Jazz, frantic with delight, lunged and scrabbled on his tether.

"Oh, all right," Julian gave in grumpily. "But just this once."

"Tell Madame Dunn," he called to the *femme de ménage* through the front door, "I've taken Jazz."

She gave him a look that said he could go to the devil for all she cared, the dog with him.

•

"Count yourself lucky," Julian snarled at Jazz as he started the engine and roared out of Ecoute-la-Pluie in the direction of Les Colombes. For want of information from Jeanne de Sauvignac, he had to make assumptions. He had already guessed that the ridge on which the château stood offered the kind of soil and the cool, wooded environment that *Cypripedium* liked. That's where he would have chosen to establish a plantation of Lady's Slippers if it had been up to him.

He had come away without any of his usual hiking paraphernalia, but at least he had his compass and maps, which he normally carried in his van. Using a Série bleue, he found a road that allowed him to approach the estate from the east. That way he could avoid crossing La Binette land, which lay to the west of Les Colombes. He had no desire to be caught trespassing by Vrac or his hulk of a mother.

He parked at the roadside near a scattering of tiny Burnt-tip Orchids. The high tree canopy offered him no view of his destination, so the first thing he did was to set a westerly bearing on his compass that would orient him roughly in the direction of the château and the ridge. Since there was no path, he would have to break his own trail, and he estimated that he had a good hour's hike ahead of him.

He set out. Jazz vanished immediately (Julian had also not thought to bring a leash). Slightly alarmed, Julian called him back. The dog took his time coming but eventually returned. This happened repeatedly. Finally, Julian got tired of calling and left the animal to his own devices. When he came across a mass of pink Heath Orchids growing in a clearing, he forgot entirely about the dog. Later he found a fine stand of *Limodorum abortivum*. The tall, handsome plants were in peak condition, with their mauve blossoms spiraling up each individual stem. He made a mental note of their location.

After about twenty minutes, Julian stumbled on a path that seemed to be trending in the right direction.

He followed it. It took him past a crudely fenced pasture where a nervous huddle of ewes and lambs broke apart at his approach, skittering away before wheeling around from a safe distance to stare at him sideways with stupid, squarish eyes. At this point, he had no idea whose land he was on. The pasture sloped down to a stream so heavily overgrown with willow brush that although he heard the sound of water he could not see it until he nearly fell into a narrow, deeply cut rivulet that rushed away at his feet.

His path ended there. A network of faint tracks led off in several directions. Referring again to his compass, he chose one that snaked along the water's course. He had not gone far when a shrill, inhuman scream brought him to a startled halt.

"Bloody hell!" he uttered. "What was that?" His first thought was that Jazz had seized on some poor, unwary animal. The sound had come from farther along the watercourse. He ran forward, breaking through a heavy screen of willows. What he saw caused him to pull up in sheer terror. Vrac stood below him on the other side of the stream, bare arms spattered in blood. In one hand he grasped a knife, in the other the thing he had just slaughtered. It was a lamb, which he secured by the hind legs while he disemboweled it. Bluish intestines spilled onto the mud. The water of the stream ran a ghastly shade of red.

For a moment Vrac stared stupidly up at Julian. The mono-lens sunglasses blanked out one eye, but the look in the other turned quickly ugly. Julian took two involuntary steps backward, spun about, and fled.

Counting on speed he did not really have, Julian crashed through the trees. Behind him he heard a fearsome bellow and the thud of heavy footsteps. The realization that Vrac had been merely poaching someone's livestock, probably for his evening chops, did not make Julian less inclined to put distance between him and his pursuer. Poaching was a serious offense in those parts, and Vrac clearly resented being caught at it. Julian did not like to think what Vrac could do with that knife of his.

Dodging branches, Julian found himself at another section of the stream, where it curved off in a wide, shallow bend. He flailed across it. The splatter of water in his wake told him that Vrac was not far behind. Gasping for breath, Julian scrambled up the steep, wooded embankment on the other side. Small avalanches of scree rattled down behind him as he surged over the top of the rise. The land fell away precipitously before him. He galloped down recklessly.

A root caught his foot. He spun sideways, rolled wildly, and came up hard against the base of a tree. The impact knocked the wind out of him. He lay fighting for air. Painfully he dragged himself on his elbows into the cover of a dense bed of ferns. Pressing himself flat against the ground, he listened. The only sound he heard was the hammering of his own heart.

Cautiously, Julian raised his head. Small white butterflies danced over a gray-green sea of bracken that spilled thickly down the slope. Light filtered lazily through the treetops. All about him the woods were quiet. He lay still for a few moments longer, then congratulated himself on a close escape. Vrac appeared to have abandoned the chase and was probably going back for his lamb. Julian judged that he would finish gutting it and make for home as fast as possible.

Julian pushed himself upright, reoriented himself, and set off again, scrambling along the steep side of the embankment. A break in the trees gave him his first, distant glimpse of Les Colombes, or, rather, its chimneystacks. It stood high on its prominence across a broad, wooded valley. He took another compass reading and headed down into the valley floor, pushing his way, often with difficulty, through the tangled undergrowth. When he came across another network of trails, he chose one trending in a westerly direction. It took him through a gloomy pine forest.

Now the land began to rise before him. Pines gave way to beeches, old-growth chestnuts, and oaks. After another fifteen minutes, he found himself in a hornbeam grove at the base of the ridge. The château stood high above him to his left. The trail veered off toward it. To his right, the ridge continued on for a kilometer or so before coming to an abrupt end in a spectacular hanging cliff.

He decided to begin his search by working diagonally up the slope face, away from the château and toward the cliff, sticking to tree cover as much as possible until he was out of sight of the château.

There was no path, and large boulders frequently blocked his way. One, as big as a house, rose up before him. He was edging around it when the ground suddenly gave way beneath him. With a startled cry, he found himself dropping into a void and managed only just in time to catch himself with his outflung arms. Panicked, he kicked about to find some purchase with his feet, which only caused him to slip farther. A shower of earth and stones struck bottom somewhere ominously far below him. He now dangled over nothingness, supported only by his hands and forearms. Gradually, as the friable soil crumbled beneath his weight, he lost even this precious hold. In a minor avalanche, he plunged down into a pit of darkness. It was as if the earth itself had swallowed him up.

•

Mara awoke to daylight. She was on the floor, where she had collapsed the night before. She felt cold and clammy. Then the sour smell of her own mess hit her. Miserably she rolled away from it and found herself staring into the dim, dusty space beneath the bed. Something shiny was wedged in a gap between the floorboards just by one of the legs of the bed. Frowning, she scooted forward and picked it out with her teeth, dropping it out in the open where she could study it better. It was a plain, narrow metal band, slightly pitted with rust and bent tightly in upon itself. A hair clip of some kind, too flimsy to be of use to her. Disappointed, she rolled away. Then faint recognition stirred. She closed her eyes and struggled to visualize. Hair. Bedie's hair, pinned back at the temples. *This was a woman's hair clip such as Mara had seen in every one of her nightmares for nineteen years:* Bedie's barrette.

Her brain in turmoil, Mara struggled to understand how it came to be there. She fought to concentrate, staring at this terrible and yet precious token of her sister. Her mind went back to the knobless door, the deadbolt lock, the dormer window that had been altered to let light in but blocked any view of the outside world. The garret was fitted out like a prison.

I know a lot about head injuries, the old woman had said. Bedie—who had been struck on the head, but who had not died, at least not right away—Bedie had been there once. Mara was sure of it. The bed bore the impression of her body; the walls, the enclosed space of the garret held her presence like a bottled ghost.

She struggled to rise, ignoring the pounding in her head. Hobbling on her knees to the barrier of the door, she fell against it, pivoted around, and hammered at it with her feet, shouting with all the force she could muster.

"Get up here, you monsters! Get up here and tell me what you've done with my sister!"

•

Julian landed heavily. Instinct told him not to move. In the dimness, he saw that he was on a limestone shelf only slightly wider than himself. It was, in fact, what had saved him, for it projected out over a chasm, the depth of which he could only guess at by the rattle of debris still on its way down. He was in an *edze*, a typical geological feature of the region, where rifts in the calcareous mantle of the earth, dissolved by rain, opened out into deep pits underlain by subterranean rivers. He sat up carefully. Apart from being stunned and shaken, he did not seem to have broken anything. Above him, he saw a ragged patch of daylight, the hole through which he had fallen.

Julian's horror and revulsion at encountering Vrac at the stream were now replaced by a strong desire to see the man again, for there was no way he could climb out without help. The mouth of the *edze* was perhaps five meters up, more than twice his own height. The shaly sides offered no hand- or foothold. To make things worse, the pit interior was wider at the bottom, sloping inward at the top. Despite his belief that Vrac was capable of slitting him open like a hogget, Julian got to his feet and began to shout.

He shouted until he was hoarse. Exhausted, he slumped down against the wall of his prison. *Get a grip*, he ordered himself and set about studying his situation. Although the *edze* was vase-shaped, he saw that it narrowed at one end. By bracing his back and feet against the opposing faces, Julian thought he might just be able to work his way to the top. However, he was also aware that the ledge he was on extended only partway across the gap. Between it and the far wall lay a maw of blackness. The rocky projection had saved him once. If he slipped, would it catch him a second time?

He rolled over onto his stomach and peered down into the darkness below. As his eyes adjusted, he discovered to his relief that the fissure, although undoubtedly deep, was not as sheer as he had thought, for the opposite wall sloped outward, forming another shelf not far below him. All kinds of rubble had accumulated on it. He made out a dark jumble of shapes. Maybe there was even something down there he could use.

Carefully, he lowered the top half of his body over the side of the ledge, extending one arm down in a sweeping motion. His fingertips brushed something. He wriggled as far forward as he dared to go and closed his hand on a hard, rough object. He brought it up, a wedge-shaped thing that he flung away immediately, for it was horrific, studded with teeth and trailing stiff shreds of woolly hide: the lower jaw of a sheep.

Julian sat back, shaken. For the first time in his life, he earnestly wished he had a cell phone.

NINETEEN

"*Vrac hit her on the head!*" Mara screamed at Henri, who stood in the doorway. Behind him, fluttering in her shawls, was Jeanne. Mara struggled to her knees to confront them. "But she was alive, wasn't she, when you brought her here! Was it was your wife, who isn't competent to care for a dog, who finished her off?"

"Shut up," Henri de Sauvignac ordered curtly, seizing her under the arms and dragging her roughly back to the bed.

"The police will come looking for me." Mara fought against him as he lifted her and shoved her facedown on the mattress. "What story will you concoct for them? It'll have to be good because they'll find evidence of me everywhere—hair, blood, vomit—it's all over the floor. Or will you simply tell them that, having covered up the murder of one sister, you thought you'd finish off the other?"

"Stop that." Jeanne hurried forward to aid in holding her still while Henri checked her bonds. "No one is going to finish you off. We just want to help you, make you better."

"Like you did my sister?"

The other woman cried indignantly, "I gave her the best of care!"

"Jeanne, *tais-toi!*" the husband ordered sharply, but the words were out.

It was like a boulder dropped from a great height into a deep pool. Mara lay still as the admission sank and lodged in the depths of her consciousness. She rolled over to stare up at Jeanne.

"And how was that, madame?" she began softly, but her voice became quickly shrill. "How exactly did you care for her? By tying her up here and refusing her medical attention? Because you wouldn't have wanted to risk a doctor, would you? By feeding her stale bread dipped in slop? How long did she last before she choked on her own vomit or died of a hemorrhage of the brain?"

"Since you insist," said Henri, with a savage jerk at her knots, "fourteen years."

Mara went limp beneath his hand. It was as if her known world had suddenly shattered like glass, sending jagged shards flying in all directions, exposing a void in which nothing made sense.

"Fourteen years? In this garret? You locked my sister up here for fourteen years?"

"You must understand, my dear," Jeanne's voice wavered apologetically above her, "it was necessary. She was terribly damaged. She couldn't speak, she couldn't care for herself. I had to do everything for her, feeding, baths, cleaning up her messes."

"You kept her caged like an animal!"

"Not at all!" The woman sounded deeply offended. "I nursed her like my own child. I used to put her head on my lap and brush her hair. I always had to pin her hair back, out of her eyes, you see. She became very agitated if her hair was in her eyes."

"And then what? At what point did you get tired of playing jailer? Were people starting to ask questions? Or were Alain's home leaves getting too much for you to manage?" Mara rolled away from them and propped herself up on her elbows, the better to see their faces as she worked out the truth for herself. "That's why you couldn't let him live here, isn't it? Why your 'poor boy' has to work abroad. You were terrified he'd learn your secret. Or was he becoming suspicious? Was that when you decided to get rid of her? How did you do it? Hold a pillow over her face? Or did you simply let her starve to death up here?"

"No, no!" Jeanne wailed, her hands flying up around her face as if warding off Mara's accusations. "It wasn't like that at all. I did my best to make her comfortable. And happy. She was happy here with me. Until"—the old woman's voice cracked, and Mara realized that she was crying—"one day, one morning, I brought her coffee up to her. She was lying on her stomach. I couldn't wake her. I rolled her over. Then I saw that she was dead. She had simply died in the night, you see."

"It took her long enough," Henri cut in brutally.

Fourteen years. Dully Mara's mind began to compute. For at least two of those years, she had lived and worked in the Dordogne, not more than twenty kilometers from the place where her twin had been held a mindless captive. For fourteen years her nightmares had been not of a sister dead but of a sister living, feebly signaling for rescue from a twilight existence. And then, like a light exhausted, all signals had ceased. A wrenching sadness filled Mara as she realized that Bedie Dunn had slipped away, had dropped her end of the string that bound sister to sister, while she, Mara, had been unable to pull her back from the brink.

"But why?" The question rose again to her lips, for the improbability of the de Sauvignacs' motive weighed once more on her. Why would a family like the de Sauvignacs take such risks to shield a bastard? And how had Bedie come to Les Colombes? For, if Julian had really reconstructed her path, then it had brought her right onto the grounds of the château. She could not have been dragged there struggling because she had stopped to take photographs along the way. Would she have willingly gone with a monster like Vrac? Or, more likely, have accompanied someone comme il faut, as Loulou had suggested, someone presentable? Not Julian, she knew that now. Someone else. Someone who was able to move about the region with ease and for whom places like Limoges, Bordeaux, and Biarritz, where other women had gone missing, were within striking distance. A man whose wife wore a souvenir of Biarritz as a shawl. Thing-in-his-pocket. The stallion in rut.

"It was the other way around, wasn't it," Mara hissed at Henri in a slow release of breath. "Not Vrac. But you. *You* hit my sister on the head."

Nineteen years ago, Henri would have been a vigorous man in his fifties. Had it begun as a simple grope that escalated into a struggle and accidental death? Or a vicious, planned attack? Just as he had struck Mara herself down, had he also smashed the butt of his gun into Bedie's skull? How many others had de Sauvignac disposed of in his need to assert his seigniorial rights? The noble rot applied to more than grapes.

"And you caught him in the act, didn't you." Mara twisted about to accuse the wife. "That's why he didn't finish her off and simply bury her in your woods. Why you had to keep her here. Not to shield Vrac, but to protect your husband's precious skin."

Jeanne was staring at her haggardly, wordless, not denying. Mara now realized that there was no limit to what Henri would do to save himself. She also realized that her own danger was made more acute by Alain's planned return. Henri would make sure his son did not find her there.

"Leave us, my dear." Henri turned to his wife and ushered her quickly from the room.

"Let me go," Mara bargained desperately when he returned to stand over her. "I won't make trouble. Even if I went to the police, what can I prove? If I haven't been able to make a case against Vrac—and I've tried, believe me—who will credit that Henri de Sauvignac, *seigneur* of Les Colombes, is a serial killer?"

"Fool!" Henri spat furiously.

"I may be a fool, but you are a monster." Mara's anger surged as she saw that all pleading was futile. "Your victims trusted you, didn't they. You, with your aristocratic air, your fine courtesy. How did you lure my sister onto your land? With orchids? With promises to show her a place where rare species grew?"

Henri laughed outright. "Madame, I have never been particularly knowledgeable about orchids and would not, if given the opportunity with a young woman, have ever wasted time talking about flowers."

"Who else, if not you?" Mara challenged, galled by his sneering indifference.

He regarded her cynically, as if assessing how much information to divulge. Finally, he spoke, with an upward curling of the lip: "My wife."

She stared at him, speechless.

"It was she, you see," he said, as he turned to leave, "who met your sister in the woods."

•

Young Carlos, the *rouleur* filling in for Gaston, swung by the house in Le Coux at the end of his Saturday-morning round of deliveries.

"How's it going, old man?"

"Hmm." Gaston pulled a face and flipped his good hand back and forth to indicate so-so. "You? What's new?"

"Didn't you hear? The patron's made a dog's breakfast out of everything. He's split your route between René and me. So now I have to do your half in the morning and somehow finish up old Geneste's in the afternoon." Carlos ran a hand through his thick, black hair. "Worst fucking roads in the region. No wonder your van kept breaking down."

"Tell me," said Gaston, highly gratified.

"Oh, by the way, looks like those old birds of yours got themselves a new car."

"What old birds?"

"Them. In Les Colombes."

"Monsieur and Madame de Sauvignac to you," said Gaston severely, offended to hear his favorites treated so offhandedly. But he was curious. "What kind of car?"

"Renault Clio. Green. Well, not new, exactly. Used, by the look of it. Saw it parked around the side the other day when I made my delivery. Finally traded in that old thing of theirs, I guess."

Gaston sniffed. "That 'old thing' of theirs was a genuine antique. Probably fetched a few sous. I tell you, Carlos, you treat the de Sauvignacs right and they'll treat you right. Always good for a *coup*. Quality shows."

•

With the first light of day, Julian began again to try to work his way out of his prison. In between unsuccessful attempts, he shouted for help. Although his body ached and he was hungry and thirsty, his head had remained surprisingly pain-free. It was the only upside to his horrible predicament.

At the moment he was stretched horizontally across the *edze*, back and shoulders pushing against one face of it, feet against the other. It was, it seemed, his thousandth attempt. *Come on*, he urged himself as he squirmed his way upward, gasping with the effort. On each of his previous tries, his progress had been checked by crumbling shale that had given way beneath his weight, causing him to slither painfully, sometimes head-first, back down onto the ledge. Each time, the small avalanche of rock and soil loosened by his efforts ricocheted off the rift walls below him, ending at some greater depth in a series of faint splashes.

He was doing better this time, had managed to work his way more than halfway up his prison wall. Already he could see the ragged edge of the pit mouth clearly above him, full of brilliant light.

Back and shoulders. Feet. Centimeter by centimeter. Then he slipped. He fell amid a shower of dirt and stones, landing heavily on his side. His legs flopped over the edge of the ledge, and the rest of his body, driven by the momentum, followed, tipping him into a void. He tried to save himself by throwing out his arms but was unable to prevent himself from tumbling down onto the lower shelf.

Julian lay still, feeling sick at the thought of how much farther he could have fallen if this second outcropping had not caught him. He was lying on top of a pile of wool and bones. The sheep's jaw no longer held any terrors for him. He realized that it was the sheep's carcass that had broken his fall.

He sat up gingerly, rubbing a painful shoulder, thankful that he was still in one piece. He judged that, with a certain amount of scrambling, he would be able to hoist himself back onto the upper ledge. As he pushed himself unsteadily to his legs, his fingers touched something. Fur? Some other kind of animal pelt? It came away in his hand. A pale hank of longish fibers. Hair. And then he saw it: wedged up against the *edze* wall and overlaid by the jumble of sheep bones, the rounded cranium with its blank eye sockets. Pushing the sheep's carcass aside, he uncovered first the entire skull, then the rib cage and long bones of a human skeleton.

•

Back and shoulders, hands clawing behind him at the sharp layers of shale. Feet. Digging the heels of his boots in, scrabbling for any niche, any irregularity in the damp, slippery rock that would gain him one more centimeter. Julian concentrated on the spot, higher up, where the *edze* narrowed. Once he passed that point, it would be easier. His best attempts so far had taken him only slightly more than halfway up before he had lost his hold and fallen in a shower of debris. This time he would not fall. He did not like what was waiting for him at the bottom.

Inevitably he fell, sliding down the interior rock face of his prison, crashing onto the top ledge, barely managing to keep from tumbling off it a second time. He lay stunned and shattered. The bright mouth of the *edze* might have been a galaxy away. He closed his eyes. Exhausted and weak, he slid into unconsciousness.

He dreamed that he was lying on an island of bones. A blood-red tide roared over him in waves of deep, rhythmical sound. The roaring was accompanied by a dribble of soil that fell into his open mouth. A pebble, striking him hard on the nose, brought him to. A shower of pebbles. The *edze* was collapsing, and he was being buried alive. He groaned and rolled over. The hail of stones and earth accelerated, bouncing off his hair and neck. Something was tearing at the mouth of the pit. A cacophony of noise echoed in his ears. He began to make sense of it: loud, anxious barking resonating all around him.

Julian staggered up, steadying himself against the rift wall.

"Jazz!" he yelled with all the force he had remaining. "Jazz!"

Back and shoulders. Brace with arms and hands. Now feet, sliding them upward one at a time, heels digging in. The dog's vociferous presence overhead gave him renewed strength. Back and shoulders. Feet. He was two-thirds of the way to the top. Already he felt the greater purchase afforded by the smaller space his body had to bridge. He could drive now with all the strength remaining in his legs and back, progressing a hand's breadth at a time. Soon he was able to make out in clear detail the trailing roots of plants dislodged by his original fall. Above him, barking a frantic encouragement, Jazz raced around and set up a powerful digging with both front paws. Earth and vegetation flew, showered down on Julian, blinding, choking him, destroying the very handholds he needed in order to surface.

"Jazz!" he bellowed. "Get off it! Down, dammit, down!"

The dog obeyed, whimpering perplexedly somewhere over Julian's right ear. Back and shoulders. Feet. The pit perimeter was just above eye level. He could make out individual blades of grass, trembling in the breeze. His head emerged into blinding sunlight. He wanted to shout aloud with joy. Then something beneath his heel gave way. Wildly, Julian threw up an arm as his left leg lost purchase and his right threatened to follow. Just as he slipped, a powerful clamp closed down on his collar. Jazz had taken hold and was pulling mightily, as only a dog of his size and strength could pull, dragging Julian up the remaining distance until he lay, half in, half out, and was able at last to crawl to safety. He sprawled, Jazz panting by his side, in warm sunshine on the sweet surface of the earth.

·

"Get up."

Julian breathed deeply. Never had the soil and its vegetation smelled so good to him.

"Get up."

A large, booted foot dug at his ribs. Jazz whimpered and moved away. Julian raised his head, too weak to defend himself. La Binette, in her straw-colored wig, her face congested by its disfiguring stain, towered over him. Next to her stood Vrac. Mother and son regarded him impassively. Jazz, a little off to one side, looked on but was not inclined to come to Julian's aid.

Between the two of them they dragged him. He made no resistance, merely allowed them to seize him under the arms and pull him along. At one point, as they crossed a source flowing from the hillside, he begged for water. They dumped him into it. He drank greedily. After that he was able to croak, "Where are you taking me?"

La Binette's basilisk eye, set in a creased and leathery face, fixed him stonily. She jerked her head over her shoulder. "To him. You're on his land." She turned to her son. "Where is he?"

"Pond," Vrac grunted and with one hand hauled Julian up again.

•

The pond lay in the forested valley bottom. Reeds grew thickly at its margin, except where, here and there, they had been broken down by the passage of water rats. In the middle of the pond was an island where irises still showed their withered yellow flags.

Henri stood at the muddy edge, staring into the still surface of the water. He carried his shotgun under his arm. A freshly killed rabbit lay in the grass at his feet. He turned as two people, dragging a third and followed by a dog, broke through the trees. Mother and son dumped Julian unceremoniously at the *seigneur*'s feet.

"Caught him trespassing," said la Binette.

With an effort, Julian heaved himself up on his elbows. He said with all the aplomb he could muster, "Which undoubtedly gives you the right to order me from your grounds. Call these two off"—he jerked his head in the direction of la Binette and Vrac— "and I'll go quietly."

De Sauvignac studied Julian's crumpled form suspiciously. "Who are you? What were you doing on my land?"

"Nosing around, he was," Vrac said gutturally. "They came together the other time. Saw them. Him and her."

Julian took in the tall, stooping man. Alain resembled his father, he thought. "Your son knows about my interest in orchids," he lied. "He said his mother and grandfather had planted some unusual species around the estate and told me to have a look around anytime I liked. So I'm not here uninvited."

"He was with her, you say?" Henri asked.

Vrac confirmed this with a growl.

"I see." Henri considered the man on the ground with an expression of distaste. "Vrac, m'boy," he said at last, "help me take care of him, will you?"

Once again Julian was hoisted roughly to his feet.

"And Binette, get rid of that cur."

The woman did so by the mere expediency of looping her finger through Jazz's collar and leading him off in the direction they had come. If Julian had been hoping for some display of canine heroics, he was disappointed. Except for a strong territoriality with respect to cars, Jazz was a remarkably easygoing dog.

·

Mara came to with a start. Jeanne de Sauvignac was hovering over her.

"Ah," murmured the old woman. "You're awake. I looked in several times, but you were always sleeping." She lifted Mara to a sitting position, propping her against the wall.

Once more Mara was aware of Jeanne's strength. This time she noticed how large the woman's hands were.

"I brought you some medicine, my dear."

Mara glared suspiciously at a glass of murky liquid. Was this it? Were they planning to drug and dispose of her while she lay senseless? *Dear Lord,* she prayed, *don't let them bury me alive. They're both crazy enough to do it.* Henri's last words came back to her, setting off a deafening internal alarm. *What exactly had happened when Jeanne de Sauvignac met Bedie in the woods?* Mara clenched her jaws and turned her head away.

The other looked disappointed. "It's not really medicine," she admitted. She sat down on the edge of the bed and put the glass on the floor beside her. "Only sugared water. I used to give it to her. The other one. It was a game we played. I would say, Now,

331

poupoule, drink this, it will make you well again. She liked sugar, you see. Sometimes I gave her lumps of sugar soaked in brandy. She loved that. It made her smile. Your smile, my dear, is just like hers."

Mara was stunned and sickened by the woman's maudlin need to nurture coupled with her total disregard of the larger issues of good and evil. She had lost a son. Was she like some demented beast, driven endlessly to find substitutes for her dead child? Between the husband and the wife, Mara did not know whose guilt was greater. But here at least was a weakness that she thought she could exploit.

"You nursed her well, madame."

The rumpled face brightened. "Like my own child."

"And yet you let her die."

The brightness faded.

"There was another death, too, wasn't there? Patrice," Mara drove the name at her cruelly. "Your little boy. My sister. And now me. I'll be dead, too, if you try to keep me here, you know. This house doesn't have a very good track record, does it? One way or the other, people die here. Do you want that? Do you really want another death?"

"Oh, my dear." Jeanne's hands flew up about her face in a characteristic fluttering.

"You know your husband intends to kill me."

"Don't be silly." Jeanne's head came up sharply. "Henri would never do such a thing."

"He will. He has to. Don't you see? He can't afford

to let Alain find me here."

The other stared at her, stricken.

Mara whispered urgently, "Untie me. All you have to do is let me get away from here without your husband knowing."

The ragged head swung from side to side. "I can't. Henri wouldn't like it."

"Damn Henri," Mara nearly shrieked. "Can't you understand? *He's going to kill me.* Madame, you have to help me, or be an accomplice to murder!"

The faded blue eyes fixed on Mara with a look of vague unease. For a second, Mara hoped as she felt the light touch of fingers on her arm. Then hope died. Jeanne's expression crystallized into a smile of almost cloying indulgence.

"It's impossible," Jeanne laughed softly. "You're far too ill to leave here, my dear. You need to rest. I'm afraid you'll be staying with me for a very long time."

There were noises on the stairs. Mara could have wept with desperation. The garret door flew open. Henri entered first, Vrac followed, hunched and burdened with something large that he threw roughly to the floor. A body. Julian's body.

TWENTY

Grissac lost to Le Buisson five to zero on Saturday. It was a hotly contested match, for revenge hung in the balance, Le Buisson having beaten Grissac badly the year before. Paul and the entire team were furious. Not only had Julian not turned up, he had not even bothered to let them know he wasn't coming. The *anglais* wasn't the most brilliant fullback, but at least he offered a damned sight more body than that weed of a José whom they'd had to drag in at the last minute. Paul swore violently all the way back to Chez Nous, where Mado, for once sympathetic to his rugby woes, made soothing noises while massaging his shoulders with a penetrating salve.

"We could have beaten that canaille if that calf's head had bothered to show up."

"Hmmm. Still, it's not like Julian. You don't suppose he's sick?"

"He'll be sicker when I squeeze his neck."

"No. I mean really sick. Too ill to call."

Paul craned around to squint up at her through a wave of mentholated fumes. The kneading of his muscles was having a relaxing effect. "How d'you mean? Dying?"

She chewed a provocative lower lip and bent forward, showing deep cleavage. "At least you could check up on him."

Paul rolled himself over on the bed, displaying a vast expanse of hairy chest and formidable-looking nether parts. He pulled Mado to him. "First things first," he growled.

Later he did drive round to Julian's cottage. The back door, as usual, was not locked. Paul stuck his head inside and bellowed, "D'you know you cost us a loss, you *voyou!*" There was no answer, not even a scuttling sound that might have told him that Julian was trying to hide. He left, slamming the door.

However, when Madame Léon, whom he happened to encounter in the lane, mentioned that Julian had not been by for his weekly dozen eggs, Paul began to wonder. Back at Chez Nous, he rang Mara, only to get her *répondeur*.

"That'll be it," he told Mado. "The two of them have done a bolt. Probably having it away in Spain."

•

"You two have created quite a problem for me." De Sauvignac stood alone in the center of the garret, cradling his shotgun over his arm. He had dismissed his wife. Vrac, after trussing Julian up by the simple expedient of slipping a noose over his head, jerking it tight, and winding the long end around his ankles and the remaining length around his wrists, had also gone.

"You've done that for yourself," said Mara. She turned a pale face to Julian. "He attacked my sister and left her brain-damaged. He and Jeanne kept

335

Bedie in this garret for fourteen years. They claim they found her dead one morning, but I think they simply finished her off when she became too inconvenient to explain."

"That explains the skeleton I found," said Julian. At Mara's startled exclamation, he went on to describe his gruesome discovery in the *edze*. He turned back to their captor. "That's where you dumped her body, isn't it. In the *edze*. Is that what you plan to do with us?"

Henri inclined his head slightly. "That of course is the question. What to do with you. No doubt you would like your freedom. On the other hand, to let you go would create considerable trouble for me. You must understand that I feel compelled to protect my interests. A dilemma, don't you agree?"

He raised the gun. Mara and Julian braced themselves. Henri noted their reaction with a bitter twisting of the lips. To their astonishment, he merely broke the barrel and tucked the weapon under his arm.

"Don't worry," he assured them cynically. "It won't be anything as crude as that." Over his shoulder, he gave them a mocking smile, "You see, at heart I am not a sufficiently evil man."

He left, locking the door behind him.

•

Mara told Julian about her stakeout of Les Colombes and its consequences; her conclusions about Vrac's parentage; and her fear that Henri would be forced to dispose of them before Alain's return.

"When does he get back?" Julian asked.

"Sunday. What's today? I've lost track of time."

"Saturday. I think."

"If we could just hang on until tomorrow."

"That assumes Alain will help us. Henri is his father, after all."

"I don't think he'd stand by and watch us be murdered," Mara countered. She added less optimistically, "Provided he knew."

"I wouldn't trust him as far as I could toss him," Julian muttered.

Julian described his encounter with Vrac and his ordeal in the edze. When he got to the point where Jazz had dragged him out of the pit, Mara cried, "Jazz? Here? What's happened to him?"

"La Binette took him away, I'm afraid. I'm sorry, Mara. I shouldn't have brought him. I never thought anything like this would happen."

"Poor Jazz," she moaned, and closed her eyes.

They fell silent—Julian because he was occupied trying to work his wrists free, Mara because the revelation of Henri's guilt now made her suspicions of Julian acutely embarrassing.

"Julian, I . . . I have something to confess," she said at last.

He swiveled around on the floor to peer up at her. "What's that?"

"I . . ." Where to begin? "I searched your house."

"Oh. That. I know."

"You know?"

"Well, I guessed. For Christ's sake, Mara, what the hell did you think you were playing at?"

"I wasn't playing," she began indignantly, and then stopped, sure that if she told him the full extent of her suspicions he would never speak to her again. "It's just that certain things made me think . . . Why, even the newspaper on your kitchen table . . ." She trailed off lamely.

"What newspaper?"

"The one headlining le Mur's death. You see, there was no way you could have gotten a copy of that edition if you'd really been in the woods looking for orchids at La Binette that day. It made me think you'd faked the search."

"Faked the search?" Julian was deeply offended. He propped himself up awkwardly on an elbow and said, with all the dignity he could muster from his position on the floor, "Mara, I would *never* fake an orchid search."

A moment later he said, "It was probably Madame Léon."

"Madame Léon?"

"She always wraps my eggs in newspaper."

"Oh," Mara said faintly and decided she had made enough damning admissions for the time being.

•

"That chamber pot," cried Julian with sudden inspiration.

Mara blinked at him. "What about it?"

"Break it. We'll use the shards to cut ourselves free."

338

It was a beautiful piece, eighteenth-century, in flawless condition, with a blue-and-green acanthus motif on a cream ground. Mara's clients would have paid good money for it. Probably use it as a planter, she thought ironically. Nevertheless, she slid off the bed and seized it between her feet, bringing it down hard on the wooden floor. It took three tries, but the pot eventually shattered into several pieces. She chose the one with the best cutting edge and scooted across to Julian. Positioning herself back to back with him, she sawed away at the rope binding his wrists. It was slow work, but once his hands were loose, Julian was able to free himself and Mara in minutes.

Their next concern was a means of escape.

"It's too bad the post won't come around again until Monday," Mara said, rubbing feeling back into her arms. "That dormer looks out on the back of the house. If there's mail, the van will drive right into the rear courtyard. We could smash the window and yell down. Except we probably won't be alive by then."

Julian rose rather shakily to his feet and looked around him. "What are the odds of breaking through that door?"

"Not good. It's as thick as a brick and fitted out with a dead bolt."

"Well, then, Jeanne. Do you think we can persuade her to help us?"

Mara shook her head. "I've tried. Although she acts as nutty as a fruit bar, she's been covering for

Henri all these years. And, Julian, I found out it was she who met my sister in the woods."

"Jeanne?" Julian broke off his inspection of the garret to turn back to her. "What are you saying? You don't think *she* hit your sister?"

"I don't know. I really can't make her out." Mara paused, troubled. After a moment, she said, "There's only one possibility. Until Henri decides how to dispose of us, she'll probably keep on bringing us food. That might be our chance. We could jump her as soon as she comes in with her tray."

"Speaking of food," Julian murmured, "I could do with some." When was the last time he had eaten? Two days ago? "Does she come alone?"

"So far. Although I have a feeling he's never far away. With his gun."

•

Henri stood on the top step of the scullery stoop, surveying the empty courtyard of the château. Above him rose the bulk of Les Colombes, where generations of de Sauvignacs had come into the world, lived, and died. Clouds scudded across a darkening afternoon sky. There would be no sunset. A storm was building up, the song of its approach strong on the wind.

A moment later, Jeanne joined him on the stoop. The wind whipped her shawls about her so that it seemed she would really fly away.

"Henri?"

"Yes, my dear?"

"I've nothing for the soup." Her voice was thin and plaintive.

Her husband turned his gaze from the panorama of the valley, where trees huddled like beasts in anticipation of rain. "Not to worry, my dear. I think we can forgo our supper tonight." He gave his wife a bleak smile, took her elbow and turned her gently into the house. "Go back in now, Jeanne. I have some things to take care of."

Alone again, he descended the stoop steps, crossed the courtyard, and stood looking down the lane. The wind brought with it a dusty smell. He felt rather than heard the muffled thunder bulging in the air. Eventually, Vrac materialized from the trees.

"Ah. Vrac, m'boy." Henri paused. He was a long time gazing at his bastard son, as if seeking to relate the clumsy body, the heavy, swollen features to himself. Vrac bore the inspection impassively, hands dangling loosely at his sides, mouth slack. Pale stubble, like stalks on a winter field, sprouted from his large, misshapen jaw. In the fading light his expression was unreadable.

"Give your mother a message, will you?" Henri said. "Tell her there are things I need her to do for me."

•

Their plan was simple: wait for Henri or Jeanne to return and make the most of what would probably be their only opportunity to fight their way to freedom.

Mara said, "If we stand on either side of the door, we can be ready to tackle whoever comes through it.

341

If it's Jeanne, and if she's alone, the important thing is to prevent her from warning her husband. We'll have to knock her out or something. And we'll have to be quick about it. There can't be any struggling or crying out. He'll have to think she's feeding us as normal."

Julian assumed it was up to him to do the knocking out. He was not sure he was equal to it. For one thing, he was weak from lack of food. For another, the only weapon he had was the chamber-pot shard, and he couldn't see any way of silencing Jeanne apart from slitting her throat. The last thing he wanted to do was kill the woman. She was the only real lead he had to the mystery *Cypripedium*.

"If he comes in with her," Mara went on, "you tackle him, I'll deal with her. If we can get his gun away from him, everything should be easy."

"Unless, of course, the pair from hell are hanging around at the bottom of the stairs."

Mara stirred fretfully. "I can't think what's keeping her. So far she's been coming up every three or four hours to check up on me. I don't like it. Something's happened."

Rain began to patter softly on the roof, growing heavier until it drummed overhead in a steady tattoo. Night fell. Jeanne de Sauvignac did not come.

•

By Mara's watch, it was approaching ten. They sat in darkness in order not to alert their captors. The rain had slowed to a steady drizzle. Still Jeanne de

Sauvignac did not come. This made them almost more uneasy than the thought of the husband bursting in on them suddenly and blowing them to pieces with his shotgun.

"You don't suppose they've decided to let us starve to death?" Julian speculated anxiously. Food, or the lack of it, was becoming a serious issue for him.

"He might, but I don't see her doing it. The feeding instinct is very strong with her. You should have seen her, spooning slop into me like a surrogate baby."

Julian was silent for a moment. "I wonder how long it would take."

"What?"

"Dying of starvation. I've heard of people surviving for weeks without food."

"I think it's the dehydration that gets you first," offered Mara.

A few minutes later Julian observed, "Things are awfully quiet."

"The château is solid stone throughout. You wouldn't hear a bomb go off."

"I was thinking maybe they've done a run."

Mara frowned. Then she added hopefully, "Julian, if they've really gone, all we have to do is hang on until Alain returns and shout for help."

"Don't forget, la Binette and Vrac are still around. Oh, my Christ," Julian burst out as an unpleasant thought struck him. "What if he's left them to finish us off?"

The possibility—which quickly took hold in their

minds as a strong likelihood—made them both go cold. It stood to reason that Henri would employ Vrac and his mother to do his dirty work. Both realized how vain their plans were for escape. It was no longer a matter of overpowering two elderly people, one armed with a shotgun. At the appointed time, la Binette and Vrac would mount the stairs. The door would open. Against those two, they had no chance.

Forgetting caution, Julian turned on the light and, using a piece of the chamber pot, began to dig frantically at the wood around the lock fitting in the door. After a long time, he saw that he had managed to gouge out only a small trough along the edge of the metal plate. The wood, seasoned oak, was extremely hard. At the rate he was going, the job would take him days.

•

They sat on the floor, one on either side of the door, anticipating their fate. They both expected it to happen sometime that night. Now Julian knew the heightened awareness achieved by people awaiting execution. Every sensation was magnified tenfold, the pumping of his heart as loud as thunder. He imagined that Vrac could break his neck with a single, effective blow.

While Mara slept, Julian forced himself to stay awake. He preferred to meet death ready rather than have it take him unawares. At last, he, too, slipped into unconsciousness. He dreamed that he was standing on a windy ridge. The *Cypripedium*, enormous and grotesque, rose beckoningly before him. As he reached his hand out to it, he saw that the plant was broken just below the flower head. A poisonous blue exudate dripped from the damaged stem.

TWENTY-ONE

"Julian."

"Hmm?"

"Wake up." Mara was kneeling by his side, shaking him. He opened his eyes. She looked pale and frightened. A somber morning light slanted into the garret.

"Something's happening."

Lightheaded and disoriented, he struggled to sit up. His entire body hurt.

"What?"

"I don't know. But I can sense it."

She was right. Something had occurred or was about to occur. The atmosphere, the very stillness of the place, held a kind of dreadful expectancy, of breathless waiting, as if past events had collected there and were waiting for their final resolution. He rose unsteadily to his feet.

Then he heard it. A sound at the bottom of the stairs. Two sets of heavy footfalls, their cadence unhurried, fateful as the knell of doom. This was it. The unholy pair were coming to finish off what Henri de Sauvignac had started. Heart pounding, Julian gestured Mara to the other side of the door. They stood, backs pressed against the wall, listening. The footsteps stopped. The key turned in the lock. The door swung open.

Julian brought la Binette down with a flying tackle that would have done his team proud. The woman crashed to the ground, but, with the agility and strength of a wrestler, slipped from his hold, overturned him, and pinned him with her full weight. He beheld the frightening spectacle of one deep-set eye glaring balefully at him out of a vivid splash of purple. At that point Mara fell on la Binette's back. The woman struck out, sending Mara crashing against the wall. Julian seized the moment to drive her off with his knees, but she grabbed him by the throat. He was on his back, crushed beneath her big, unwholesome body. He clawed at her face. She slammed his head against the floor so hard that he saw stars, punched him until blood spurted from his nose. He choked on his own blood. Someone was shouting. Another body moved across his line of sight. He managed to roll free, but the woman was on him again, slamming and punching. The walls and ceiling of the garret spun before his eyes.

"*Assez!* Enough!" bellowed Loulou, struggling to separate the two. His normally cheerful face was red, and the tail of his shirt trailed out of his trousers.

La Binette stood up and dragged Julian to his feet. He hung limply in her grip. With a grunt of disdain, she dropped him. He fell heavily to the floor.

"*Sacrebleu*, you two are prepared to sell your lives dearly," Loulou panted. He helped Mara up and then bent over Julian. "*Ça va, mon vieux?* That was quite a welcome you provided. Didn't think you had it in you."

347

Julian attended to his bleeding nose at the kitchen sink while la Binette stood grimly by, arms folded, watching his every move.

"I'm not going to pinch the silver, if that's what you think," Julian snapped.

La Binette thrust her jaw out, but Loulou stepped in quickly to prevent another eruption of violence. "*Doucement*. Madame is only carrying out instructions."

"What, to break my head?"

"You did go for her first," interceded Mara, who seemed to have a better grasp of the state of things than he.

"Wait a minute," Julian objected. "I thought that was the idea. And what the hell are you doing here?" he demanded of the ex-*flic*.

"Ah," said Loulou, looking pleased with himself. "I was sent to collect you."

"Collect—!" Julian stopped trying to staunch his bleeding nose and stared warily about him.

"That's right, *connard*," snarled la Binette, hurling two sets of bright, metallic objects at them. They fell noisily to the stone floor. Their car keys. "Your dog's outside. Now get lost."

"It's all right," said Mara. "We're free. We can go."

"Exactly," crowed Loulou. "My friends, Henri de Sauvignac is in custody at Périgueux Police Headquarters right now. He has confessed."

348

For the third time in as many months, Mara was in the *commissaire*'s office, sitting on a hard chair, watching Boutot roll a pencil between his palms. As before, Loulou strolled about the room. Julian was elsewhere, being interviewed by Boutot's second-in-command.

"You're saying he simply turned himself in?" Mara was incredulous.

The *commissaire* nodded gravely. His mustache drooped. The pouches under his eyes were blue. He looked as if he hadn't slept the night before. "He had no choice. You had learned the truth about your sister, his son was about to return, and Monsieur Wood had found a skeleton on his estate."

"Just walked in and handed across a written statement," declared Loulou from his position behind her at the bookshelves.

"However," continued Boutot, "he claims it was an accident."

"He's lying!" Mara cried.

"According to him, nineteen years ago, your sister found herself in the forest adjacent to Les Colombes—"

"Courtesy of la Binette's taxi," snickered Loulou, coming into view.

Mara was uncomprehending. "La Binette's taxi?"

"That's right," Loulou grinned. "De Sauvignac said Bèdie had been hitchhiking and the Rocher woman had given her a ride. However, reading between the lines, this ties in with complaints we've received over the years about a pair resembling

349

Madame Rocher and her son who like to pick up hitchhikers, drive them to inconvenient places, demand a fee, and leave them to find their way back."

"In any case," resumed Boutot wearily, "Mademoiselle Beatrice was in the forest, and that is where she met Madame de Sauvignac. We assume your sister's interest in orchids was strong enough to offset any inconvenience she had suffered at the hands of the Rochers. Madame, who is herself a serious amateur, recognized a fellow enthusiast. She directed your sister onto the estate, telling her about an orchid walk, created by Madame and her late father-in-law, that runs along their land." The *commissaire* put down his pencil. "I'm given to understand that it was old Monsieur de Sauvignac's ambition to plant Les Colombes with every wild orchid native not only to the Dordogne but to all of Europe."

"I see," murmured Mara, a piece of the puzzle slipping into place.

"Henri de Sauvignac happened to be out hunting that day. He says he ran into Mademoiselle Beatrice, fell into conversation with her, made a pass, and she resisted."

"Always looking for a bit of *frou-frou*," elaborated Loulou. "A real skirt-chaser in his day."

"Quite," the *commissaire* murmured dryly. "He says there was a struggle, she stumbled, fell backward, struck her head on a stone—"

"No," Mara cut in hotly. "I think it was an intentional, brutal assault."

"Hmm. De Sauvignac's version might be difficult to disprove after so much time."

"Not if you have a body," said Mara. "Don't forget Julian's skeleton."

"She's right," Loulou contributed. "Forensics can check the skull for injuries consistent with a fall as opposed to, say, a crushing blow to the head."

"Possibly," Boutot conceded. "At any rate, Henri claims he was horrified at what had happened. He says he brought your sister to the château."

"Why didn't he call a doctor?" demanded Mara.

Boutot nodded. "Indeed. This is where the man accepts full blame. He admits he made no attempt to get your sister medical attention. First, because he didn't realize at the time how badly she was injured. Second, because she was a foreigner and he was afraid that it would not be so easy to buy her family off, as apparently he was accustomed to doing whenever his sexual excesses caused a local scandal. He hoped instead that he and his wife could nurse Mademoiselle Beatrice back to health themselves."

"But fourteen years!" Mara cried. "And his son? Where does—where was Alain when all of this was going on?"

"In Abidjan. Working on a water-containment project. That, of course, can be checked. Alain knew nothing of your sister's injury or incarceration. In fact, Monsieur de Sauvignac said that he had to forbid him access to the château, except for brief visits home, while your sister was alive, for fear that he would discover her presence."

Mara let her breath out softly.

"Even now Monsieur Alain has no idea of what has transpired." Commissaire Boutot referred to a note on his desk. "He's returning from Paris this evening. Two of my men will meet his train. He'll be informed, and we'll need to take a statement from him as well. His mother, unfortunately, is in a state of collapse and can't be questioned. The Rocher woman is caring for her."

Mara shook her head. "Jeanne de Sauvignac is tougher than she looks, believe me. And Julian?" She thought tardily of the man she had so recently denounced. "I take it Henri's confession clears Julian?"

"Ah," said the *commissaire*. Something in his voice caused Mara to sit up.

"That one's not so simple," pronounced Loulou, pulling up a chair and plumping his fat bottom onto it. His expression was bland, but his complexion had gone pink with suppressed excitement. "De Sauvignac's confession clears Julian of involvement with Mademoiselle Beatrice, certainly. But there's still the little matter of Julie Ménard."

"But surely Henri—"

Loulou wagged a finger back and forth. "Nothing sure about it. De Sauvignac claims to have no knowledge of any of the other missing women. And we have no evidence linking him to them."

"What have you said to Monsieur Wood about your suspicions?" asked Boutot.

"Well, very little," replied Mara uncomfortably. "I mean, it's not the kind of thing one wants to talk about."

"Just as well," chuckled Loulou. "Because there's more. Tell her, Antoine."

Boutot sighed and blinked lugubriously at Mara. "One of my men just took a statement from a neighbor of the late Madame Charlebois. It seems that this person remembers a gardener who used to work for the old woman. She thinks it might have been around the time Mariette disappeared, and she had the impression that he only came a few times and then stopped. Described him as a foreign chap, English, she thought. Her description of this man fits Monsieur Wood almost exactly."

"Julian?" Mara murmured, all her old doubts reviving.

"But the final straw"—Loulou jumped up, no longer able to contain himself—"is that another woman's gone missing!"

Mara gaped at him.

"Arlette Cousty," Boutot informed her. "Legal secretary, forty-five years old, married, no children, resident of Toulouse. Her husband reported her missing last week. She hasn't been seen or heard of since. Her car was gone, some of her clothes as well. The husband admits to their having marital difficulties but believes that even if she had left him something must have happened to her subsequently because she would not have failed to contact him. She was a very responsible type, you see."

Mara shook her head. "But Toulouse is in the south. It's a hundred and fifty kilometers away. How can this tie in?"

"Hear me out. The interesting thing is that Madame Cousty's credit card was used to purchase gas on the evening of the day she went missing. Can you guess, Mara, where this purchase was made?"

Beynac, Carennac, Souillac, La Bique. The place names came back to Mara.

"Somewhere along the D703 or D25?" she hazarded.

"Exactly. At a station just outside of Beaumont. Shortly after seven on the evening in question, somebody purchased thirty-seven liters of gas at a Total station. Unfortunately, the cashier was one of these young cretins with earphones plugged into his head. Couldn't recognize his own nose, let alone identify a photograph of Madame Cousty as the bearer of the card. Nevertheless, you see what this signifies, don't you? Beaumont puts Arlette Cousty's last known location right within our zone of interest!"

Mara stared first at one man and then the other. "What's being done about it?" she asked at last.

Boutot fingered his pencil. "It's being treated it as a case of domiciliary abandonment. So far."

"Ha!" barked Loulou. "But you realize what all this means for Julian? He already has some explaining to do regarding Julie Ménard. Now, supposing he's identified as the man who worked for Madame Charlebois, and if he just happened to be cruising the area around Beaumont on the night in question, I'd say *he's still very much in the frame!*"

TWENTY-TWO

Mara wrote to Patsy.

> They've made a positive identification of the skeleton based on old dental records. So that lays Bedie to rest. Although I'd always hoped somehow to find her alive, at least this gives me closure, me and everyone who loved her—Mum, Dad, and especially Scott, who's suffered as much as any of us from all these years of not knowing. Henri's sticking to his story that it was an accident, but I don't believe him. He insists that Bedie's eventual death was "natural." Since there seems to be no evidence to the contrary, I guess I can at least be grateful that Henri and Jeanne let Bedie die in her own time.

The police have reopened investigations on Julie Ménard and Mariette Charlebois, and they're checking into the latest woman to go missing, Arlette Cousty. So far, they haven't questioned Julian directly. Loulou says they're purposely playing their fish until—tac!—they have enough evidence to pull him in. Meantime, Commissaire Boutot has asked me to stay clear of Julian and take basic precautions, although I think he's less concerned about my safety than worried that I'll give something away. At any rate, it hasn't occurred to

him to offer me any armed protection. For the rest,
I'm just getting on with my work and trying to put
Bedie behind me . . . <

Mara glanced out the window at trees, a blue sky, and sunshine. There seemed nothing more to say. She signed off, got up, and wandered restlessly about her studio. The unfinished plans for a kitchen renovation (another of Prudence's referrals) lay on her workbench. In a corner stood a recently acquired nineteenth-century cheval glass mounted in a beautifully carved walnut frame. She had bought it quite reasonably from a *brocante* in Monpazier with another client in mind. Now she wasn't sure she wanted to part with it. She stood before it, staring at her slightly tarnished reflection. Her eyes met those in the mirror. My face, she thought sadly. Bedie's face. Hesitantly, she reached out to trace the contours of her image with a fingertip that met only the flat, cold hardness of glass.

My god! she whispered as the realization hit her.

Rushing back to the computer, she logged on again.

> Patsy, I've just thought of something. It's a minor
detail, but if it means what I think it means, it
could turn everything upside down . . . <

A shadow fell into the room.

"Hello." Julian stood in the open doorway.

"Oh," said Mara and sat very still.

Jazz, who had been snoring on the floor, gave a grunt, heaved himself up, and ambled over to greet their visitor. Julian scratched the dog's ear. He did not come farther into the studio but spoke from where he stood.

"We have unfinished business, Mara."

"What—what do you mean?" She snapped her fingers for Jazz to return to her side. The dog ignored her.

"The *Cypripedium*." Julian seemed exasperated at having to spell it out. "I mean, you've got what you—that is . . ." He trailed off awkwardly.

"I've found my sister but you still haven't found your orchid. Is that what you're trying to say?"

"Well, I wouldn't have put it quite like that. But we did have a deal."

"So?"

He looked a little surprised at her ungraciousness. "Look, I'm not asking you to hike the forest with me. Unless, of course, you want to. But I need your help."

"How do you mean?"

"Jeanne de Sauvignac and her late father-in-law tried to establish a plantation of *Cypripedium calceolus* at Les Colombes. I think the mystery Lady's Slipper was a mutant of this attempt. There's a slim chance that it continued to propagate. I have to find this plantation. Jeanne is the only person who can tell me where it is. I understand she's pretty incoherent right now, but time is running out fast. I mean, the flowering season, and without a flower, I haven't a prayer of proving my theory. I thought if you could ask Alain to get some sense of the location from his mother, even generally, it would narrow down my search tremendously. I happen to know that Géraud is also on the hunt, and I'm damned if I'm going to let that *voyou* beat me out again."

She nodded. Julian had told her of Géraud's scoop at the Société Jeannette meeting.

"All right," she said. "I think I can do that for you."

•

"Of course you realize it's risky?" Loulou warned when Mara called him later.

"I do, but I think it's the only way. Certainly you can see how what I've just told you puts things in a different light? It could be one of them, or both."

"Hmm," said the ex-cop. "I'll talk with Boutot. He might just agree that your idea has some interesting possibilities."

•

"Are you sure?" Julian adjusted his glasses and scratched his head.

They stood in the forecourt of Les Colombes, peering at a hand-drawn map held by Alain. It was the second time Julian had spoken with the son, and he liked him no better, even though the man had obviously gone to some trouble to get the information Julian needed.

"It's the best Maman could do, I'm afraid," said Alain. "She's in a state of shock, and her memory never was very good at the best of times. I could ask her again, if you think it would help."

Julian considered this.

Mara, dressed in a baggy sweatshirt despite the warm day, said, "We may as well check the spot out first. If we don't turn up anything, maybe you could talk to her again, Alain."

He nodded. "Yes. That would be better. She's still in a pretty bad way at the moment. I hadn't realized how dependent she's become on my father over the years. She's frantic with anxiety. Binette and I had to restrain her physically from trying to go to Papa last evening. Speaking of which, I'd better return to the house. We're sitting with her in turns, and Binette needs to get back to her cheesemaking."

He left them.

"It doesn't make sense," Julian grumbled as they walked down the road leading away from the château.

"Why not?" asked Mara. This time she had left Jazz at home.

"Well," he scowled at the map. "This puts it in low, wet land, under pine-forest cover. If I'm not mistaken, there's a lot of bracken, which suggests acid soil, and"—he struggled to recall his first meeting with Henri de Sauvignac—"a big pond nearby. Lady's Slippers like semi-shade and drier, alkaline soil." Julian directed them onto a path snaking down in the direction of the valley he had crossed the day he fell into the *edze*. "If Jeanne and her father-in-law knew anything about orchids, and we have to assume

360

they did, they'd never have tried to establish the root-stock there."

"Watch where you're going," warned Mara, scrambling after him down the steep slope. "You don't want to fall into another pit."

They descended to the valley floor. It was hot and windless there. The woods at noon were very quiet.

"This should be the spot," said Julian after another twenty minutes or so. Deciduous trees had given way to conifers and ferns. "Really," he muttered after a few minutes of pacing the ground, "this is damned odd. You don't suppose she'd purposely try to mislead us, do you?"

"Why would she do that?"

"Because, from the sound of it, she's round the twist." He stopped and turned back to Mara. "Or because there's something she doesn't want us to find. Quite honestly, I don't know about you, but I never really bought Henri de Sauvignac's confession." He shook his head. "It's too convenient, somehow. Almost as if—as if he were protecting someone."

Mara looked up sharply. "What do you mean?"

"Well, you said it was Jeanne who met your sister in the woods. I asked you before if you thought it could have been her and not Henri who attacked Bedie. She sounds crazy enough to have done it, you know. What if she has a sick need to find substitutes for her dead child? Or maybe she's driven to punish young women because of the maid who let her little boy drown."

It was a troubling hypothesis that called forth some of Mara's own doubts about Jeanne de Sauvignac. She remembered the woman's surprising strength, and the thought crossed her mind once again that behind Jeanne's goggling appearance there was a purposeful intelligence, albeit functioning fitfully, like a faulty switch.

"Are you saying she's setting us up for something?"

"Who knows," muttered Julian. He resumed his pacing. "Anyway, I don't see anything here that faintly resembles an orchid. Dammit, the habitat's all wrong. Still, I suppose we ought to make a thorough search." He sought a landmark and selected a tall pine tree standing in a small clearing. "We'll take this as our point of reference. You remember how we squared off the ground when we were looking for the *Neottia?* Well, this time we'll do it a little differently, and we'll have to cut it finer. We're no longer looking for an extensive colony of plants but possibly a single plant. You know what it looks like—dark-pink slipper, two long, spiraled petals springing out from the sides, blackish-purple sepals, fifty to sixty centimeters high. In case it's past its flowering, keep your eye out for anything with three to five broad oval leaves, deeply veined, coming out of a single stem."

He indicated two imaginary lines extending due east and west of the pine. "These will be our guide lines. We'll start out back to back at the tree. I'll go north twenty paces, you go south the same amount.

Be sure to look to either side of you as you go. When you've done your twenty, go five to your right, then right again, and return twenty paces, which should bring you back to the pine but in your case five paces farther west along your guide line. I'll be five paces farther east. Then we repeat the procedure, each time ending up five paces farther away from the pine. After four repetitions, we'll have each walked a twenty-by-twenty square. If we haven't found any-thing, we'll meet back at the pine, set the guide lines running north and south, and pace to east and west. At the end, together we'll have walked a forty-by-forty square. It's slow going, but it's the only way to handle the search in such heavily overgrown terrain. Are you with me?"

Mara said she was.

"Good," said Julian. "And—er—Mara, if anything happens, remember I'll never be very far away."

She glanced uneasily at him. "What can happen?"

"Oh, if you should get lost or something," he said casually.

Yes, she thought. *Or something.*

They set off.

After two turns, Mara lost sight and sound of Julian entirely. She went carefully, poking at the undergrowth with a stick and stopping from time to time to listen to the forest. The profound silence made her nervous. After her fourth turn, she fol-lowed her line back to the pine tree. Julian was wait-ing for her.

"No luck?" she asked.

He shook his head. "A nice crop of cèpes, but I'm not very interested in mushrooms at the moment."

They reset the guide lines along a north-south axis and resumed their pacing, Julian going west and Mara east. Her way was frequently barred by tangled undergrowth that she had to beat aside with her stick. At one point, through the trees she saw the glint of water. The pond Julian had mentioned. She completed her square without seeing anything of interest and again followed her line back to the tree. This time Julian was not there. She sat down on a log to wait. Time passed, but he still did not appear. She, who had been on the alert for something to happen at any moment, was frankly puzzled. Had he found something, or was he at that very moment moving up silently behind her? The thought made her glance uneasily over her shoulder. A cuckoo called. It was the first birdsong she had heard since they had been in the forest.

"Hello, Mara."

The voice behind her made her jump.

"Oh," she said, turning, a lead weight sitting on her heart. "It's you. I was wondering if you'd show up."

"Could you doubt it?"

"I suppose you've decided to join the hunt?"

"I've been looking forward to it."

"Who's with your mother, then?"

Alain smiled. "Drugged to the eyeballs. I doubt she'll know I've gone. Have you found your orchid?"

"I haven't. I don't know about Julian. We've been pacing off the area in opposite directions. He should be meeting me back here any minute."

Alain shook his head. "He won't be coming."

Mara frowned. "What do you mean?"

"I mean he's *hors de combat*. Out cold."

Mara stood up, giving a nervous tug at her sweat-shirt.

"In any case," Alain assured her, "for what we are about to do, we don't need him."

Mara felt herself go clammy. "What are we about to do, Alain?" she asked quietly.

"I think you know," he said, moving close enough so that she could see a flicker of excitement burning in his dark-blue eyes. He was breathing hard. "*Cache-cache*. You run, I chase. You see, I'm giving you a fair chance."

"Like the game you used to play with Vrac? You're not a child anymore, Alain."

He smiled. "I know. I've learned to reverse the roles."

"Is that"—Mara stepped back—"how it happened with my sister? She ran, and you hunted her down like an animal?"

"Does it surprise you?"

Mara took a deep breath. "No. I knew it had to be one of you. I admit, you did everything to make me believe it was Julian. Very plausible. But you made one small mistake."

"Oh?"

"You said that Julian would have been shaken to see me because I was the spitting image of a woman he'd killed."

"And what was wrong with that?"

"I told you Bedie and I were twins, Alain. *But I never showed you her photograph and I never said we were identical.* Unfortunately, I didn't get the significance of this until just the other day, and even then I couldn't be sure if it was just an assumption on your part, or if it meant only that you'd seen my sister in the garret, or if it was really you and not your father who had met her in the forest."

He laughed harshly. "And do you have your answer?"

"Yes," said Mara, watching him closely. "I think I do. There's one thing I don't understand, though. Why didn't you finish Bedie off at the time? In some ways it would have been better for her if you had."

Alain shrugged. "Vrac caught me at it. The stupid fool took her back to the château, slung over his shoulder like a gutted sheep. You can imagine the state Papa was in."

"But he did nothing?"

"How could he? There was the precious family name to protect and Maman to deal with. She'd already lost one son, you know, because of him. If he hadn't been rolling that fat slut of a nursemaid in the grass, we wouldn't have played the game that day. Patrice wouldn't have gone down to the pond. He was always very good at hiding, you see, and he

366

thought he could fool me by crouching in the reeds. But he didn't think about his footprints in the mud. After all, he was only seven. I was ten. All I had to do was track him down."

Mara stared at him speechlessly. At last she asked in a faint voice, "How exactly did your brother drown, Alain?"

He looked at her inquiringly. "Patrice?" His gaze shifted momentarily. "The rules of the game. And the water in that pond is very deep. But we were talking about your sister. I told Papa I'd swear it was Vrac who had attacked her. If she died—and at the time I didn't think she'd last out the hour—it would have been the word of an idiot against mine. They didn't have the means of DNA testing in those days. No one would have believed him over me. That stopped Papa cold."

"Of course," agreed Mara acidly. "Vrac is also your father's son."

"His by-blow!" Alain sneered. "In the end, Papa and I struck a deal. I stayed away, paid their upkeep, and he kept silent. Voilà, all nicely arranged and the family name untarnished."

"Except that you were free to go on murdering women," Mara cried. "Because I'm sure that's what happened. In Africa and here. Women went missing every time you returned on home leave, didn't they? The periodic cycle. Surely your father saw the connection. And yet he protected you—goes on protecting you."

"Of course. I am the last of the de Sauvignacs. Besides, what proof had he? Women go missing all the time. I don't have a monopoly on evil."

"On the contrary. You are a monster. You know, when I was in that garret, I thought the deadbolt lock was put on the door to keep my sister in. But I'm not so sure now. She was a vegetable. She couldn't have escaped. I'll bet it was there to keep you *out*."

"You're very good at this," said Alain, a note of mocking admiration in his voice. "But enough teasers. We must move on to the principal course, which is where the main enjoyment is to be had. Shall I give you a minute's head start? Don't worry. I won't rape you. One has to be careful about evidence nowadays. Or perhaps two minutes? You'll have to run for your life. Literally. I know these woods like the back of my hand."

Mara held her ground. "I'm not running, Alain." She turned away. With a sudden movement, she whirled around, clutching her stick with both hands and using the momentum of her body to smash it with all her strength across his face. He reeled from the blow. Then she ran, screaming.

He was on her in seconds, throwing her to the ground, was now on top of her, gripping her wrists, while she fought against him with all her strength. When he felt the hardness below her breasts, he yanked her sweatshirt up, revealing a small tape recorder strapped to her torso and a tracking device clipped to her belt. He hesitated, taking in the significance of these things, just long enough for her to drive her knee up as hard as she could into his groin. With a roar of pain he rolled off.

"*Putain!*" he howled. "Filthy whore!"

She scrambled up, but he seized her leg. She fought him, kicking, clawing, screaming, as he dragged her to him. His hands were on her throat, squeezing. She felt her eyes bulge, thought her brain would burst. Her tongue was thrusting from her mouth when Alain released her abruptly. She was now in danger of being trampled under the heavy feet of two desperately struggling men. Her vision cleared in time to see Julian land Alain a mighty clout in the face that sent a pinwheel spray of scarlet spinning through the air.

Then the area was all at once busy with running uniforms as gendarmes surged out of the trees. Commissaire Boutot appeared from a different direction. Two agents fought Alain to the ground and handcuffed him. Last but not least, Loulou came trotting up, puffing with exertion.

"What took you so bloody long?" Mara tried to yell at them, but the best she could manage was a broken croak.

TWENTY-THREE

June came on the Dordogne, with sunshine and tourists. The spring flowers had finished, except for a remnant poppy here and there, showing scarlet among the young wheat. Many of the orchids had reached the end of their blooming, but roses and honeysuckle garlanded every wall.

They were gathered at Chez Nous, eleven end to end. Mado and Paul had pushed the tables together to form a banqueting board running the length of the bistro. The windows stood open to catch the cool night breeze. Julian, with bruised face and a splinted ankle—he had sprained it badly in his struggle with Alain—and Mara, her neck in a brace, sat at one end; Loulou and Gaston at the other. In between were Prudence, Gaston's wife, Géraud, and Iris. Julian had included Géraud only because of Iris, who had given him his lead on the mystery *Cypripedium*.

Next to Mara lounged a large, long-legged body in a green pants suit—Patsy Reicher, arrived the day before from Manhattan. Her broad face with its topping of iodine hair turned from side to side as she followed the story told piecemeal by everyone. Places were set for Paul and Mado, but they occupied them only in between sallies to the kitchen. They were assisted by Bernard Léon, Julian's erstwhile bulldozer, who performed the tasks of underwaiter with surprising aptitude. Jazz moved down the company, thrusting his head hopefully into everyone's lap.

At this point in the meal they were eating scallops in cream sauce, accompanied by a chilled dry Bergerac.

"You see," Loulou addressed the gathering at large as he waved a forkful of scallop, its bright-orange comma of roe attached, in the air, "Henri de Sauvignac was not just protecting the family name. He was trying to make up to his wife for the loss of one son by salvaging the other."

"Guilt and atonement," murmured Patsy, ignoring her food.

Mara said, "The irony of it is that I think Alain killed his own brother. I think he hunted him down at the pond and pushed him in. Or held his face underwater."

"*Mon dieu*," shuddered Gaston's wife.

"They've moved Jeanne to hospital, you know," Iris said. "They say the poor woman may never recover."

Loulou wagged his head. "Nevertheless, both she and her husband will be charged as accessories after the fact, although in her case there will probably be a plea of reduced responsibility. The evidence Mara got on tape makes a strong case against Alain, despite his story that it was a casual sexual fling that went wrong."

"Lying bastard," muttered Mara to no one in particular. "I can't believe I trusted him."

"But it wasn't just Mara's sister," Mado called from her end of the table. She was slightly flushed with all the rushing back and forth from the kitchen, which perhaps accounted for the inner glow that lit her face. "What about those other women?"

Loulou raised a hand. "Denies any involvement with them. However, the lads have established that Alain was in France at the time of Hanneke Tenhagen's murder. And Valérie Rules and Mariette Charlebois's disappearances both coincided with later visits home. By the way, they plan to drag the pond in the forest. Who knows what they'll find?"

"*Mon dieu*," repeated Gaston's wife, clutching her throat.

"And while we're on the subject, reports are coming in from Abidjan, Dakar, Yaoundé, and Douala. Seems there's quite a trail of missing and dead women everywhere our Monsieur Alain was known to have worked."

"I had a mass murderer at my party," murmured Prudence wonderingly. "How can someone so sick look so good? I mean, he was a damned sexy man. *Incroyable!*"

"Serial killers are often extremely persuasive and charming," said Patsy. "It's a skill they develop to get close to their victims."

Mara touched her neck brace and shifted unhappily in her chair.

"Well, I still think Julian owes us an explanation about that Ménard woman," roared Géraud. "What's this about you trying to hide the fact that you'd worked for her, eh?"

"I didn't," Julian said hotly. "Try to hide anything, I mean. I never met her. It was her husband who hired me, he paid cash, and I only ever knew him as Jackie. How was I supposed to connect?"

"There. You see?" said Iris, jabbing her paramour in the side with her elbow.

"Hmph," grunted Géraud, unconvinced. "And la Charlebois?"

"The neighbor had it wrong," Loulou declared, mopping up sauce with a bit of bread. "Turns out the fellow in question was Portuguese and not a gardener at all but a man come to fix the fence. As for Julie Ménard, the lads are also digging up Monsieur Jackie's rock garden in Souillac."

"At my suggestion," Mara murmured dryly.

"Bloody hell," Julian exclaimed, more upset by Loulou's news than he was at Géraud's insinuations. "I built that rockery. In the days before Bernard." He jabbed his chin in the direction of the underwaiter, who had stopped in his tracks sometime ago, mouth agape. "Are you telling me they think she's buried under it? Damned shame. I planted some unusual varieties of dwarf rhododendron in that rock garden, as I recall."

"Maybe you ought to rethink the rockery Julian's putting in for you," Paul addressed Prudence with a malicious glint in his eye. "All those trenches."

"I get these headaches," Julian confided to Patsy,

shifting topics. "Thumpers. When I'm tired or stressed. Now, the funny thing is, while I was in that *edze* and then in the garret, I was fine. I mean, my head was. In fact, I haven't had a headache since."

"You were concentrating on more important things," Patsy said, amused. "Like survival."

"What happened to the woman, Arlette Cousty?" Mado asked, rising to clear the course and giving Bernard a sharp shove in the direction of the kitchen.

"Ah," said Loulou. "That one. She turned up. Yes indeed. She turned up. Apparently ran off with her lover, but couldn't bring herself to tell her husband about it because, *tenez*, the lover is a woman. She thought he wouldn't be able to handle it. Turns out he's been having a same-sex relationship on the side himself. Both are greatly and mutually consoled."

Paul, getting up as well, called over his shoulder, "So nothing happened to her?"

"Nothing apart from running out of gas," affirmed Loulou. "She said a kind monsieur stopped and gave her a couple of liters, just enough to get her to a station outside Beaumont."

"Oh." Julian looked startled and choked on his wine. "That was Arlette Cousty?"

"*Mais oui,*" said Loulou, glancing at him curiously.

"Did I tell you the police are also looking more closely at my accident?" Gaston announced. "They found a log near where I had my accident that had bits of glass and plastic embedded in it that match the parts broken off my van. The suspicious thing is that it was piled back in with a stack of cut wood at the side of the road. They've had a conversation with Vrac about it, but he put on his idiot act, so they couldn't get much out of him, and all la Binette would say was, '*Allez-vous faire foutre.*'"

"Speaking of them," Loulou broke in, "you might be interested to know that a German hitchhiker made a complaint a month or so back about a pair answering the description of la Binette and Vrac. Said they picked him up and tried to extort money from him."

"Something needs to be done," said Gaston's wife angrily. "That pair are a menace to society. My husband could have been killed."

"For Alain it was the thrill of the chase as much as bludgeoning his victims to death," Mara was telling people at her end of the table. "A sick perversion of a childhood game."

"Hoo boy," marveled Patsy. "This one should make psychoanalytical annals."

"And he would have hunted you down and left Julian to take the blame?" cried Mado, back from the kitchen. "*Quel salaud!*"

Mara went on, "It was simple for him to fake the map and then slip down to the forest to wait his chance. But Julian knew something was wrong from the start."

"Hah!" snorted Géraud.

"And if it hadn't been for Julian," Mara went on with a severe look for both Géraud and Loulou,

"Alain would have killed me. So much for the lads."

"Nonsense," Loulou called down to her, "they had you covered every centimeter of the way."

"Well, they took their damned sweet time getting there."

Julian shook his head at Mara. "I can't believe you actually suspected me of doing away with your sister. And a string of other women as well!"

She blushed into her plate.

He leaned meaningfully across the table. "You owe me, Mara."

Her dark eyes flashed. "I already apologized."

Julian shook his head. "Not good enough. Jeanne de Sauvignac can't remember where they planted the rootstock. It could be anywhere." He lowered his voice. "With my ankle, I'm going to need help if I'm to beat out that *chameau*"—he jerked his head in the direction of Géraud—"for the Prix Vénus."

"Oh, now wait a minute. If it's that bloody *Cypripedium* again—"

Géraud, whose ears had caught the mention, sneered, "Figment of your imagination, *mon vieux*. It never existed."

Julian ignored him and reached for Mara's hand. "A friend in need?" His look was appealing.

Her face softened. Laugh lines reasserted themselves over the frown. "Okay," she gave in. "You're on, damn you."

"Watch out, kid," warned Patsy over the rim of her wineglass. "He'll have you speaking Latin."

"*Cypripedium*? Greek, actually," announced Julian. "From kypris, which relates to Aphrodite or Venus, and—er—*podion*, little foot."

"Rubbish," snapped Géraud. "It's from the Latin *pedium*, for 'shoe.' "

"Whatever," Julian sighed.

"*C'est très ironique*," Prudence remarked to the company at large. "All this interest in *pigeonniers*, and no one ever thought about Les Colombes. I mean, *colombe* means 'dove,' doesn't it, which is a kind of pigeon?"

"*Ah, ça.*" Loulou cocked his head, impressed. "*C'est très bon, ça!*"

Mado and Paul came from the kitchen to announce the *plat principal*: tender, juicy squabs, studded with truffles and simmered in a rich wine sauce. The birds were presented in individual lidded clay casseroles. Bernard helped with the serving up. When the covers were lifted, a heady aroma wafted out, causing an ecstatic ripple of approval. There were also platters of asparagus and Julian's favorite, pan-fried Sarladaise potatoes, dressed in garlic and parsley. Paul moved swiftly from glass to glass, pouring out a fine chilled Chablis.

Julian hobbled to his feet and rapped for attention. "Friends, I think we should all toast the culinary artistry we've been privileged to experience tonight." He raised his glass. The others did the same. "I name this superb dish *Suprême de pigeonneau à la Mado*." There was laughter and loud applause.

Paul leaned over the head of the table to give another thunderous rap. "Listen up, everyone. Important announcement. Mado's given up smoking."

"I don't believe it," cried Julian. "What brought this on?"

"Has to, doesn't she?" said Paul in a choking voice. He went the color of raw beef. "Got a bun in the oven!"

Loud cheers and general pandemonium. Everyone kissed Mado, who was immediately made to sit. Gaston's wife and Iris would have had her recumbent if she had not protested.

In the middle of all this, Bernard hissed in Julian's ear, "Old Hilaire's here. He wants to see you."

"What? Now?"

The young bulldozer grinned and gave a massive shrug. Old Hilaire pushed through the bead curtain. He looked as he always did, like a pickled walnut, and, as usual, brought with him a whiff of goat.

"I found her!" he bellowed over the noisy company. His face was wreathed in triumph and delight. "*Ma petite* Edith. She turned up at the animal shelter in Bergerac."

More cheers. Everyone who knew Edith had great affection for her. Those who didn't shared in the general enthusiasm all the same.

The farmer went around, shaking everyone's hand. When he got to Julian, he stopped, looking self-conscious.

"Monsieur," he spoke with a kind of awkward ceremony. He fished around in one of his capacious pockets. "Voilà, monsieur. For you."

It was small, round, and fawn-colored, with a snub muzzle, bright eyes, black-tipped ears, and chubby white paws. A diminutive white blaze was just discernible on its chest. Julian received the pup, thinking that he really didn't want a dog. Edith, now that she was back, was enough for him. But the pup made small murmuring noises as he held it and nibbled his ear with painfully sharp little teeth. It was warm, and its fur smelled of straw. Jazz saw it and, with a sharp bark, came up to investigate. Carefully and gently he sniffed the tiny body.

"Oh, the darling!" cooed Mara, reaching out.

Julian handed the pup across to her. She nuzzled it.

"Nine of them." Hilaire was prouder even than Paul. "This one's the pick of the litter. With Maman Edith's compliments."

"Hilaire, I'm honored." Julian rose and shook the farmer warmly by the hand.

Jazz stood by, amiably wagging his tail.

Julian looked down at him. "Why, you old son of a bitch," he growled fondly at the dog, who cocked at him a smug and knowing eye.

BE SURE NOT TO MISS THE NEXT THRILLING NOVEL
IN THE "DEATH IN THE DORDOGNE" SERIES . . .

The Orchid Shroud

Available now from Anchor Canada

Turn the page for a sneak preview . . .

PROLOGUE

APRIL 2004

The man in the greasy beret dropped his burden to the ground. He glanced over his shoulder. As usual, he, André Piquet, was up to no good. Nothing serious, mind. Just the kind of routine skulduggery that the Piquets, a noted clan of *tricheurs*, generally practiced.

With a quick slash of his hunting knife, André severed the cord that secured the mouth of the sack. It sagged, spewing some of its contents over the damp litter of pine needles and last year's fallen leaves. Sheathing the knife, he upended the sack. Smelly kitchen peelings mixed with dried maize tumbled to the ground.

Baiting *sangliers,* the tough wild pigs that hunters in the Dordogne prized above all game, was frowned on as unsportsmanlike, not to say damned sneaky. The idea was that the *sangliers,* which roamed freely through the deep valleys and dense forests of this region of southwestern France, became accustomed to feeding at the baiting stations, with the result that, when the hunting season opened, *voilà*, you had a ready population of pigs in place for the kill. If you were quick off the mark, you could bring down an animal or two before anyone got wind of what you'd been up to. It was the Piquets' guiding principle. Do it the easy way, secretly and fast, and your neighbor would never be the wiser. Also, it meant not having to share out your kill, taken on the quiet like that, with other hunters and local residents.

As he rolled up the sack and stuffed it under his jacket, André heard a sound. He looked about him. The woods in early evening were chill and gloomy. It occurred to him that everything was uncommonly still. Normally starlings and crows made a racket around this time. Suddenly he felt a little nervous. Was someone spying on him? Or maybe it was the speed with which the darkness was moving in.

Again, his ears caught the noise, a kind of scraping that was not the drilling of a woodpecker, or the creaking of branches in the wind. It seemed to be coming from somewhere to his right. Now curiosity vied with caution. Treading softly, he pushed through the thick undergrowth in the direction of the noise. He parted a curtain of pine branches and stepped into a small clearing. What he saw outraged him: a juvenile boar, freshly killed by the look of it. It lay head-on to him, one of its underdeveloped tusks driven into the dark, rough earth.

"Putain!" André, thrust suddenly onto the unaccustomed moral high ground, gave vent to his disgust. Baiting pigs was one thing, but hunting out of season, especially if someone beat you to it, really went against the grain. Funny, though, he hadn't heard a shot. And there did seem to be an awful lot of blood about. The ground all around was churned up and soaked with it.

Then he realized that the wild pig had not been shot. Drawing closer, he saw that it had been brought down by something that had slashed its haunches, severing the hindquarter tendons to disable it before going in for the kill. Feeding had already begun, for the belly had been partly torn open, the slippery guts spilling out. André whistled through a gap in his stained front teeth. Whatever it was had to be big. A boar, even young, was a tough adversary for most dogs. Maybe a pack of dogs? he wondered. He hunkered down for a closer look, balancing on the balls of his feet.

It was then that the long gray form came on him, hitting him from behind with tremendous force. He sprawled forward, driven face-down into the blood-wet earth. He felt a visceral shock as something ripped deep into the flesh of his shoulder.

"Nom de dieu!" André shrieked. A hunter, he knew the ferocity of the wounded boar, the dangerous valor of the stag at bay. Never had he encountered anything like the savagery of this attack. Desperately he rolled over, shielding his face and throat with one hand while attempting to free his knife from its sheath with the other. He stood no chance against it. With a snarl conceived in hell, the creature came in for the kill.